SCORCH CITY

ALSO BY TOBY BALL

The Vaults

SCORCH CITY

TOBY BALL

ST. MARTIN'S PRESS

NEW YORK

SCORCH CITY. Copyright © 2011 by Toby Ball. All rights reserved. Printed in the United States of America. For information, address St. Martin's Press, 175 Fifth Avenue, New York, N.Y. 10010.

www.stmartins.com

ISBN 978-0-312-58083-4

First Edition: September 2011

10 9 8 7 6 5 4 3 2 1

For Mom and Dad

ACKNOWLEDGMENTS

I am indebted to Faith and Jonathan Ball and Glenda Kaufman Kantor, who all read early versions of this book and provided valuable insight and encouragement.

Thank you to my agent and friend Rob McQuilkin, and to his colleagues at Lippincott, Massie, McQuilkin. Once again, Michael Homler was the steady hand steering this book from manuscript to what you have in your hands. Many thanks to him and to Jeanne-Marie Hudson, Loren Jaggers, and Emily Fry at St. Martin's.

There are a number of other people who deserve mention for their support, enthusiasm, and friendship: Susanna, Peter, Jackson, and Julia Kahn; Terrence, Lisa, Owen, and Sophie Sweeney; Martin Sweeney and Heidi Kim; Julian, Kate, and Meghan Gross and Jill McInerney; Paul, Riley, Adelaide, and Leo Nyhan and Samantha Neukom; Nick and Maria Aretakis; Carter, Julien, and Charlotte Strickland and Nicole Gueron; Michele Filgate, Liberty Hardy, and everyone at RiverRun Bookstore; and my friends at the Durham Public Library.

And, mostly, thank you to Deborah, Jacob, and Sadie.

SCORCH CITY

1.

Moses Winston had learned from years of being a stranger everywhere he went—such was the life of an itinerant musician—how to recognize trouble and how to avoid it without backing down. It never did him any good scrapping in a place where he wasn't known. So, as he walked through the smoky shantytown alleys, breathing fumes from the tar roofs baking in the sun, he kept his head up and his eyes on nothing in particular, save the occasional passing woman who, even today, earned his glance. This day, of all days, was one to stay out of trouble.

He moved quickly through the maze of shacks, the route playing with him, disorienting him. The way out never seemed quite the same. The configuration of the alleys seemed to be constantly changing, like dunes shifting in the wind.

Children appeared out of the smoke like apparitions. Winston moved to the side to make way, stepping into the threshold of a shanty. A baby was crying inside.

He walked toward where he thought the way out was. His skin prickled in the heat, his eyes burned red from the smoke. On his back he carried a guitar case with a rope rigged as a strap. He'd left Billy Lambert's shack minutes before, after several hours spent rooted to his bedroll, paralyzed into inaction, watching Lambert's bruised body across the room, chest expanding and contracting with each sleeping breath.

Inside the little shack he'd felt isolated, even protected, as if history didn't exist there. But he had a gig tonight and had reluctantly left, trading static anxiety for the uncertainty of the shantytown alleys.

Winston turned a corner and found himself at the far end of an alley from a group of four older men who were sharing a pipe and watching his approach. Winston knew of these men and his pulse quickened. *Trouble.* He kept his head up and eyes focused beyond the men, down the shantytown alley. These were big, hard men with indifferent expressions but malevolent eyes. Winston didn't worry about much, but men like these concerned him more than the teenage kids who roamed the shanties like jackals, looking for isolated prey. The kids had material wants. Who knew what the hell these men wanted? Maybe nothing.

Their gazes as he passed them had a physical quality, repelling Winston into a new alley, this one a confusion of chickens pecking wildly in the dirt and a tethered goat lying either asleep or dead.

Eventually he found his way out, emerging from the shantytown into a field defined on one side by *the river* and on the opposite by crumbling low-rise buildings. The fresh air hit him like waking from a dream; but with this wakefulness, fear.

Winston was playing that night at a broken-down joint called the Checkerboard, located in the midst of several seedy blocks of bars and clubs—the streets haunted by hustlers, whores, and working-class drunks—where the edges of Capitol Heights drained into the Negro East Side. The Checkerboard was run by a fat white cat by the name of Cephus, who kept the drinks weak and ran a half dozen whores who looked better than the usual fare on the street.

Winston arrived early. The bartender unlocked the front door to let him in, locked up again. Winston grabbed a shot of rail whiskey and a bottle of beer from the bar and sat on the tiny wooden stage, playing with the amplifier, tuning his guitar. It was just Winston on the stage and the bartender stocking his bar for the evening when Cephus rolled in from the back wearing a Hawaiian-style shirt that could have doubled as a pup tent. The collar and underarms were dark with perspiration, and the top buttons were undone to reveal a mass of damp, white, hairless flesh.

Winston watched Cephus amble over and register the empty shot glass and half-empty beer sitting on the stage. Winston didn't normally drink before playing. Cephus knew that.

"You don't look so good, Moses," Cephus said in his high, wheezy voice.

Winston kept to his tuning. "No?"

"No, you don't. And the drinking . . . Something wrong, boy?"

Winston looked up, not liking this fat-ass cracker calling him "boy." But something in Cephus's face, some kind of ignorant sincerity, made Winston think that Cephus probably called his white musicians "boy," too. Probably. And now that Winston had a good look, Cephus didn't seem to be doing so well himself, his face an alarming shade of red under a sheen of sweat. The early-evening heat was taking its toll.

"Nothing wrong," Winston said, forcing himself to hold the fat man's eyes for a couple of beats before turning back to his guitar. *Nothing wrong.*

Cephus shrugged. "I must be mistaken." He thought for a moment, then asked, "You need something from the bar, Moses? Another whiskey, or a beer, or something?"

"I don't believe so."

"Suit yourself." Cephus gave a concerned scowl, seemed to contemplate saying something further. Instead, he made a kind of clucking sound, checked his pocket watch, and headed to the front door. Winston watched him go, heart pounding.

2.

Frank Frings's apartment smelled of marijuana smoke, the half-smoked reefer stubbed out in an ashtray on the coffee table. Frings leafed through the early edition of the *Gazette*, taking his time with a bottle of beer. He didn't have a column in the day's paper, so he skimmed through the headlines, perused the obits, read up on the horses. He checked his watch—ten past one. Renate wasn't home.

Frings finished with the paper, picked up his beer, and walked to the window, looking down onto the street. A couple of cabs crept along, looking for fares. A group of young men, their ties loose around their necks, made drunken, boisterous conversation as they jostled down the block. Two derelicts huddled in a doorway, sharing a smoke. Frings finished his beer, took it and the newspaper into the kitchen, and left them on the counter next to the sink.

She would have been off the stage by eleven forty-five and home by twelve thirty. That's the way it always was, except when she didn't come home. Frings sighed, drank a glass of water. He didn't wonder whom she was with tonight. He was annoyed that he'd stayed up waiting for her and would be tired the next day. He was annoyed that he would be alone in his bed tonight. But he didn't think about her in another man's bed. It didn't matter to him.

He undressed, set his alarm clock. The phone rang.

His shirt pasted to his back with sweat from the cab ride, Frings walked into the Palace, shook hands with the bouncer, and glanced around at the crowd—maybe a couple hundred people—which seemed to be suspended in the thick air. Years ago, a few whites had been regulars at the Palace, but tonight there wasn't another white person in the joint. Frings felt eyes on him and then, because he was a regular, the attention returning to the stage. He watched as the owner came his way, weaving gracefully between tables, nodding, smiling, giving the occasional brief handshake. Floyd Christian was about Frings's age, but could have passed for ten years younger if not for the beginnings of gray in his hair. His body was still lean, the coal black skin of his face unlined. He might have been the only person in the place not sweating.

"How are things at the *Gazette*, Frank?" Christian asked by way of greeting, gripping Frings's hand, flashing a grim smile.

"Good. Fine. You know what time it is?" It was a rhetorical question; they both knew it was two in the morning. Christian had rung him, pulling him out of bed, the urgency in Christian's voice getting Frings here in yesterday's clothes, no time to pull out new ones. He was rumpled, his face greasy from the pillow. Christian didn't make calls like that, dragging the best-known newspaperman in the City over to his club during the wee hours. Frings wondered what the hell was going on.

Christian said, "Sorry to pull you away from the lovely Renate."

"You didn't pull me away from her."

Christian raised his eyebrows, concerned.

"It's nothing," Frings said. "She's young."

Christian frowned and clapped Frings on the shoulder. "Come on. Let's go back to my office." Frings followed him along the back row of tables. Frings, at just under six feet, was shorter than Christian and a little thicker around the waist, too. But despite an unmemorable face, Frings had a smile that drew people in, and the presence that sometimes comes to those who are comfortable with their celebrity.

Christian turned his head and yelled over his shoulder, "What do you think of them?"

Onstage a band was playing languid jazz, the musicians dressed in maroon tuxedos. The crowd murmured dozens of low conversations and smoked and drank. Frings wobbled his hand. *So-so.* It wasn't his kind of thing.

Christian knocked twice on his office door, which opened from within. Christian went in first. Frings followed.

He eyed three Negroes sitting at Christian's meeting table; two men, one woman. His mouth went dry. He'd met one of the men before and could guess who the other two were. Something was really wrong. Christian wouldn't have brought Frings together with these people at this time of the night and in secret unless it was big. He didn't like it. Christian could have filled him in, warned him about what he was walking into.

The man in the middle stood up—tall, very thin, black-framed glasses, close-cut hair.

Christian said, "I think you know Mel Washington."

Frings had met Washington before, smart, elegant, rumored homosexual. Frings's editor's, Panos's, take on Washington: *Black, queer, and Red? God doesn't hate nobody that much.*

Mel Washington extended a slender hand with long, pianist's fingers. They shook. "Nice to see you again, Mr. Frings."

"Frank." Frings saw the tension in Washington's jaw.

"Okay. Do you know Warren Eddings and Betty Askins?"

"Only by reputation."

The other two nodded in silent greeting. Washington, Eddings, and Askins: the City's three leading Negro communists. Frings looked at Christian. Christian nodded, acknowledging the difficult situation he'd put Frings in—better to have done this during the day, in public. Right now things *looked* suspicious.

Frings and Washington sat. Christian stood by the door, overseeing, removing himself from the conversation. The room was furnished in black leather; a one-way mirror looked out on the club floor. Barbershop fans pushed the stifling air around the room to no effect. Eddings and Christian smoked Luckies. It was hard to breathe.

"Frank," Washington began, elbows on the table, fingers steepled, "we asked Floyd to bring you here to meet with us because we have a very difficult situation. A *very* difficult situation. We're hoping you'll be . . . discreet. We're coming to you because we know you are sympathetic to our cause. *Can* we trust you to be discreet?"

Frings looked at Washington, then turned in his seat to give Christian a questioning glance.

"Frank, I wouldn't bring you . . ."

Frings nodded, trusting Christian. He turned back to Washington. "Okay. We can talk."

"Two men over at the Community were fishing tonight on the riverbank. They found a dead woman in the rocks. A dead *white* woman."

"On Community land?"

"More or less."

Betty Askins nodded along with Washington. Warren Eddings scowled at his hands folded in his lap.

"Yeah, that's not good." A dead white woman by the all-Negro Uhuru Community was trouble.

Washington continued, "We don't know what happened yet, but it doesn't really matter, does it?"

Frings shook his head. It didn't. Frings knew how perception worked in the City. Anticommunists and the blue press would make lurid speculations, and these would be digested by many people as unquestioned truth. The Uhuru Community, he thought, would burn.

Betty spoke. She was younger than the two men and attractive in a finishing-school sort of way; her hair in a chaste bob. "We have people trying to find out if it was someone in the Community that did this. We can't rule it out, but . . ."

"What would a white girl be doing there?" Frings said.

"Exactly," agreed Washington.

"Working girl?"

Betty Askins looked down at the table, embarrassed.

Washington said, "Could be. But our understanding"—he looked uncomfortably at Betty—"is that . . . this type of commerce is generally kept within the Community."

Frings nodded.

Warren Eddings wore a skullcap. He had high cheekbones and a narrow patch of beard that hung a couple of inches below his chin. His voice was low and controlled. "This is a setup, white folks putting this on the Community."

Washington looked pained. "Frank, I realize this might put you in an awkward position."

Frings's pulse hammered in his ears. "Jesus, Mel, I don't know why you say that." *Why was he here?*

Eddings and Betty looked to Washington. "We need this to be kept quiet." They'd said that. "That's going to be difficult."

Washington said, "I'm afraid I'm not getting to the point. We need this situation taken care of. We can't let this crime be associated with the Uhuru Community. The Community's the most successful Negro endeavor in this City's history. Its existence is at stake. You know that white folks won't tolerate the Community if this news gets out. They won't. And I'm worried that, like Warren said, this is a setup, specifically to put the Community at risk."

Frings nodded. "I get the situation. I'm not clear what you think I can do about it, though."

"We'd like you to talk to someone on the force, convince them to alter the circumstances of the body's . . . disposition."

"Wait a second. If I'm hearing you right, you want to move the body?" Frings was incredulous. "Why didn't you just do it yourself; keep it simple?"

Eddings snorted a cynical laugh.

Washington removed his glasses and rubbed the lenses on the front of his shirt. Rivulets of sweat eased down his temples. "We thought about that. Two reasons we didn't. First, we feared that if someone had, in fact, planted the body in the Community, they might have in some way documented this fact and our moving the body would simply further implicate the Community in the crime. Second, we want a police investigation."

Frings ran his fingers back through his hair and pulled them away wet. "Really? You want the police to doctor the crime scene to absolve the Uhuru Community but also conduct an actual investigation into the crime? That's your plan?"

There was a pause before Betty said, "Yes. And we'd like you to make it happen."

3.

Frings sat in a booth at an all-night diner, waiting for Piet Westermann, a cop. The bright lights showed the place's filth. Frings couldn't imagine eating here, but the coffee was strong. The only other customer was an older man wearing a tweed suit despite the heat, mumbling manically to nobody. Frings half-read a flyer someone had left on the table.

Truffant for Mayor
End the Communist Threat
Restore Christian American Values to the City

He rolled the flyer up and then twisted the roll until it was tight. He'd just met with part of the "Communist Threat." He was aware that in Truffant's eyes, he might even be part of the Threat. But it was hard to imagine Washington, Eddings, and Askins posing much danger to the City. He thought about the humiliation—maybe even anger—they must have felt coming to him for help. It made him uncomfortable; put real urgency into this meeting.

Looking over the opposite side of the booth, he saw Westermann push through the door. Frings tossed the twisted flyer into the empty booth behind him.

Westermann, foggy-eyed, slid onto the bench across from Frings, looking wrung out, his sweat-damp hair pushed back, showing a creeping widow's peak. He was a big guy, lean, movie-star looks, but with a softness about him, too. Frings couldn't put his finger on it exactly—maybe it was what Frings knew about Westermann rather than what he saw—but it was unusual for a cop.

"Frank, I'm eager to hear what would compel you to get me out of bed at this time of night." Westermann also had the movie-star baritone.

Frings laughed cynically. "You'll like this." Frings laid out the scenario that he'd heard earlier at the Palace, leaving out the request to move the body. Westermann sat relaxed, listening with his arms spread across the back of his bench. When Frings was done, Westermann was silent, thinking.

"Awake yet?" Frings asked.

"Getting there, Frank. This couldn't wait?"

"Let's walk this through, okay? First, on its face, do you think this crime was probably committed by someone in the Uhuru Community?"

"Doubtful, but possible, I guess. Look, there's almost no reported crime in the Uhuru Community. They are either basically crime-free or they don't call the police. I have my guess about which one's true, but either way, we don't get out there much. If they have crime—and they must have *some*—it's contained within the Community population. That doesn't mean Community people don't commit crimes outside the compound, but it just doesn't make sense to bring this woman or I guess maybe her corpse back to the shanties. Why ask for trouble? That's hardly rock solid, but at first glance, I'd say it's more likely not to involve someone from the Community."

"So the body ends up in the Community compound either by chance—washing up onshore—or someone puts it there deliberately, probably trying to implicate the Community."

Westermann nodded. "That sounds right."

"The second consideration," Frings said, motioning to the waitress for more coffee, "is what happens if this situation goes public."

"Right. I think the Community would be in a lot of trouble. A lot."

"I think there's a consensus on that point. Mel Washington and his people wanted me to talk to you, to convince you that we need to take steps to prevent any connection between the Community and the body."

The old man at the counter barked out a short, wicked cackle and returned to his mumbling.

Frings made sure he had Westermann's eyes. He needed Westermann to see how serious he was. "They want the body moved. But they don't want to do it."

Westermann smiled—or maybe grimaced. "Jesus. Listen, you know Mel Washington is communist, right? I mean, it's one thing to be tampering with a crime scene. It happens. But for Mel Washington?"

Frings kept eye contact, letting Westermann protest enough to satisfy his conscience, but knowing he'd acquiesce eventually. Frings would leave him no choice. He let Westermann keep talking.

"I have no issue with Mel Washington. But the force . . . he's not real popular."

Frings nodded dismissively, thinking, *Neither are you.* "Look, the other piece of this is that they want an investigation. Not a sham investigation, but a real one. They think this is a provocation and I'm inclined to agree with them. They need this person, these people, to be caught."

Westermann nodded. Frings watched him think, Westermann rubbing his eyes with the heels of his hands, still trying to chase away the fog of sleep.

"This is a hard one, Frank. I don't know."

"It sounds queer now. It did to me, too. But it grows on you."

"Yeah . . ." Westerman was deep in thought.

Frings leaned forward, ratcheting up the pressure.

Westermann said, "What's this to you, Frank? You've got a thing for the Uhuru Community?"

"Sure," Frings said, not wanting to let Westermann change the focus. "People trying to get a little taste of freedom. That a problem?"

Westermann closed his eyes. Frings knew that Westermann didn't really have a choice, didn't even have time to see what he was getting into.

Westermann opened his eyes, looked wearily across the table. "All right, let's go take a look."

As they walked out, Frings tossed a couple of dollars in front of the old-timer. This seemed to jar him from his mumblings and he started yelling in some language Frings didn't know.

4.

The heat seemed to suck the stench out of the river and into the stagnant night. Humid air clung to Frings's face like a hot towel. The moving water reflected a shimmering full moon, and the scene at the riverbank was nearly twilit. Westermann had a flashlight anyway as he, Frings, and Washington followed an older Negro—one of the pair who'd found the body. The Uhuru Community shanties were on a plot of flat land where the river took a sharp bend just downstream from a large abandoned industrial compound. The shantytown ended about fifty yards from the shore, maybe to get some distance from the odor.

The older man worked his way along the rocks on the shore while the others watched from higher ground, until he shouted that he'd found the body. Frings could see the corpse's outline in the moonlight, stuck on the bank and partially submerged in the current. She was clothed, and even with her thin dress matted up against her by the water, Frings could see she was too thin.

Until now, Frings had felt the urgency of the Uhuru Community's plight and the risk he and Westermann were about to take. But this situation had had a vagueness as he thought it through. Seeing the body made everything concrete. His body tingled from the stress, even as his confidence in the choice he'd made strengthened. *You are your deeds.*

"I'm going down to have a look," Westermann said. Frings and Washington caught the implication and hung back on the bank.

They watched Westermann conduct a closer examination of the body, following his progress as the flashlight beam made a circuit of the corpse, starting with her pale, fragile face, her eyes open, staring at the moon; then her thin arms—Westermann zeroing in on them, putting his face up close; then where the sodden dress lay plastered to her chest; and finally her legs and bare feet. There wasn't much to the dress; probably a pro, Frings thought.

He leaned toward Washington, eyes still on Westermann and the body. "What does Father Womé have to say about this?"

When no reply came, Frings turned to face Washington. "Doesn't he know?"

Washington kept his eyes on Westermann below them. "It's complicated, but, no, he doesn't know."

Frings shook his head at this piece of subterfuge. He could pick out a faint orange glow to the east; the first hint of sunrise. He reached into his pocket and pulled a cigarette pack from his jacket and tapped out a reefer. He lit it with a battered metal lighter, took a drag, and held it out to Washington.

"I don't smoke."

"I get migraines," Frings said, feeling the need to explain, and this was *technically* true. Then: "Why is it complicated with Father Womé?"

"We're at cross-purposes in many ways. He wants to create a separate Negro community. We want to create a separate Negro community. But the Father, his eyes are to heaven. We are trying to work here on earth."

"But this *is* his community, right?"

Washington sighed. "It wouldn't be here if it weren't for the Father, no question. The thing is that he's content to provide for his people and leave them to their own devices as long as they are free. What they do with that freedom . . ." Washington let the thought trail off. "But you can't keep a community together that way. Not this kind, at least. There needs to be organization. Right now the Community needs to be protected from the City. That's not what Womé does. He simply doesn't understand or think about it. So, it's complicated."

Westermann climbed up from the rocks to join them. Frings stubbed the reefer out on the sole of his shoe and slipped the stub into his pocket.

Westermann caught the whiff of marijuana smoke as he climbed up the bank to Frings and Washington. He'd seen dozens of dead bodies and there was nothing particularly different about this one. She did have sores— maybe measles or something like that. He'd taken his time with the examination; thinking through the next move. The choice to move the body had been made. It was a career-ending decision if he was caught, but Frings could end his career—would end his career—if he didn't. His real choices were how to move the body, and where.

"I can't tell for sure, but my guess is she drowned. No blood, though that could have been washed away by the water. No wounds that I could see. But in the dark . . . a coroner really needs to take a look. It's strange, though, she has these blisters. I didn't want to touch them, but they're all over her body. And she's so thin. There's something wrong with her. She's sick. Or she was."

Frings asked, "How'd she end up on the rocks?"

Westermann shook his head. "The river maybe? Washed up? Could be overland. Just park back there"—he nodded in the direction of the road, one hundred yards or so in the distance. "She can't weigh ninety pounds."

"What do you suggest we do?" Washington asked, his fingertips brushing his lips, his body hunched with exhaustion.

Westermann looked downstream. "Easiest thing to do is push her back out into the river, see where she ends up. Just like she never washed up here in the first place, or maybe got pulled loose from the bank." There wasn't much of a crime scene down among the rocks. The current was continuously washing away any evidence, even of his own presence. He could just shove her back out into the river, "discover" her body wherever it ended up, and conduct the investigation from there. It wasn't perfect, but it wasn't terrible and had the benefit of being simple.

He looked at the two men. Washington seemed fatigued, Frings energized for some reason. "What do you think?"

Washington nodded, lost in thought.

Frings shrugged. "You're the cop."

This bothered Westermann, Frings putting all the responsibility on him when they were both complicit. He caught Frings's eye and wondered if, maybe, this squared their debt.

5.

Westermann caught two hours of sleep, woke up in his clothes, and made it to headquarters in time for Frings's anonymous call reporting the body on the riverbank in the vicinity of a cluster of derelict warehouses just downstream from the Uhuru Community shanties. There were some jurisdictional complications, but this was not a promising case and no one objected much to Westermann's claim.

Without the dark to fill in the spaces, the area around the Uhuru Community was remarkably empty. The Community shantytown, from the outside, was a low amalgamation of scrap lumber, sheet tin, and assorted other found building materials. It spread for more than two hundred yards across flatland. Several hundred yards of weed-infested asphalt, abandoned road, and empty lots teeming with bugs and rodents lay between the Community and a district of warehouses abandoned when the railroad supplanted the river as the main route for cargo transport. Vultures and crows hovered above, searching for a meal.

The sun out here was merciless. In the field near the shanties, two young Negro girls, their hair in braids, fanned a cow with leafy branches. The cow was white and brown and sickly. Westermann saw that three of the cow's legs were brown and the fourth was white. Odd, to notice something like that.

Uniformed cops were already at the site, taking photos and sifting through the surrounding weeds for evidence that Westermann knew did not exist. He walked across the no-man's-land with two of his detectives. Westermann had six detectives under his authority and he'd brought the two best with him, Larry Morphy and Torsten Grip. They cut an interesting profile walking toward the riverbank. Westermann and Morphy were both well over six feet, but where Westermann was lanky and languid in his movements, Morphy was broad shouldered and strutted with a big man's confidence. By contrast, Grip was just over five and a half feet, built like a keg, and walked as if he were trying to punish the ground with each step.

"How'd you pull this case?" Grip asked, his voice rasping with cigarette damage.

"Statistically anomalous homicide," Westermann said, forcing a half smile, trying to hide the anxiety. Grip chuckled. Morphy, not generally one for a lot of conversation, took in the surroundings as they walked. Smoke came from different points in the Community, and the smell of burning wood and spiced meats drifted across the field to them.

They arrived, dripping sweat, at the riverbank. The uniformed cops taking photos of the body and examining the rocks made way. Westermann flashed on six hours earlier, the same body but lying differently. This time she'd made shore facedown, held in place against the current by jutting rocks, black hair fanned out in the water like a starburst. He had the animal urge to grab her, get her away from the water; destroy a crime scene that, however improbably, could point to him.

"The fuck are these assholes doing?" Grip said, jerking his head toward the uniforms searching the brush farther off the shore. "They think someone dragged her all the way over here, dunked her, and then pulled her back up on the bank? Jesus. They get paid for this?"

Morphy snorted and shot a contemptuous look at the uniforms.

"No stone unturned," Westermann said, climbing down on the rocks to get a better view of the body.

"Right. Turn over every fucking stone," Grip said. "Hey, you assholes done taking pictures of the girl?"

One of the police photographers answered in the affirmative and Westermann watched Morphy, sitting on a rock, take off his shoes and socks and then stand, remove his jacket and his pants, and fold them neatly on top of his shoes.

"What the hell are you doing?" said Grip.

Morphy, in shirt, tie, and boxer shorts, looked back at Grip. "You going in the water?"

Grip shook his head, muttering, "Jesus Christ," and walked upstream.

Westermann watched Morphy wade into the river to get a better vantage on the corpse. Westermann had done much the same inspection just a few hours prior and knew what Morphy would find. No trauma. Presumed death by drowning. But those blisters and her weight . . . *Wait for the coroner's report.*

It was goddamn hot out in the sun without any cover. Westermann took off his jacket and held it by a finger over his shoulder as he walked closer to the body. "What do you think?"

"Drowned." Morphy didn't look up as he moved the woman's chin. Westermann noted leaves and other small debris stuck in her snarled hair.

Emaciated. Ended up in the Uhuru Community. He had moved the body. Was it too late to take it back? What if he confessed now, to Morphy? He caught himself. Fatigue. It kept him from thinking straight. Calm down.

Morphy climbed back up onto the bank, amber water dripping from his legs. He shrugged at Westermann. "The coroner can do his job."

The uniforms got to work bagging the body for delivery to the morgue.

Morphy dressed, sitting on a rock to pull on his socks and shoes. Westermann paced, uncomfortable with nothing to do, ready to get out of there. He looked upriver and saw Grip standing on a rock at the river's edge, watching as the current pulled detritus downstream.

Back at the station, Westermann sent Morphy and Grip to handle the paperwork and headed to the bathroom to douse his face and neck with cold, rust-tinged water from the tap. He checked himself in the mirror: bags under his eyes, two days' growth. He ran his wet fingers through his hair, smoothing it back into place. He'd made it through the first step. He needed sleep so that he could think more clearly.

The bathroom door swung open and a cop in uniform entered and took a sink two down from Westermann's. Westermann rolled his neck and noticed the cop glaring at him in the mirror. He knew this guy, an anticommunist fanatic named Ed Wayne.

Westermann said, "Something I can help you with, Sergeant?"

Wayne sneered.

Westermann checked out their reflections side by side in the mirror—Westermann tall and broad shouldered; Wayne stocky, a little overweight, but with a brawler's look about him; thick neck under his fat, red face.

Westermann turned to leave, walking by Wayne on his way to the door. The two men exchanged stares until Westermann winked and walked out, heart pounding, forcing a chuckle.

6.

Off duty that night, Grip was at the wheel of his DeSoto—all four windows down to get some air—creeping through a neighborhood of low buildings with heavy doors. It was twilight here, a jaundiced light rendering every color false. Two men accompanied Grip. Ole Koss rode shotgun, working a toothpick, listening to some preacher on a Christian radio station. He was a big, muscular vet, close-shaved head, weird scar on his mouth that made his upper lip move a little funny when he talked. Grip wasn't sure what Koss did for work, but he always seemed to have time for these things. Grady Filkins sat in the backseat, a corporate geek on his first time out, looking to get his thrills. Grip had picked up that Koss didn't like Filkins; the geek physically frail, a desk zealot still in bow tie and straw fedora.

Koss read off street numbers as they eased along through sparse traffic. Grip saw cops every few blocks, walking with their hands on their truncheons. Campaign posters for the mayor were plastered onto brick walls along with posters for his opponent, Vic Truffant, and anticommunist propaganda: giant, vaguely Asian eyes captioned THE ENEMY IS AMONG US; shady, Semitic-featured men lurking under the hammer and sickle. Above them, the night clouds were lit red and purple from below.

On the radio, the preacher was going on about the Antichrist or something; Grip hated that shit, but there was never much profit in arguing with Koss. Filkins chain-smoked in the back, nervous as hell. He wasn't the type of guy you'd peg for rough work.

"Yeah, up here," Koss said, indicating a cinder-block building with a cargo door and an entrance to its right.

Grip glided to a stop at the curb. Koss pulled a sack from under his seat and produced two guns. He secured one in the back of his waistband and tossed the other to Filkins, who recoiled as if it were a live grenade landing in his lap.

"Put it in your pocket," Koss said. "We're going to leave you at the bottom of the stairs. Someone shows up, you stick the gun in his face and bring him to us. Don't be weak with the piece. If someone gets his hands on it, I'll have to kill them and that would be too bad."

"I don't . . ."

Koss sucked in his lips.

"You won't have to do anything," Grip said gruffly, trying to head this off before it turned into a disaster. "Stand at the door, maybe have your gun out. Don't talk, just stand there. Nobody's going to show up. We'll only be up there for a couple minutes."

Filkins seemed uncertain. Koss turned in this seat and shot him a withering look. "You going to get it together?" It came out like a question, but it wasn't.

They waited in the car for ten minutes, listening to Christian radio while Filkins made humming noises in the backseat, trying to get his nerves under control. The wall was peppered with Truffant posters—maybe the Reds thought this was some kind of camouflage.

A heavy guy in a white shirt padded down the street and approached the door to the cinder-block building. He stopped, pulling keys from his pocket with a surreptitious look both ways. Grip was out of the car quickly, moving on the guy with practiced efficiency—a cop move. Koss followed him. The guy turned, surprised, and Grip stuck a pistol in his ribs.

"Open up, real quiet."

The man's eyes were wide with fear, but he unlocked the door and Grip followed him through. They left Filkins, hands shaking, on the ground floor while Grip pushed the fat guy up the stairs with a pistol in his back. Koss followed, gun drawn.

At the top of the landing they listened; heard a sliding sound that came at long intervals, and muffled conversation. Grip motioned the guy to go in, the guy looking as if he were going to be sick. Grip moved his pistol up to the man's head and he swallowed hard and opened the door. Grip pushed him into the room and followed tight behind.

Inside, three men looked up, stunned. They were working a small printing press, churning out commie posters: crude block prints of Mao; a blond guy with a scythe looking heroic in front of a field of wheat; WORKERS UNITE.

Two wore Lenin beards; they were all small, wiry. Grip thought Koss could probably take all three of them at once, no problem.

"What the hell?" one of them sputtered as they instinctively retreated to the far side of the room. Koss pushed the fat guy toward them. Grip covered them with his gun, closing the distance. They didn't look to have the nerve or the ability to put up any resistance. Still, you never knew.

Koss took the press, flipped it on its side, and began stomping on it, splintering the frame, red ink pooling on the floor, the chemical smell filling the room. One of the guys began to protest, but Grip sighted the gun on his forehead and he backed down. The fat one was sitting on the floor, shaking.

The press in shambles, Koss gathered posters, throwing them on the shattered press. He paused with one, a block portrait of a wide-browed Negro above the slogan THE UHURU COMMUNITY MUST LIVE! Koss showed it to Grip. Grip shook his head in disgust.

Koss asked the Reds, "You in bed with the Uhuru Community?"

They looked back at him, intimidated into silence. Koss laughed—a nasty sound. Koss threw the whole stack of Uhuru Community posters on the pile. He pulled a tin of matches from his jacket pocket.

One of the Reds said, "Don't."

Grip turned on him. "Shut it."

Koss lit a match on the sole of his shoe and tossed it on the pile of paper. Then he tossed another. And another. The posters caught, flames rose.

The small, scattered flames began to find each other and the fire grew. Koss's face was neutral. "Come on," he said, and walked toward the exit.

Grip nodded at the flames. "Good luck with that," he said to the Reds.

Later, Grip sat with Ed Wayne at a bar called Crippen's, chasing whiskey shots with beer in sweating glasses. A dozen or so men—and one woman—smoked and drank balefully. Filkins sat at a separate table with a Mexican prostitute, leaning into her and speaking quietly in her ear. Koss, an alleged teetotaler, had gone home.

From somewhere came the sound, half static, of someone ranting on the radio. This bar was a headquarters of sorts for anticommunists, run by a World War I vet below a seedy Italian joint.

Grip recounted for Wayne the incursion on the printing press, embellishing a little; the Reds needing more physical coercion in his telling.

Wayne nodded along to all this drunkenly. He was a stupid prick, but their shared politics made conversation tolerable.

"Shit, I nearly forgot," Wayne said, nearly slurring his words, "I saw your boss this morning."

"Yeah?"

"Yeah. Restroom at the station. Making himself pretty."

"Okay, Ed. Whatever you say."

"Whatever I say?" Wayne laughed. "How about this? I say your boss is an asshole."

Grip reddened. "Know what, Ed? Shut the hell up about shit that you don't know about, all right?"

"Get fucked," Ed growled.

Grip stood up, leaning over the table. "Fuck you." They locked eyes, Grip daring Wayne to stand up and do something about it.

Finally, Wayne broke and returned to his beer. "He's still a bastard," he muttered.

"Jesus," Grip said, holding up two fingers for a shot and a beer.

Filkins and his whore got up from their table holding hands. In a weird euphoria driving back from the press, Filkins had babbled on about rewarding himself for his night's work with this girl—Grip couldn't remember her name now—until Koss had finally snapped at him to shut it and Filkins had spent the remainder of the ride huddled in the corner with a little grin on his face. Grip wondered if he could somehow work it out so that he'd never have to see Filkins again.

7.

Lou Souza walked the dirt alleys of the Uhuru Community shantytown carrying a handkerchief that he used to mop his brow every few steps. It wasn't just the heat. The smell of the shanties was getting to him, too: spices, exotic-wood burning, sweat, baked dirt, marijuana, and, underlying it all, sewage and rotting garbage.

"I'm having trouble breathing," Souza said to Remy Plouffe as the two detectives trod warily through the claustrophobic alleys on the edges of the shantytown.

"It's in your head, Lou."

Negro children in ragged clothes scattered laughing when they saw the two white men in suits and straw fedoras approaching. Something about these kids bothered Souza, made him uneasy.

"I'm telling you, there's something in the air. Something's working on my lungs."

Plouffe shook his head. "What's in the air is this shit smell and the heat."

Souza mumbled something under his breath and Plouffe said, "What did you say?" and Souza told him to never mind and nodded up ahead of them where four men stood, passing a huge reefer between them.

The morning had been frustrating. They wore their badges clipped to their jackets, neither one comfortable in the shanties and counting on their authority to give them some kind of protection. They'd been met with silent wariness, fear, and hostility. Their attempts to question people had consistently been rebuffed, the people either ignoring them or claiming ignorance.

"*Have you seen or heard about a young white woman around the shanties the last few days?*"

"*I'm sorry, sir, but I haven't.*"

Souza saw Plouffe's increasing frustration in the set of his jaw and the narrowing of his eyes. Souza didn't much care if they came away with nothing from this canvas. Some whore found dead? Was it that important? And

23

there was something he didn't like about the group of men they were approaching, the way they dominated that end of the alley; the way the other
Negroes seemed to walk down side alleys so as not to walk past them.

Souza and Plouffe stopped a few feet from the group of men. Up close,
Souza saw their matted hair and yellowed eyes. The men met the two detectives with a heavy-lidded, menacing silence.

Plouffe said, "We're investigating a missing person. White girl; word is
that she was seen around here. Any of you seen a white girl hanging around
here? Or heard about one?" His voice had an edge, the morning's frustrations creeping in.

The men stared back without expression, but their eyes burned.

"Maybe you didn't hear me," Plouffe said, moving forward a stride, stepping up the tough-cop vibe. "I asked if you'd seen or heard about a white
girl around here the past couple days."

One of the Negroes stepped forward. He had a good five inches on
Plouffe and tilted his head back to look down condescendingly.

"We've heard nothing." Deep voice. Island accent.

Souza saw Plouffe's back tense. Plouffe wasn't real fond of Negroes to
begin with.

"Rem," Souza whispered. Plouffe was in a staring match with the big Negro and ignored Souza. Souza saw people beyond the other three Negroes,
out of their shacks to see what was going on. He looked over his shoulder
and saw more standing in the alley, checking out the action. Souza rolled
his left shoulder back a little, pulling the jacket away from his shoulder
holster in case he needed to go for his gun. Behind the standoff, the crowd
parted to allow a short, thin man with coal black skin move up front. He
wore round sunglasses. Souza felt the man's eyes upon him.

The big Negro said, "You asked your question, Mr. Cop, and got your
answer. Now you can go."

Souza moved up quickly next to Plouffe, trying to head off Plouffe's response.

Souza whispered in Plouffe's ear, "Rem, look around. We've got to be
smart here."

Souza saw Plouffe break off the staring match and look down the alley.
The onlookers weren't belligerent, but Souza didn't know how they'd react

if the confrontation escalated. The little man was still there, standing motionless.

"Come on, Rem. Let this one go. They probably haven't seen anything anyway."

Plouffe nodded. He looked at the big man. "Next time."

The big man snorted and then laughed. His friends joined in. Souza felt his face flush and he grabbed Plouffe by the elbow as they retreated down the alley. The crowd seemed to understand what was going on—or they were looking to buy some favor with the four men—because they began to laugh as well, the noise gathering volume as it echoed through the narrow confines of the alleys. Souza cleared a path through the people with his right arm as he pulled Plouffe along with his left. Plouffe had his hand on the gun still holstered under his arm, and Souza thanked God that he had the good sense not to pull it.

They walked back toward where Souza thought they had come in, but the alleys didn't seem the same somehow. Or maybe they did. Plouffe was calming down and they walked in silence, not bothering to question the people they passed. Souza looked down an alley of dilapidated and makeshift huts and thought he saw the man with the sunglasses moving parallel to them. But as soon as the man disappeared from view, Souza thought that maybe he hadn't actually seen him. His memory of the way the man moved seemed wrong.

Souza began to feel as if they had walked more than far enough to reach the exit, but there was no way they could have missed it. He looked at Plouffe and saw that he, too, was trying to work it through.

They passed a small lot between two shanties. It looked as if a shack might have stood there at one point and been torn down or stolen or whatever happened to shacks here. At the far side of the tiny space was a wall made of corrugated tin, and through the cracks in the tin, Souza could see the fields outside the shantytown.

"Goddammit," Souza said, took two steps, and put his shoulder into the wall. It sagged. Plouffe joined him and they kicked at the wall until it finally ripped away from where it was attached to the plywood wall of the adjacent shanty.

8.

Grip had been mildly disappointed that morning to find that he and Morphy had drawn the task of trying to establish the dead woman's identity. He'd been looking forward to poking around the Uhuru Community, getting the line on some of the communists there. He also had some thoughts about how the body had ended up where it had, but he could look into that on his own time.

The City Morgue was painfully bright and clean and smelled sweetly of formaldehyde. Grip's and Morphy's footsteps echoed on gleaming tile floors that shone so that the room seemed to be illuminated from every direction. Six stainless steel examining tables were lined up in the room and only two were empty. On three lay bodies covered with white sheets, and at the fourth a small, round man with rimless glasses over his surgical mask peered into an open chest cavity. It wasn't cool in here the way it was supposed to be. Grip suppressed thoughts of what the heat was doing to the cadavers.

Grip cleared his throat and the man jerked his head up. He'd been lost in his examination of the corpse of an obese Caucasian man. Grip felt slightly sick, not from the grisly sight of the opened chest, but from his contempt at the condition this man had been in while alive. Disgusting.

The coroner, an ageless man named Pulyatkin, opened his palms in inquiry. Sweat misted the tops of his lenses.

"Jane Doe. Came in yesterday," Grip said.

Pulyatkin nodded. "One moment please." He walked back to a sink, and Grip and Morphy watched as he scrubbed his hands and forearms with powdered soap and hung his surgical mask on a peg. Then he came back to the two officers. He didn't offer his hand.

"This is one of them," he said, and pulled a sheet back to reveal a woman's waxen body. "There's two others. One of them's older, maybe sixties."

"This is her," Morphy said, cocking his head slightly as he looked at the woman's uncovered face.

Grip's first impression—he hadn't seen the body up close at the riverbank—was that she must have been attractive in life. The structure of her face was delicate and her body had probably been pretty good before she had begun wasting. Then he noticed the blemishes on her skin.

"We did an exterior exam," Pulyatkin was saying, "and came up with nothing indicating external trauma. The water, of course, would have washed away most of what we would normally find in the way of fibers and such. There are no external signs of anything potentially fatal, though there are needle marks in her arms."

"Hophead?"

Pulyatkin grimaced at the thought. "Not unless she just picked up the habit. There isn't the scarring normally associated with any kind of regular use."

Morphy had left the conversation and was pulling back the sheets to look at the faces of the other two corpses. Pulyatkin gave him a disconcerted look, but continued.

"What about these marks?" Grip said, pointing to the blemishes on her face.

Pulyatkin nodded. "She actually has these same marks all over her body. They appear to be blisters of some sort, though I haven't had a chance to examine them more closely. We're very busy here, Detective. The heat . . . there are always more bodies when there's heat like this."

Morphy was back and had pulled back the other end of the sheet, giving her feet a close inspection.

Grip asked, "How do you think she got these blisters?"

"An allergic reaction, maybe. Again, I haven't had a chance to examine them more carefully, but their dispersal around the body indicates that their origin is internal—systemic—rather than external."

Morphy pulled the sheet up, covering the corpse's face. "When are you going to give the body a closer look?"

"Today, sometime. Maybe after lunch."

"Be sure you get back to us," Morphy said.

Pulyatkin nodded wearily. He knew his personal stake.

"You hear from your relatives back in the motherland recently?" Grip asked, almost as an afterthought.

"I haven't been in contact with anyone from the USSR in well over a decade."

Grip smiled in an unsettling way. "You know what to do if you ever *are* contacted by one of the comrades."

"My first call, in that case, would be to you."

Grip winked at him.

"We'll be waiting to hear from you," Morphy said, "about the corpse."

9.

Frings woke to his alarm clock, slamming the top to stop the ringing. He lay back against his pillow and turned to the empty space next to him, remembered that Renate hadn't come home. Sunlight came through the east window, illuminating the framed concert posters—BRAZILIAN SENSATION RENATE CONCECAIO SINGS THE BOSSA NOVA—he had given her on her birthday, her twenty-fourth.

He took a quick shower, water lukewarm; shaved; pulled on a brown, summer-weight suit; smoked a reefer while he waited for the coffee to percolate; read the obits and the police log in the morning paper. The reefer tasted good, felt good; his body relaxing, his mind easing into the day.

He read the front section of the paper with his coffee, noted Truffant going after the mayor for being insufficiently vigorous in his efforts to root out communists in the City government. Frings doubted there actually were communists in the City government. But it was always something, every day, the drumbeat of criticism, all in the service of painting the mayor as a corrupt patsy of communists. Frings sighed, frustrated that the paper ran these bleatings as if they were news, instead of invective.

He finished his coffee, tossed the paper on his metal-topped kitchen table, and decided to pick up a bagel at Sheffer's around the corner from the station.

The *Gazette* had moved into a brand-new building only three years before, yet Panos, the managing editor, had managed through some strange alchemy to turn his office seedy and musty in this short time. Panos himself had the haunted, gaunt look that previously fat people sometimes have. He was alternately sucking on a Cuban and hacking a wet cough. His mustache drooped unhealthily beneath his sad eyes.

Frings had watched Panos's physical decline from the bearlike man he had been only a decade ago, to this new, wasted body. His Mediterranean skin had gone sickly yellow. Panos was not forthcoming about his health, but Frings knew something had been wrong for a while now.

"Frank," Panos said to Frings, sitting in the chair opposite, cradling a mug of black coffee. "There's something you want?"

"You know the Uhuru Community, Chief?"

"Sure. Of course. Over by the river."

"You know we've never given them any ink. Not them; not Father Womé."

Panos's shoulders sank as he shook his head. "We haven't given any ink. Is there a story here, Frank? Something that's more important than the election?"

"The election? Plenty of time for that. Listen for a second, this is the kind of stuff that will sell papers. Cult community in the City? Weird rituals, the whole bit. People will eat it up. Voodoo, Panos."

Panos brushed this last bit away with a wave of his hand. "I'm sorry, Frank, where is it we are headed with this?"

"I want to interview Father Womé."

"Frank—"

"Listen, Panos," Frings interrupted. "This is an interesting story. I'm telling you, we run something, the other papers will be all over it, but we'll be there first. People will eat it up."

Panos squinted. "I'm surprised by this, Frank. I expect this type of thing from Latapy, maybe. All flash. But you, Frank?"

Frings didn't say anything.

Panos thought. "I'm sorry, the Uhuru Community, it is communist, no?"

"Don't look for a reason not to do this."

"So I am right."

"There are some communists involved in the Community, yes. Mel Washington, you know him. But the Community as a whole? Father Womé? I don't think so."

Panos frowned. "This is serious, Frank. We cannot be the newspaper that is friendly to communists. It hurts circulation—"

Frings began to protest, but Panos waved him away.

"More important, if we do this, we can't go after Truffant in the race. He'll accuse us of being communists, and then what do we say? We will be impotent."

Frings exhaled in frustration. "Communism is such a small—"

Panos held up his hand and shook his head. "They could be goddamn Boy Scouts; the public thinks they are communists so that's what they are. We cannot be the newspaper that supports this communist experiment."

"Look, let me talk to Womé. You want, you run an editorial criticizing the Community for their commie ties, okay? I wouldn't do it, but maybe you need the cover."

Panos studied his cigar, which was how he dealt with misgivings. "Frank, do you forget we have a mayor's election? *This* is news. The Uhuru Community?" Panos showed his palms, indicating that the Community, in his eyes, did not rate particularly high. "I thought I'd be pulling you off that fascist Truffant, that you would tear his throat out. But this?"

"Don't worry, Panos, I'm going to get my teeth into Truffant. But at least let me interview Womé first. I'll write it up, run it by you, and then you can make the call. You don't have to run it. You're the chief."

"I'm the chief," Panos echoed dubiously. "Frank, you go ahead, but remember that this story, I don't know . . ."

"Of course. Thanks, Panos."

Frings was out the door before Panos could reconsider.

10.

Westermann sat slumped, knee jiggling, in a windowless, third-floor conference room along with the deputy superintendent, a wraith of a man name Kraatjes, and a mathematician from the Tech who contracted part-time with the force.

Westermann was distracted, worrying about what his men might be doing in the field. Even if he weren't in this meeting, he could do precious little other than monitor developments—he couldn't be everywhere. This was the balance he had to find, giving his men enough leeway to conduct a real investigation while making sure they didn't find the truth about where the body had originally lain. His chest was tight.

They sat around a detailed map of the City, divided into quadrants and covered in dots of various colors of ink. The paper was damp from the humidity, books on each corner keeping the map flat. The men had pulled off their ties and sweated into their open collars. Drops of perspiration fell on the edges of the map, raising little wet welts.

Kraatjes, who oversaw the compiling of the crime data that produced the dots on the map, talked in his high, nasal voice, identifying areas of the City that had seen a notable increase or decrease in crime over the past month. The mathematician took fastidious notes in the ruled notebook that he always brought to these meetings.

This was a System meeting. The System was Westermann's brainchild and it had brought him equal measures of reverence and disdain. Fortunately for his career, the reverence mostly came from the administration and the disdain from the cops on the street.

The System was a mathematical method for deploying police assets throughout the City, putting police in high-crime areas. This idea, on the face of it, was simple enough. The problem was that if you moved the cops from low-crime areas to high-crime areas, you risked criminals' becoming savvy to this redeployment and crime increasing in previously safe neighborhoods. The System was a complicated mathematical formula that prescribed police deployment largely to high-crime areas while also maintaining a presence in relatively safe ones. It also mandated that the presence in low-crime areas be deployed without a pattern, so that observant criminals were not provided predictable windows of opportunity.

The System was implemented as an enhancement to the traditional cop-on-the-beat modus operandi that had dominated the force for decades. But despite its maintaining a credible number of beat cops, the duties of a large group of uniforms were radically changed. This, along with a presumption that the System was an attack on the fundamentals of good traditional policing—community relations, instinct, presence—left Westermann deeply unpopular with a large percentage of the cops on the beat, particularly the old guard, who saw the minor corruptions of protection money and patronage suddenly become nonviable.

Westermann did not intend the System as an inherent criticism of traditional police work or an instrument to mitigate police corruption. It was simply a way to allocate resources, and the effect on crime rates since its implementation four years prior had been substantial. But, truth be told, he was ambivalent about his unpopularity in some quarters. He hadn't sought hostility and did not feel he deserved it. Yet, in some way, it validated the profundity of the change he'd advocated. And he would rather be reviled than ignored.

The penance he paid for the System was this monthly meeting with Kraatjes, whom he genuinely liked and respected, and the mathematician. The irony was that while Westermann disliked these meetings, this work was where his talent lay—not the cop work on the street. He was self-aware enough to understand this and have it bother him.

The mathematician and Kraatjes discussed how the body found on the riverbank should be treated as an anomaly and not factored into the next month's deployments.

Westermann's mind was on the two detectives he'd felt compelled to send to the Uhuru Community to question anyone who'd been on the riverbank that night to find out if they'd seen or heard anything. There was no way to avoid taking this risk—the investigation required it—yet it was also the first and conceivably most likely point at which the original location of the body might be disclosed, and with it, the moving of the body.

Souza and Plouffe, counting the weeks until their pensions, were the least likely of his men to uncover anything during a canvas. It was the best he could do at the moment. He turned his thoughts to the river and the flow of detritus caught in the current and how intently Grip had watched.

He shuddered involuntarily, realizing that he had, without their knowing, alienated himself from his own men.

"Too cold for you, Piet?" Kraatjes asked.

11.

Pulyatkin, the coroner, pulled a sour face when he saw Grip and Morphy return. Grip sucked on a toothpick and surveyed the room under heavy lids, as though something or someone might be trying to hide from him. Morphy, as always, was more laconic, disconcerting Pulyatkin with an unblinking stare.

"You figured anything out, comrade?" Grip asked, close to the old man and leading with his chest.

Pulyatkin took a step back. "Something, yes. I haven't been able to identify her, but, well, let me show you."

The two cops followed Pulyatkin to the far examination table where Pulyatkin pulled back the sheet to expose the corpse's face. Grip was again taken with how attractive she must have been when life had animated her features. In death, she retained the quality of beauty that one might find in a statue.

"So, again, this is her," Pulyatkin said. "I can tell you this, no identifying birthmarks or major scars. I'm waiting on fingerprints, but it will take a while. Dead prostitute, no sign of foul play. . . ."

Grip was fixed on her face, mottled with the little sores. "You said you were going to show us something."

"I don't know for certain, but I would guess she's not American. Not originally, at least."

Grip jumped on this. "She's foreign? From where? How do you know?"

Pulyatkin looked over at Morphy, who was slowly walking around the room, his head tilted slightly as if at a better angle for hearing.

Pulyatkin hesitated; Morphy's wandering had thrown him off. The humming sound of the lights filled the void. "I took a look at her possessions, what was found on her body: a necklace, a cross with an inscription in Cyrillic letters."

Grip said, "Yeah?"

"It didn't say anything interesting, Detective. You aren't that lucky. A good-luck charm that would be common in rural Russia."

Grip nodded, his eyes eager. "Could she have gotten it here? Maybe from a relative?"

Pulyatkin shrugged. "Could be, but I don't think so. You get a sense of bodies when you're in this business as long as I've been. You can tell things. She isn't American. Her body doesn't have that history."

Grip nodded, not sure he was convinced. He looked to Morphy, but Morphy was leafing through a folder he'd pulled off a metal table by the wall.

"Detective," Pulyatkin called to him. Morphy finished reading the paper and tossed the folder back on the table.

"There's another thing you might find of interest." Pulyatkin reached into a bowl and pulled out a pink-and-purple mass.

"Jesus," Grip said. "The hell's that?"

"Her liver."

"Fuck," Grip said.

Morphy walked over, hands behind his back. "What are those white marks?" he asked, nodding to the slightly raised white welts that formed a lattice over the organ.

"Lesions of some sort. I haven't seen anything quite like them before." Pulyatkin replaced the liver and pulled a second organ from a different bowl. "Her heart, also with the white lesions."

Morphy took a close look, his face inches away. Satisfied, he straightened up. "That doesn't look healthy."

Grip gave a quick, truncated laugh.

"No," Pulyatkin said gravely. "I suspect that she would have died very soon if she hadn't drowned."

"So, what does all this mean, in your opinion?" Grip asked.

Pulyatkin replaced the heart. He turned from them and walked to the washbasin, talking over his shoulder. "She had some kind of disease, something that I have not seen before. Based on that and the necklace, I would surmise that she picked it up abroad, and I would think not from the USSR. One hears about diseases like this; Africa, maybe South America. I don't know. It's just a guess."

Pulyatkin turned on the water and began to wash his hands.

Grip looked at Morphy. "Doesn't tell us a whole hell of a lot."

"I saw the necklace when she was in the river." Morphy frowned and asked of Puyatkin's back, "There's nothing else?"

Pulyatkin shrugged without turning. "There's no identification, no personal effects except for her clothes and the necklace. Maybe someone will come and identify her."

Something about the coroner's dismissive tone angered Grip. He stalked over to the washbasin and grabbed Pulyatkin's shoulder and turned him so that the two men faced each other.

"Listen, comrade. This is a very important case, right? We don't have time to wait and hope that someone comes in to identify her. We need to know now. What else can you tell us?"

Pulyatkin stared back at Grip, keeping his gaze steady, not backing down. They stared at each other for a few moments, then Pulyatkin dropped his eyes to Grip's hand on his shoulder. Grip pulled it away.

Pulyatkin spoke quietly. "If someone comes to claim the body, I will let you know. Beyond that there is nothing I can tell you about this woman. Now I have some work to do."

Grip continued to stare at Pulyatkin. Morphy put a hand on Grip's shoulder. "Come on."

Grip kept his eyes on Pulyatkin, hesitating as if he had something else to say, but he just shook his head and followed Morphy to the door while Pulyatkin, motionless, watched.

12.

The police station smelled of perspired alcohol. A dozen cops tried to steer eight protesting Negroes through the lobby and into booking. Westermann, just arriving back from lunch, paused to watch and noticed Sergeant Ed Wayne, sweating, red-faced, furious. Wayne noticed Westermann and, sneering, gave a fierce jerk to the cuffs of one of the prisoners, drawing a bark of pain. Westermann flashed Wayne a wink and continued on to his squad room with the familiar feeling in his gut—he didn't know how to deal with guys like Wayne. His efforts were hollow and they both knew it. He and Wayne didn't share a common background, and as police, they were playing on Wayne's turf: tough, working-class, vet.

Westermann's detectives were waiting for him—three teams of two—sitting in folding chairs in their squad room. Kraatjes frequently reminded Westermann that this was the hardest squad he'd ever had to assemble, given Westermann's unpopularity in so many police circles. Westermann wasn't sure if Kraatjes was joking. Regardless, he had a group that was at least neutral toward him—some even loyal—if not consistent in their abilities. And he'd betrayed them.

Everyone smoked cigarettes except for Grip, who was chewing on an unlit cigar, and Westermann, who didn't smoke. They dispensed quickly with reports: the search warrant carried out on an East Side apartment to find evidence supporting a homicide confession; the questioning of suspects in the murder of a vagrant in a Theater District alley; and so on.

Souza and Plouffe briefed the squad on their morning in the shanties, changing the details to preserve some dignity but admitting that they had come up empty. Grip and Morphy chuckled at this, and Souza pinched up his face and bulged his eyes but didn't say anything.

Grip and Morphy reported last, with Grip, as always, doing the talking. He related the two trips to the morgue and then, anticipating Westermann's questions, continued.

"So, no progress as far as actual identities, but the disease angle has possibilities. Maybe this woman, this possibly Russian woman, was in Africa or South America and picked up the disease there, but maybe she wasn't. It's possible she caught the disease here from someone else."

"Like someone just off the boat in the Community," Plouffe suggested.

"Maybe," Grip said.

Westermann was about to say something, try to move this in a different direction, but decided against it. He couldn't control things to the degree he wanted and he had to accept that.

"Not necessarily," Morphy said, which seemed to end that particular line of inquiry.

"No missing persons that match. We're going to look into if she might have been a working girl, see if that turns up anything."

Westermann nodded.

"Also," Grip said, "we're going back to the river to check the crime scene again."

"Why's that?"

"I've got a thought. Let me get back to you when I've had a chance to look into it."

"Okay," Westermann said, sensing danger. Grip got ideas in his head and more often than not they bore fruit. He mentally ran scenarios of uncomfortable conversations with Grip—trying on diversions, counterarguments, deliberate misinterpretations—while Grip and, sometimes, Morphy responded to questions from the other detectives.

A fuse blew—probably all of the fans running—and they were plunged into darkness and a din of impressively varied profanity.

13.

Frings watched City blocks go by from the back of a jitney. They passed through a neighborhood of low buildings and signs in Chinese characters. The streets here were narrow and the sidewalks teemed with women in wide, conical hats who made way for crouched older men, shuffling along with purpose. Frings caught quick glances of people gazing out of second-story windows, their faces blurred by the sun hitting the glass.

He thought about something Mel Washington had said the other night, that Frings was *sympathetic to their cause*. This had gnawed at him—*sympathetic to their cause*. Frings, contrary to some people's belief, wasn't a communist and not even a communist sympathizer, though he preferred them to the rabid anticommunists whom he saw more and more frequently—Truffant their best-known face. Frings was, though, sympathetic to racial justice, and he rationalized that this was the "cause" he'd struck the deal with Washington to support. Mel's communism was his means to achieving freedom and equality, and Frings didn't necessarily have a problem with that. He wondered, though, if this distinction—his support of justice, not communism—would make much difference if their plot was uncovered.

The cab dropped Frings in front of Father Womé's brownstone, in an elite neighborhood of high-level bureaucrats, lawyers, and doctors. A group of maybe a dozen clearly impoverished Negroes sat on the stone steps below the stoop, where two imposing guards stood impassively, sweating in dark suits and bowlers. Frings's arrival brought an end to whatever activities had been taking place as everyone's attention turned to him. Frings gave them a stoned grin and turned to the two men on the stoop.

"Hi, fellas, I'm expected."

"Frank Frings?"

"That's right."

"Clear the stairs," the man ordered, and to the extent that a dozen people can be a sea, they parted.

Frings ascended, half grin still in place.

It was, Frings thought, an ostentatious home for a man leading a community of the destitute. Inside, the place was appointed with a seemingly random assemblage of objects—a greenish vase on a pedestal; an embalmed leopard rearing unconvincingly on its hind legs, front claws extended and face in blood ecstasy; colorful, wall-hung hammered-tin masks; a bust carved from dark wood, its face elongated; and so forth. It was the type of place that should have been dim and dusty, but all the surfaces shone. Frings paused, checking out the artifacts, noticed the guard waiting for him, and took a couple of quick steps to catch up.

He followed the man as they climbed a broad staircase into a hallway with honest-to-God flaming sconces—in this heat?—and waited as the man knuckle-rapped three times on a heavy oak door. Apparently hearing an answer, he pushed the door open and stepped aside to allow Frings to enter.

Father Womé sat in a chair that he probably considered a throne, high-backed with dark wooden arms ending in lion-head finials that Womé cupped in his small, well-manicured hands. He had, Frings thought, a very African face—high, wide cheekbones and dark eyes set far apart. His forehead was broad and sloped gently back. His smile, as he greeted Frings, was brilliant. Sitting across from him, Frings could feel Womé's energy. It was similar, he thought, to the odd sensation of putting your finger between two repelling magnets. Or maybe it was the reefer.

"Forgive me for being surprised by your decision to visit," Father Womé said. "We don't enjoy much notice in your newspaper."

"I should be the one to apologize." Frings wasn't sure what to call the man. "I'm afraid we've been negligent in our duties where you are concerned." He wondered why he was speaking so formally. He felt as if he were in church, overdoing the deference to compensate for his atheism.

Womé motioned, putting the palms of his hands up as if to say that these small injustices happen. "What brings you here today?"

"As I said, we've been negligent. You must be aware of the rumors and lies about the Uhuru Community. I think we have a duty to investigate the truth."

Womé smiled. "I'm gratified that you find our Community newsworthy."

Frings smiled back, not sure how to interpret this response. Was he being mocked or thanked? Frings pulled his pad and pen from his jacket pocket.

"Maybe we can start with why you created the Uhuru Community in the first place."

"Mr. Frings, I know that you aren't oblivious to the struggles faced by Negroes in this City and, in truth, this country. In bad times, in times of war, the Negro's status is elevated—he is called upon as an equal to help defend his country of residence. We fought in the war and we saved Europe. The Negro fought—whether he was British, French, yes, if he was American. But in times of peace, the Negro is once again consigned to inferior status.

"There is no justice, Mr. Frings, but through strength. And there is no strength but in freedom. As long as we are deceived into believing that Negroes can be strong and receive justice in a society where they hold no power, we are trapped.

"We are endeavoring to create our own enclave where Negro peoples can achieve success. Does this answer your question?"

It was a well-rehearsed sermon, and Frings found himself moved despite the lack of spontaneity. He was tempted to ask Father Womé to repeat it, but more slowly so that he, Frings, could get all the words. Or, better yet, maybe Father Womé had a printed copy available. Instead, Frings tried to get beyond the rhetoric.

"But you aren't oblivious to the fact that the very people who are doing the organizing that you talk about are admitted communists. Is this really how you want your Community to be governed?"

Father Womé squinted his eyes in a merry expression. "I bring people together, Mr. Frings. I give them a safe place. I provide them with sustenance. I give them freedom from oppression. What they do with this freedom . . ." He shrugged. "That is their prerogative. And I suspect"—here Frings detected a gleam in Womé's eyes—"that your feelings about the political philosophy of some of my people are not as negative as your statement would suggest."

Frings laughed, wondering if Womé had intuited this or knew more about Frings than he was letting on. "Let's go back for a second. You said that you wanted a place where Negroes had freedom, power, justice; have you achieved this in the Uhuru Community?"

Womé's face went serious. "We have no justice in the Community."

"Why do you say that?"

"An example: just this week, three assaults against my people. Groups of young Negroes coming back to the Community, attacked on the street in the night by men in masks."

"Masks? Like the Klan?"

Womé shook his head. "My children said they wore stocking masks or masks around their eyes."

"Did you notify the police?"

"They call the police. The police come, but they do nothing. No investigation. No arrests."

This didn't sound right. "You're sure there was no investigation?"

"Of course I'm sure," Womé thundered, giving Frings a peek at another facet of the man's charisma. "They did nothing."

Frings ratcheted back. "Father, the impression that a lot of people outside the Community have is that you are worshipped by members of the Uhuru Community. That they consider you to be divine in some way."

This seemed to change Womé's mood and he laughed deeply, his hands on his stomach and his head tilted back. "I may not think of the divine in the way that you do."

Frings didn't think about the divine at all, but that was beside the point. "How do you mean?"

"I will bring you to the Square sometime. I think you would find that interesting. *That* would give you something to write about for your paper."

"The Square?"

"In the Uhuru Community. I'll bring you there and you can see what you think. God works in mysterious ways. But you must do something for me in return."

Frings raised his eyebrows.

"Find out why these assaults are not being investigated, Mr. Frings, then you'll understand why we need the Uhuru Community."

14.

The Uhuru Community had a storefront business office between a butcher shop and a newsmonger's in a low-rent neighborhood just outside Capitol Heights. No sign identified it as such, but the window front was plastered with signs supporting the Community. Grip glanced at them with a sneer, Father Womé's face prominent in block print. A campaign sign for the mayor was positioned above them, and Grip didn't think that the mayor would be too happy about that.

Morphy was already through the door. Inside, four desks sat scattered in a seemingly random configuration around the front room. Three were empty, and behind the fourth sat a middle-aged woman with coffee skin and her hair wrapped in a red scarf. She looked up at the men with nervous eyes.

"Can I help you?" Definitely Caribbean.

Morphy flashed the badge. The woman's eyes turned down to her desk. A ceiling fan squeaked rhythmically above her.

Morphy said, "We're trying to find Mel Washington. Is he here?"

The woman kept her gaze fixed on the desk; her hands trembled, but she was otherwise motionless, maybe thinking that if she didn't show signs of life they'd go away.

"Ma'am," Morphy said, his voice soft, the way it often was around women, "Mel Washington?"

The woman turned her head slightly toward a door leading back. Morphy nodded and Grip went to the door, hand on his holstered Colt. He opened without knocking. Mel Washington sat at a table with two other Negroes, both in suits, papers spread out before them.

"What the hell?" said one of the men, fat, with red suspenders and pants hiked up so that a strip of skin showed between socks and pant hem.

Grip showed the badge. "I'm here to talk to Mel Washington. You two, screw."

The two men looked at Mel Washington, who nodded slowly, not looking at Grip. The man who wasn't the fat man scooped the papers on the desk into a leather satchel and the two men stood, paused briefly to look at Washington, and, reluctantly, made their way out. Morphy escorted them out of the building, locking the front door behind them.

"Hold Mr. Washington's calls," Morphy said to the woman at the desk, and joined Grip, who was now sitting across from Washington. Morphy stood by the door.

"Comrade Washington," Grip said, a nasty grin on his face, "I don't know if you heard, but we pulled the body of a white woman from the river just downstream from your shanties. You heard about that?"

"I have." Washington was leaning forward with his elbows on the table and his palms together prayer-style, the tips of his index fingers touching his nose.

"What do you make of it?"

"I don't make anything of it."

"You know what I make of it?"

"No. But I imagine you're going to tell me," Washington said neutrally.

Grip brought his fist down hard on the table. "Don't have a piss with me."

"Okay." Washington leaned back in his chair now, massaging his neck absently.

"I think some of you commie degenerates had yourselves a good time with a white woman and then killed her to cover up your perversions. How does that sound?"

"I don't know anything about that. You have some evidence to support this . . . conjecture?"

With both hands, Grip tossed the table over to the side. He grabbed Washington's legs and flipped his chair backward so that he lay sprawled out on the ground, his glasses skittered against the wall.

"I'll get the fucking evidence. Don't worry about that, comrade. There are people in this City that know what is going on in the Uhuru Community. Patriots. The clock is ticking."

Washington lay still on the floor, looking in Grip's direction, but without his glasses on, his eyes were unfocused.

Grip took a step so that he was standing directly over the prostrate Washington. "All I'm looking for is a wedge, just a little wedge, and I'm going to use it to pry open your whole goddamn operation. You hear me?"

Washington just looked up at him.

"You hear me?" Grip repeated louder, nudging Washington hard with the sole of his boot.

"I hear you," Washington said, keeping his voice strong.

"I thought so." Grip turned and went out the door.

Morphy walked over to where Washington's glasses had slid and picked them up. He knelt down next to Washington and placed the glasses over Washington's eyes and gently tucked the arms behind his ears.

"I thought you might have a hard time finding these," he whispered, then blew gently in Washington's ear.

15.

Frings leaned against the doorframe of Panos's office, cradling a cup of coffee and watching this new kid, Art Deyna, looking satisfied with himself.

Panos was leaning back in his chair, his eyes bright with amusement. "Deyna here thinks he has a scoop."

"That right?"

Deyna was slender, with a delicate face, like a girl's. Probably didn't shave. He said, "A source called me, said there was something going on with a dead whore; cops giving it a lot of attention. He said the police consider it, quote, *very important.*"

Alarm bells. "A dead prostitute?"

Deyna nodded, the eagerness plain in his eyes. His first big hunch story right there.

Panos said, "Deyna tells me your buddy Westermann is on this case. I remember the story you wrote on him and I think maybe you might have some things you can tell him; help him with the background."

Frings pulled out a pack of cigarettes to buy some time. He offered them around, found no takers, and put one to his lips, worried that his hand might be shaking. It wasn't.

He looked at Deyna. "Who's the prostitute?"

"Goes by the name of Jane Doe," Deyna said with a half grin.

Fuck you.

Deyna continued, "They found her on the bank by the abandoned warehouses a little downriver from the Uhuru Community."

"The Uhuru Community?"

Deyna nodded. Frings looked at Panos.

Panos said to Deyna, "Frank, here, just interviewed Father Womé."

Frings watched Deyna do the mental calculations and didn't like what he saw.

"You know, Panos, since I know Westermann and I've just interviewed Womé, it might make sense for me—"

Deyna was out of his seat. "Hold on. Are you poaching my story?"

Frings ignored Deyna as much as he could. "Panos?"

Panos scowled. "Really, Frank? You want to take this story, this story about a dead whore, from your young colleague?"

Frings's breathing was shallow. Deyna glared at him.

"You two can talk later." Panos looked to Deyna. "Frank *will* help you. But now I must speak with him alone."

Deyna nodded at Panos, gave Frings a cocky smirk, left.

Now just the two of them.

"Frank, why do you try to take his story? It's not what I expect from you."

Frings shrugged, pissed off by Deyna's arrogance. "I don't know, Panos. The kid rubs me wrong."

"What? People you don't like can't have stories? Listen, Frank. You know I love you and the work you do. But lately, you smoke the reefer; have other things in your life. You're a writer now, Frank. The best we've got. But I don't know that you're a reporter anymore. I give you slack, let you do what you want; but we need reporters at a newspaper. Deyna is a reporter. He finds stories, works sources, investigates, hustles. You used to do that, Frank. You don't anymore and that's fine. But let Deyna do the reporting. You just write."

Frings stared at Panos, wondering if he agreed with this assessment and, if so, what he thought of it.

16.

Westermann walked from headquarters through a night unsettled by a hot wind careening through the streets, carrying debris on crazed, rudderless journeys. Men on the sidewalks seemed cowed by its force, staring bleakly at the ground or taking deep pulls from bottles held in paper sacks. Women and children stayed off the streets, and the night pulsed with violent possibility. Westermann took the journey at an easy stroll, enjoying the effect that his size and physical confidence had on other men. He neither sought nor avoided eye contact, but never conceded once engaged. His pulse pounded; his body coiled like a spring; desperate energy.

He thought about the girl lying in the morgue. He thought about Grip watching flotsam riding eddies in the river. He thought about a note left on his desk by one of the duty officers, asking him to return the call of an Art Deyna from the *Gazette*. He didn't know that name. What the hell did he want?

Westermann walked without conscious direction, but there was, on some level, no doubt as to his ultimate destination. He wandered through neighborhoods that he'd never before visited, signs in unfamiliar languages, stocky men smelling of garlic and liquor. He passed through an abbreviated neighborhood, maybe two blocks square, where women clad head to foot in dark robes—only their brown eyes visible beneath their chadors—were accompanied by men with long beards wearing flowing white robes and sandals. The neighborhood smelled of tea, and two sets of street signs hung on the poles, one in English and the other in Arabic script.

He left this behind, feeling the sweat soak the back of his shirt, and entered the blue-collar environs of Praeger's Hill. Here they dispensed with paper bags to cover the bottles they drank from. Here packs of boys roamed the streets, jacked on adolescent adrenaline, looking for action. As the streets became more alive with possibility, Westermann moved with more swagger, almost a dare; no badge to hide behind.

A thought forced its way into his mind. *Pushing the girl's body into the river, her skin stiff.* He shook his head to rid himself of the memory.

He came to a block of row houses and walked about halfway down, checking to see if the curtains were still open in a particular one. They were; the signal that he had been hoping for. He climbed the steps and, despite himself, looked up and down the block before knocking. He heard the pad of footsteps inside, and the door opened as far as the security chain would allow, then closed again, before opening wide.

"Hello, Lieutenant." The woman across the threshold was wearing a silk nightgown that seemed a size or two too small and over it a sheer robe of some sort. Her red hair was pulled into a pile on top of her head, and the streetlight picked up the sheen of perspiration on her pale skin. The word that Westermann associated with her was *ravishing*, and it was as apt tonight as it had ever been.

He stepped across the threshold, sliding his hands onto her hips. "Hello, Mrs. Morphy."

17.

At the same time, partway across the City, Carla Bierhoff hosted Frings and three other men at the apartment she lived in with her husband, Gerhard, a wealthy physicist at the Tech, one of the City's best-known intellectuals. Frings knew Carla from years back, at a time when she was a labor organizer and agitator. She hadn't aged much since then; her hair was longer and she was a little heavier, a little fuller, but she still had that something, not beauty exactly, but an exoticism with her dark hair and complexion and her turquoise eyes. She'd settled down when she married Gerhard, no longer putting herself in harm's way; no longer openly agitating. Now she did it behind closed doors. Partly this was because she no longer had the recklessness of her youth, but part was because of her marriage to Gerhard and the attendant acceptance in his circles; acceptance that wouldn't likely survive an arrest.

Carla's apartment was in a building at the peak of a hill overlooking the City, and her windows revealed, through a gray heat haze, the sprawl beneath them. The men at this meeting were professionals who believed that part of the responsibility that came with their success was to help the poor and the disadvantaged of the City. It wasn't exactly a group, more a loose conglomeration, in constant flux, of people who could be called on to help with left-leaning causes on the condition of anonymity. There was no profit in the public knowing your politics. Over the years these businessmen had begun to identify each other and meet semiclandestinely in plain sight—at cocktail parties, dinners, small gatherings like this. They had become a recognizable clique, but no one knew the common purpose that united them. Or so they hoped.

The small group meeting tonight was intended to work out the details for providing a number of Community needs: clothing, medical examinations, certain types of food, and the like. These things were necessary to keep the Uhuru Community, the impoverished utopia, functioning.

Gerhard was working at the Tech tonight. He supported Carla's endeavors but did not generally participate himself. He kept a distance to spare the Tech some headaches.

The men drank whiskey. Carla sipped wine. As usual, there was music on—some horn-heavy jazz—because it was supposed to help beat the bugs. Frings didn't actually believe that this music would mask their conversation in the unlikely event the apartment *was* bugged, but people seemed to find comfort in the effort.

Carla pitched them on the urgency of the matter. The men—two businessmen, Spencer and Wright, who would donate money for food and clothing, and Berdych, a doctor who would conduct medical exams and round up medicines and vaccines—drank and listened. They were committed; it was only a matter of logistics.

The whiskey bottle circulated again. The men gave estimates of the time it would take to secure the needed supplies and arrange for their delivery. Carla listened and pushed. Could they do it quicker? Frings watched silently. He was there for support, to put another *name* in the room. He'd smoked a reefer on the way over, calming down after the meeting with Panos and Deyna. Deyna was a potential problem, but Frings knew that overreacting would be the worst possible move. He had to see how things played out. It was a nervy game and he knew that the reefer was masking a real fear.

Things wound down. The three men caught the hint and left, animated conversation receding in the hallway. Carla's husband, Gerhard, would return soon from the Tech.

"I had a sit-down with your buddy Father Womé today," Frings said.

This seemed to surprise Carla. "Going straight to the source?"

"To hear you tell it, the source would be Mel Washington."

"Mel's *my* source, but don't make the mistake of thinking that Womé's just a figurehead and Mel and his people run the show. Nine out of ten people in the Community, they'll tell you they're there because of Womé. They've probably never even heard of Mel. Have you ever been in the Community?"

"No."

"You should go. I can take you or get Mel."

Frings smiled. "I don't think being seen with Mel helps my carefully crafted reputation for impartiality too much."

Carla heard the irony and laughed. "That's probably true. Let me take you around. Tomorrow? The next day?"

"Well," Frings said, getting to his original point, "I *do* want to look around. Womé mentioned that there have been attacks on Community people in the night. Have you heard anything about that?"

"I haven't seen any of the people who were assaulted, but I've heard. I know one of the boys. You want to see him?"

"Yeah, I think so."

"Okay. Not tomorrow. The day after. You want to meet outside the shanties at eleven?"

18.

The next morning, Westermann hit his alarm clock and lay in bed, eyes closed against the light, wishing he could summon up some self-loathing after his visit to Jane Morphy but finding it just wasn't there. Guilt didn't eat at him as he felt it should. Instead, he pondered the question that hung over this affair: why? There were so many other women in the City—he'd been involved with a number—but he was insistent upon this one woman, who was married to, of all the people he knew, the man most likely to kill him if their tryst was ever discovered.

Jane Morphy never asked him why. She had theories that she took a cruel pleasure in explaining to Westermann, knowing that her insights cut him. One night, she'd said, "You get bored with girls of your class— rich girls and college-educated girls. They're not exciting to you. You can take them out and they make nice conversation. Some of them are probably even good fucks if they fuck at all." Westermann had winced at this, not used to women who spoke like Jane. "But they don't excite you. They don't challenge you. You know their world, Piet. You don't know mine. I'm a working-class girl and you sleep with me because it excites you and you know that you don't have to marry me. You don't even need to take me out."

He'd looked at her, thinking there was a bit of truth in this, but trying to see if this was her way of expressing some kind of hurt. But she'd been amused; even happy. She didn't mind it. He'd asked her once why she would cheat on her husband. She'd said, "How else is a girl going to get a little excitement?" For some reason Westermann hadn't felt up to challenging her and let it go.

Westermann showered and soft-boiled two eggs that he ate with toast. His apartment was vast and elegant and nearly unfurnished. Westermann kept it to the minimum—dining room table and four chairs, a couple of easy chairs in the living room, a bed, bureau, a few bookcases, mostly filled. His father had given him the apartment as a graduation present, and while he couldn't refuse the gift—nobody refused Big Rolf—the bare walls and near-empty rooms were his protest. He couldn't confront his father head-on; he had to get in his jabs at the margins.

He stopped for his mail, found an invitation from his father to an event at the swank Helios Club, the day after tomorrow. *Thanks for the notice.* But for all he knew it had been sitting in his mail slot for days. He wished now that he hadn't checked. He thought about sliding it back, but his father would know. Somehow he always knew.

Leaving his building, Westermann made the Negro kid by the time he'd hit the bottom stair. The kid—maybe ten or twelve, thin, loose-limbed, with funny symmetrical scars on each cheek—followed from a distance for half a block, probably nervous. Westermann took the walk slow, giving the kid a chance to find his courage and catch up. At the crosswalk, Westermann paused to let a truck rattle past and heard the kid's soft voice.

"Mr. Westermann?"

"That's right."

"You dropped this." The kid handed over a piece of paper folded in quarters. Westermann fished in his pocket, gave the boy a quarter, then crossed the street, leaving the boy staring at the coin in his hand. He read as he walked.

COMMUNITY AT 10 AM. WATER SIDE. WE NEED TO TALK.

Westermann tore it into eighths, carried it to the next public trash bin, and dumped it.

The streets were full and Westermann let the crowd pull him along. He was exhausted. The nights with Jane Morphy left him drained; part sleep deprivation, part carnal release, part anxiety. Jane seemed to thrive on the anxiety; it made her jittery, wild.

Morphy did not return early last night. Another bullet dodged. Could he dodge them forever?

Out gambling, she'd said. It was what she always said. Westermann didn't know whether he believed it, or if he thought she believed it. Westermann couldn't tell with Morphy. What the hell would a guy like that do for kicks?

Westermann took an unmarked car from the pool at Headquarters and drove to the Community. He had the windows down and hot air whirled wildly around the interior. His shirt clung to his back where it met the seat. Little puddle mirages preceded him in the streets, the asphalt soft under the tires.

Washington was waiting outside the shanties on the river side, maybe a hundred yards from where the girl's body was originally found. He wore an untucked short-sleeve shirt and his black-framed glasses. Warren Eddings was with him, skullcap in place. Westermann caught their tight expressions as he approached. He shook hands with the two men. Downriver, he spotted two men in suits and hats, probably cops, walking around the area where the body had "officially" been discovered. One was taking photos—maybe forensics guys come back.

Eddings scowled at Westermann. "Things aren't shaking out right."

"What do you mean?" Westermann spoke loudly to be heard above the rush of the river.

"Detectives Grip and Morphy—they work for you?"

Westermann nodded. "Sure."

"They paid a visit to Mel yesterday."

Westermann turned to Washington. "They did?"

Washington nodded. "Wanted to let me know that we were in their sights."

Shit. "You know I can't keep you totally out of this, Mel. We have to run a legitimate investigation and that means giving the Community a look. I'm trying to keep those two away from this side of the investigation."

Washington said, "Yeah, well, we weren't surprised to see the other detectives—Plouffe and Souza, I think their names were—asking questions in the shanties. Normal cop stuff. But this visit from the other two, that was an attempt at intimidation. Let me emphasize that it was an *attempt.*"

Westermann thought for a minute, considering his words. Crows were making a racket, pulling at something in the weeds. "I'll speak to them. Detectives Grip and Morphy are good investigators. Detective Grip, however, also has very strong political beliefs that were probably a factor in their decision to visit you. I'll talk to him and make sure that it doesn't happen again."

Eddings said, "It shouldn't have happened in the first place."

Washington held out a calming hand. "It's not just the visit they paid me that's concerning."

Westermann raised his eyebrows.

Eddings said, "They were down by the water yesterday. The kids were watching them. A couple came and found us and told us what was going on, that we should come have a look."

Behind Washington and Eddings, the men from downriver were ambling their way. Westermann kept half an eye on their approach.

Washington said, "They were taking boards and logs that they'd found and putting them in the water at various points on the riverbank and watching where the current took them."

Westermann's pulse pounded. "Did he—"

"Find the spot?" Washington finished the thought, shaking his head. "Close. He narrowed it down. All those sunken docks and debris under the water, they cause some funny patterns in the current. I think by the time they left, they had a pretty good idea of where we first found her."

The two men in suits were twenty yards away, clearly coming over to talk. Westermann lifted his chin toward them and Washington and Eddings turned. The men stopped. The one without the camera was thin, a boyish face below his fedora. Smooth jaw—probably never had to shave.

"Lieutenant Westermann," the man said.

"That's right."

With practiced speed, the man with the camera—unshaven, unkempt— snapped a photo of Westermann with Washington and Eddings.

"What's—," Westermann started.

The photographer wound and shot a second photo.

"What the hell?" Eddings made a move toward the cameraman, but Washington stopped him with a hand on his shoulder. The cameraman walked back downstream in a hurry.

The other man stayed behind, fixing Westermann with a grin. "I left you a message, Lieutenant. You didn't get back to me, but we do need to talk sometime. Sometime soon. Call me at the *Gazette* when you get a chance. Ask for Art Deyna."

19.

It had been a morning of wall-to-wall meetings, and Frings took advantage of a brief break by sitting out on the fifth-floor fire escape, sharing a reefer with a young beat reporter named Latapy. A group of four pigeons—the same four pigeons that always came—perched on a metal railing. Frings and Latapy blew marijuana smoke at them.

Frings liked Latapy. Latapy was young and eager—Frings didn't necessarily like him for that—but smart and savvy enough to listen to the more experienced reporters. And he was funny. He wasn't a prima donna, trying to rewrite the rules. Had Frings been a prima donna at that age? Probably, to be honest.

Frings asked, "Do you know Art Deyna at all?"

"Deyna? Sure. Don't you?"

Frings took a hit off the reefer, holding the smoke in as he shook his head.

Latapy said, "Why? What's up?"

"He a decent gink?"

"*Gink?*"

"What? Am I dating myself? Is he a decent 'chap'? 'Bloke'? 'Guy'?"

Latapy laughed, exhaling a plume of smoke at the pigeons. "He's fine. Not my cup of tea, but fine."

"Why? What's the problem?"

"I don't know. He's a little serious, I guess. Looks out for himself. Not the kind of guy to be friends with, really."

"He good on the beat?"

"*He* thinks he's good. And he's probably right. Look, Frank, what's the story?"

Frings shrugged, not wanting to make this a bigger deal. "We're working on different parts of the same story. I just wanted a sense of him."

"You two are working the same story?" Latapy was genuinely surprised.

Most of the younger reporters looked up to Frings; were even intimidated by his reputation. One of that generation actually competing for a story with Frings was a big step up. "I don't know how he'll be with you, Frank. But if it was me, I'd keep my eye on him. He'll go after the story hard. He likes to compete and you would be a big trophy."

Frings sighed, staring at the stoned pigeons.

In an editorial meeting, Frings's mind wandered to Westermann, the man he had chosen as a coconspirator. He liked Westermann, to a degree, and considered him one of the smarter cops Frings had known—maybe the smartest. But Frings also knew how weak Westermann could be; had seen it himself, doing research for a feature he'd written on Westermann just as the police were rolling out the System.

There was a story Frings could have written, should have written; the story would have sold papers, put him back in the spotlight, rendered the *truth*. The story would have sent Westermann back to a desk somewhere or out of the force entirely, and this had stopped Frings. Not so much what would befall Westermann, but the fate of his *system*. The events of that night didn't call into question anything about the System, but they called into question everything about Westermann as a cop, and Frings knew that the System's opponents would use its creator's failings to impeach the thing itself. So he'd written a different story, one where heroism and cowardice were inverted.

What happened: Frings was spending the night as a ride-along with Westermann, getting material for a story on the force's controversial "Golden Boy." *Smart, good-looking college boy with a world of possibilities chooses to be a cop and soon has the majority of the force despising him.*

Then there was his father, Big Rolf Westermann, maybe the best-known lawyer in the City, with a penchant for rich clients and headlines. Cops hated Big Rolf's grandstanding, his belittling of police, but Big Rolf evoked fear, too. No one wanted to look like a fool, or worse, corrupt, on the stand. His son, Frings thought, might be an attractive proxy.

Westermann rode shotgun, talking over his shoulder to Frings, while his partner, a two-decade vet named Klasnic, steered the prowl car through block after City block. It was fall—a cool night, light breeze. Westermann came off cocky, as if he had it all figured out. Frings knew how to read people, though, and Westermann was hiding something behind the bravado. Westermann talked and Frings took notes, ignoring the words and jotting impressions, psychological conjecture, and philosophical musings about class and law enforcement and entitlement. Frings's head was buzzing with thoughts. He was stoned to the gills.

Klasnic took a call. A disturbance, apparently, in a tenement a couple blocks away, two men arguing; a chance for Frings to catch Westermann in action. They hightailed it to the scene, siren and lights off. A tattered notice condemning the building was nailed to the front door. Westermann led them up narrow, shadowed stairs with Klasnic in the rear. Frings sensed that this was not their usual order.

The place was in terrible shape, doors missing off the dim hallways; puddles of stagnant water on the landings; sounds of despair, anger, and psychosis echoing around the walls. These places had to be squats. No way anyone paid money to live like this.

Shots exploded above them, unsettling a pack of rats that fled down the stairs, scrambling under the feet of the men as they ascended. Frings's skin prickled; his adrenaline flowed. The human noises above them had stopped. No one wanted to attract the attention of a man with a shotgun.

They took the remaining two flights of stairs three at a time and arrived at a hallway lit by a bare bulb that flickered like a frenzied strobe. Westermann and Klasnic advanced with their guns drawn, Frings trailing. The carpet in the hall was damp under their feet, smelled of mold. Bugs crawled where floor met wall. The two cops found the right door and pressed against the wall on either side, listening.

Only one voice seemed to be coming from inside: ranting, howling expletives and threats, the words barely comprehensible. The guy in there was either drunk or insane or both. Frings watched Klasnic nod to the door and hold up three fingers, then fold each one in turn until none remained and he pushed against the door, easing it silently open, the voice now coming louder into the hall. Klasnic disappeared through the door. Westermann waited a five count and then followed. Frings walked over to the threshold and looked in, but there was only an empty foyer, so Frings kept on edging down a short hallway to his right.

The tone of the ranting changed, like a drop in air pressure; a sudden focus, words sharper.

"Who the fuck are you? Drop the piece or I'll blow his fucking *head* off. I *will* blow his fucking head off."

Westermann's voice: "Drop the weapon. Drop the goddamn gun."

Klasnic's voice, high with tension: "Shoot him. Shoot."

The ranting voice: "Shut your goddamn trap. You shut your goddamn trap."

Frings rounded the corner and took in the situation. The light in the room was mostly dim, but shotgun smoke defined sheets of bright light knifing down from slits in the ceiling. Klasnic stood in the opposite doorway, pistol at his feet, staring wide-eyed at a man, spotlit in the center of the room, a sawed-off trained on Klasnic. The man—tall and lean, red hair flaked with gray, huge sideburns—Frings recognized as Blood Whiskers McAdam, a criminal and habitual murderer with who knew how many victims, mostly mob guys. At McAdam's feet lay what was left of a man who'd just caught two shotgun shells from close range. Westermann stood just in front of Frings, visibly trembling, his gun all over the place.

Klasnic's eyes were on the shotgun, his voice desperate. "Fucking shoot him."

"He doesn't have the balls," McAdam growled.

Westermann tried to steady his gun with a second hand. It was quiet for a minute. Frings heard a radio playing big-band music in some other apartment; cars honked on the street; a baby cried a story below.

Growing anxious, McAdam said, "Goddamn it," and adjusted his grip on the shotgun.

Klasnic flinched and McAdam fired, blowing a hole in Klasnic's chest. Westermann fired six times, hitting McAdam with four of the shots, driving him to the floor, his body half in light and half in shadow. He seemed to smile before dying.

Later, Frings sat on a stoop opposite the tenement, drinking a cup of coffee he'd been given by a cop, and watching orderlies carry the body bags out to the police van, the figures ghoulish in the blue police lights. His mind ran through the—what? Five seconds?—in which it had all happened; trying to alter his memory so that it fit the story he'd given the police. In this story, Westermann arrived as McAdam pulled the trigger, catastrophic fractions of a second too late. Westermann was almost more heroic, in this telling, for the tragedy of the timing.

Westermann walked over to Frings. It had taken him a while, but he seemed to have his legs back and was making at least a show of confidence. Cops patted his back and gave shallow smiles. They still hated him, but they weren't so cold as to abandon him after something like this. In days this benefit of the doubt would evaporate as the whispers on the street concentrated on Klasnic's death, and Westermann's unpopularity, even then, made it easy for cops to place the blame on him. Only Frings, though, knew the truth.

Westermann sat. Frings offered a cigarette. Westermann shook his head.

"You're going to be okay," Frings said, not looking at Westermann.

"Am I?"

"As far as I'm concerned."

Westermann stared dully ahead. Frings could see him puzzling over this, trying to figure out the tally book between them. He gave up.

"What do you want?"

Frings shrugged. "Nothing. Maybe someday. I don't do blackmail, Piet. That's not how I got where I am. But this is a big one."

"I know."

"So, maybe you'll remember it someday."

Westermann nodded. "Yeah, this isn't one I'm going to forget."

Meetings finally over, Frings was back at his desk, smoking a Camel and leafing through the day's *Gazette* without taking much in, contemplating which contact to call at Headquarters to get a handle on who, exactly, had been handling the assaults near the shanties. He knew a fair number of cops and had chits that he could call in, but this was a tricky one. Cops got suspicious about giving out this kind of information. The inference would be that Frings had cops in his sights, and cops got mum real quick when this was the case, protecting their institution—the police—above all else. He settled on a records clerk named Klein and flicked through his contacts book until he located the name and gave him a call.

Frings recalled Klein as a good-looking blond kid, kept off the beat by a missing eye, gouged out while he was trying to bring order to a near riot on a block of bars. He had no depth perception anymore. He was a big guy, though, muscular. Frings had heard that he boxed and wondered how the hell he made that work.

"Klein, it's Frank Frings with the *Gazette*."

"Hey, Frank, how are you?" Klein seemed genuinely happy to hear from him.

"I'm fine. How're the wife and kids?"

"Good, Frank. Real good. What's up?"

"Listen, I was wondering if you could do me a favor."

"You bet. As long as it doesn't come back to me."

"Has it ever?"

"Okay, shoot."

Frings explained the nighttime assaults on the Community people. "I want to know who was assigned to those cases."

There was a brief silence. "Jeez, I don't know, Frank. This doesn't sound kosher to me. You looking to nail cops? 'Cause if that's what's up, you know, I can't help you."

"It's not about the cops. It's about whether these attacks really occurred and whether anything was done about it. I'm not looking to name names. Have you known me to pull one over on a cop? If I was trying to take someone down, I'd tell you. I live on my rep."

There was a brief pause, Klein thinking it over on the other end of the line. "Okay, Frank. Your word is good here. I'll take a look for you, get back to you sometime tomorrow."

"Thanks, Klein. I owe you."

20.

The storm arrived suddenly, a sun-scorched afternoon quickly becoming twilight beneath a towering, purple-and-blue thunderhead. The heavy air came to life, crackling with latent electricity, huge volumes of air barreling through the canyons formed by high buildings. Grip drove with Morphy shotgun and Westermann reclining comfortably in the backseat. They rolled the windows up as the first marble-size drops were annihilated against the windshield.

Westermann watched adults scurry for cover while children stayed, faces lifted to the sky, welcoming the relief.

"The fuck'd this come from?" Grip asked.

Westermann registered Grip's nervousness, talking to break the silence. A clap of thunder came from somewhere close, sounding like a bomb detonating.

"How'd yesterday afternoon go?" Westermann asked.

There was a pause.

Grip said, "We went back to the river. I had an idea I wanted to try out. While Morphy was taking his fucking clothes off the other morning, I was watching the currents, how shit was flowing down the river. It gets kind of funny by the banks because of all the docks and everything that fell into the water. So I noticed that maybe the girl had to have been put in the water in a certain place to wash up where she did, you know?"

"Okay."

"So we tested it out."

Morphy said, "We tossed logs in the river, is what he's trying to say. Saw where they ended up."

"And?"

Grip said, "Looks to me like she probably got dropped in the water a little upstream from the Uhuru Community."

"If she wasn't just put on the bank where we found her, you mean."

Grip shook his head. "That doesn't seem right, Lieut. Why just dump her in the rocks? Why wouldn't you put her in the river, get the body away from the scene, wash the evidence off her?"

It made sense, of course. But had she been put in somewhere farther upstream, only to wash up where Westermann had found her before pushing her back in the water?

"Are you sure," Westermann asked, "that the body would float the same way your logs would?"

Grip shrugged. "Why not?"

Westermann straightened in his seat, leaning forward to get his head between Grip and Morphy. "So what's your conclusion?"

Grip chose his words carefully. He was already on thin ice because of his treatment of Mel Washington. There wasn't any angle in having Westermann think he was targeting more Negroes, commie Negroes at that. "That there's a distinct possibility that someone put the murdered girl in the river at a point near the Uhuru Community. This would seem to point to the Community as a possible source of the perpetrators."

"Souza and Plouffe couldn't find anyone who'd seen a white woman around the Community."

Morphy laughed.

"Jesus," Grip muttered.

Left unsaid: Even if Souza and Plouffe had done a competent job of canvassing, there was no reason to believe that the Community people would tell them anything, even if they had seen the woman. And this, Westermann realized, was the unknown; where he might have made a terrible blunder. If she *had* been killed near the Community, he had tried to cover up a real crime; and he had failed.

Westermann thought about Art Deyna and the photographer and was about to ask Grip and Morphy whether they'd heard from the press when Grip pulled to the curb.

They left the prowl car parked by a fire hydrant and took the stairs down to the basement, where Pulyatkin kept his office just down the hall from the morgue. They found Pulyatkin smoking at his desk, his door open. Westermann led the other two in, leaning over the desk to shake Pulyatkin's hand. Westermann knew that Pulyatkin liked him, considered him moderate and judicious. He assumed that Pulyatkin had asked him to come to chaperone Grip and Morphy, who made everyone nervous.

Pulyatkin said, "I'm sure that Detectives Morphy and Grip reported to you that the woman you brought in the other day was very sick."

Westermann nodded.

"I'd never seen anything quite like that before, the way the disease was attacking the organs. She couldn't have had much time left. But I remembered something I'd heard from the doctors at City Hospital. We talk sometimes if we run across something unusual. 'Compare notes,' I think they say. Well, I remembered that they'd called a couple of weeks ago about a young woman who had come to the hospital, very ill. Blisters, like your girl. She was vomiting, in pain. No one there had seen this combination of symptoms before, so they took blood and tissue and considered quarantining her." Pulyatkin paused to take a sip of coffee.

Westermann looked over at Grip and Morphy, wondering if they knew what was going on. Grip shrugged and Morphy raised his eyebrows.

"I remembered this conversation, so I sent blood and tissue samples from the girl over to City to have them compared with the samples from that woman."

"And they matched?"

"I don't know. They seem to be having a difficult time laying their hands on the original sample. I don't know if they haven't looked hard or maybe it's gone. But this unusual set of symptoms recurring in this short time frame—it's hard to believe it's not the same disease."

"Who's the woman? Is she still there?"

Pulyatkin laughed ruefully. "No. She left the hospital soon after the samples were taken. It was at night—no doctors on the ward—but the nurses said a man came and got her and they had no choice but to discharge. The doctors were furious, of course."

"Was she . . . ?" Grip asked.

"The same as our woman? No. I checked the physical description. Different altogether."

"How about a name? An address? She must have registered."

Pulyatkin nodded and pulled a folder from the top of a pile on his desk. He read from a page. "Mavis Talley. Eighty-six Newton Avenue."

The rain had stopped and steam rose off the streets as they rolled down Newton Avenue, eyeing tired row houses and storefronts with bars over the front windows. Westermann knew the stats—assault, rape, robbery, murder; all occurred with alarming frequency here. It wasn't the worst district, but not far removed from it. Morphy and Grip could have told you the same thing just by looking around at the young men, idle and menacing on the stoops and the street corners; the absence of women on the street; the defiant postures as the prowl car passed. Hell of a place for a young woman to live.

Eighty-six Newton Avenue was a row house in a block of row houses marked by peeling paint and sagging stoops. Grip parked out front. Not many cars at the curb in this neighborhood.

"You think we'll find it in one piece when we get back?" Grip asked, maybe rhetorically.

Morphy rapped on the door and stepped back to stand with Westermann. Grip stood below them, at the foot of the steps. When no one answered, Morphy pounded, yelling, "Police. Please open the door."

Slow footsteps sounded from inside and Morphy stepped away again, fingering the grip of his Colt. Seeing this, Grip did the same. The door opened against a security chain and Westermann saw a small face, crabbed with age.

The voice was a woman's, gravelly and suspicious. "What d'you want?"

"Mavis Talley?" Westermann asked.

"What you want Mavis for?"

"Just need to speak with her. Nothing serious." Keeping it calm, projecting authority.

"That makes two of us need to speak to her," the old woman said. "Haven't seen her in a couple weeks."

It took some cajoling from Westermann, but the woman—a broad, stooped widow named Mrs. Levesque—eventually let them in to see the room that Mavis Talley rented. There were four doors off the third-floor landing, one to the shared bathroom and the other three to rented rooms. Mavis Talley's was the middle of the three. Clearly, no one had been there in a while. Roaches crawled over a molding half loaf of bread placed next to a stack of papers and pamphlets on a small, round kitchen table. The bed was carefully made, the blue sheets faded and threadbare with age. Morphy began opening drawers in her bureau and Grip opened a narrow closet. Westermann picked up the stack of pamphlets on the table and brought them down hard, scattering the roaches.

He took a look at the pile. There were anticommunist pamphlets—"They Live Among Us," "The People Who Abandoned God," "The Threat to Freedom"—programs from the Church of Last Days, and letters signed "Mom" or "Juliet."

"Torsten," Westermann said, waving a handful of the pamphlets. "She seems like your type. A fellow God-fearing patriot."

Grip walked over. "There's nothing in the closet." He took some of the pamphlets and looked them over, tossing them on the table when he was done. "Typical shit. You can find it anywhere."

"How about this?" Westermann read from one of the church brochures: "'Will Christ Return to the New Israel?' Let's see." He sifted through the brochures. "'Is the Antichrist Alive and Among Us?' What do you think?"

"About the Antichrist?" Morphy asked, still looking through drawers.

"What church is that?" Grip asked, ignoring Morphy's crack.

"The Church of Last Days. You know it?"

"Sounds familiar," Grip said, thinking that it sounded familiar because of Ole Koss; that maybe it was his church, or that he listened to it on the radio.

21.

Westermann had Morphy and Grip drop him at City Hospital before they went back to the station and then home. City Hospital seemed always on a knife's edge, the chaos caused by the sheer number of patients threatening to overwhelm what little order the staff could maintain. In line at the check-in desk, a Negro was leaking blood from some kind of wound in his arm; a stout white woman in Gypsy clothes was kept upright by two younger men with trim beards; a drunk had his eyes swollen shut and his lips misshapen and bleeding. Maybe two dozen people sat against the walls in various states of medical distress. A baby cried. Westermann moved past them, flashing his badge. He only had a question.

"Records?"

A gray woman eyed him over her bifocals. "Fifth floor." She nodded back toward a bank of elevators before turning to a man whose hand, Westermann saw to his alarm, was being consumed, slowly, by a large, brownish snake.

Westermann hastened to the elevators and ascended with an elderly couple who stared silently at the floor and shuffled out at the fourth floor. The fifth floor, the administrative floor, was quiet. An orderly smoked against the opposite wall, ignoring Westermann. The tentative sanitation attempted in the lower floors was absent here. The linoleum floors were filthy, the air reeked of stale cigarette smoke and urine. A second orderly made slow progress down the hall with a cart full of files. Westermann asked him for Records and he pointed vaguely down the hall.

"The door says RECORDS."

Westermann followed the corridor past dozens of closed doors. He paused at an open door, thinking he might ask directions again. Inside, two small men in white lab coats were examining a fleshy mass suspended in clear liquid in a specimen jar. The men looked up at Westermann and he saw that they must be identical twins. Westermann opened his mouth to speak, but the two men had returned to the jar.

He walked down another empty corridor, took a corner, and arrived at the door marked RECORDS. The room was huge, rows of shelves guarded by a service counter on which file folders sat piled in uneven stacks. The place hummed with the sound of the overhead lights. Westermann banged on a bell and waited. A bald kid, face scarred with burns—maybe from a grease spatter—emerged from the stacks.

Westermann flashed the badge. "I need the file for a Mavis Talley."

The kid squinted at him. "She a patient?"

"Was."

The kid hesitated. He hadn't seen a warrant yet. The badge alone didn't compel him to get the file. Westermann pulled a five from his billfold and tossed it on the counter. The kid palmed it and turned back into the stacks, walking with a strange roll to his hips, as if he were pulling his feet out of mud. Westermann leaned against the counter with his back to the files, watching as an orderly peered through the wire-reinforced window in the door, saw Westermann, and disappeared again. Westermann drummed his fingers absently on the counter until he heard footsteps from behind him and the kid returned with a file and dropped it on the counter.

"You can't take it out of this room," he said sullenly.

"You bet," Westermann said, and gave a grateful smile. The kid apparently didn't trust Westermann enough to leave him alone, so Westermann opened the file while the kid watched.

The doctors' puzzlement was clear from the records. Mavis Talley had been admitted with a fever near 105 and pain in her abdomen and chest. She was coughing up blood. The attending doctor noted the blisters covering her body. He also detected swelling in multiple organs—spleen, liver, kidneys—during his physical exam. They took blood samples and stuck her in an intensive-care room. Shortly after, she had apparently been discharged into the care of her doctor, a Raymond Vesterhue. That was it. Westermann read through the papers again, noting that Mavis Talley was twenty-three years old, that she was born right here in City Hospital, that she was five feet five inches tall, and that she weighed ninety-three pounds at intake. Westermann flashed on the corpse in the river, how the wet dress clung to her emaciated ribs.

"It says in here that they took a blood sample from her, but there's no report."

The kid shrugged.

"Where would that report be?"

"Probably didn't do it."

"What do you mean?"

"There's always a backlog of tests. Patient dies or is discharged, they usually don't get done."

"But this case, they were dealing with an unknown disease. They considered quarantining the patient. You think they'd scrap the test, even in that circumstance?"

The kid shrugged again. "Probably."

"Any way of finding out for sure?"

The kid waited, looking at the counter. Westermann pulled a card with his name and phone number from his pocket and put it on the counter.

"You find that file, give me a call, and there's a tenner in it for you. Understand?" Westermann couldn't get the kid to make eye contact.

The kid picked up the card, studied it, put it in his pocket, and retreated with that peculiar walk of his, silently back into the stacks.

22.

Grip brought Morphy along to Crippen's, both men slumping into chairs, drained by the day. The door to the outside was open, fans blowing, making no difference. Angry rhetoric and static blared from the back, the hate tangible even if the words weren't. The bartender brought over whiskey shots and bottles of beer. His right arm was amputated at the shoulder— Belleau Wood, or so he claimed. He set the tray down on the table.

Wayne was sitting at another table with a couple of younger guys that Grip recognized but didn't know. Grip could feel the energy radiating from their group; hot and dangerous. Wayne looked over at Grip and nodded, then eyed Morphy warily. Morphy wasn't a regular here and guys on the force tended to be unnerved by him, his strangeness.

"Seen the door?" Wayne said.

"What's that?" Grip asked.

"The door."

"What about it?"

"Have a look."

Grip walked over to the open door. Morphy watched, tilting his beer bottle into the corner of his mouth. The bartender watched, too, as Grip took a look.

"Yeah?"

"Other side. The outside side," Wayne said.

Grip opened the door and checked the other side. "The fuck?"

Beneath two TRUFFANT FOR MAYOR signs that had been nailed up there weeks ago, someone had, in black paint, traced the outline of a top hat above two rounded triangles and, below them, four vertical lines; the whole thing maybe two feet high.

"What d'you think?" the bartender asked.

"It's a skull in a fucking top hat. Who did it?"

The bartender frowned. "Damned if I know. It was there when I showed up this afternoon."

"Jesus." The figure gave Grip the creeps.

When Grip sat back down, Morphy was smiling. "Nice place."

Grip held up two fingers. He needed another shot.

23.

It was cool in the German Street Cabaret; almost too cool when you came in from the night heat. Frings kept his jacket on as he sat at a table near the stage, drinking a beer and smoking with Lenny Moskin, who owned the joint. The place was full. Onstage a pianist and saxophonist accompanied a blond singer, her voice as smoky as the room.

"She's still got it, Frank. Twenty years on and she can still sing. Her voice ain't the same, but it's better. And the people love her."

"Yeah," Frings said vaguely. Her voice had changed; she had changed. Just look at her, still beautiful but thicker; her face softer; weight in her shoulders and back. All this had changed since they were together, over a decade ago.

Moskin looked at him funny, asked, "How is the lovely Renate?"

Frings could tell by Moskin's tone, his expression—he knew about Renate's philandering; the news was around.

"She's fine." Frings took a drink, ending that line of conversation. It didn't bother him, people knowing about her affairs. It was, he thought, almost expected of people like her, couples like them; some association of glamour with different moral calculations—sex, drugs. And it was accurate where he and Renate were concerned.

Nora Aspen leaned on the baby grand, purring some tune.

Moskin moved to a new topic. "You must be spending your time on the election."

"Some of it."

"You know, I'm not the mayor's biggest fan, but this Truffant . . . he scares the piss out of me. Is there any chance he could win?"

"Your guess is as good as mine. It's not out of the question, I think."

"The problem is, with the mayor, it's like the City is a sinking ship and he's trying to plug up each little leak, like if he keeps doing that the ship will stay afloat."

Why did everyone want to try out their shit metaphors on Frings? *Jesus.*

Moskin kept going. "Truffant, he says to hell with it, let it sink and we'll build a new one."

"That's not bad," Frings lied.

"Yeah, but what's that new ship going to be like?"

"That's the question," Frings said as Nora ended her set, mercifully bringing this conversation to a close.

Nora made her way over to Frings, smiling at the tables of people as she passed by. Frings stood and kissed her chastely on the cheek. Moskin surrendered his seat, kissing Nora's hand extravagantly as he left.

A waiter brought Nora a glass of white wine. "It's nice to see you, Frank. What brings you over?"

Frings smiled. "It's always great to see you sing. I forget. I should do this more often."

"You're blowing smoke, Frank." Nora gave him a smile that carried years of familiarity and the remnants of love. "But did you really enjoy the set?"

"Very much."

"Such a gentleman. Why are you here *tonight*, though, Frank?"

Frings looked at her; little lines spidered out from the corners of her eyes. She put on a pout. "I think maybe I know."

Frings raised his eyebrows.

"Word gets around, Frank, in the music world."

"I guess so."

"She's a nice girl, and God knows she's beautiful, but she's a tramp. You know she's slept with her bandleader—I can't remember his—"

"Warren. Dickey Warren."

"That's right." Nora shook her head. "With Dickey, with other men in the band."

Frings nodded.

"Are you going to kick her out?"

Frings shook his head.

Nora rolled her eyes. "Of course not."

"She's an adult. She can make that kind of decision. I'm supposed to tell her she can't?"

"You're a weird guy, Frank."

"The thing that bothers me, I don't like being alone at night; or at least I like to know if I'm going to be alone or not. I like company."

"So get some, Frank. There are a lot of women in the City. If she's sleeping around . . ."

"Too complicated."

Nora smiled sadly. "I'm not going to have an affair with you, Frank. I love you, but we've been down that road."

Frings laughed. "I don't think either one of us needs that."

"Frank, you haven't changed—that's a good thing. But you still haven't told me: Why did you come here tonight?"

"I don't know. To see you. See how you're doing."

"I'm doing fine, Frank."

"I know," Frings said. "I can tell."

24.

Moses Winston was second on the bill at the Checkerboard that night. He came in through the back and stepped out from behind the stage and into the bar. The joint was nearly full, and smoke—some tobacco, some mesca— was heavy in air that carried dozens of conversations, threatening to over- whelm the duo on the stage, a skinny cracker with round glasses playing the house piano while a big woman with her hair piled on top of her head caterwauled her way through some jazz number.

Winston scanned the crowd and saw more Negro faces than he'd seen here before, though that number seemed to grow a little each night. He was used to being popular, even revered in some small towns that he'd played. But he hadn't known how things would work out in the City. Now he was beginning to see.

He left his guitar case by the stage where he could keep an eye on it and maneuvered his way to the bar, aware of people pointing at him, feeling the occasional clap on his back. He'd smoked some mesca that Billy Lambert had bought off kids who'd starting hanging around the perimeter of the shanties, offering wares of this sort and that. It had been good smoke. Win- ston felt it in his body, and the crowd seemed somehow like a single, huge organism, the faces and bodies blended together, the place pulsing.

The bartender had a glass of water with a brownish lime waiting for him. Winston's shirt was unbuttoned but clung damply to his back. Ce- phus was behind the bar, too, dripping perspiration into the drinks that he was imprecisely preparing, looking up now and then as if to assure himself that this crowd was, in fact, really there.

Winston leaned against the bar, listening to the girl onstage as she strug- gled with the realization that the crowd mostly wanted her to finish up. The crowd cheered a little, jeered some more, but mostly ignored her. He felt bad for her in a way. But it wasn't often that white people had given way to him, and though it didn't exactly give him pleasure, there did seem to be some kind of justice.

He felt a paw of a hand on his shoulder and turned to see Cephus's enormous face beaming at him through the rivulets of sweat.

"You see this crowd, Moses?" Cephus was nearly yelling so that Winston could hear him over the crowd.

Winston nodded, looking into the crowd, roiling like the sea.

"They're here to see you. Do you see what we've done?"

This was something that Winston was familiar with in dealing with white people, too. As far as he could tell, Cephus's role in "their" success was simply to own this broken-down joint. Winston's playing had brought people into this oven to drink Cephus's shitty drinks and listen to the music. It was really what Winston had done for Cephus.

Winston smiled at Cephus, but not particularly kindly.

"I'm going to have them off the stage after their next number. You going to be ready to go?"

Winston nodded. "Sure."

Cephus turned to walk away, then turned back to Winston, putting his hand on Winston's shoulder again.

"Moses?"

"Yeah?"

"I know you two are friends. You seen Lenore lately? She hasn't shown up around here."

Winston felt a tingle in his hands and legs. He stared at Cephus until Cephus became uncomfortable and said, "I guess not," and went back to making drinks.

25.

Westermann arrived at Headquarters early the next morning to find Morphy sitting on Souza's desk, jawing with Grip, who sat on his own. Grip was telling some story about a fight he'd witnessed at a bar the previous night. Morphy drank coffee and listened, looking bored. Westermann walked over to them and Grip let his story die.

Grip said, "We're on the Jane Doe this morning."

"Any leads?"

"We're going to make some leads."

Westermann was about to ask Grip to explain what he meant by that when Kraatjes came through the door, grim, moving fast. Kraatjes was wearing the bow tie that he kept in his desk for visits to the mayor's office.

"Detectives," Kraatjes said, acknowledging Grip and Morphy. "Piet, the Chief needs to talk to you."

"Okay." Westermann searched Kraatjes's face for a hint of what was up, but saw only stress. He turned for his office, to drop off his briefcase.

"Now, Piet."

Westermann nodded and handed his briefcase to Morphy, who seemed to be thinking this through.

Kraatjes led Westermann down the stairs and into the lobby where the Chief was waiting, talking to a couple of uniforms; smiling, but without much conviction.

The three of them walked briskly out the door, down the stairs, and onto the street, ignoring the cops who made way before them. The Chief talked the whole while.

"Piet, your Jane Doe case on the river, there's been a development. A second body turned up several hundred yards upstream. Another white woman. Young. I haven't seen photos, but the report indicated that this woman was severely underweight, sores covering her body. Sound familiar?"

Westermann felt his face grow hot. "Of course."

"What do you think this means, Piet?"

Westermann was trying to figure this out, but was struggling to slow down his thoughts. A second girl murdered, and he had to assume at the same spot as the girl they had moved. This time Mel Washington hadn't found out before the police found her. Westermann tried to focus on the Chief's question.

A police cruiser pulled up and Westermann followed the Chief into the backseat. Kraatjes sat up front with the driver.

"Piet?" the Chief prompted.

"They have to be connected. It gives us a chance to look for a connection between the girls—"

Kraatjes had turned in his seat. "We can see the obvious," he said, asserting his rank, something he rarely did. "What do you think this means? Does this implicate the Uhuru Community?"

"I don't know, but I think we need to sit on this for now. If this gets out—"

"If it gets out that we were sitting on two homicides, that's not going to reflect very well on us, either."

"Is this why you're headed to the mayor's office, to tell him about the second body?"

Kraatjes looked to the Chief. The Chief said, "You know the politics here, Piet. If this comes out, Truffant is going to go after it full bore. The mayor needs to be on top of this, whether he wants to keep it quiet or release the information on his terms. If he releases the information, he'll be wanting to go hard after the Community; try to preempt what's going to come from Truffant. But it's more complicated than that."

"What do you mean?"

"The officer at the scene was Ed Wayne."

Westermann sighed, trying to seem casual, his heart pounding.

Kraatjes said, "He's under orders to keep this tight, Piet. But with Wayne . . ."

The Chief lowered his voice a little, ratcheting down the intensity. "I think the mayor is going to want us to do everything possible to keep it quiet. If this gets out, there's going to be trouble down at the Uhuru Community, and that doesn't do his campaign any good, either. Sergeant Wayne knows the consequences if he talks. But Wayne, you know how he thinks. He probably figures if he plays this right, he comes out a hero."

Westermann nodded.

They were nearing City Hall. Kraatjes turned in his seat and mumbled something to the driver. The Chief gently gripped Westermann's arm. This close, Westermann could see the tension in the Chief's jaw, the stress lines spreading from his eyes. "You need to clear this case, Piet."

Westermann held the Chief's gaze and nodded. The Chief didn't even know.

26.

A yellow haze hung low in the City, refusing to dissipate, obscuring the tops of the taller buildings even in the slum just west of Praeger's Hill known as the Cauldron. Morphy drove with Grip riding shotgun, a literal description in this neighborhood where even cops felt their backs tighten and the usual prowl-car banter fell mute. Morphy crept the car along, letting Grip get a good, menacing look at the action on the street. If there was a truly heterogeneous neighborhood in the City, this was it. All manner of color, creed, and nationality were here, having only poverty and desperation in common. On one corner they saw three men with long beards and turbans sitting Indian-style passing a flask and talking in high, staccato voices. More typical were the furtive transactions taking place on the sidewalks. Deft exchanges only halfheartedly disguised as handshakes or embraces. Whores were out, too, even at this hour—just after noon. Grip recognized a few from the station, in particular a red-haired Irish girl whose high cheekbones and startled eyes had transfixed him.

"Weird thing yesterday with the boss giving us the up-and-down for bracing Mel Washington," Grip said. It had been at the back of his mind.

"Yeah," Morphy replied without much interest.

"Not usually his way, you know, second-guessing his men."

"No," Morphy agreed.

"I mean, how did he even know about it? Who the fuck told him?"

Morphy shrugged. "I don't know. Who the fuck cares who told him? One of those guys we ran off. Maybe Washington. We know the lieut doesn't like the heavy stuff."

"Yeah," Grip muttered.

"He's not going to start running a tight ship, Torsten. It's not in him."

Grip nodded without the confidence that Morphy seemed to have. He thought about burning the commie press operation, about Ole Koss scaring everyone in sight.

They crossed Wolffe Boulevard and entered a block of town houses that, although squalid, were practically palaces compared to most Cauldron residences. They drove by the address they were looking for, took a right at the end of the block, and parked the car at the curb.

Three boys materialized from nowhere, their clothes hanging from their slender frames and their eyes, even at this age, hard.

"Watch your car for a buck," the tallest of the three said.

Morphy ignored him and opened the trunk of the car. Grip gave the boys the once-over.

"A buck," Grip said, making a show of mulling it over, "to watch the car."

"Each," the boy shot back.

Grip spat into the gutter. "A buck total. You want it or not?"

The boy frowned judiciously, then shrugged. "A buck."

"When we get back," Grip said, and saw that Morphy was holding a crowbar now.

Morphy said, "You make sure no one gets out the front."

Grip nodded and marched around the block to the front of the house. Morphy strolled down the alley that ran behind the row houses. Trash was everywhere, huge rats enjoying it, ignoring Morphy. A couple of young kids playing with an old tire saw Morphy coming and beat it. An old-timer with a long gray beard lay in a large crate, snoring, wearing a jacket made for fifty degrees cooler.

Morphy swung the crowbar lazily in his right hand while he hummed something by Mozart under his breath—he didn't know the name, but the tune was his favorite, he having heard it at a gala affair in Admiralty Park, carried away to the point that he had almost forgotten that he was on security. And composed by a kraut, he thought, which was generally a negative in his book (it was doubtful that the distinction between Austrians and Germans would have made much of a difference to him). He had done his bit against the Germans in northern France and into Belgium and Holland.

He came to the right house and walked up four wooden steps to a small stoop by the back door. He paused for a moment, listening. There were voices, but not natural ones—the radio. He lifted the crowbar above his head and gave three vicious hacks to the doorknob, destroying it and ripping a small hole in the door.

He heard a man's voice yell, "Hey, what the hell?" and heard a feminine whimpering.

Morphy switched the crowbar to his left hand and without rushing pulled his gun from his shoulder holster. He held the gun outstretched at shoulder height and nudged the door open with his foot. He took three steps and was at a door to his left when through it walked a man wearing only boxers and carrying a pistol. His momentum stopped when his forehead hit the business end of Morphy's gun. The man's eyes looked up. Morphy gave the man's gun hand a tap with the crowbar and the gun rattled to the floor and the man barked in pain.

"Back in the room," Morphy ordered, and backed him into the room with the pressure of the gun barrel on the man's forehead.

"Okay, Jack, okay," the man said, hands in the air.

He had come from a bedroom and on the bed cowered two women, barely more than girls, the sheet pulled up to their chins. Morphy could tell from the outlines beneath the sheet that they were both naked. A radio played in the corner—one of those serials.

"Who else is here?" Morphy asked the room.

One of the women—dark-skinned, maybe Italian—shook her head violently.

Morphy engaged the man's eyes. "You have already pulled a gun on me. I could kill you right now and it would be self-defense all the way. Now you have five seconds. Is anybody else here? If you lie, I will kill you."

"Come on, Jack, ain't no one else here. Don't pull the fucking trigger." The man was sweating now as if he'd run a goddamn marathon.

"Okay," Morphy said, looking at the women this time, "get in the fucking bathroom." He nodded toward a door leading off the bedroom.

The women struggled for a moment with the sheet, not sure how they could both use it and move at the same time.

"Leave the sheet," Morphy said slowly, as if to children, "I won't look." To demonstrate his disinterest, he turned his attention back to the man.

"You Kaz Plansky?"

The man nodded. Kaz Plansky was a known pimp, part of a pipeline for young women just off the boat. He was a broker, accepting the women when they arrived and then funneling them to the crime organizations that controlled prostitution in much of the City or to smaller-time freelance pimps.

He was just over five feet tall and, in his boxers, looked like a standing god-damn hedgehog. He rubbed his hand, which Morphy noticed was ballooning and turning an angry shade of yellow.

The women had made it to the bathroom, pulling the door closed behind them. Morphy grabbed a chair and propped it hard under the doorknob.

"Okay, let's go to the front door."

They walked down the hallway, Plansky in front, hunched over a little from the pain in his hand. Morphy followed a couple of paces behind, gun trained at the shorter man's head.

When they got to the front door, Morphy shouted, "Officer Grip, it's Officer Morphy. Kaz Plansky is about to open the door. Do not kill him. Do you understand?"

"Don't kill him?" came the response from outside.

"Correct."

Plansky looked nervously back at Morphy, who nodded toward the door. Using his left hand, Plansky fumbled with the lock and then pulled the door open. Grip stood in the doorway, an unpleasant smirk on his face.

"All right," Morphy said, "let's head on back."

They went back to the bedroom and made Plansky sit on the bed. Morphy and Grip stood before him, a little closer than necessary.

"Shit, Jack," Plansky said, "I think you broke my fucking hand."

"Yeah, that don't look too good," Grip confirmed cheerfully.

"Look, if this is a shakedown, I'm already paying off LaRue and Riise. Maybe you should—"

"Shut up," Grip said.

Morphy put his face down at Plansky's level, their noses almost touching. "This isn't a shakedown, Kaz. We need some information. And you call me Jack one more time, I'm going to put a fucking bullet in your head."

It didn't seem possible, but Plansky looked even more worried. "Okay," he said uncertainly.

Morphy produced a photo from his breast pocket—head and shoulders shot of the corpse from the river. "You recognize this girl?"

Plansky squinted at the photos. "She's dead."

"No shit," said Grip. "You ever see her alive?"

"Jesus," Plansky said slowly, shaking his head. "I don't know. I see a lot of girls. And her, look at her shoulders, it's like someone didn't feed her. And the shit on her face."

"Think hard," Morphy asked. "Because if you're wrong, and this girl has crossed your path, we will find out and we will come back here and fucking kill you. Do you understand that I'm serious when I say this? I will kill you and I will walk because it will be so goddamn ugly that they'll say no way a cop could ever do this. Get it?"

Plansky nodded his head quickly. Morphy could almost see the thought process on his face. Plansky was desperately trying to come up with something that would be useful.

"This the bird they found on the riverbank?"

That got Grip's attention. "Yeah, why?"

"Just wondering."

"What is it, Kaz?" Grip asked with a grin that showed his teeth.

"Shit. You know, a lot of girls come through here, but I sell them off to other guys who work them on the street."

"What're they, fucking slaves?"

Plansky looked at him funny. "They're whores. Anyway, maybe this one looks familiar. Like I said, she don't look like she's in such good shape."

Grip nodded encouragingly and Morphy just continued to stare.

"Well, I don't know that I remember the girl's name or anything. But she might just be with Joey Stanic down in the Theater District. You know Joey?"

Grip shook his head, looking at Morphy. Morphy shrugged.

"Ask around down there, you'll find Joey. People know him."

"And you think this girl, whatever her name is, you *sold* her to this Joey Stanic?"

Plansky shrugged. "Like I been telling you, it's hard to tell with her all skinny and those sores. But, yeah, I think I might have."

Morphy shook his head, tapping the crowbar against the bedroom wall. Grip looked his way, eyebrows up.

"Come on, Jack," Plansky said; then paused, wondering if Morphy would really shoot him. When he realized he would survive the next thirty seconds, he continued, "LaRue and Riise, they said that I pay them, I'm good with the force."

"What do you think?" Grip asked Morphy.

Morphy frowned. "We find Stanic and it turns out he doesn't know what the fuck's going on, I'll come back and take my time with our chum here."

"Fuck," Plansky said, clearly hoping that his memory was right, but having his doubts under this pressure.

Grip and Morphy turned to leave.

"Wait," Plansky said. "Don't mention my name down in the Theater District. It don't look good, people think I'm peaching on Joey Stanic."

Morphy laughed and kept laughing. He laughed all the way out the broken back door, Grip shaking his head behind him, thinking about Plansky shitting himself back in the bedroom.

The three boys were still there, sitting on the curb by the front of the car, looking harder than any kids that age should.

The one who had done the talking before got up as Morphy and Grip approached. "No one touched your car."

Grip took a trip around the car, putting on a show of judiciously inspecting it from all angles. When he was done, he fished out his wallet. He took three bills and gave one to each boy.

"Keep this in mind if we ever need you again. We need good men from time to time."

Morphy looked at Grip as if he'd lost his mind.

27.

A block from the Uhuru Community shantytown, Frings leaned against a burned-out light post and smoked a reefer, his hat tilted back on his head, feeling the sun on his face. He was here early, not wanting to make Carla wait, what with her doing him a favor.

He'd stopped off at the office before coming over and been rewarded with a call from Klein over at Police Records. The Community assaults had been assigned to a Sergeant Ed Wayne, who had that beat. The name rang no bells. He'd run it by Westermann, see if he was familiar with Sergeant Wayne.

He saw a cab several blocks off, headed his way. He took a last drag off the reefer and tossed it down a storm drain. The sky, he noticed, was a particularly deep blue, with high white clouds hanging almost motionless. He wiped his forehead with his sleeve and tilted his hat down to get the sun off his face. A hell of a lot of birds were chirping away up on the power lines and pecking around in the field by the shanties. Frings didn't like birds. He wasn't sure why.

The cab pulled up and Carla stepped out, looking, Frings thought, very prole with a scarf over her head and her modest, brownish clothes. Frings kissed her on the cheek.

Kids hung around the perimeter of the shantytown, throwing a makeshift ball of twine back and forth while younger kids chased. Carla smiled at them and they stopped, waiting for the adults to pass before they picked up their game again. Frings winked at the kids and followed Carla through a gap between two sheets of corrugated steel and into what felt like an oven. The stagnant air was heavy with the smells of spices, cooking meat, exotic incense, and cannabis smoke.

The alleys between the shacks were narrow, and Frings saw that most doors were open, allowing a view into hovels where women in bright dresses cooked over open fires and children played on the dirt floors. People, sweat beading on faces, eased sideways to let them by in the narrow passages.

Some people clearly knew Carla, people nodding to her, some calling her by name. But Frings was aware that others looked at them with wariness and even hostility. It was understandable, he thought. There were no other white faces.

They ventured farther into the maze, Carla navigating between shanties made of cardboard, tin, and scrap lumber. Symbols were painted on many of the doors—intricate patterns, crosses—sometimes numbers, or words in French. On some walls hung plates of tin painted in bright colors, simple portraits of Negro men and women—their heads huge and topped with halos—framed by complicated and colorful patterns. Sometimes names were painted below the portrait. Senjak. Senjon. Samedi. Mama Loa. Brown.

"These are interesting. What are they?" Frings asked.

"Religious symbols. Portraits of saints. Many of the people here are from the islands. They brought their religion with them."

"How does this fit with Father Womé?"

Carla laughed. "I don't think he worries very much about it. From what I've heard, he seems to embrace the Square."

"What's the Square? Womé mentioned it, too."

"The Square? I can show you the *place*. It's where the islanders hold their rituals. I'm told the whole Community comes out sometimes. It's kind of the center of the Community. The Square and Father Womé, of course. It's over here."

She led him to a dirt plaza, maybe twenty yards to a side, bordered by shanties. Chairs were placed sporadically along the edge, and large, unlit candles sat bunched in the center. A group of older men had pulled chairs in a circle and were chatting and drinking coffee from battered tin cups. They turned in their chairs, postures wary, to see Frings and Carla.

Carla waved. "I'm here to see Billy Lambert."

One of the men, thin, wearing a bowler and dark glasses, asked, "What you want that boy for?"

"I'm his friend. I heard he was hurt."

The old man nodded. "He was beat down good. In yonder house." He motioned with his head to the opposite side of the square.

"I know where he lives," Carla said. "Thank you."

Frings flashed a smile and noticed they were passing a pipe. No one smiled back.

* * *

Billy Lambert lived in a tiny shack amid dozens of other similar shacks. While they were essentially the same size, their construction was incredibly diverse because they had been pieced together from whatever materials were available in whatever quantity: tin, steel, wood, cardboard, canvas, plank, parts of abandoned cars. Again, the symbols and the paintings. Lambert's door was marked with a symbol that looked like a cross on a stand, outlined and then filled in with loose cross-hatching.

Carla knocked lightly on the door. "Billy?"

"Yeah. Come."

Carla pushed the door open and they entered the dim shack, a cot taking up about a quarter of the floor space. On the cot lay a young man with very dark skin, wearing only a pair of slacks.

"Billy," Carla said again, tentative.

"Mrs. Bierhoff." Billy raised himself up on an elbow. His voice was slurred, the words indistinct around the edges.

"Oh my God, Billy." Carla said it calmly, more in sympathy than in shock. Frings took a closer look. Somebody had really had a go at the kid. Both eyes were swollen, the right one basically shut. His lips were bruised and puffy, and an angry gash ran above an eyebrow. If the rest of his body was in the same shape as his face . . .

Carla fussed over him, folding his pillow so that it propped him up a little. She retrieved a bottle onto which someone had shellacked a newsprint image of a saint—Frings thought it might be St. George slaying a dragon. Billy accepted it, took a couple of shallow sips, and lay back into the pillow. She noticed a guitar case and bedroll in the corner and asked Billy if he played.

"No, ma'am, I've got a guest." He looked at Frings.

Carla introduced Frings as a newspaper reporter. "He's trying to learn more about the attacks outside the Community."

Billy nodded, friendly but wary.

Frings didn't even have to ask; Billy told the story, his island accent pronounced even though his swollen lips slurred his speech.

"Me and Tom Belgrave was coming back from passing out papers down by City Hall. We'd been there all day. It was night, you know, and there's a couple blocks were there's no streetlights and it's real dark; real dark. Me and Tom were walking down on these blocks and hear a car behind us, running slow, and we get real nervous 'cause a few others been beaten this last week. But you can't outrun no car, no? So we just walk along and the car gets right up next to us and is just cruising right beside us and we can't see inside the windows 'cause it's so dark. Well, the car stops and those doors open and out comes three men with bats and we didn't have no chance to run. Those men just start swinging and down we went, and they give us several whacks while we down on the ground, covering our heads, like, and they're screaming *nigger* and *commie* and *commie nigger* and all, and I'm just praying that they stop before they kill me." He paused to take another sip from his bottle.

Carla asked, "Do you know who they were?"

"No. They's wearing something over their faces, makes it hard to see what they look like. They're ofays, though. No doubting that."

Frings again took in the damage to Billy Lambert. This was what he'd really come to see, the seriousness of the crime. No way the police would ignore an assault like this on a *white* kid. Lambert's story was useful, but essentially just confirmed what Frings had already assumed. The important part was the police reaction.

Frings asked, "Did you talk to the police?"

"Yeah. Sergeant came with another man, but they just asked a couple questions, that's all. Never heard from them again. They didn't even talk to Tom, look around where we got beat. Those kids that play on the street say the coppers just get back in their car and drive away. If there's a copper car around, those kids see, they let me know. Cops came back last night, but not for this. Kids say they were down on the river, searching."

Frings nodded. "You remember the name of the sergeant you spoke with?"

"Nah." Billy shook his head. "I was still hurting then, not keeping track of the names."

"Maybe Sergeant Wayne?"

Carla looked at Frings, as if she was wondering what he knew.

"Yeah," Billy said. "Coulda been."

"How's your buddy?"

"What? Tom? Like me, I guess. Laying low."

Frings thought for a moment, then looked over at Carla. She frowned, nothing more to add.

Frings said, "Billy, I'm really sorry about what happened to you. You've been very helpful. Thank you."

"Yes, Billy. Thank you so much," Carla added. "I hope you get back on your feet soon."

Billy nodded. "You going to get those bastards what did this?"

"We're going to get the police to get them."

Billy snorted cynically and went back to his bottle.

28.

By prearrangement, Frings and Westermann met after lunch at Veteran's Park, a modest triangle of grass nestled in the angled intersection of two streets near the *Gazette* building. A statue of a World War II soldier carrying an apparently windblown flag stood high on a pedestal overlooking a grassy common and the occasional wooden bench, most of them occupied by sleeping derelicts. Beneath the statue, a crowd had gathered around a Negro in a sleeveless T-shirt, bowler, and dark glasses, who was speaking with great animation into a microphone attached to an amplifier that spit out his words, distorted and angry. From this distance, Westermann couldn't make out what he was saying. Another man distributed leaflets to the crowd, which seemed evenly split between whites and Negroes.

Frings arrived and shook hands with Westermann.

"You know what's going on over there?" Westermann asked.

"One of the reporters checked it out. They're Community guys, trying to get donations. Proclaiming the Gospel according to Father Womé."

Westermann blanched at this unexpected Community presence.

"You all right?" Frings's tone was more challenging than sympathetic.

"Yeah, I'm making it."

"Do we have a problem?"

"What do you mean?"

"One of our reporters, Art Deyna, looks like he's taken an interest."

"Maybe you can tell me."

"I can tell you that he's got a photo of you and Mel in front of the shanties. I can tell you that he's not stupid. But that's all I've got."

Westermann was surprised that Frings wasn't more concerned about this; putting it all on Westermann. "What are you—the *Gazette*—going to do with the photos?"

"Nothing right now. Sit on them. But I've got no guarantees about later. It might be a matter of days. Or a day."

"Shit. You know what that'll do to me."

"I'll do what I can, Piet. But this isn't in my control."

Westermann closed his eyes.

Frings said, "How about on your end? Anyone getting close?"

Was anyone getting close? Grip? "One of my guys, he's interested in how the currents work down there; tossing sticks in to see where they end up."

"Really? He find the spot?" From the tone, it seemed that Frings was more interested in this news from a technical viewpoint—how did Grip figure it out?—than he was alarmed.

"I don't think he's got it that exact, but he thinks he knows basically where the body came from." Westermann decided to keep the second body to himself for now; he was beginning to feel the weight of desperation, and this was the only leverage he held.

Frings nodded.

Westermann said, "There's no reason for him to connect me or you to it."

Frings thought that this was probably true. "I was down in the Community today, talking to one of the kids who was jumped the other night. There've been several assaults on Community people over the past week. They don't seem to think the police are taking it all that seriously."

"Wait." Westermann saw all the crime stats and he hadn't seen anything about assaults near the Community. "You sure? Several assaults?"

"I saw the kid myself. Somebody'd done a number on him."

"There's no record of it."

"Well, it was called in and an officer, at a minimum, interviewed the victim. Like I said, there wasn't a whole lot of confidence that he did much else. Guy named Sergeant Wayne."

"Wayne?"

"Yeah."

Westermann shook his head in disgust. "I know him. He was the guy put on the Community assault case?" It wasn't hard to imagine Wayne burying it. "I'll look into it."

"Let me know what you find."

Frings didn't think Westermann looked so sure about that.

"Don't jerk me around, Piet. Jesus. Cops, you'd let anything happen before you'd put the brakes on another cop. What's more important, Piet, some bent cop or justice?"

Westermann winced.

"Because institutions, Piet, you start making them more important than people, that's how things get balled up. You're smart enough to understand that."

Westermann nodded and changed the subject. "You run anything about the girl in the *Gazette*?"

Frings gave him a long look, then decided to move things along. "Couple of grafs buried in the middle. Jane Doe on the riverbank. You know . . ."

They noticed by its absence that the amplified speech had come to an end and the small crowd was dispersing. The speaker and the man who'd been passing out leaflets were gathering their things and preparing to leave.

Watching this, Westermann said, "I don't like the way the Community's looking for attention."

"Nothing we can do about that, but I think we're okay. Even if someone figures where the body was originally, it's a long step to connecting it to us."

"Maybe not to Mel Washington."

Frings shook his head. "Mel? Maybe, but I don't see it. What's his connection?"

Except that he *was* connected, Westermann thought. He was very much connected and so was Frings and so was he.

29.

The night heat had transformed these marginal blocks just off Capitol Heights into a scene from a more lawless era. Bar patrons gathered on the sidewalks, their sheer numbers forcing them into close quarters. Voices overheard in passing carried the tense pitch of latent violence, the people's faces set in angry concentration, lit blue, yellow, red, by storefront neon. And on every block, whores, looking weary and spent, going through the motions of enticement.

Westermann and Grip were in short sleeves and straw fedoras, badges visible, clipped to their belts. It was the kind of night where you didn't want to have to take the time to find your badge.

Morphy was home tonight with his wife.

Westermann scanned the crowds, looking for Joey Stanic. He carried a photo of Stanic in his pocket, a small guy with delicate features, almost like a girl but with a trim mustache. Difficult to picture a guy like that as a hard case, but a couple of uniforms at the station told Westermann not to take Stanic lightly; that a healthy caution was wise.

Grip walked with his arms slightly out—gunfighter style. "That body they found?"

"Yeah?"

"Souza filled me in a little. No ID. Same sores as our girl; same underweight."

"That's right."

"Souza also told me where they found her."

"He did?" Westermann bumped a heavy guy, spilling the guy's beer on the sleeveless T-shirt stretched over his gut. The guy turned on Westermann, eyes lit with booze and rage. Westermann showed him the badge. The guy didn't back down, kept eye contact, but didn't press it.

Grip picked up as if nothing had happened. "Yeah. And it sounds like they found her about where I think the body must have been before she was tossed in the river."

"*If* she was tossed."

"Right. But, Lieut, I think we need to focus on the shanties. That's two with at least one of them on their doorstep. Probably both."

Westermann nodded thoughtfully. They continued on, concentrating on the crowd.

"What do you think?" Grip said, nodding to a couple of drunks getting surly, grabbing each others' shirt, fists balling.

"You been drinking?" Westermann asked, catching a whiff of scotch on Grip's breath.

"Just a nip before we headed out. We're working late, Lieut."

Westermann shook his head, leaving it at that. This was how he preferred to handle things, letting the men know if they crossed some line, but not dwelling on it. Move on; give them the opportunity to make adjustments themselves.

"The fight?" Grip asked.

"We start making busts, we'll be here all night. Let's find Stanic."

They walked another block, people clearing out of their way, making them as cops, or at least people you didn't mess with.

Westermann's adrenaline was jacked; his chest tight. He talked, trying to chase off the feeling. "You know a Detective Wayne?"

"Yeah. Ed Wayne," Grip said, still walking and peering into the crowd.

"He a friend of yours?"

"Nah, we drink at the same bar, have the same politics. He's an asshole."

"What about as a cop? He a good cop?"

Grip thought for a moment. "I don't know. He's smart enough, I guess. I don't know . . ."

"Don't know what?"

"I don't know. I've got no idea how he does police work, but I know him a little and I wouldn't be surprised if he pushes the limits sometimes."

"Think he's bent?"

Grip stopped. "Where are you going with this, Lieut?"

Westermann shrugged. "His name came up."

Grip shook his head. "I don't know. Like I said, he's an asshole."

Westermann was satisfied with this and they moved on to the next block, crowd noise vying with a guitar keening from the open door of the Checkerboard. Westermann saw two Community Negroes standing on a corner, handing out pamphlets. Passersby mostly ignored the proffered sheets, but some took them, mostly Negroes. Westermann wondered how many Community people might be out tonight.

"Shit." Grip was focused on a spot in the distance like a hunting dog.

Westermann peered into the crowd where Grip was looking, but didn't see anyone resembling Stanic. "You see him?"

"Yeah, pretty sure." Grip was already moving faster, clear of the crowd and doing a half trot in the street.

Westermann followed, adrenaline kicking in. He saw Stanic—small and slender-hipped—as Grip got to him. Stanic was wearing some kind of cowboy getup—boots, yoked shirt, flat-brimmed hat. There was the boyish face and the tight mustache from the photo, and now, in person, Westermann could see two parallel vertical scars in one eyebrow. He was almost pretty.

Grip sidled up to him. "You Joey Stanic?"

"You a cop?"

"What gave it away?"

"I ain't causing no trouble."

"Save it. I'm not interested."

Westermann hung a couple steps back, letting Grip work. He eyed graffiti on the wall above Stanic. BETTER DEAD THAN RED.

"What the fuck d'you want?"

"We fished a girl out of the river the other day, thought maybe you'd know her."

"How's that?"

"Hunch. This girl was pretty, dark hair, but real skinny. And she was sick, sores, the whole thing."

Westermann saw Stanic giving Grip a blank face while he worked out the situation, trying to figure Grip's angle.

"Yeah, I don't think I'm going to say any more until I see a lawyer."

Grip looked back a Westermann, putting his all into a can-you-believe-this-asshole look. He turned back to Stanic. "You think you're under arrest here? You're not under arrest, I'm just asking you a question."

"If you're not arresting me, you can take a walk." Stanic squinted at

Westermann and his voice changed from brash to genuinely curious. "I know you from somewhere?"

Westermann reddened, caught off guard.

Grip got up into Stanic's face and spoke quietly. "Keep with the program, pal. I just asked you a question. I'm waiting on an answer." Grip pulled away.

Stanic made eye contact with Westermann. "I thought he was going to kiss me there."

From behind, Westermann could see Grip's shoulders tense. He stepped in, putting a hand on Grip's shoulder. To Stanic, Westermann said, "Let's take a walk."

Stanic laughed, his chin raised to Westermann in a provocation.

Westermann smiled. "You going to make me work for this?"

Stanic smiled back at Westermann. "'You going to make me work for this?'" Stanic mocked. "I'm paid up. You want to talk to me, work it out with Riordon and Mossberg, they work this block. Now take a walk, you've wasted enough of my time."

Westermann turned away, trying to keep his cool. The mob scene on the street gave them some camouflage, nobody much paying attention to the three men facing off. But on the periphery, maybe twenty feet away, he saw two men watching. *Something about them . . .*

Facing Stanic again, Westermann said, "Okay, I've changed my mind, punk. We're arresting you."

Stanic squinted at him. "For what?"

"Suspicion of murder."

"You're crazy," Stanic said, smile still in place, but the confidence ebbing from his posture.

"Turn around."

Grip came forward, cuffs out. He pushed Stanic hard into the wall, kicked his feet apart, and kneed him in the groin from behind. Stanic's body sagged a little, but he didn't make any noise and even turned his head, forcing his grimace into a half smile. A flash exploded and all three men turned to the source. Westermann took a better look at the two men and now recognized Art Deyna and his cameraman. The cameraman got off another shot as they stood there. Grip looked to Westermann.

Westermann said, "I'll handle it."

While Grip cuffed and frisked Stanic, Westermann strode over to Deyna.

Deyna smiled. "Lieutenant, good to see you again."

"What are you doing here?"

Deyna raised his eyebrows and pointed to himself. "Me? The question here is why you're pulling a pimp roust. This isn't your usual beat."

Westermann shook his head.

Deyna said, "I don't want to keep you from anything, Lieutenant. We've got our story and our photos. But I would like the chance to meet. Soon."

Westermann stared at Deyna for a moment, then walked away.

Deyna called after him, "This story isn't going away, Lieutenant. You want to give me your side, you call me."

Westermann ignored him, but thought, *What story?*

Grip had Stanic by the back of the collar, pushing him into the wall. Grip gave Westermann a questioning look. Westermann frowned and shook his head. With a rough yank, Grip pulled Stanic from the wall to face Westermann.

Stanic, still queasy from the knee to the groin, said, "It's like I've been telling him, I'm paid up. Talk to Mossberg. What the fuck's wrong with you?"

Grip said, "Shut up." They'd finally attracted attention, a small crowd eyeballing the action. Stanic kept his stare hard, working on his rep.

They walked Stanic off the block and down a residential street.

"Where the fuck you taking me?" Stanic asked.

"I don't know. Maybe nowhere," Grip said. "Why don't you make life easier on yourself, you dumb asshole."

Stanic didn't like this answer. "You say you found a body in the river?"

Westermann blinked. He couldn't get Deyna out of his mind, trying to figure out why he was here, what it meant. He wasn't focused on what he was doing, feeling his arms push Stanic hard in the back. Stanic, unable to pad his fall with his arms behind his back, fell hard on his face.

"Shit."

"You feel like talking now?"

"The girl, she had sores on her?" Stanic's voice was up an octave in panic.

Westermann lifted Stanic's chin off the street with the toe of his boot. He saw Grip looking over, worried for once. Westermann knew he wasn't a natural with the hard stuff; had no sense for it. He knew Grip had seen this before, Westermann either going too soft or, like now, going too hard; or at least too hard for out here in the middle of the street.

"Lieut, there's people watching out from their windows."

Westermann pulled his foot from under Stanic's chin, which dropped to the pavement. Grip walked over.

"You got a name for us?" Grip asked.

"Lenore."

"Lenore got a last name?"

"I don't know. Lenore. It's probably not even her real name. Shit. But it must have been her, all sick and with those sores. Haven't seen her in a few days."

The girl, moonlit, turning slowly in the current as she floats downstream.

Lenore, moonlit, gently turning in the current as she floats downstream.

Grip knelt down so that his face was closer to Stanic's. He noticed the blood running from Stanic's nose and lips. "Lenore got a place?"

"Yeah."

"Okay. I'm going to help you up and then you're going to take us there. Got it? Or the lieut gets another pop at you."

"Yeah, I got it," Stanic said, resigned. "I'll take you there."

30.

Moses Winston couldn't see the crowd—the stage lights hit him in the
eyes, everyone behind the lights was invisible—but he could hear them and
he could feel them, the place shaking. He had his head tilted back, squinting
against the sweat flowing into his eyes. Behind him, a fat white cat played a
stand-up bass. The guy had shown up with his instrument earlier; asked if he
could back Winston up. Winston had said, "Show me," and damned if the
cracker didn't play a hell of a bass. Winston didn't change it up for the bassist, just playing like hell. But the cat went with it. No problems.

They'd smoked some mesca back in the alley. There must have been
something in it or it was some kind he hadn't smoked before, because his
thoughts seemed to fray, even as he played. He closed his eyes and saw a
newsreel he'd caught at a picture show years ago: bombs exploding one
after another somewhere in Germany, the perspective from above, in an
airplane. He played in rhythm to the bombs in his head, each pick of a
string another detonation. He was playing the music of violence, of destruction. He played different kinds of music: desire, violence, despair, pain.
He played devotion sometimes when he was playing at a church or, lately,
the Community. Tonight there were explosions in his head and he broad-
cast them into the world with his guitar.

Winston didn't see Cephus giving him the signal to end the set, so the bassist gave him a little tap on the shoulder and Winston stopped almost imme-
diately. The cheering came to him as an almost physical thing; a wave of
sound. The stage lights were dimmed and the houselights turned up and
the crowd was suddenly visible. Winston gazed out over the faces, Negro and
white intermixed. Each face seemed to stand out to him through the smoke,
though one more than the rest. His breathing went shallow. He heard the
bassist behind him, saying his name. He turned away from the crowd, felt
some of the tension ease.

The bassist said, "Look over there at the bar. You see that guy, nice clothes, between those two lookers?"

Winston took in the bar, letting his eyes glide down the people sitting there, until he thought he saw the right cat.

"Negro, got some salt in his hair?"

"That's right. You know who he is?"

Winston shook his head, still staring at the man as he talked to one of the ladies sitting next to him.

"That's Floyd Christian, Moses. He owns the Palace. You heard of it?"

Winston had heard of the Palace from other musicians. It was the pinnacle of the City's Negro music scene. Yeah, he'd heard of it—his destination, eventually. He was confident of that.

The bassist continued, "He's here to see you, Moses. Word about you is spreading around. If he likes what he sees, you could be playing the Palace this time tomorrow."

"You think he likes what he sees so far?" Winston asked. But he knew the answer. He'd had cats like Christian catch his act before and they never left disappointed.

"You joking?" the bassist said.

They were silent for a moment; the question unspoken.

The bassist said, "You don't need me at the Palace. You need to do for yourself."

Winston nodded, shook the bassist's hand. He felt the man's respect and returned it.

The bassist said, "Cephus is going to try to talk you out of leaving, maybe say some shit about the Palace. Don't listen to him."

Winston looked at Cephus behind the bar, slinging drinks, his face like a goddamn tomato.

"Hey," the bassist said, stepping down from the stage to get a drink. "Looks like you got a friend wants to talk to you."

Winston turned and saw a huge cracker with a blond army cut and a scar on his upper lip. Lenore had pointed him out one time on the street. *Koss.* Winston had remembered that, thinking if someone mentioned that name, he'd want to know they were talking about this enormous man with the leopard tattoo.

He walked to the edge of the stage, knelt down so that his face was closer to Koss's. Too loud to hear otherwise.

"Can I help you with something?"

"Yeah, I think you can," Koss said.

"Okay."

"You seen Lenore lately, Moses?"

Winston felt the chill. "No," and cut himself off before he said *sir*, a habit he was trying to break.

"I think maybe you did about a week ago. Am I right about that?"

Winston stared at him, too high to really feel the impact the words.

Koss kept on. "But you haven't seen her since, have you?"

Winston had nothing to say.

"I've seen her, though. Keep that in mind."

Koss walked away with a grin. Winston shook his head, wondering if that really hadn't made sense, or if it was the mesca. He looked up and lost himself in the sea of faces.

31.

Frings sat at a table in the back of the Cairo, sipping a whiskey on the rocks and chatting with a gink named William Ebanks, a Bohemian of sorts. Up front, Renate, decked in a long, tight emerald dress, sang a seductive number in Portuguese. Frings sat in the back to avoid her notice. She hadn't been home in a week. He didn't want to talk to her, just enjoy the music and talk with Ebanks.

The Cairo was run by a private club called the Pharaohs that occupied the building next door. Ebanks was a third-generation Pharaoh, a guy whose bohemianism was supported by family wealth. As far as Frings knew, Ebanks had never worked a day in his life, though he seemed to collect a new academic degree every few years.

They'd smoked a reefer earlier in the Pharaoh's library, an imitation of a London gentlemen's club library, Frings thought, with dark, floor-to-ceiling bookshelves holding leather-bound books; well-padded chairs; and heavily shaded table lamps. Ebanks had long since failed to shock the other Pharaoh members with his open marijuana use, now considered a club eccentricity along with Fitz Dalgliesh's extended and intense conversations with empty chairs and ancient Hamish Strachan's habit of arriving for dinner from his upstairs room without some essential piece of clothing.

Ebanks knew of Renate's affairs, but was not the type to bring it up.

Frings asked, "You ever been down to the Uhuru Community, Bill?"

Ebanks smiled broadly, widened his eyes, and raised his eyebrows—a signature expression. "But of course. Wherever there is a chance to sample something unusual, Frank, I explore."

"What'd you think?"

"What, the shantytown?"

"That's right."

Ebanks shook his head. "Poverty, Frank. You wonder how a place like that is ever going to rise above it. What kind of hope is there for those people?"

"Did you go in alone?"

"No. I had a chum—a Negro—who went with me. Not a big deal, but we kept our eyes open. Why do you ask?"

"I went in today. It's an interesting place."

"No doubt about that. Interesting cats there, interesting reefer, but a little spooky, too. Did you pick up on that, the weird Caribbean vibe—like voodoo or something?"

Frings had picked up on something in the shanties, putting it down to the poverty and the foreign roots of most of the people. Ebanks had traveled, though, and if he found it weird, maybe there was something to it.

Renate's set ended and, along with it, talk of the Uhuru Community. The conversation drifted. Another reefer appeared from Ebanks's jacket pocket and they passed it back and forth while Ebanks enthusiastically related his recent interest in Buddhism, his discovery of a guitarist who was tearing up the Checkerboard, and some hash he'd tried a couple of weeks ago.

Frings listened and watched Renate talking with a couple of her musicians onstage, experiencing that weird feeling he sometimes had after smoking reefer, that distance from people he wasn't actually interacting with. His nights with her seemed a vague memory.

"Listen, Bill, are you going to donate any money to the mayor's campaign?"

Ebanks laughed. "That fascist?"

"He's hardly a fascist." Ebanks's politics were strange, but mostly revolved around his being able to do whatever the hell he wanted without any hassle. Anything that got in the way was "fascism." "You've got a problem with him, wait until you see Vic Truffant."

Ebanks rolled his eyes. "Really? Frank, you know that there's nothing I find more excruciating than politics. I really can't get too excited about the choice between one fascist and another."

Frings sighed, ordered another drink, and talked into the night, knowing that his apartment would be empty when he returned.

32.

Joey Stanic lead Grip and Westermann to the flop that Lenore shared with two other prostitutes: two filthy mattresses on the floor, a threadbare couch, broken door to the bathroom.

"Jesus," Grip said, pushing Stanic down on one of the mattresses.

"Where are the other two?" Westermann asked.

"Better be out on the street," Stanic mumbled, sulking. A rhythmic pounding sounded from upstairs, as if someone were ramming a pole against the floor again and again. A red neon light flashed across the street, the rhythm not in sync with the pounding above.

Just then, the bathroom door came open and a young woman walked out, wearing a ragged dress. She looked nervously at Stanic—registering the cuffs—then at Grip and Westermann. She didn't say anything. The veins in Stanic's neck shone blue through his skin.

"What's your name?" Westermann asked, showing his badge out of courtesy.

The woman looked to Stanic for guidance.

"Don't worry about him," Grip said. "He knows what'll happen if he touches you after this."

She didn't seem too sure, but said, "My name is Belle."

"Belle," Westermann said, keeping his voice soft, "I'm sorry to have to tell you this, but Lenore is dead. She was murdered."

Belle frowned a little, more, it seemed, because it was expected than because she was upset by this news.

Westermann and Grip exchanged looks. The pounding continued. The flashing lights. *Art Deyna.*

Westermann continued, "Do you have any idea who might have wanted to kill her?"

Belle looked to Stanic again. Westermann wondered if this was instinctive, getting his permission to talk, or whether he was the first person to come to mind. Westermann didn't figure Stanic for the murder; didn't think he was playing it the way a murderer would.

"No ideas?"

"Could be anyone," she said, her voice barely audible.

"But no one in particular?"

She shook her head. "She didn't know anybody. Not really."

Westermann moved closer to her, bending a little to make sure they were in eye contact. "Do you know anybody?"

She frowned.

"What kind of fucking question is that?" Stanic asked from the bed.

"Shut the fuck up," Grip barked at him.

"Belle, did Lenore have any possessions? Any things?"

Belle pulled out a drawer from a battered bureau, removed a pile of papers and a book, and handed them to Westermann. Grip came over, standing next to Westermann at an angle where he could also see Stanic. Westermann worked his way down the stack, handing items to Grip: Holy Bible; picture of the Virgin Mary torn from a magazine; handwritten letters in Cyrillic; and, at the bottom, three pamphlets from the Church of Last Days.

Grip whistled. "What are the odds?"

"Long."

"I guess I know where I'm headed tomorrow."

"Let me think on that. Maybe I'll take that one myself." Westermann turned to Belle. "Anyone else you know missing? Someone you haven't seen around?"

Belle looked confused.

Stanic said, "Whores are always missing. They come back after a few days with a john or a hop jaunt. They come back."

Grip said, "You didn't hear me last time? Shut it."

Stanic made an exasperated noise and Grip was on him, pulling him roughly to his feet by the back of his collar and pushing him hard against the wall. As he unlocked the cuffs, Grip said, "I am going to come by here every few days, asshole, and if I see that anything has happened to Belle here, I don't care if it's some john that done it or what, I am going to rip your fucking balls off and make you chew them up. Do you understand?"

Stanic gave a dismissive laugh. Grip cuffed him on the back of the head and his face hit the wall.

"Shit," he said. "Yes. I get it."

Westermann handed Belle his card, but was sure she would never contact him; too much to lose. Grip opened the door.

Stanic said, "Hey, I know how I know you. You're the guy, your dad's a lawyer. Big Rolf Westermann. What're you doing rousting pimps like me?"

Westermann put his hand in Grip's chest, keeping him from going after Stanic. "Let's get out of here. We're done."

The sidewalk still teemed. Grip could feel the tension in the atmosphere rising as people grew increasingly drunk. The police presence was more visible now; cops everywhere. Another consequence of the System—lots of cops in place before the trouble starts. Grip knew plenty of beat cops who hated Westermann—most cops felt the way Wayne did—but Grip fucking loved what the guy had done; it made for better policing. If guys were uncomfortable, fuck them. *Shut up and do your goddamn job.*

"So, what do you think?" Westermann asked. Another thing Grip loved about Westermann, always asking and listening; smart enough that he wasn't defensive about other people having their insights.

"About the church?"

"Yeah. Is there any way it could be a coincidence?"

"I don't think so. You're the numbers guy. But, Lieut, I think maybe you're making this more complicated than it needs to be."

"Tell me more."

"Well, like I said before, I noticed those currents by the riverbank and me and Morph tested it out to see how stuff floated downstream. And like I said, we found that unless someone carried that girl over to the riverbank to drown her right there, then she must have got pushed in the water over by the Uhuru Community. So now there's another girl turned up in basically that exact spot, so I feel like I was right on that. Two dead girls on the riverbank by the Uhuru Community. Okay, so that's one connection. The next connection is that this girl, Lenore, and the second girl, they've both got some kind of crazy disease, maybe African. Now I don't know if there's many Africans in the Community, but you can't tell me there aren't any. So that's connection number two."

"So, you're saying . . ."

"I'm not saying anything, but it seems like the place to focus our efforts is the Uhuru Community. This thing about the church of what?"

"Church of Last Days."

"Yeah. It's interesting; maybe not a coincidence. But against what we've got over at the Community, now that we have a second body? We need to check them both out, but the Community's where the action is. But it's your call, of course."

Westermann thought about this as they walked, balancing the protection of the Community against further arousing Grip's suspicions. He didn't see how he could dispute Grip's argument. "Okay. I'll think about it. Maybe you and Morphy head over to the Community tomorrow and work that angle. I'll follow up on the church connection. Like you said, we can't just leave that alone."

Ahead, the next block up, something was happening; a different distribution of bodies; a different pitch to the din. Westermann and Grip sped up to a trot; saw other cops converging ahead of them.

They pushed their way through a crowd to where there was some room. A space had been cleared by a fight. Two Negroes were facedown on the ground, cops kneeling on them, getting out the cuffs. Two other Negroes, one bleeding above an eye, hovered, breathing hard. Two cops were holding back a group of six white men. They were young, crew-cut. Two had blood on their shirts, another held his hand to his mouth, blood sluicing through his fingers.

A fire hydrant by the curb was cracked, leaking water in a thin spray. The standing water was lit red by the storefront neon and mixed with blood where the Negroes lay. Westermann heard Grip mumble under his breath.

"What's that?"

Grip nodded over to a group of men, two white men, one fat, one obese, and a powerfully built Negro between them. "See the Negro over there?"

"Sure."

"I think I saw him down in the shanties the other day."

"Okay."

"It's just interesting. He don't look like he's passing paper."

Westermann was thinking about this when he saw a white guy from the crowd rabbit-punch one of the Negroes still standing from the fight, putting him on his knees, bringing roars of approval and protest. More skirmishes broke out. Westermann turned to see the two white men and the Negro walking into a club called the Checkerboard.

Pieces of paper littered the street—Uhuru Community flyers and others. Grip picked one up, looked at it, handed it to Westermann. It was simple enough, the white paper red in the fake light. The same block print of Womé's face as on the Community flyers. Above the print, the word ANTI-CHRIST.

33.

Westermann lay in bed, a deluge of thoughts keeping him awake. They had a name now, Lenore, and a potential second front in the investigation, an alternative to the Uhuru Community. But his thoughts strayed to his problems. Why hadn't he told Frings about the second girl? It was a stupid play, childish, petulant, desperate. It was only a matter of time, maybe even just a few hours, before Frings found out anyway. What had he been thinking? Asserting some control over the situation? Spite? He wished he could have it back; make a different decision. But what was done was done.

He was puzzled by Art Deyna's reappearance. What the hell did it mean? Did Deyna have any idea what was going on? Had he seen enough to draw any conclusions? Couldn't Frings keep the *Gazette* off his back?

He worried about how the location of the second body confirmed Grip's theory about Lenore's original resting place. He wasn't surprised that Grip had figured it out. Westermann wondered where Grip would be now if he had grown up as wealthy as Westermann had, gone to good schools and then to university. But Grip had been raised by a grandmother in a hardscrabble block of Praeger's Hill, and he had done what the boys who hadn't already fallen into habitual criminality did, he joined the army, and when his time was up, he became a cop.

Westermann got out of bed, looked around his empty apartment, wiped the sleep from his eyes.

In the shower, trying to slow his thoughts, he flashed back a decade, when the City had practically vibrated with possibility. After the assassination of Mayor Henry and the end of his successor's term, the people of the City had found the good judgment to elect an aging millionaire named McCree. In hindsight, the golden age that McCree seemed to auger never quite came to pass. His reforms—changing the City government to a council with a figurehead mayor, modernizing the police force—had since slowly eroded under the relentless stream of government corruption.

Six councilors proved no less corrupt than one mayor. The police chief's progressive notions had been crushed by the sheer volume of crime in the City. The System was one of the few remnants of this brief period of reform, and Westermann had come to defend it with grim resolve rather than the pride of success he felt it deserved.

Westermann had been pitched by the mayor and the Chief, personally, in the mayor's office. Westermann was what the new City was all about: innovating, taking advantage of the most original thinking. He would be a big part of the City's renaissance.

How could he refuse the chance to see his theory, created in the halls of the Tech, tested in the real world? But he hadn't wanted to sit at a desk studying stats, putting pins in maps. That was something that people hadn't seen at first, his wanting to be a part of the action. The brass fast-tracked his training. He'd learned the craft during the day, and at night he'd worked with statisticians and cop brass to figure out how the System would work. They needed a couple years of stats to create a plan, so they'd started compiling.

Kraatjes had struggled to pull together a small squad of detectives who were willing to work for Westermann. Some refused the assignment. Others undermined the work or quietly boycotted, putting in empty hours. Eventually Westermann and Kraatjes sifted these people out, and the men that remained were willing to work with Westermann. Some did this because their pensions were coming up and they didn't want to make waves; some because they really believed the innovation that the System represented. Morphy was willing because he didn't give a shit about much and found a certain pleasure in being associated with the least popular man on the force. Grip liked working for one of the rare cops who he considered at least as smart as himself. And Grip was very smart, which was why Westermann lay awake, staring at the topography of his ceiling, worried that his deception would be undone by one of his own men.

34.

"Have you been to Godtown?" Westermann asked Plouffe from the passenger seat. They had the windows down, the heat this morning again suffocating.

"No, sir." Plouffe was nearing his pension. Westermann knew that Plouffe was getting a little extra in his monthly checks for working Westermann's squad. Plouffe wasn't a great cop, but he didn't dislike Westermann, which was something.

"You been down here?" Plouffe asked.

Westermann shook his head, watching out the window as people made their way on yet another blistering day, wondering when the heat would finally break.

Godtown, as it turned out, was rather hard to miss, two square blocks of reclaimed row houses on the eastern edge of the Hollows, the houses painted in bright colors: purples, yellows, oranges, blues. Beyond them, the blocks of abandoned buildings that made up the Hollows

"What's this?" Plouffe said, pulling to the curb. No one was about, the sidewalks empty and clean, planters bookending many stoops. By any standard it was a cheerful-looking place. But the deserted streets were strange, like a movie set.

"Let's find the church," Westermann said, as Plouffe drove on slowly, eyeing the row houses, expecting one of them to be the church. In the next block, though, they saw a steeple a block west, rising above the low houses. It was clear why Prosper Maddox had chosen this area to bring his people: this fine old stone church apparently abandoned until his flock had acquired it and fixed it back up. A man in a suit was at the near corner of the church, scrubbing stones with a sponge and soapy water where someone had painted graffiti on the wall. He didn't look up as the prowl car passed.

Westermann told Plouffe to stay with the car and took the steps up to the heavy wooden double doors. He paused for a moment, not sure if he should knock. He decided to just go in, but found the door locked.

He banged on the door and waited. It took a minute, but he eventually heard the scrape of footsteps, and the door opened a crack. Westermann tilted his head to look in. The man at the door was young and big, his blond hair shaved military-style.

"Can I help you?"

Westermann looked past the man into a dim vestibule and a set of closed wooden doors on the far wall. He showed his badge. "I'm looking for Prosper Maddox."

"Can I ask what for?"

"Just some questions."

"Pertaining to?"

Westermann noticed a scar tugging at the man's upper lip when he spoke. "Is Mr. Maddox here?"

"Dr. Maddox."

"Okay."

"Hold on." The man shut the door. Westermann heard the lock slide. He waited.

The door opened again and this time a man came out—medium height, slender, tan suit, blue eyes, very clean.

"Prosper Maddox," he said, offering his hand. "How can I be of service?"

Westermann shook hands and introduced himself. Maddox had a round, childish face, and his grip was dry and weak. His hair was carefully parted and stiff.

"Dr. Maddox, is there somewhere we could sit down?"

Maddox gave a regretful smile. "Unfortunately, we are presently having a Bible study and I am reluctant to interrupt it. Is there a problem, Lieutenant Westermann? I'm sure we can talk out here." Maddox noticed the cruiser and ducked a little to get a better angle from the steps to see in.

"That's my colleague, Detective Plouffe," Westermann said, getting Maddox's attention back. "I guess we can talk here. I don't know if you read about it in the newspaper, but a couple of days ago we found the body of a young woman washed up on the riverbank. We've found out that her name is Lenore; we don't have a last name. Dark hair, attractive, very thin. Seemed like she might have been sick; had these sores on her body." If Maddox recognized the name, he hid it well. "We took a look at her place and found some church materials from here, so we thought maybe you could help us with an ID."

"Lenore?" Maddox said, looking up at the sky as if seeking divine assistance with his memory. "I don't recall a Lenore at our church, Lieutenant. Of course, it is possible that one of our people might have passed on these materials, helping to spread the Word."

Westermann nodded. "That's possible. You know, it might be a coincidence, but we found materials from your church in another place; this time the apartment of a woman who's turned up missing. Her name was Mavis Talley. That ring a bell with you, Dr. Maddox?"

Maddox smiled sadly and shook his head. "I'm certain I would remember a name like Mavis Talley, Lieutenant, but I'm quite sure that I haven't heard it before. And you say she had materials from this church? The Church of Last Days?"

Westermann nodded, angry at Maddox's casual dismissal of his questions. "So you would say it is a coincidence that these two women, one missing and one dead, had programs from your church?"

"I'm not saying that at all, Lieutenant. I'm simply saying that I do not know who they are. It is entirely possible that someone in the congregation knows both of them and gave them both materials."

"Well, then, we'll probably want to talk to your congregation."

"I could save you some time by making an announcement, asking anyone who knows either one of these unfortunate women to come forward. I could even start now with the Bible-study group."

"I appreciate the offer, but I think we're better off doing the questioning ourselves. I'll send some detectives over, get a list of congregants from you, with addresses."

For the first time, Maddox seemed bothered. "Lieutenant, you understand, of course, that you are asking for confidential information. This puts us in a very awkward position. Would your detectives be bringing a warrant?"

"We can arrange that."

"I think it would be better if you did. For both of us. You understand, of course."

"Mr. Maddox, I have a dead girl and a missing girl who seemed to know your church. Two nights ago we found a second dead girl that we believe might be connected to the other two. Do you understand the urgency?"

Maddox frowned. "Of course. If you bring a warrant, we will do our utmost to assist."

Westermann hid his frustration, bowing his head a little in mock supplication.

Maddox clasped his hands in an act meant to bring the conversation to a close. "Lieutenant, I look forward to speaking with you again. May the Lord walk with you."

35.

Winston sat with a group of elderly men in an area of shade carved into the square by the low shanties, hiding the morning sun. He was working on a guitar that lay in his lap, its tuning post loose, unable to keep the tension in the string. He could have been doing this in Billy Lambert's shack, but he liked listening to the old men talk, their funny patois, their conversations reminding him a little bit of home.

One of the old men—a talker with a patch over his left eye—was going on about cops walking the shantytown alleys, asking about a white girl found dead on the riverbank. The other men murmured their agreement. Winston kept on with his work, but he felt the heat in his arms and face.

One of the geezers, wearing a formless straw hat, said, "I hear they found another girl, night before last. This one was on the river where those boys fish. Right by the Community."

Winston was confused by this, but kept his head down, adjusting the tuning posts and tweaking strings.

The man with the patch said, "I've heard no such thing."

"I heard it from old Letourneau, who heard it from his boy what saw the police down on them rocks. Said he saw them pull away a body; a white girl, same as before."

Winston realized that he was squeezing the tuning post hard, grinding it into the wood of the guitar neck. He eased off.

The man with the patch adjusted in his seat. "Like I said, I've heard nothing to that effect."

The tuning post fixed, Winston played quietly, testing to see how his repair work would stand up to actual use. He was half-listening to the geezers, hoping and fearing that the girls would come up again. His real concentration was on the pitch of the guitar strings until he heard the old-timer with the patch say something about *the young man* and realized that he had now been brought into the conversation.

"Ask the young man. I've seen him playing that drum at the ceremonies." The man with the patch banged a few times on an imaginary drum, his head cocked back. "He's been there. Ask him."

He was talking to a cat who was a little younger than the rest; skinny, very dark skin, with an accent Winston couldn't place. Not Caribbean. African, Winston thought. Winston knew the man's name was Glélé, but he'd also heard him called Samedi. He seemed to carry some weight in the Community, though Winston didn't know why. He seemed to command the same respect that Winston sometimes received when he was onstage—a fierce, highly emotional adulation. But Glélé did not have to perform to earn it. His mere presence seemed enough. Winston had never spoken to him, but respected and feared him in the way that a stranger always fears men with power.

Glélé's eyes were hidden by dark glasses, but he turned his head toward Winston. "You a religious man?"

Winston stopped playing. "I suppose."

"I suppose not."

Winston raised his eyebrows.

Glélé's voice was direct, making statements, not expressing opinions. "Religious men don't suppose."

Winston nodded, keeping his eyes low, not wanting to look the man in the eyes.

"You don't fall for the white man's religion, no? You don't pray to no white God, keeps you in your hole."

Winston nodded. He felt his breathing go shallow. Glélé was right, though Winston hadn't thought of it quite that way, that the church in his home had promised him a better life in the hereafter; that it kept people from seeking to improve their earthly lives.

The old-timer with the patch was grinning broadly now, apparently enjoying this interaction.

Glélé said, "Young man, you've been at the ceremonies, you've seen the African gods made flesh."

Winston looked up at Glélé despite himself.

"You know. You've seen me mounted by Samedi. You've seen others: Legba, Senjak. Tell me you've not."

Winston kept looking at Glélé. He wasn't sure that he'd seen it, but he wasn't sure that he hadn't. He had no experience to compare to what he'd seen in the Square.

"What has the white God brought you? Huh? You see those young men in these here shanties, Samedi's boys?"

"Your boys?"

Glélé spit theatrically into the dirt; the old men laughed.

"Do I look like Samedi to you? Do you think I'm mounted?"

Winston shook his head because he knew that was the correct response, though he didn't know why.

"Samedi is an African god. He's the Africans' past and the Africans' future."

Winston went back to picking at the guitar strings, playing a faint tune.

"Think on Samedi, young man. Dream on him. Talk to his boys. Samedi brought me to this place from Africa. Samedi brought this Community here—to the City. There is a purpose. I have a purpose. The Community has a purpose. You can be a part."

Glélé turned his attention from Winston, and after a brief silence, the geezers started in again with their gossiping. One of the men pulled out a pipe and lit it, the smell of mesca suddenly filling their little space as the pipe made its way around the circle.

36.

Grip wore a straw fedora to keep the sun off his face as he and a hatless Morphy navigated the narrow passageways of the Uhuru Community. Grip was exhausted and sweating whiskey he'd downed just a few hours ago at Crippen's, winding down from bracing Joey Stanic. Morphy seemed fresh, but his hair was damp with sweat.

Negro kids had been playing outside the shantytown entrance when they'd arrived. Young boys and girls engaged in some kind of tackling game with a ball made from a stuffed sack. The same two girls Grip had seen before stood in canary-yellow dresses with their cow, watching from a distance. The cow, Grip noticed, seemed to be putting on weight, though it was still thin through the back and shoulders. Grip waved to the two girls, but they didn't wave back.

Grip and Morphy made their way to the shacks closest to the river, feeling their way along by a kind of dead reckoning. Kids ran past them, laughing, and women with bright scarves on their heads made way for them, keeping their eyes down. Morphy smiled and excuse-me'd and Grip, for once, let him do the talking. Grip eyed the symbols painted on the doors and walls: weird crosses, elaborate designs with triangles, ovals, stars, weird arcing lines, and, on some, tiny phalluses.

"You see these drawings?"

Morphy nodded.

"What do you think?"

"Weird island shit, I guess. Who knows?"

"Not much like that thing painted on the door back at Crippen's."

"Not much like that, what we've seen so far."

"So far," Grip echoed.

Grip was feeling sick from the combination of the heat and the alcohol still in his bloodstream. His hand rested on his gun as they moved along. He didn't consider himself a racist. In fact, he reserved a special disgust for racists. But he had an idea of what America looked like and this wasn't it.

He and Morphy were in plainclothes, but no one in the shanties mistook two crackers in suits for anything other than cops. They hadn't run into any other white people and they attracted a lot of attention as they moved through the alleys. Older kids—teens—sometimes hurled taunts at them, playing courage games. Morphy and Grip ignored them, though Grip could see from Morphy's tensed shoulders that he was becoming irritated.

"Let's just get to the river side of the shanties," Grip said, trying to keep Morphy's mind on the objective.

Morphy grunted. They walked on.

They came to an intersection and saw, to their right, a group of five men, younger than Grip, standing in an alley, drinking from mason jars filled with some kind of cloudy liquid. The men caught sight of Morphy and Grip and their conversation stopped, all attention on the two cops.

"Let's go, Morph. We aren't going to accomplish anything here."

Morphy stared back at the group.

"Come on." Grip grabbed Morphy's arm and pulled him down the alley away from the men. As they passed out of sight, Grip could hear the men's laughter. He looked nervously at Morphy, whose face was impassive.

They walked to the next intersection and Morphy paused, surveying the paths of the alleys. "Wait here."

"Come on, Morph, let's not get sidetracked."

But Morphy was already headed down a perpendicular alley, intending, Grip had no doubt, to come up on the group of men from behind. Grip found a spot in the shade. He leaned back against a tin wall but it began to buckle under his weight and he stood straight.

Grip waited, expecting to hear yelling or a scuffle or some other Morphy-initiated mayhem. Instead, Morphy appeared back in the alley he had walked down. He looked pissed off, but that wasn't unusual.

"What the hell?" Grip walked over to meet him. "I didn't hear anything."

Morphy frowned. "I didn't do anything."

"You go soft all of a sudden?"

"I was going to start a little fire in one of their shacks."

"Morph," Grip said, alarmed.

"You set one of those things on fire, the whole place is liable to burn down. So I didn't."

"But you know you could have. If you'd decided to."

"Yep."

"Maybe you're not going to rot in hell."

Morphy shrugged. "Let's go."

They happened upon the Square by accident, suddenly walking out into it, surprised at the expanse after the cramped alleys. A half dozen men, mostly old, sat in chairs arranged in a rough circle, passing a pipe. A younger guy sat with them, plucking quietly on a guitar with his fingers and playing a slide over the frets. Grip thought he recognized the guitar player from the street fight the previous night. He filed it away, unsure of its significance.

The smell of marijuana wafted slowly toward Grip and Morphy in the stagnant air. Grip snorted. Morphy elbowed him and pointed to a dark patch, maybe two feet in diameter, in the middle of the square.

"What's that?"

They approached the spot and the old men stopped passing the pipe to watch in silence. Morphy flashed them a broad smile and got down on a knee while Grip watched. Morphy stirred the discolored dirt a little with his finger, pulled it up stained with rust-colored residue.

Grip narrowed his eyes. "Blood?"

Morphy frowned. "Could be." He turned to the group of men. "Excuse me. Any of you gentlemen know what made this stain here?"

The men looked at each other, communicating something with their red-rimmed eyes. An old-timer with a patch over one eye spoke. "That's blood right there."

"Blood?"

"That's right. From the meeting last night. Blood."

Grip and Morphy exchanged a look. Morphy asked, "Whose blood?"

"Got no name, so far's I know."

"No name?"

"I don't know how you do, but the people down here don't often name our roosters." The man with the patch kept a straight face but the other men broke up in laughter. Morphy, too, laughed.

"Jesus Christ," Grip said, shaking his head.

They stood and strode over to the circle of men. One of them was making a cock-a-doodle-doo sound, to everyone's amusement.

Grip spoke. "You gentleman hear about the girl's body they found two days ago down at the riverbank?"

The men quieted down, exchanging glances, noncommittal. The pipe made the rounds again.

"You see a white girl around here two days ago?"

There was a collective shaking of heads, the men avoiding eye contact. The guitar player seemed to be ignoring them, focusing on the guitar and, when it came around to him, the pipe.

"How about a week or so ago—another white girl?"

The geezer with the patch seemed to be their spokesman. "No, sir. Just like we told those boys come round the other day. No white woman been through here for months, save Mrs. Bierhoff, and since we seen her yesterday, I'm pretty sure it wasn't her body they found on them rocks."

Morphy asked, "Who's Mrs. Bierhoff?"

"She's a girl, works with us. Helps out in the Community."

Grip shook his head. "Carla Bierhoff?"

"That's right."

Grip turned to Morphy. "She's Red."

Morphy nodded, not thinking this was as important as Grip did. "So you all don't know anything about this girl who they found on the riverbank?"

The man with the patch shook his head. "I was you, I'd ask those men go fishing down at the riverbank. Anyone know about it, it'd be them."

"Where're they?" Grip asked.

The man with the patch recoiled as if it were the dumbest-ass question he'd ever heard. "Riverbank. Where else?"

They didn't follow the same path out, getting off track almost instantly in the seemingly identical alleyways. Grip noticed different kinds of graffiti on the doors of some places, more representational, like the skull and hat, but not that exact design; elongated brown faces with eerie, liquid eyes; crimson hearts that seemed to vibrate where they were painted against the wood; bearded men with three-horned hair and halos. The torrid air seemed to impede him, the tin reflecting the sunlight into the alleys, washing out the colors. The scents of marijuana smoke, sweat, and spices inundated him as they walked. He was getting shaky, not sure how to get out of the maze, bile rising into his mouth, the acid taste of whiskey coming up from his stomach.

"You know where we're going?" Grip asked, his voice pitched high as it came out, sounding to him as if someone else were speaking—someone far off.

"Hmm?" Morphy asked.

"You know how we're going to get out?"

"Yeah." Morphy sounded distracted.

Grip's heart pounded. Kids ran past laughing, voices echoing off the close walls; women watched silently with suspicious eyes from inside their shacks. Morphy made turns seemingly at random, Grip following close behind, fearful of getting separated; the two of them silent. Morphy seemed to be walking faster. Grip had to take a skip every third step to keep up. His vision tunneled.

The exit came upon them out of nowhere, a rectangle of green and brown and the distant skyline. Grip followed Morphy into the open, sweat pouring down his face and soaking his shirt.

"Jesus." He looked at Morphy, who was smiling, but not very convincingly.

37.

"You been in the shanties, Lieut?" Grip turned his head slightly, keeping an eye on the road while speaking to Westermann, who sat in the backseat of the prowl car.

"No."

"It's different in there."

"Grip didn't like it so much," Morphy said.

"I have no problem admitting it."

"Can you explain?" Westermann asked. Grip didn't have a problem with Negroes, so far as Westermann knew, and was never reluctant to get in the face of anyone he thought had some Red in them.

"I don't know."

Morphy said, "It's these narrow, little alleys that get confusing, and the symbols and pictures they've painted on their doors and walls. Nerve-racking. And hot as hell."

Grip nodded. "That's not the only thing, though. Something weird."

"A lot of reefer being smoked," Morphy suggested.

"Maybe," Grip said.

"Any luck?" Westermann asked.

Grip shrugged. "Not really. We talked to some older ginks in the shanties and they sent us to these guys that fish down by the riverbank. Said if anyone'd seen a body on the rocks, it would have been them. Went down and found about a half dozen and talked to them one by one. They didn't have much. One guy said he saw someone down by the rocks the night that the second girl was killed—said he was drinking at the time—but that the guy was too far off to give any kind of description."

Westermann felt the tension ease in his shoulders, but kept on with the questions. "Nothing? White? Negro? With a girl?"

"I gave you the whole thing, Lieut. Someone on the rocks—too dark to see anything else."

Westermann saw Morphy nodding along to Grip's account. "So, nothing useful."

"No," Grip agreed. "But that feeling about the shanties, something about it . . ."

"Okay," Westermann said, trusting Grip's instincts, wondering what he was picking up on and if it had anything to do with Lenore. "Pull over here."

Morphy pulled to the curb on the edge of Godtown, behind two other prowl cars.

Westermann had sent Plouffe off to work on getting a warrant to bring back to Prosper Maddox's church. In the meantime, Westermann wanted to let Maddox know that he wasn't going to be backed down, so he'd returned with his men to canvass the neighborhood. Grip and Morphy moved down a block and Portillo and Breda worked the houses across the street. Westermann was with Dzeko, who normally paired with Plouffe. Dzeko was tall and lean with narrow shoulders; a gray mustache under a beaked nose. He was a somber guy, Westermann thought, or maybe just dull.

They banged on two doors without reply and then on a third—a purple row house with a periwinkle door. They waited, not expecting anything, but the door jerked suddenly open, then closed, then opened again. Westermann saw the broad, red face of a woman through the crack in the door. Her eyes showed panic.

"What do you want from me?" Her voice was tremulous, pitched high.

"Ma'am," Westermann said softly, "my name is Lieutenant Westermann with the City police."

The door closed and then opened again. The door shook as she held it open with unsteady hands. From inside came the smell of boiling potatoes.

"Ma'am?"

"What do you want from me?" Her voice approached hysteria.

"Ma'am, what's your name?"

"Mary Little. What do you want from me?"

"I'm with the—"

"In the name of Jesus—" Something over his shoulder seemed to catch her attention and she went suddenly silent. He kept his eyes on her, trying to get a read from what he could see of her through the crack in the door.

"Lieut?" Dzeko said.

Westermann turned toward the street to see Breda and Portillo, holding his cigar at his side, facing a big man with a blond military cut and Prosper Maddox. The door closed again. Westermann and Dzeko crossed the street toward Prosper Maddox. Two other men were converging, too, hats low, one carrying a bulky square bag.

Shit.

"Mr. Maddox," Westermann said, extending his hand.

"Dr. Maddox," Maddox corrected, shaking Westermann's hand with a fixed smile but hostile eyes.

"I see you've met Detectives Portillo and Breda. This is Detective Dzeko." Westermann looked past Maddox's shoulder; Deyna and his cameraman, ten yards off. The cameraman was unpacking his camera.

Maddox ignored Westermann's pleasantries, but kept his smile in place. He seemed unaware of Deyna's presence. "Lieutenant Westermann, my understanding is that you were going to return with a warrant. Your detectives indicated to me that you do not, in fact, have a warrant."

"We're canvassing the neighborhood, Mr. Maddox. It's fairly routine in these types of cases. No one has been compelled to talk to us, we're merely asking questions."

"I'm afraid I'm going to have to ask you to desist."

Westermann looked at the big blond man, thinking it was probably he who had initially opened the church door on Westermann's first trip to Godtown. "Who's this?"

Maddox's smile was nearly gone. "Do not ignore me, Lieutenant."

Westermann darted a look at Deyna, who met his eyes. Back to Maddox, keeping his voice down. "I'm not ignoring you. I hear your every word. I want to know who this is." He pointed hard at the big man. "Who's this?"

Something about the big man had Breda and Portillo on edge; maybe his stance, as if he were waiting for something to happen. In the periphery of his vision, Westermann saw the two detectives, hands hovering by their holstered pistols. Their attention switched from Maddox to Deyna. Back and forth. Back and forth. Their nervousness made him nervous.

Maddox said, "Ole Koss. He's with the church. Now Lieutenant Westermann, I insist that you stop questioning my people."

"Your people?"

"Yes. Everyone in this neighborhood is in the congregation."

"And because of that, you speak for them all."

"Yes, as a matter of fact. Many of these people are country folk, Lieutenant. They, quite honestly, do not have the guile that comes from a lifetime in the City. They will not weigh their words."

"What's to weigh, Mr. Maddox? Our questions are very straightforward. Do they know Mavis Talley or a woman named Lenore? No guile required. Are you afraid of something?"

Deyna's partner was snapping photos. Maddox saw Westermann's distraction and turned to see the two *Gazette* men for the first time. He turned back to Westermann.

"Newspaper," Westermann said.

Maddox's eyes widened. "First it is the police and now the newspapers? This is your doing, this intrusion of the world—*your* world of vice and sin— into our little congregation. You and your detectives have brought the world that we have worked so hard to protect these holy children from."

Behind Maddox, Westermann could see a prowl car heading their way. Maddox and Deyna both turned to see the car.

Westermann said, "It was nice talking to you, Mr. Maddox. We'll be back to the church with a warrant. Right now, we have some more doors to knock on."

Maddox smiled. "You may want to wait a minute."

Westermann watched as the car entered their block and pulled up to them. The driver rolled down his window.

"Lieutenant Westermann?"

Westermann stepped to the car and leaned over, one hand on the roof, aware of Deyna and Maddox watching, photos being taken.

The driver said, "Y'all've been called back to Headquarters."

"What's that?"

"You're to stop the canvass and come back to Headquarters. Orders are to do it right now."

"Orders from who?"

"The Chief."

"You sure?"

The driver nodded.

Westermann heard Maddox's voice from behind him. "Lieutenant, I believe it's time for you to go."

Westermann turned to him, teeth clenched, furious. Maddox's smile was back in place, Koss smirking next to him.

"We'll be back," Westermann said.

Maddox's gaze shifted over Westermann's shoulder, his eyes unfocused. "I'm sure you will, Lieutenant. I'm sure you will."

Climbing into the back of Grip and Morphy's prowl car, Westermann saw Deyna, notebook open, speaking with Maddox.

38.

Frings still found it jarring to drive into the Hollows and find a place like this: blocks and blocks of abandoned buildings, slowly crumbling in on themselves. Some not so slowly. Past these blocks, a huge fallow field—maybe a dozen acres—and scattered about, like motionless livestock, rusting railway cars. The rails themselves, long out of use, lay half-hidden in the weeds. Frings met Warren Eddings, Mel Washington's right-hand man, at the edge of the field. Eddings wore a dark suit and bow tie, sweat beading below his skullcap. Behind him, waves of yellow humidity rose from the tall weeds.

They walked into the field, through the loose maze of train cars. Some, Frings noticed, seemed to serve as homes of a sort, clothes hanging off roofs, makeshift furniture visible through the sliding gates.

"Mel couldn't make it." Eddings left it at that.

"That's okay," Frings said. "Why did he . . . why did you want me out here?"

Eddings laughed a little, but his face stayed tight. He didn't look at Frings.

"Mel's concerned that you might not understand about the Community. You know, Mel feels like you think he's got the Community wired. Like Father Womé just attracts all these people and then Mel takes over; that Womé's okay with that arrangement somehow. It's not like that, bo. And Mel wants you to see that. You know, we do what we can with the Community and we're proud of what we've done, but if you think it's about us—about Reds—you don't have the picture."

"Okay," Frings said, wondering what was out here that would give him the picture. His collar was soaked. His shirt was pasted with sweat to his chest. He took off his straw fedora to get some air on his head and wiped his face with his sleeve. He watched a thick black snake push its way through the weeds to their right.

Eddings continued, "So, Mel wanted to make that clear to you. Father Womé isn't just some cat with a hoard of money and a shantytown full of people he supports. He's more than that. He's got his ideas that we have to work around. That and the Square."

Frings gave him a questioning look but Eddings's eyes were straight ahead.

"Okay, you've got my attention. What are we here to look at?"

"You'll see."

They walked around a line of boxcars, each identically labeled TRANS-CON in a feminine cursive, each rusting through. On the other side, looking as out of place as diamonds in the mud, were four passenger cars, gleaming an immaculate black in the sun. A thin horizontal stripe of gold ran under the scarlet-curtained windows. Above the windows in the center of each car BLACK COMET LINE was written in golden block capitals. Negroes were at work on these cars, crouching on the roofs, working on the undercarriages, entering and exiting through narrow doors, maybe three dozen in all.

"Wow," Frings said, using his hand to shield his eyes from the sun. "What is this?"

Eddings nodded a greeting to a group of workers who were drinking water from a ladle they pulled from a wooden trough.

"Nice to see you, Mr. Eddings," one of the men said, casting a curious look at Frings, who hung back a little, still taking in these elegant railcars marooned in this field.

Eddings shook hands with a few of the men, not bothering to introduce Frings.

"Come on." Eddings led Frings to one of the cars, grabbed the handrail, climbed up. Inside, a narrow corridor was lined with doors on either side spaced at short intervals—a sleeper car.

"I hear you've talked to Womé, so maybe you know a little about where he's coming from; how Negroes need to have our own, separate institutions if we're going to have any measure of justice or equality. It's an interesting thought and I'm not sure I disagree. That's what the Community is all about, as I guess you know."

Eddings pushed open a door to a sleeping compartment. It was almost comically luxurious: upholstered seats, wall sconces with maroon shades, maroon curtains on the windows, a narrow Oriental rug on the floor.

"Amazing," Frings said. "But I'm not sure I get it."

"Like I was saying about Womé, he thinks we need our own institutions to be equal, and one of the things he thinks is important is that Negroes be able to travel like the wealthy white folks. So he decided to create the Black Comet Line so that Negroes can travel in luxury."

"Wait. Are there that many Negroes who can afford to travel like this?"

"More than you'd think. But that's not the point. The tickets will be cheap. He'll see to it."

They stepped back out into the corridor.

Frings said, "So, Womé thinks he's going to further Negro equality by subsidizing luxury train rides on his special rail line? Really?"

"Crazy, right? You think that me and Mel and Betty, we're worried about people sitting in luxury sleeper cars? It's beyond crazy. But that's Womé. He's got his ideas and he's got the money to make it work. You ask him, 'How're you going to move these cars around? You going to buy an engine? You going to hitch it up to someone else's engine, get connected to all those ofay cars?' You ask Womé that and he just smiles and says that it'll all work out; you know, trust in Father Womé. Crazy. But, you see, this is what the Community is about. It's about Negroes finding their own, separate place; and it's also about the Square. What we're trying to do—creating a just and principled community—it's way down the list."

They walked back across the broad field toward Frings's car. Frings felt de-hydrated, dizzy. The ambient noise of crickets in the weeds seemed oppres-sive. Had the noise been there when they arrived, or had some cricket instinct kicked in, causing them to create this din? Frings noticed rats, too, scattering as he and Eddings made their way through the weeds.

Frings asked, "You been thinking about the girl?"

Eddings nodded.

"Come up with anything new?"

"Nothing new. It's not Community people."

"You sure about that?"

Frings hadn't meant it as a challenge, but Eddings stopped and faced him. "It's not Community people." Eddings shook his head. "Something as big as this . . . Look, most of the violence in the shanties is because someone messed with someone else's wife or kids being kids. *That* kind of secret don't last long at all. You think someone murders a white girl and nobody knows anything?"

"Closing ranks?"

Eddings shook his head in disgust. "You've been down in the shanties, you know what they're like. There's no locking doors. You think folks down there want some killer walking around, could just walk in any door at night? You think they aren't the most anxious people out there to catch this guy if he's Community?"

Frings conceded the point. Of course, this wasn't actually proof of anything, merely a good argument and based on a premise—there are no secrets in the Community—that sounded dubious. But, all the same, Frings thought—or maybe it was hoped—that Eddings was right.

Eddings said, "You know if Westermann's making any progress?"

Frings shook his head. "You know, you'd have to ask him. He's keeping me caught up, but who knows if he gives me everything."

The car was a hundred yards or so ahead, the waves of heat making it look as if it were beneath the surface of water slightly disturbed by the impact of a stone. It was kind of an interesting effect, Frings thought.

"How do *you* feel about all this?" Eddings asked Frings.

"What? The girl? Pushing the body back in the river?"

"Yeah. That, and now with the second girl—"

Frings stopped. "Second girl?"

39.

Westermann stalked through Headquarters, Grip and Morphy in his wake. Uniforms cleared out of the way and whispered among themselves after the three had passed. Sweat dripped from the tips of Westermann's hair onto his collar.

Grip said, "Go easy, Lieut. You need to calm down before you go in there."

Westermann ignored him. Grip looked in frustration at Morphy, who smiled back in amusement. Morphy loved this kind of thing: conflict in the upper echelons.

They approached the Chief's office, guarded by his secretary, an elderly former cop named Merchant. Merchant seemed prepared for Westermann's arrival, standing before they arrived. Smiling.

"The Chief says to go right in."

"Lieut," Grip said, somewhat desperately, giving it one last shot.

Westermann again ignored him and opened the Chief's door.

The Chief was standing at his desk, smiling warmly. "Piet, I'm glad you came straight here." Though he was still fairly young—early forties, Westermann guessed—the Chief had been on the job for almost eight years now. He was fit and handsome and wore an unfashionable walrus mustache that gave him the aura of some kind of viceroy. Westermann considered him to be smart and a freethinker, not beholden to traditional procedures the way some past chiefs had been. But, like any chief, he wasn't impervious to the realities of political pressure.

"Chief, I—"

The Chief held up a hand. "Before you say anything more, have a seat. Let me explain some things. Then you can say your piece."

Westermann nodded and took a seat, as did the Chief. The office was small and bare, save for a massive desk, and on it, files placed in well-ordered stacks of varying heights. His windows were open, street noise filtering into the office along with air that was, if hot, at least fresh. Kraatjes stood by one of the windows, blending into the background as he often did, a cigarette hanging from his lip.

The Chief said, "So a little less than an hour ago I get a call from the mayor, saying that a group of my detectives is poking around Godtown, harassing the people there."

"Chief—"

The Chief held up his hand again, turning his cheek, not wanting to hear anything yet. "You know who runs Godtown? Prosper Maddox and his church. You probably *do* know that; that's probably the reason you were down there, would be my guess. But I wonder if you know much about Prosper Maddox. For instance, do you know that he's tight with Vic Truffant? Truffant goes to Prosper Maddox for *spiritual guidance.*" The Chief gave the last two words a sarcastic edge, as if he knew it was bullshit. "And because he has Truffant's ear, the mayor keeps a special eye on him, doesn't want to give Truffant some kind of edge, you know? For the election. So the mayor gets a call that some detectives are poking around in Godtown and Prosper Maddox isn't happy about it, and he calls me to say that I need to get you the hell out of there. So I do. Follow?"

"Yes, but—"

The Chief talked over him. "But while I'm waiting for you to come back here with your nose all out of joint, I call in Detective Plouffe, who you had over at the courthouse trying to get a warrant signed. I bring him in here, ask what the hell you're doing down in Godtown. You, of all people, know that there isn't any fucking crime in Godtown. But Plouffe fills me in about the bodies by the river and the connection to Maddox's church and Maddox stonewalling you. So, I think I have a fair understanding of what is going on here. Would you agree?"

Westermann nodded.

"So, I have the mayor pressuring me to keep my people out of Godtown, and I have you conducting an investigation into one, maybe two, murdered prostitutes—you don't even have a name for the second—with a tenuous Godtown connection. So what am I going to do?"

Westermann sighed in frustration.

"Piet," the Chief said, the irritation plain in his voice. "Are you going to let me finish?" Satisfied that Westermann would wait, he continued, "Is the mayor my boss? No. Is the City Council my boss? No. That was part of the reforms, so that the police wouldn't be subject to political pressure like this. So when the mayor calls me and asks me, *as a favor,* to pull a squad of detectives out of a neighborhood that never sees any crime, I say sure. Look, the mayor is in a tough election and he can't be seen going soft on the Reds because Councilor Truffant will kill him—*kill him*—with that issue. So, I get where he's coming from. But if my people are conducting a proper investigation, I don't care if they upset the mayor's goddamn grandmother, I will not hamper the conduct of a legitimate investigation. Not for the goddamn Virgin Mary herself. Right?"

The Chief paused, looking at Westermann. Westermann met his eye and nodded.

Pushing Lenore into the moonlit current.

"But, Piet, you need to handle this carefully. Just because the mayor and Truffant don't have any authority over the department doesn't mean that their interests can just be ignored. They can cause plenty of mischief, and that needs to be part of any calculations that *you* make going forward on this case. They have, in fact, already made mischief. Piet, they can vote down our budget for chrissake. I don't mind holding my ground, but not everyone is going to take risks for a couple of dead whores. I'm not saying it's right, but that's the way it is.

"By the way, Plouffe struck out with the judge. Asplundh's not going to sign a warrant, cross the mayor—or the next mayor—for this kind of case. So you can kiss that avenue good-bye."

Westermann rubbed the sides of his face with his hands.

"Are you following me, Piet?"

"I think so."

"We won't be chased off this investigation, but we need to tread carefully. I know you can do that and I need you to get your men on the same page. That means Grip and Morphy, too. There's talk around the building that they paid a visit to Mel Washington. You know about that?"

"I talked to them."

"That's the old force, Piet. We don't do things that way anymore. Doesn't matter who they're visiting. Even if they're Reds. Even if they're pains in the ass like Prosper Maddox. *Especially* Prosper Maddox. Don't put me in a bad position."

Deyna's cameraman shooting him with Mel Washington.

"I get the picture."

"Good. So, tell me, why are you digging so hard on these girls? The location? Kraatjes showed me the stats for the warehouses and the Uhuru Community. Quiet. Nobody home."

"That's how it started," Westermann said, the question leaving him feeling vulnerable. *The location.* "Murder in that part of town; no precedent for it. And then the connection to Godtown, also crime-free."

"Free of reported crime," the Chief corrected.

"Exactly. And then you add Maddox being obstructive."

The Chief nodded. "Your report mentioned that this first girl"—he looked down at a paper on his desk—"Lenore, was ill, and my understanding is that the second woman seems to have the same disease."

"I hadn't heard that for sure."

"Now you have."

"Okay."

"And I hear there was another woman at City Hospital who they think might also have had it, the same disease."

"Right."

The Chief thought about this. Westermann looked at Kraatjes, was met with raised eyebrows, and said, "I think we might have a public health problem here."

"Three women, working girls; that's a public health problem?" the Chief snapped.

Kraatjes stepped forward, looking warily at the Chief. "We probably need to at least acknowledge that it *could* be an issue. Even if it doesn't leave this room."

"You think the mayor, in an election year, needs a public health crisis? We need to be pretty damn sure. We're going to err on the side of caution, and caution is not making a mistake and screwing the mayor. I'll stand up to him for the investigation, but I won't instigate something like this. Understood?"

Westermann nodded. "Understood."

The Chief exhaled loudly through his nose. "Right."

From the street below came a sudden cacophony of sirens as squad cars deployed. Westermann and the Chief exchanged looks.

"Piet," the Chief softened his voice. "Tread carefully, but if you run into any problems, you come straight to me."

Grip and Morphy were leaning on the wall outside the Chief's office, drinking coffee and smoking cigarettes, shooting the shit with some uniforms they knew. They looked up expectantly as Westermann emerged. Westermann smiled at them and winked.

"Lieut?" Grip asked as Westermann strode away down the hall.

40.

Frings had his shirt and tie off, washing his face in the men's bathroom sink at the *Gazette*. Even in this new building, the water tasted of rust. He rubbed his eyes with the heels of his hands, wondering what to make of the Black Comet Line out there in a grown-over lot in the Hollows. As Eddings had said: crazy.

The bathroom door opened and a kid whose name Frings had either forgotten or never known stopped in the doorway.

"Mr. Frings?"

Frings glanced over at him.

"We've been looking all over for you. The editor wants to see you in his office."

"Okay." Frank turned back to the mirror, combing his wet hair back with his fingers.

"I'm sorry, Mr. Frings. He wants to see you right now."

Frings looked back at the kid, but the kid didn't have a clue.

Panos looked up wearily from his desk as Frings came in. "Where have you been, Frank?"

Frings was about to answer, but saw Deyna sitting in one of the leather chairs, a folder in his lap and an ugly grin on his face.

He kept his eyes on Deyna. "Later," Frings said to Panos slowly.

Panos thought about this for a moment. "Fine. Listen, Frank, Deyna here has been working hard, keeping an eye on your friend Westermann; watching his actions, which, truth to be told, are quite odd in some ways."

"I guess I don't understand."

Deyna started to speak but Panos held up a hand. "Before we talk, see these photos that Deyna has brought with him."

Deyna held out the folder. Frings had to take a couple of steps to reach them.

"Sit down, Frank. Please," Panos said. Frings heard the tension in his voice. This was not a meeting Panos wanted to have.

Frings sat and opened the folder, aware of the two sets of eyes on him. A small stack of photos. The first showed Westermann, Warren Eddings, and Mel Washington, puzzled looks, turning toward the camera. Shanty walls in the background to the left indicated where the photo had been taken. Frings looked at the next one; same subjects, same place, puzzled looks replaced by angry ones. Next photo: Westermann and another cop bracing a little guy in a cowboy getup. There's a crowd around, but no one paying attention. Next: same subjects, same place, this time the cop's knee is up in the cowboy's groin, the cowboy wincing. Perfect front-page fodder. *Shit.* Next photo: same place, Westermann advancing, looking murderous. What the hell was he doing? Next: Westermann and several other men in suits talking with Prosper Maddox and a big blond gink. Maddox looking placid, Westermann stern. Next: same subjects, same location, Westermann pointing at Maddox. Next: same location, Westermann leaning on the roof of a prowl car, talking to the cop inside. Last photo: Westermann climbing into the shotgun seat of a prowl car, Maddox and the big gink in the blurry foreground.

Frings kept his eyes on the last photo, gathering his thoughts. The sum of the photos was not pretty, the portrait of an enraged cop. There was nothing wrong with the photos themselves. It was the innuendo that would be the problem: Westermann buddying up with commies and castigating a preacher; Westermann condoning or encouraging police violence.

Frings replaced the photos and tossed the folder on Panos's desk. He shrugged. "So?"

Panos held his eyes. "Deyna?"

Deyna said, "Your friend Westermann—"

"Don't start with that."

Deyna smiled, looked at Panos. Panos opened his palms, urging Deyna to be more politic.

"As I told you, before, Lieutenant Westermann seems to have placed quite an emphasis on the investigation of an unidentified whore picked up from the riverbank. That seemed interesting to me, the Golden Boy giving a shit about a case like that; maybe there's a story there. The day before yesterday, two things happen that seem like there's definitely a story here: One, they find a second body on the river, this one up by the Uhuru Community. The last one was a little downstream, if you remember. Second, I come across your . . . Lieutenant Westermann palling around with two known communists with Uhuru Community ties. Seems interesting, doesn't it?"

Deyna paused for a moment to let that sink in. "Okay, so next thing, the lieutenant heads down to the bar district with another cop, named"—Deyna looked at his notes—"Grip. Torsten Grip. Anyway, I think you saw the picture. Lieutenant Westermann and Detective Grip find this pimp"—again to the notes—"Stanic, and they rough him up a little. Fine. Dead whores, find a pimp. Knee him in the jewels? He's a pimp, right? No problem. Not the image that Westermann puts out there, though. Not exactly the System.

"So then, for some reason, Lieutenant Westermann heads to Godtown not once, but twice. Godtown. You saw the photos, he's harassing Dr. Maddox, a preacher. I talked to Dr. Maddox and he said that he'd promised to cooperate with the lieutenant, but Westermann starts banging on doors despite Dr. Maddox's specific request that he not. Then, and this is the interesting part, a police cruiser arrives and Westermann and his people up and leave. Just like that."

Frings looked at Panos. "So?"

Deyna said, "You're the genius, Frings. What does it mean?"

Frings didn't look at Deyna. "Is there a story here? Cop investigates murder?"

Panos winced. "Frank, why are you like this? We are simply asking what you think."

"There's nothing to think, Panos."

Deyna said, "Golden Boy cop, lawyer's kid, cuddling up to commies and bullying preachers? That's nothing?"

Frings looked to Panos. "What? We're going to start attacking people for their associations based on a photograph? He's investigating a crime, talking to community leaders where the body was found. What's he supposed to do? Panos, I don't care one way or the other about Westermann, but we have some standards here, right?"

Deyna's voice rose with his irritation. "We may have a communist in a position of authority in the police department. Maybe that doesn't bother you, but it sure as hell bothers me."

41.

Even with the windows down, Grip felt trapped by the heat in his car, as if it were physically restraining him. He sat in the driver's seat with Ole Koss next to him. Ed Wayne was in the back, taking a pull from a flask of whiskey he was sharing with Grip. They were parked at the curb in the Negro East Side of the City. The buildings seemed lower here, the streets wider.

"Nearly shit when I saw you today," Grip said, dangling his arm out the window, cigarette in his hand.

"Yeah?" Koss was eyeing the sidewalk traffic, giving a hard stare to anyone who looked at the car too long. It was getting on in the evening, probably ten-ish, though none of them had a watch.

"I knew you were in with Maddox, but I didn't realize you're that close."

"What're you saying?"

"Nothing, Ole. Just surprised that it would be just you and him."

From the backseat, Wayne asked, "What the fuck are you talking about?"

Koss ignored him. "Surprised to see cops in our neighborhood, myself. I didn't hear about a crime or anything, and suddenly you guys are crawling all over the place."

"Yeah, well," Grip said, not willing to go down this path.

They sat in silence for a while, watching pedestrians but mostly a storefront a half block away and across the street, waiting for the lights to go off and the people to leave. Grip and Wayne passed the flask back and forth. Grip felt light-headed, his body charged with energy. Koss sat relaxed in the shotgun seat. He looked placid enough, but Grip sensed something in him and decided not to engage him again. Grip was getting restless, though. He needed to move.

Grip asked, "Ed, you ever been down to the Uhuru Community?"

"What d'you mean?"

"What don't you understand?"

Wayne grunted a half laugh. "As little as I can get away with. Bunch of colored Reds? Not my idea of a good time."

"Yeah? I thought it was your beat."

Wayne shrugged. "Like I said, not my thing."

"Well, I was there this morning."

"What the fuck were you doing down there?"

"What do you think?"

"What was the call?"

Grip stole a glance at Koss, who didn't seem to be listening. "Dead girl on the riverbank a week back. You must've heard. And then two nights ago . . ."

Wayne leaned forward, his hands on the seatbacks, excited. "That was my call. You should have seen her; sores all over. Never seen anything like it. Couldn't have weighed a hundred pounds."

"Same as the first girl."

"That right?" Wayne seemed to mull this over. "You figure one of those Uhuru Community Negroes for that one, too?"

"What, you got a suspect for your girl?"

"Nah, they took me off the case; said you guys were on it. But it's got to be one of those commie Negroes, right?"

"Yeah, well, that's not real clear at the moment. The lieut is working a few different angles."

"*The lieut*," Koss said, mocking, "needs to keep out of Prosper Maddox's business."

The conversation ended. They sat in silence, Grip staring out the windshield, the tension in the car up a notch.

Koss said, "Here we go."

Grip turned to Koss, then followed his sight line to the storefront. Lights out. Man locking the door.

"About goddamn time," Wayne said.

Koss shot him a furious look, the Lord's name taken in vain.

Ole Koss didn't believe in doing these kinds of jobs by stealth. Instead, the three men walked to the unmarked storefront, and Wayne and Koss stood facing the sidewalk while Grip jimmied the lock. It was a decent lock, so it took Grip nearly a minute of delicate fiddling. Wayne didn't like doing things this way and became more and more agitated as the seconds rolled by.

"Hurry up. What's the fucking problem?"

Grip ignored him. Koss had his arms folded, his muscular chest pushing them out before him. Nobody in his right mind would mess with Koss. Grip slipped the bolt and pulled the door open, holding it for the other two. When they were all in, he pulled the door closed again and locked it with a latch from the inside. Wayne was already at one of the desks, pulling drawers out and emptying their contents on the floor. Street light filtered in through the storefront glass, just bright enough to illuminate everything in monochrome.

Koss found the door to the back room and tried the handle. When it didn't open, he kicked the door down with three strong stomps.

Grip sifted through the crap that Wayne had dumped on the ground, moving papers around with his feet. It was barely light enough to read. He wasn't looking for anything in particular and didn't actually expect to find anything of interest. This visit was about sending a message to the Reds in the Uhuru Community. Any information they turned up would be a bonus.

Wayne finished with the desks and took a wooden chair by the back, swinging it hard against the wall, splintering it on impact and leaving a small hole in the wall. He found another chair and did the same. Loud crashes sounded from the back room as Koss threw file-cabinet drawers. Grip peeked in. Koss had turned on the light and papers were everywhere. Koss sensed Grip in the doorway and looked over.

"You almost done out there?"

Grip nodded. "Anything interesting in here?"

Koss shrugged. "Could be. It'd take hours to go through this."

Wayne joined Grip in the doorway, holding a lighter in one hand and a burning sheet of paper in the other.

"The fuck you doing?" Grip asked, alarmed.

"Let's burn this place."

It wasn't part of the plan. "The fuck's wrong with you? Put that thing out."

Wayne looked to Koss. Koss didn't hold any kind of actual authority beyond that which came with being the guy nobody wanted to mess with.

"Ole," Grip said in a let's-be-reasonable voice.

Koss said, "Put it out. Let's stick with what we set out to do."

Wayne spat, dropped the piece of paper, and stomped out the remaining flames.

Grip stepped back out into the main room and froze. Looking in through the front glass from the street was a skinny Negro with very dark skin, a bowler, and sunglasses. He stood motionless, arms by his side. Something was familiar about him; maybe from the Community. Grip's breathing went shallow.

"Fuck," he said, voice unsteady.

"What's wrong?" Koss asked.

Grip didn't answer, still staring at the man looking in on them.

Koss and Wayne walked in from the back room, saw the man. Koss gave a kind of gasp and started for the door. The Negro turned and walked jerkily out of view, his gait almost unnatural. Koss got to the door and yanked on it twice before realizing it was locked. He tried to turn the key in the lock but was too anxious and fumbled with it, not coordinating the key in the lock with the doorknob. They finally made it out to the street, but the Negro with the bowler and sunglasses was nowhere to be seen. Koss seemed rooted to his spot on the sidewalk, clenching and unclenching his fists, head darting to look up and down the street, his face gone white.

42.

Westermann shared an elevator with an elderly couple who he recognized but couldn't place, giving them a warm, whiskey smile—he'd had a couple at the bar across the street, steeling himself for this party. The woman was wearing a fortune in diamonds. Westermann was in a tux, required for any party at the Helios Club. The elevator doors opened to the sound of a swing band grooving over dozens of conversations. The air was cool.

Westermann followed the elderly couple into the room, scanning the crowd for familiar faces. He wasn't sure of the occasion for this party, but you didn't turn down an invitation from his father. A Negro waiter approached with a tray of champagne glasses and Westermann took one.

He walked into the midst of the party. Powerful men and women who were either beautiful or once beautiful socialized, gossiped, and made deals over cocktails. This had been Westermann's world for the first twenty years of his life, as far from the world of the street cop as you could get in the City. He was comfortable here; he found that troubling.

He saw his father first, his balding head high above the crowd, and then his mother beside him. They were talking with a banker named Finnerty and his wife, a looker maybe twenty years his junior. Westermann headed toward them. His father, Big Rolf Westermann, was a lawyer who only represented people of a certain class; the class Westermann himself been raised among. Big Rolf was successful because he was smart, relentless, and ruthless. He brought those same qualities to bear on his family.

Westermann's mother caught sight of him as he weaved his way through the crowd. He edged past a woman, sleeved in a gold dress, who had been his father's mistress. Maybe still was.

When he reached his mother, her eyes were bright from drink and he gave her a kiss on the cheek.

He shook his father's hand. "Hi, Rolf."

"Piet. So glad you came."

"You knew I would."

His father smiled the same way he'd smiled at Westermann as an obedient ten-year-old. Westermann greeted the Finnertys, the wife holding his eyes for an extra beat. He took down the rest of his drink and looked at his mother, still beautiful but withering somehow. She was half in the bag and nattered at him about her concerns over his safety. He'd heard it before, repeated his usual empty assurances. His father continued his conversation with Finnerty. Westermann watched Big Rolf grow impatient with his wife's incessant chatter in the background. A waiter came by. Westermann exchanged his empty glass for a full one. Mrs. Finnerty tried to catch his eye. His mother talked.

A judge named Asplundh joined the group along with his beautiful wife and even more beautiful daughter: dark eyes, dark hair, tall and slender, maybe twenty years old. They were introduced. Her name was Cora.

"I hear you're a police officer."

Westermann downed his drink, exchanged the empty for another.

He learned that she was at the Tech. He told her some cop stories, noticed Mrs. Finnerty still eyeing him, smiling conspiratorially when their eyes met.

Lenore, rotating slowly in the moonlit current.

Cora told him about her summer in Europe. The rest of the group had moved off a few feet to give them some privacy. Westermann flagged down another drink. Cora wasn't drinking.

While she talked, Westermann watched a man he recognized approach his father, get his attention, then engage him in conversation, both men looking over at Westermann. Cora noticed his wandering attention and turned to see Big Rolf and the other man walking toward them.

Big Rolf made the introductions. "Cora Asplundh, this is Vic Truffant." Truffant kissed her hand.

"And I think you know my son, Piet."

Westermann shook hands with Truffant. "When you were younger, Piet. Still in short pants."

There's a photo of me with Mel Washington.

Big Rolf turned to Cora. "Would you excuse us for a moment? I'll make sure Piet finds you after we talk a little business."

Cora looked to Westermann. He smiled and shrugged. She retreated to join her parents, who were still talking with his mother and the Finnertys.

Westermann grabbed a drink from a passing waiter. He was drunk, feeling good.

Truffant said, "Let me get right to the point. I have a constituent . . . well, a friend . . . who says that you have been—and I want to be careful with what I say—but that you have been harassing him and his people about a crime that he has, to his knowledge, only the most tenuous connection."

"Does your friend have a name?"

"Dr. Prosper Maddox."

Westermann laughed. He was aware of his father's gaze on him, an appraisal being made. There were expectations; but what were they? Stand up to Truffant? Show respect to his father's contemporaries, his elders?

"What do you want from me, Mr. Truffant?"

"To think about why you want to pressure Dr. Maddox, who, it is my understanding, is truly peripheral to your investigation. Surely it's not worth upsetting him and his congregation."

"I've hardly pressured him."

"That's not his impression."

Westermann laughed again, looking to his father. "Mr. Truffant, I asked Prosper Maddox for cooperation in a *murder* investigation. He declined."

"The investigation of a murdered whore."

Feeling very drunk, Westermann stared at Truffant.

Big Rolf said, "Just tell the boy what you want, Vic."

Boy?

"Stay away from Dr. Maddox, Piet. A word to the wise."

Westermann's ears rang. He stared at Truffant murderously.

Big Rolf said, "Come on, Vic, you've told him what you wanted."

Truffant extended his hand. Westermann didn't even look at it.

Big Rolf was a couple of steps away now. Truffant leaned close, his lips inches from Westermann's ear, whispering, "Don't fuck with me, boy. I'll take your head off. I don't care who your father is."

Westermann watched his father put his arm around Truffant's shoulders, steering him toward Westermann's mother and Judge Asplundh and his wife. Westermann watched Truffant kiss his mother on the cheek; kiss the judge's wife on the cheek; shake the judge's hand, leaning in to whisper something. He felt Cora's eyes on him, turned to her, caught the questioning look across twenty feet. He had to get the hell out of there.

* * *

The cabbie was barking something at Westermann. He must have passed out on the ride; his head spun, his shirt was soaked with sweat.

"I said, which house?"

Westermann squinted at the block, not sure at first where he was. He didn't remember giving the cabbie an address. But it became clear.

"Just go a half block down. Slow."

The cabbie did as Westermann asked. They came to Morphy's house and Westermann saw, almost to his relief, that the curtains were closed.

"Never mind," he said, and gave the cabbie his address.

The cabbie turned to him. "You sure you know what you're doing?"

43.

Grip woke in the night, something disturbing him, bringing him to consciousness. His eyes were hazy from sleep, the room dark. He registered the familiar silhouettes of his apartment: table, chairs, wardrobe, the brighter squares of shaded windows. He registered the silence, none of the normal street noise. In his semiconsciousness he found it vaguely strange, but not particularly troubling. And there was something else, a presence in the room. Another person? He thought he might have seen a silhouette, but he wasn't sure, and anyway, he was overwhelmed by fatigue, unable to stay awake.

His dream came intensely. A woman, as there often was, but a Negro—beautiful, tall, dark. It didn't make sense, this dream; no coherence; no logic; but there was lust and there was fear.

He woke when the sun came through his window, the dream still with him in its essence, its impressions; the details lost. His head throbbed from dehydration and last night's whiskey. He wondered if this might be causing the dread that seemed to wrap itself around his chest, constricting him. He drank a couple of cups of tepid tap water that pooled, stagnant, at the bottom of his stomach.

He showered and shaved, nicked himself below his chin. He put on a lightweight suit and knotted his tie loosely. The day was already hot. He shut his windows in case of rain, shrugged on his shoulder holster, and slipped in his Colt. He looked around the apartment before leaving, decided not to make his disheveled bed.

Out in the hall, he pulled the door shut behind him, turned to lock it, and saw that someone had painted the same skull-in-top-hat on his door that he'd seen at the bar two days before. His mouth went dry, the tepid water and whiskey bile churned in his stomach.

"Oh, fuck," he said. His sweat ran cold.

44.

THE *GAZETTE*
August 8, 1950
Editorial Page

A CLEAR, HONEST CHOICE

By Frank Frings

It is confounding that in their ill-conceived crusade against all things bearing even a speck of Red, certain elements within the City—most notably mayoral aspirant Vic Truffant—have cast their rapacious gaze at the Uhuru Community.

To those unaware of the Uhuru Community, this clapboard hamlet is an experiment in Negro self-government and relative isolation. This endeavor is presided over in a rather remote and idiosyncratic fashion by a visionary named Father Womé. I had the occasion to hobnob with Father Womé and receive explication of the purpose of this movement. The crux of the Uhuru Community's existence is the extension to Negroes therein of a degree of freedom not achievable in Caucasian-dominated municipalities. Freedom.

Truffant and his ilk will, whether with deepest sincerity or the most craven deviousness, point to a small cadre, numbering less than ten, of alleged communists associated with the Uhuru Community and, with this anemic justification, demand the dismantling of the Community and the dispersal of its residents.

This is a piece of foolhardiness that only people with a cruelly misguided appraisal of their own cogitative abilities and moral sense would advocate. Who can predict with any certainty at all the consequences of leaving the Uhuru Community to its own devices? The answer to this is clear as is the essential choice to be made in this instance: whether to allow the Negroes in this Community to be free or to deny them freedom. This is the choice. There is no other choice to be made.

This choice should not be considered within external frameworks constructed by opponents of the Uhuru Community that do not bear on the essential choice. This choice should not be delegated to others who stake capricious claim to knowledge that is both unfounded and unknowable. Delegation of the choice is not a choice.

So how to make this choice between freedom and not-freedom? This, as with all choices made by an honest man, must be made on universal principles. If we are to deny these Negroes freedom, it is because we choose to deny all men freedom. If we choose to grant them leave to pursue their freedom, it is because we would afford freedom to all men.

Consider these principles and I trust the correct, that is, honest, choice is clear.

45.

Eleven in the morning and Westermann was a little disheartened to see a smattering of prostitutes out in this neighborhood of run-down shops and workers' tenements. They seemed deflated, leaning against walls, smoking or chatting listlessly, not working the pedestrians. This time of day, anyone looking for a trick would have to come to them.

He found Vesterhue's business address, a storefront clinic called Wilhelm Health Center; Wilhelm because of the street it was on. Also on the block: a butcher's, a Christian reading room, a barbershop, Madame Pristina's Palm Reading and Fortune Gazing, and a place called Dreiburg's— chintz in the window under a maroon valance. Half sheets of paper littered the sidewalk, as if someone had thrown them up into a wind and let them lie where they fell. He read one: "Your Mayor Is Asleep at the Switch, No to Communism, Yes to Truffant."

Earlier, Westermann had pared down the investigation team to just Grip, Morphy, and himself, releasing the others to work on ongoing cases or new ones that came in. No eyebrows rose. Even with a second girl murdered, investigations into dead prostitutes simply didn't merit much attention. Five or six—then you had something worthy of a real delegation of manpower. He'd reminded Grip and Morphy of the Chief's admonition to play it subtle. They'd nodded and given at least a show of getting it.

The coroner's report had come back on the second girl: still no identification; near certainty that she carried the same disease as Lenore; cause of death—*asphyxiation by strangling.* Different from Lenore. Lenore had drowned; her lungs had been full of water.

Westermann wondered what this meant. Was this second girl dead before she reached the river? Why would she be left in the same spot as Lenore? Westermann chewed on his lip while he walked, thinking this over.

Pushing Lenore into the current.

No turning back.

* * *

All eight chairs in the waiting area at Wilhelm Health Center were filled. An old guy in an expensive but ancient suit coughed phlegm into a white handkerchief he kept over his mouth, even during the brief periods when he was not hacking. Two mothers—clean, young, blissed-out expressions— had three young children between them, sitting in chairs, playing with tin army men. An elderly couple sat holding hands, watching with inscrutable expressions as the kids battled.

Westermann nodded to the two mothers, who smiled demurely back. A heavy woman with her hair piled up on her head and bifocals perched on the end of her nose sat behind a desk, eyeing Westermann.

Westermann flashed the woman his badge. "I'd like to see Dr. Vester-hue, when he has a moment."

The woman barked a short, sardonic laugh. "You, me, those two women over there, Dr. Phillipi, others who came yesterday; we'd all like to see Dr. Vesterhue."

"Pardon?"

"Dr. Vesterhue didn't show up for his hours today. Or yesterday, or the day before. Dr. Phillipi's trying to pick up the slack, but he can't do it himself. We sent some patients down to City Hospital, mostly the working girls." As an aside, she said, "Dr. Phillipi doesn't like to see them."

"You tried to get in touch with Dr. Vesterhue at home?"

"Of course. You think we wouldn't? Nobody there. No word to us that he was sick or anything like that."

"This happen before?"

"No."

"You worried about him?"

She shrugged, not seeming very concerned. "Be nice to have him show up" was all she could manage.

Westermann sighed, taking a look around the room again as he gathered his thoughts. Again, the two mothers caught his eye and smiled. He nodded a little.

"Listen. I know Dr. Phillipi must be extremely busy, with Dr. Vesterhue not here, but I need five or ten minutes with him, and quickly. Like after his current patient. Also, I need records for Mavis Talley and a woman named Lenore; I don't know her last name."

The woman looked back at him with undisguised exasperation. "Really, I hardly think . . ."

Westermann put his hands on her desk and leaned over so that he was near her ear. He whispered, "We are conducting a murder investigation. We can argue about this in front of your patients, but I don't think that does anyone any good, do you? Ten minutes, tops, with the doctor. You pull a couple of files, maybe have to do a little searching for one of them. You want to make a big deal of this?"

The woman reddened considerably, though it was unclear whether she was angry, embarrassed, or chastened. Without another word, she stood and disappeared through the door behind her. Westermann turned from the desk to look at the magazines spread across the waiting-room coffee table. *Reader's Digest. Life.* And a number of anticommunist rags: "Is This America's Future?" A woman shielding her two apple-cheeked boys from sinister-looking men in gray suits, her face contorted in horror. Westermann was bending to pick it up when the woman returned.

"Dr. Phillipi will see you," she said curtly.

Westermann straightened and followed her back down a short hallway with four doors, three of them open. They passed one on the right, file shelves to the ceiling, and then on to the next room on the right opposite the closed door. The woman stood aside for Westermann to enter, then left without a word. Westermann studied a wall chart, a person in profile, the organs detailed along with the muscles in the arms and legs. Westermann pegged the figure as a man, though it had no genitalia. There was a rap on the door and Westermann turned to face a small, trim man with sunken eyes and wide mouth, maybe in his fifties.

"Lieutenant Westermann?"

"Thank you for meeting with me on such short notice, Dr. Phillipi."

He nodded, hanging in the doorway. His graying hair was disheveled; he looked stressed.

"Could we talk in private?" Westermann asked, nodding at the open door.

Phillipi gave an annoyed shrug, but stepped in, closing the door behind him. Strange.

"I understand that your partner's been missing a few days."

"My partner?" Phillipi asked, confused.

"Dr. Vesterhue."

Phillipi puzzled on this for a moment. "I'm not sure I'd describe him as my partner. But, yes, he hasn't been here for three days. Damned inconsiderate to be honest, leaving me to deal with his patients."

"Aren't you concerned that something might have happened to him?"

"Concerned?" he said, as though it hadn't occurred to him. "I suppose. *Has* something happened to him?"

"I don't know," Westermann said, squinting at Phillipi, trying to get a grip on his reaction. "We have some questions for him about a couple of his patients."

Phillipi spoke with venom. "I see. Are they whores or people from *that church*?"

"Excuse me?"

Phillipi took a breath. "I'm sorry, that wasn't called for. Lieutenant, I'm sorry if I seem callous. Dr. Vesterhue and I share rent on this property and split Mrs. Lansing's salary. Beyond that, we are not partners. We have very different clienteles and, I dare say, different philosophies of care. Vesterhue mostly sees people from that church in the Hollows."

"The Church of Last Days?"

"Yes, that one," Phillipi said with distaste. "Those people and also prostitutes. Do you know how unsettling it can be for my patients—they're mostly elderly, some younger but chronically ill—how unsettling it can be to share a waiting room with prostitutes and cultists?"

"Cultists?"

"I'm sorry. Again, maybe too strong. They are devout Christians, I suppose, but their manner . . . I think there might be a couple of them out in the waiting room right now."

"I saw them."

"A strange bunch, I can assure you."

"So, Dr. Vesterhue . . . ," Westermann prompted.

"I don't know what I can tell you, Lieutenant. He hasn't been here in three days. No notice to me. Mrs. Lansing went by his apartment, but no one was home."

"No one answered?"

"That's right. No one answered."

"So, he could have been home."

"And not answering the door?"

"Or maybe not able."

"I see," Phillipi said. "Mrs. Lansing can give you his address."

Mrs. Lansing did have his address, but not much else. She slid a thin folder, Mavis Talley's, across her desk to Westermann, who noted the expression on her face: something close to pleased with herself. The folder was empty, save for a sheet of paper stapled to the inside with an address, date of birth, and vitals; except for the date of birth, he already had that information.

"Nothing for a Lenore?"

Mrs. Lansing was working through some papers on her desk. She didn't look up when she answered. "Not that I found."

"Someone took out the contents of this folder?"

She looked up at him, exasperation in her eyes. "Dr. Vesterhue, he kept some of the files to himself. I insisted that he leave at least that information for my sake, but he kept some of his patients' files—the real files—with him."

"That normal? Does Dr. Phillipi do that?"

Still absorbed in her work. "Normal? No, it's not normal. Neither's Dr. Vesterhue."

46.

Grip and Morphy met Westermann at a Greek diner across the street from Vesterhue's apartment. They waited as Westermann finished his coffee, then the three of them crossed the street to Vesterhue's building, soot-stained brick. Westermann scanned the street for Deyna—the guy had been turning up everywhere—but he wasn't there.

Vesterhue's apartment was on the second floor, above a grocer's run by a first-generation Latvian couple. Two doors on the second-floor landing led to a front apartment and a rear apartment. Vesterhue's was the front. Grip pounded the door with his fist.

"Dr. Vesterhue. Police."

No reply, no sounds of motion from within. There was another sound though, a sound that was familiar to Grip though it was too faint for him to place.

Grip pounded again. Yelling this time. "Dr. Vesterhue, this is the police. Please open the door."

The door from the back apartment opened and Westermann noted that Grip jumped, hand going for his gun.

An old man—head shaved, gray stubble on his chin—leaned through the open door, the whites of his eyes ringed with angry red.

"No one been in that apartment for half a week."

"Sir?" Westermann said.

"No one in or out of that apartment in four, five days."

"You sure about that?"

The old man nodded. Westermann could see it: the old man sitting in his quiet apartment, picking up every sound on the landing and probably the apartments above as well.

"Thank you," Westermann said. "We may want to speak with you."

The old man closed his door without answering, the sliding dead bolt audible. The police shared a look, Morphy chuckling a little, Grip still pale.

Westermann said, "Which one of you wants to do the honors?"

Grip needed it more, so Morphy stood aside. It took three stomps before the hinges gave way and the door fell in.

The smell came at them hard, familiar, but not the smell of death; rotting food in a sealed-up apartment, stagnant air, almost a furnace. The sound Grip had heard was a radio tuned to the same anticommunist station they played at Crippen's. They did a quick recon. Grip found the radio and turned it off. The silence was sudden and stark.

No one home; dirty dishes in the sink, food gone moldy. The guy hadn't exactly been getting rich as a doctor. The furniture was old and shabby, the walls bare, except for a couple of crucifixes tacked to the wall—one in the living room and one in the bedroom. The whole place was outfitted like something temporary, as if Vesterhue wasn't planning on staying long or maybe just didn't care. The apartment had been tumbled, not by an expert, but by someone who was nonetheless trying to be careful. Books were replaced in the bookshelves, pillows stacked back on couches, a halfhearted attempt at making the bed—maybe an accurate imitation of Vesterhue's own standards. But there were signs: dust lines that didn't quite reach to the front edges of books; couch cushions replaced with their darker, bottom sides up. They spent some time, working in silence, trying to find the files for Mavis Talley and Lenore and maybe even the second girl. To no one's surprise, they came up with nothing.

Morphy had opened a window to get some air circulating, and they met there to exchange impressions and breathe some fresh air.

Morphy said, "He was expecting to come back. Didn't anticipate whatever happened, even if he left on his own for some reason."

Grip agreed. A police siren keened from blocks away.

Westermann said, "And he took those files with him or else someone came here and found them."

"Unless they couldn't find them either. We could tear apart the couch, pull up floorboards," Morphy suggested.

Westermann shook his head. "Medical files. Frequent use. He's not going to open up his couch or pry up floorboards every time he needs them."

Morphy nodded. "So?"

Westermann gazed out the window, thinking. Grip and Morphy were used to this, the lieut taking a minute to think things through, and they waited patiently, taking stock themselves.

Eventually, Westermann laid it out for them. Interview the geezer across the hall and then do a telephone canvass of the hospitals, see if Vesterhue was checked in anywhere. Westermann would get back with Mrs. Lansing at Wilhelm Health Center to get a physical description of Vesterhue and then run that by Pulyatkin at the morgue for any John Does that fit the description.

Grip went to use Vesterhue's john, and Westermann took the opportunity to talk to Morphy, whispering, "What's got Grip spooked?"

"Lieut?"

"He's jumpy; not talking."

"Yeah. I'll feel him out."

"Let me know."

Grip emerged from the john, zipping up and giving them a suspicious look as if he knew what they'd been talking about.

47.

Carla sat along with Mel Washington's compatriot Betty Askins and two other women in the shack of a round woman named Eunice Prendergrast, originally of Barbados and now something of a force in the Community. The air inside was stale but shaded; the aroma of strong coffee rose off a pot just pulled from the coals outside her door. Carla conducted a semiregular meeting with women in the Uhuru Community to get a sense of the Community's immediate needs.

Eunice filled and passed clay mugs of coffee. They discussed the condition of a plot of land the women were trying to farm between the Community and the river. The ground wasn't suitable for the crops they were accustomed to growing—mostly in the Caribbean or in the South—but they were making slow progress.

Eunice said, "Some of the kids are having diarrhea. It's getting passed around."

Carla nodded. "We're working on getting a doctor here, having a children's clinic sometime very soon. Also, we'll get the kids vaccinated, and the adults, too—mumps, pertussis, smallpox. A lot of people in the City will be more comfortable with the Community—forgive me for saying this—if they know that you aren't going to be a breeding ground for diseases; if they know the people here have been inoculated."

Eunice gave her a sour look, but nodded. "It's all for the good, I suppose."

Betty said, "There's no reason why the people here shouldn't receive the proper medical care, same as everyone else."

Carla took a sip of coffee, puckering at its acidity, feeling her face flush even more from its heat; new sweat beads formed at her hairline. "I'll let you know as soon as we work out the details, but, as I said, very soon. Days. If those kids still have diarrhea, take them to City Hospital. Let me know if you do this, and I'll arrange for payment or whatever needs to be done."

Eunice frowned. "We can pay or Father Womé can pay. We don't need your money."

Carla met her eyes for a moment, then nodded in acquiescence.

This led to a bout of gossip about particular people within the Community who were sick or feeling the acute effects of old age. Carla let the women talk, once exchanging a smile with Betty, both acknowledging the minor travails of trying to help the Community.

When the gossiping seemed to have run its course, Carla asked if they had any news about the night assaults over the past week.

Eunice's two friends made tutting sounds and shook their heads, casting their eyes to the ground. Eunice's face was a mask of contempt. "Those police don't do from nothing; like back home. No police for the poor. I wasn't expecting that here, in America, where everyone is *equal*."

Feeling the need to respond to Eunice's sarcasm, Betty Askins said, "It's not *supposed* to work that way here," but her dubiousness was clear in her voice.

Eunice snorted in disgust.

Carla said, "We have a friend in the police who's working on getting the police back out here."

Eunice said, "You going to save us, dear?"

Carla was stopped cold.

Eunice smiled. "Don't worry about the police, Carla."

"Okay, Eunice," Carla said, tentative.

"When we make up our minds, the Community can take care of ourselves."

Carla nodded, wondering what Eunice meant by that.

48.

Ed Wayne smoked a Camel and drank coffee from a paper cup, waiting for
Westermann in a framed-out room on the unfinished seventh floor of the
new police headquarters. Unfinished because the money had run out before the building was completed; too many palms to grease, too many
people with too much leverage. Light shone through the windows, casting
long shadows across the wall-less floor.

Art Deyna was waiting for Westermann on the steps of the police building, his fedora rakishly tilted, his eyes predatory. Westermann saw him,
went tense despite himself. He walked directly toward Deyna, hoping with
his aggressiveness to catch Deyna off guard.

It didn't work.

"Lieutenant Westermann." Deyna held his arms out as if delighted to
see an old and dear friend.

"What do you want? I have things to do."

Deyna laughed. "Down to business, right? Okay, why don't you tell me
why you're harassing citizens down in Godtown?"

Westermann flashed on Mary Little's panic; on Maddox's obstruction;
on being called back by the brass. "You know I've got nothing to say on
that."

"Suit yourself. How about this? Why are you meeting with Negro communists?"

"I'm not going to comment on an open case."

"Are Mel Washington or Warren Eddings suspects?"

Westermann glared. "What did I just say?"

"What were you meeting with them about?"

"Do you have any questions that I might conceivably answer?"

Deyna licked his lips, barely containing a smile. "I don't think you're going to answer any questions, no matter what they are."

"That's right. Nice talking with you." Westermann walked away to the sound of Deyna's laughter.

Westermann sat at his desk, noting the time, already late for his meeting with Wayne. Let the bastard wait.

Westermann made some calls, leaving a message with Pulyatkin's secretary at the coroner's office, checking to see if Pulyatkin had ID'd either of the bodies and leaving a description of Vesterhue for him to check against John Does.

Westermann saw that someone had left the day's *Gazette* on his desk, opened to a page in the middle of the front section. He saw a photo of himself in Godtown, jabbing a finger at a calm-looking Prosper Maddox. *Jesus.* He called Frings.

"What the fuck is this?"

"I know, Piet."

"'Mystery Sweep in Godtown'?" The headline.

"Piet—"

"Golden Boy Lieutenant Piet Westermann led a deployment of detectives into Godtown despite no crime report having been filed in this quiet, churchgoing neighborhood in weeks."

"I know what it says, Piet."

"It has a fucking quote from Prosper Maddox saying I've got some kind of vendetta against Christians."

"Piet, shut the hell up for a second. I don't run the paper. We've got a reporter—"

"Art Deyna."

"Right. I don't know how he got them, but he's got photos of you—"

Jesus. "Not on the phone."

"Right. Let's meet tonight. Come by my building. We can talk on the roof."

Westermann left his jacket at his desk, loosened his tie, damp with sweat, and grabbed a cup of coffee on the way to the seventh floor. It was private there. No chance of someone walking in on them.

Wayne was good and pissed by the time Westermann arrived, their respective ranks the only thing keeping Wayne under control.

"How are you this morning, Detective?" Westermann asked, his pleasant greeting incongruent.

Wayne stared back at him, arms crossed, fingers white from pushing down hard on his biceps; probably some means of anger control. Westermann noticed the scarred knuckles, confirming what he had heard and seen—Wayne plied his policing on the edge.

"I want to talk to you about a couple of calls you took, down by the Uhuru Community. Assaults, a week or so ago. This sound familiar?"

"If you say so." Wayne focused his eyes over Westermann's shoulder.

"I say so."

Wayne shrugged sullenly.

"What's the disposition of the case at this point?"

"You Internal Affairs now?"

"Why would you think that?"

Wayne shrugged.

"What's the disposition of the case?" Westermann asked again.

Westermann watched Wayne's face as the sergeant went through the mental process, figuring out if Westermann had jurisdiction, what kind of trouble he would be bringing on himself if he stonewalled. Westermann wondered what he would do if Wayne *did* stonewall. But Wayne was forthcoming.

"Nothing to do. Couple of interviews, best they could say was assault by a group of Caucasians, didn't see faces, no thoughts on suspects. Didn't see much prospect, no reason to waste manpower."

"This was a series of assaults, correct?"

"If you say so."

Westerman saw rats behind Wayne, picking at something hidden behind a stack of unused beams. A siren came from the street. Westermann kept his voice even, a benign blankness to his face. "You're not doing yourself any favors, making this difficult."

"Two, three assaults; you want to call that a series, you go ahead."

"You didn't stake the place out a couple of nights?"

"For a couple of assaults?" Wayne was genuinely incredulous at the suggestion.

"Look, we both know that the vics were passing out propaganda for the Community. These assaults were political intimidation; a little more important than a couple of random beatings."

Wayne focused his eyes on Westermann's. "What're you, Red on top of everything else?" White spittle beaded in both corners of his mouth. "You want the society of the future to go with your policing of the future?"

Westermann stared back at Wayne, willing himself to be placid; unsettle Wayne by not rising to the bait.

"So the extent of your work was . . ."

Wayne raised his voice and his words came echoing back. "Interviewing the vics. I determined it was a lost cause, moved on, saved manpower. That's by the book."

Like many disingenuous arguments, this was, on its face, defensible. Wayne returned to gazing over Westermann's shoulder, looking pleased with himself.

"So if there's a complaint that you didn't follow up on these two cases, it would be accurate."

Wayne answered aggressively, punctuating his points with finger jabs in the air. "Lieutenant, I don't know how much clearer I can be. I determined they were loser cases. Could I have staked it out? Maybe. Maybe we'd get lucky and the perps would come back to the same place and jump some more Negroes. But, to be honest, there are other fish to fry out there and this ranks pretty fucking low in my book. You have a problem with that, take it up with the Kraatjes or the Chief. But, even if they don't agree with what I did, they'll see it's not unreasonable. You see it, too. I can tell."

Westermann had nothing to say to that.

Wayne said, "Is there anything else?" Sounding as if the battle were won.

Westermann shook his head.

"Then I'll get back to work." Wayne walked past Westermann toward the fire stairs, his steps scraping and echoing on the silent floor. Westermann watched him strut, his body soft in the middle, but hard in the shoulders and neck. Wayne paused at the doorway, giving Westermann the half-lid tough-guy look. "You are Red, aren't you? A commie symp. Jesus."

Westermann stared hard. "You'll lose, you mess with me."

"That don't sound like a denial to me," Wayne said, smirking, and left.

Deyna's cameraman shooting him with Mel Washington.

Westermann stood alone on the empty floor, trembling with anger and anxiety.

*　　*　　*

Later, Kraatjes made his way through the squad room like a prince among the paupers, making quick, concentrated comments in response to some remark or other, but nothing holding his attention or getting a longer response.

Westermann stepped out of his office when it became apparent that Kraatjes was there to talk with him. Kraatjes put his arm around Westermann and steered him back into the office, shutting the door behind them. Westermann braced himself for the fallout from the newspaper article.

Kraatjes seemed to sense this anxiety, probably the stiffness in Westermann's posture. "Take it easy, Piet."

Westermann exhaled, pulling away from Kraatjes so that he could face him. "What's the story?"

"No one's happy about the *Gazette* piece, but you could have guessed that, right?"

Westermann nodded, his stomach knotting.

"People aren't happy, but, fortunately for you—for us—the incident took place before you met with the Chief."

"Fortunately," Westermann echoed softly.

"But, Piet, this means we are on very thin ice. Very thin."

"Right."

Kraatjes studied Westermann for a moment. "Okay, the other reason I'm here is that the Uhuru Community storefront, down on Penrose?"

"Yeah, I know it."

"Somebody tossed it last night."

Westermann shook his head. "Really?" Suddenly paranoid about Kraatjes coming to him with this, thinking about Wayne's parting shots and the connection between the *Gazette*'s implication of anti-Christian leanings and his association with communists.

"Thing was, someone picked the lock. Not your usual vandals."

"Okay." Westermann searched Kraatjes eyes.

"Thought you might want to know, what with you working those girls they found on the riverbank. The Community connection, you see."

"Thanks."

"Rolle and Vidic picked it up. In case you want to stay up on it."

"Okay," Westermann said, trying to read Kraatjes's ulterior motives, but seeing only the man doing his job, keeping the right people in the loop. He and Kraatjes were close, too, as much as men with their difference in rank could be. No way he'd be feeling Westermann out. No way.

Kraatjes strolled out, pausing briefly to exchange a few words with a detective new to the force about something, then leaving altogether.

Westermann paced his office, thinking he should get in touch with Washington, find out what the hell was happening. He walked to his window, looking out on the busy block, cruisers parked on the curb, cops in and out of uniform, frail indigents hoping that proximity with police headquarters would deliver safety.

On second thought, though, Westermann decided maybe he better not contact Washington. His attention was caught by a conversation on the street—two men talking intently.

Deyna and Wayne.

49.

Morphy and Grip were back in the prowl car. The old man across the hall from Vesterhue had been a dead end.

Grip aped him in a geezer voice as they drove, "'Many times he's entertained ladies of the night. These here walls aren't thick...'" Letting the phrase hang there the way the old-timer had.

Morphy grinned at this and responded, mimicking Grip but exaggerating his officious tone, "'Sir, would you be able to identify any of these women if we showed you pictures?'"

Grip-as-geezer: "'Son, you think I stand at my door peeping through my spy-hole all day?'"

Both laughed as they recalled the old man catching Morphy's smile and kicking them both out of his apartment. Their laughter died down, and as they drove, Morphy eyed Grip's brooding again.

"There a problem?"

Grip looked over at him. "No. No problem."

Morphy spit out a disdainful laugh. They both knew there was *some* kind of problem.

"All right. Fuck. Look, you remember that weird skull that's painted on the door at Crippen's?"

"Skull with a top hat?"

"That's the one. This morning, I open my door and there's the same fucking thing. On my door."

Morphy's eyebrows went up. "Really?"

"'Really?'" Grip said, mimicking the tone. "The fuck you think?"

"Front door of your building, isn't it usually locked?"

"Yes. Always. And better yet, how the fuck does whoever it is know where I live? And why did they paint that goddamn thing on my door?"

"That's strange."

"That's one word for it," Grip said sullenly, thinking about his strange dream; about the man who might or might not have been in his room; about the symbols and murals in the Uhuru Community and that feeling he'd had trying to leave.

50.

Frings waited for Westermann on the roof of his building, hoping to catch a breeze eight floors above the street. Someone had left chairs up there, weather-beaten now, and Frings sat with his feet propped on the raised ledge that ran about the roof's perimeter. He smoked a reefer, letting the tension run from his body, and soothed his throat with beer from a sweating can. The sun was a low red ball over the artificial horizon of silhouetted high-rises to the west. From the east came the rhythmic pounding of bridge supports being driven into the ground. Iron on steel. Again and again and again and again . . .

Renate had returned, not that he'd actually seen her—only evidence: wet towel on the bathroom doorknob; cigarette butts—her cigarette butts—in the ashtray; her smell hanging in every room. She'd be back tonight, he knew. That's the way it worked with her. Whatever it was she'd gotten into, it was over. He was glad that she'd be around again because he liked it better with her around.

Frings had noticed that the theater across the street was screening something called *I Married a Communist*, Robert Ryan and some bird locked in an embrace, the bird looking away with an unreadable look, making it unclear what she thought about being married to a Red: scared, resigned, brainwashed. Tagline: *Her beauty served a mob of terror whose one mission is to destroy!* Next to the movie poster, three for Truffant, stacked one above the other.

The utility door behind him creaked on its hinges and Frings, without turning, raised a hand to Westermann.

"Grab that chair."

Westermann twisted the cap off the cone-top can Frings had brought up for him. Frings studied Westermann's face: tight, stressed, the accumulation of deception and pressure getting to him.

"You going to make it?"

Frings had to wait for a beat while Westermann finished a pull on his beer.

"Yeah. We're making progress but I don't know if we're getting very close to figuring anything out. One thing I can tell you, though, it's not a normal dead-pross case. Too much background noise pulling in too many directions."

"Background noise?"

"Yeah. Other things brought into play."

"Like a second body."

Westermann froze with his beer almost to his lips.

"What'd you think, I wouldn't find out?"

Westermann took a pull off his beer, looking past Frings to the indigo skyline.

"What were you thinking, Piet?"

"I've been wondering that myself."

Frings shook his head softly. "This changes things."

"I know."

"Why?"

Westermann shrugged.

"Damn it." Frings seethed with the realization that Westermann's holding back had simply been out of petulance. Frings sighed hard. "Okay. So where are we?"

Westermann kept Frings's eye, feeling defiant, but cornered. He told Frings about the second girl—where she was found, the sores, the different cause of death.

Frings stopped him. "Why?"

"Why what?"

"Why kill a second girl and put her in the same place? What's the point?"

"That's the question."

"You think it's a matter of convenience, this gink kills them close to home or at his drinking spot or whatever?"

Westermann frowned, as unconvinced as Frings about this line of reasoning.

"Because," Frings continued, "it seems to me like the person that did this is trying, specifically, to tie these murders to the Community."

"And since it would be stupid for someone actually in the Community—"

"Right. Either that or maybe a copycat."

"But who knew about the original location of the first body?"

Frings nodded, conceding the point. "What else?"

Westermann filled him in on Godtown—though not about the pressure from the mayor—the pamphlets found in the apartments; the connection with Vesterhue.

"You did a story on Maddox, right?" Westermann asked.

It smelled like hot tar up on the roof. The fumes made Frings light-headed on top of the reefer. "The paper did, not me per se."

"You know about him, though?"

"Preacher out in the sticks until six or seven years ago. One of our reporters—can't remember who now—went out there. Fort Deposit, I think. I took a piece of it; a couple of interviews to flesh the story out. Anyway, this reporter says he poked around a little, talked with the people at his old church. The thing he played up was the snake handling—'serpents' they called them. I remember the guy—O'Hare, now that I think about it—saying the snakes were pretty tired, no life in them. We didn't play that part up in the story. Drinking strychnine was another thing. But the reality, O'Hare said, was that this was a detail, that the services were long: music, testifying, speaking in tongues. A real experience."

"But he's in the City now."

"Yeah, well, there's a story there, but I'm not sure that I know it. You know, they're not playing with snakes here. He's gone a different direction. You caught one of his sermons?"

Westermann shook his head.

"End-of-the-world stuff. Not what he was doing out in the sticks. Not sure what caused the change, but there you go."

Westermann flashed to knocking on Mary Little's door in Godtown and her reaction to him—maybe not panic, maybe terror. "You got another beer?" Westermann asked, trying to reestablish their partnership.

Frings returned to find Westermann watching the traffic below, so absorbed in his thoughts that Frings had to touch him with a beer can to get his attention. Frings sat down again, but Westermann stayed leaning against the ledge, legs crossed but not relaxed.

"You get anywhere with Womé's complaint?"

Westermann nodded. "What he says is basically true."

Frings frowned.

"I don't need to tell you that the force's manpower doesn't . . ."

"Doesn't allow you to investigate every reported crime to the fullest extent, et cetera, et cetera. I know the line."

"So, that's basically what happened here. A couple of assaults, no suspects . . ."

"Negro vics."

"Frank."

"Communists."

"Come on, Frank, that's not—"

"So this cop—we'll get to that in a minute—this cop takes a look, doesn't like the reward he's going to get for his work, and drops it."

"He'd say he didn't want to tie up resources in an investigation without prospects."

"What? Are you trying to defend this son of a bitch? Look, Piet, there just aren't assaults around the Community. Ever. There's hardly any crime at all. You know that. Call it self-policing, call it failure to report, call it one of the safest places in the goddamn City; but you get two, three assaults and the force doesn't feel the need to follow up; doesn't see it as something new, something they might want to get a handle on?"

"Like two dead prostitutes?"

"Yeah, actually. There's been a lot of violence in the Community, lately."

Westermann nodded. "Frank, I'm telling you what I heard."

Frings settled a bit. "This cop who took the calls, he okay?"

Westermann didn't answer, looking at his shoes.

"He dirty?"

"I didn't say that. He's got a rep."

"A rep like maybe he'd sit on this case."

Westermann shrugged. "There're a lot of guys heavily into anticommunism on the force. He's one of them."

Frings shook his head, angry. "What the hell do you guys think about, putting a cop like that on a Community case? This cop, he got a name?"

Westermann gave him a pleading look.

"What? You want to protect this gink? Is this some kind of cops-covering-for-cops thing? You've already fucked with me once. My patience is wearing thin."

"Your patience is wearing thin? You don't have a fucking photo in the newspaper, being called an anti-Christian bigot."

"That's out of my hands. He got his way, he'd have run shots of you with Mel and Warren by the shanties; you and one of your guys working over some gink in a cowboy costume. Rogue cop. Commie rogue cop. I had to talk them out of that."

"You need to get Art Deyna out of the picture."

"What? Have him done?"

"Don't be an asshole, Frank."

Frings laughed cynically. "I don't see how I can make that happen."

Westermann stood. "I've got to go."

Frings smiled. "You owe me something first."

Westermann raised his eyebrows.

"The cop. The name of the cop who took the Uhuru Community calls."

Westermann looked skyward, a few stars beating the ambient light from the City. "Ed Wayne."

"Wayne?"

Westermann nodded.

"Don't you feel much better now," Frings said, and drained the rest of his beer.

Westermann took a pull off his beer. "Now that you know his name, you should probably know a couple of other things."

"Okay."

"I saw him talking with your buddy Art Deyna."

Frings shook his head, sucked in his lips. He could see the look in Westermann's face, the cruel relief to be sharing some of the pressure.

Westermann said, "And Wayne found the second girl."

Shit.

51.

"You ever seen anything like this?" Grip asked, voice low, thinking that it might echo on the empty street.

Morphy shook his head. They were on the first block of Godtown, looking down its length; nobody on the streets. Both men did scans, trying to pick up something in the shadows where the illumination waned between streetlights, wondering what was going on. You could find deserted streets such as this at night in some of the warehouse districts or, of course, in the abandoned blocks of the Hollows. But a residential neighborhood? The row houses all had lights on, but no silhouettes were in the windows.

"What do you think?"

Morphy shrugged, wary. "Let's knock on some doors."

They began where Westermann had started days earlier, where Mary Little had panicked. Their footsteps echoed, bringing the emptiness of the streets into relief. Indoor lights backlit strawberry-print curtains. Grip banged the door and they waited. He banged again and said, "Police," his voice unnervingly loud on the quiet street. Morphy looked back over his shoulder, despite himself. Still nothing from inside.

"Next one," Morphy said, and climbed down from the stoop. They repeated this routine on the next two houses with the same result.

Morphy said, "You figure they're not answering the door or there's just no one home tonight?"

"I don't think there's anyone in there." Grip usually got a feeling when someone was on the other side of the wall, willing the police away. He wasn't getting it now. They stood on the third stoop and looked out over the block, trying to get a handle on the situation. Grip couldn't shake the sense that he was seeing something moving about in the shadows. But it was like something in his peripheral vision that disappeared when he turned his head toward it.

Grip was about to say that maybe they should move down to the next block and start again, then he saw Morphy go tense.

"What?" Grip whispered.

"Next block, about a third of the way down, opposite side."

Grip found the spot and squinted and damned if there wasn't someone standing in the shadows, not really hiding but not standing in plain sight either. Just watching.

"Jesus," Grip said, then, recovering, "Okay," but Morphy was already down the steps and halfway across the street.

They approached the man from opposite sides of the street, both detectives fingering their pistol grips. When they were within thirty yards, the man stepped forward into the light. Both police drew in response to the sudden movement.

Grip recognized Ole Koss. Koss was in suit pants and a blue, open-collared shirt, his hands out from his sides, empty palms facing the cops.

"Shit," Grip said. "What are you doing out here, Ole? The fuck is everybody?" Then to Morphy: "It's okay, I know him."

Grip noticed that Morphy kept his hand by his gun.

"What are *you* doing here?" Koss asked; his voice cold.

"Police shit," Grip said. "Where is everybody?"

"Service."

"Church?"

Koss nodded. "Every night."

"Every night?" Grip asked, shooting Morphy a can-you-believe-this-shit look. He noticed Morphy's physical confidence wasn't quite there, maybe shaken a little by Koss, bigger than Morphy and holding himself as if he knew what to do if things went south.

Koss said, "Just about." He kept looking away from Morphy and Grip, eyes darting up and down the street.

Morphy said, "You. What are you doing?"

"Keeping an eye on the place."

Grip said, "With everyone at church?"

"That's right."

"You got a piece?" Morphy asked.

Koss shook his head.

Grip said, "Jesus, Ole, it's weird you hanging in the shadows. You ever catch anyone? Anybody ever come here?"

"Not often, anymore." Koss turned suddenly, as if something in the shadows had caught his eye. He turned back.

Grip gave him a second to explain and, when he didn't, said, "All right. We're just going to do a walk around." They started to move off.

Koss shrugged. "The street's public."

Grip stopped. "Opposed to what?"

"Houses. The church."

"The fuck's that supposed to mean?" Grip asked, not liking Ole taking that tone with him in front of Morphy. They were cops for chrissake.

Koss shrugged. "Nothing you ain't already heard."

Grip gave him a hard look, angry now. "There something you want to say?"

Koss returned the stare, not aggressive but not backing down. Grip would have to make the first move.

Morphy put his hand on Grip's shoulder. "We've wasted enough time with your friend."

Grip kept the stare going for a few more seconds before breaking away.

Halfway down the next block they began to hear the noise, not identifiable at first, but as they approached the church, it became clear that it was singing coming from inside. On the empty street with its unpredictable echoes, the singing seemed to come from everywhere, like the voices of hundreds— men, women, and children—rising and falling together. A hymn. Grip recognized the tune but didn't know the words. He looked over at Morphy, who stood with his eyes closed, his face turned up slightly, letting the sound wash over him.

Grip waited him out. Morphy eventually opened his eyes and, without a word, scanned the street, looking for Koss. But they were alone.

As they walked to their prowl car, Grip said, "Unusual for you, the lieut giving you a night detail."

Morphy shrugged. "I'm sure he has his reasons."

52.

Westermann lay naked in Morphy's bed, Jane Morphy next to him, drinking from a glass of water.

"You don't have him off somewhere dangerous tonight, do you?"

The question made Westermann uncomfortable and he found himself looking around the room for his discarded clothes. "Of course not. Just a nighttime walk-through in Godtown. Safest place in the City, if you look at the stats."

"Which you do."

"Which I do."

"The reason I asked is that it probably wouldn't look too good if something happened to him while you're carrying on with his wife; you sending him out so you can make time for yourself."

She was needling him and he tried to let it roll off his back, but couldn't manage it entirely. He didn't feel like talking, but she kept at it.

"If you don't mind my asking, why are you doing a walk-through of our safest neighborhood?"

"Long story, but they're not being helpful with an investigation."

"An investigation? I thought you said it was safe."

"Might be peripheral, we don't know yet."

"So, what, they don't want you poking around in their church?"

"Something like that," Westermann said, feeling uncomfortable making pillow talk with Morphy's wife while he, Morphy, was out on the beat.

"You know, it might have to do with them not wanting you in their affairs, more than having a problem with the investigation, as such."

"I'm not sure I see a distinction."

"Well, you might not have been brought up religious, but I was. Some people, they like to make a real fine separation between their church and the rest of the world. They don't like the rest of the world leaking into their church community, no matter if they don't have anything to hide. They think it's like an infection."

Westermann nodded, rolling out of bed, going for his clothes. "Well, that's fine, but I still have to conduct this investigation and I need some cooperation from them."

"I'm just . . . I just thought maybe you wouldn't know."

"Okay," he said, pulling on his pants, needing to get out of there; trying not to imagine Morphy's footsteps on the stoop outside.

Jane sat up in bed, exposing her breasts to Westermann, and lit a cigarette.

"Are you in love with me, Piet?"

Westermann grunted something noncommittal.

Jane ignored his nonanswer, talking dreamily. "Men, I don't know what it is, but they all fall in love with me. Larry, of course, and you. You do love me, right, Piet?"

Westermann didn't speak. Jane, as she so often managed, had the edge on him.

"Larry says that Tor Grip only visits whores with red hair. He says, 'What do you think of that?' And I say, 'What do you think? He wants me, he finds whores that remind him of me.'"

Westermann, feeling cruel, said, "But he's not man enough for the real thing?"

Jane laughed. "Man enough? Oh, he's man enough. You're man enough. But neither one of you is the man that Larry is. He's out of your league. No, Tor is smart and he's not going to kick the hornets' nest just to prove that he can. He knows his way in this world. You don't, so you kick the nest to find out what might happen."

53.

Winston sat in the deep shadows beneath a wall whose original purpose wasn't entirely clear. Across the road lay the expanse of open ground up-river from the Uhuru Community; an expanse marked by the low silhouettes of weeds and shrubs and, farther on, rocks that had been built up on the riverbank as protection from the occasional floods.

Winston looked to each side, spying a half dozen or so other faintly sketched human forms, knowing that there were others that he couldn't see. He was in the minority—both among this group and in the Community as a whole—in that he wasn't from the Caribbean islands. He was from the South and had moved North, under the vague impression that his lot in life would improve with each northward step. His disappointment had come in realizing that the increments by which his life improved were very small. And this had led him to the Community, where he had found, well, a community that was not dependent on the tolerance of whites.

He flexed his fingers, reminding himself to be careful with his hands. He'd been in plenty of scraps when he was younger where he'd hurt his hands and ended up playing slide for a couple of weeks until his fingers could move freely again. Now he was a little more careful. Maybe this was what happened as you got older and wiser, or maybe it was just the steady paycheck he'd been getting from Cephus and, starting tomorrow night, from Floyd Christian over at the Palace. Anyway, he was starting to put together a little chunk of money and didn't want to ball it up by breaking his fist on some crazy ofay's head.

Another hour passed and he felt himself getting sleepy, his mind wandering to his life down South; memories coming to him as abstractions of rage, sadness, and, mostly, fear. This reverie was interrupted by a shrill whistle and a surge of adrenaline. In the open space he saw the silhouettes of two men and a woman walking in the direction of the Community, gaits stiff with tension. A block and a half away, headlights approached at a crawl.

Winston adjusted the stick in his hand, getting his grip tight and comfortable.

The car entered his block and rolled past, less than a dozen yards from him. He watched the car move beyond the group walking in the open space and then stop, the occupants now in position to cut the walkers off from the shanties. Winston watched as four men emerged from the car, holding things—bats, tire irons. The men moved at a trot on a course to intercept the walkers if they tried to make a run for the shanties. Winston's pulse pounded, blood pumped in his ears, eyes wide and unblinking.

The guy giving the signals waited until the men were too far away to get back to their car, then whistled again. Winston charged, sprinting along with a dozen other men. It was surprisingly quiet, this violent rush; just the slapping of feet on pavement. But it was enough to get the attention of the men from the car and they froze, looking in Winston's direction. Then they scattered, running in panic.

In some kind of instinctive division of forces, the Community men split up to chase the men from the car, who had, wisely, run in different directions to avoid being caught together. Winston sprinted after a guy, medium height, a little overweight, carrying a tire iron. He was surprised by how nimble the guy was, really moving. But Winston was fast, too, and the overweight guy tired quickly, eventually turning on Winston with his tire iron up, trying to get in a surprise shot. Winston was ready, though, and brought his stick up hard onto the man's forearm and he dropped the iron, let out a yelp, grabbed at his arm. Probably broken. Winston cracked him across the knees with the stick and the man went down; not fighting back, going fetal and covering his head with his good arm.

Winston caught a blur in his peripheral vision as a kid whose name he didn't know brought a bat down into the prone guy's ribs. Winston gave him a couple of shots to the spine and then lost his heart for it. No satisfaction in beating a man when he was down; reduced you to his level. The kid gave the guy a good kick in the face and Winston put a hand gently on the kid's chest. The kid accepted this and backed away, gasping for air.

The guy was unconscious and bleeding a little from the mouth. Winston and the kid each grabbed an arm and dragged him back to where the Community posse was assembling by the road. Reaching them, they laid the man out next to his three unconscious companions, lined up in a row like sardines by the street. The men talked in their Caribbean patois, but were more somber than boastful. This was work, not sport.

Something up the street caught the men's attention, and Winston looked to see another set of headlights several blocks away, creeping in their direction. The men backed a few feet away from the bodies, forming a semicircle around them. The car decelerated gradually as it approached and came to a stop next to the bodies—a black Rolls. The window rolled down and behind it was Father Womé, wearing a homburg. He looked at the bodies, frowning thoughtfully, then up at the assembled men. He nodded to them, turned to face forward, and the window rolled up again.

54.

Grip arrived at Crippen's around midnight, carrying his sweat-wilted jacket over his shoulder. The streets in this part of town were mostly deserted tonight. People were just too goddamn exhausted, Grip thought. Himself included. He'd grabbed a shot and a beer with Morphy at a dive on the edge of the Hollows, fending off the local working girls and trying to shake the weird sensation lingering from the empty streets of Godtown; the strangeness brought into relief now by what empty streets really felt like: not *really* empty, not *really* quiet. But Godtown, if there were crickets in that part of the City, you would have heard them tonight.

Whatever attempt had been made to clean the skull-and-top-hat graffiti from Crippen's door had been largely unsuccessful, and it stared back at Grip as he approached the door. The bar was nearly empty, just a couple of old-timers with crew cuts sitting at one table and a geek named Reinholdt—or something like that—talking with the bartender, waving his free hand about while cupping his beer like the Holy Grail itself.

Grip nodded to the old-timers, wondered if Reinholdt would come over to him if he sat alone at a table, and decided that if Reinholdt did, he would just drink up and leave. Grip was exhausted, probably wouldn't have even come here if he'd given it any thought.

He threw his jacket over a chair and sat down in another, resting his forearms on the table. He looked over to the bartender and was a little annoyed when the guy waved him over. Grip shot him a pissed-off look, but the bartender persisted and Grip hauled his ass out of the chair and over to the bar. At the bar, he stood with his back to Reinholdt, cutting him out of the conversation.

The bartender looked at Reinholdt and then at the old-timers, who had stopped their conversation and were watching Grip.

"This afternoon I come in to open the bar, yeah? Door's locked, same fuckin' skull shit on the front, couldn't get it off yesterday. So I come in—

door's locked right, have to open it with my key—and guess what I find on the bar, set up so it's greeting me?"

Grip held his hands up, how could he possibly know?

The bartender stepped aside and gestured with his hand as if he were a magician introducing his assistant. Behind him, on the back bar, was arranged a shot glass filled with something amber—maybe whiskey—in front of a pair of dark sunglasses against which leaned, pointing forward, three black feathers. A half dozen human teeth were arranged in a semicircle in front of the shot glass.

"The hell's that?" Grip asked.

Reinholdt started laughing, a little too loud.

The bartender shrugged. "That's it. Don't know what it means, yeah? Who put it here, how they got in. None of it."

"Who else has a key?"

"Owner upstairs. I talked to him. He don't know anything."

"You think the guy who painted the skull?"

The bartender shrugged again, finding this amusing; Grip not sure that he should. "That'd be my guess."

Grip decided to have a shot along with his beer.

Grip ended up having several shots and several beers. He'd felt his thinking go fuzzy and his stress grow, and, therefore, his anger, until he finally snapped and pushed the yammering Reinholdt so hard that the geek flipped off his chair and fell into an empty table. He stood up moaning something about his ribs. The bartender sent them both home, making Grip wait ten minutes so that Reinholdt could get good and clear.

Grip made his unsteady way home, wishing he would come upon Reinholdt; feeling as if a good workout with his fists would restore some normalcy to his life, cleanse his psyche. But Reinholdt's place wasn't on his route home. He found himself on his own block, surprised in that he didn't recall parts of the trip, as if he somehow managed to skip five blocks. An elderly Asian couple walked on his side of the street, as they often did at early hours of the morning. Beyond them, and across the street, a Negro man stood beneath a streetlight. Grip saw him with great clarity: very dark skin, skinny, wearing a thin white shirt unbuttoned to his stomach, threadbare pants, and some sort of sandals. His face had wide cheekbones above sunken cheeks, and large eyes, whites showing all the way around the pupils. *Fuck.* Grip recognized the guy who'd looked in at Wayne, Koss, and himself at the Uhuru Community headquarters. Him again.

Grip shuffled to the door of his building and the man still stood there, maybe thirty yards away, maybe watching Grip. Grip froze at his door, not sure of his next step, his back tense, some instinct telling him not to go over to the Negro, not to pound him into the sidewalk. Without warning, the man turned and walked away with a strange, jangly-limbed gait, as if he were a marionette. Grip had never seen anyone move like that and he stared, transfixed and troubled.

55.

The next morning arrived with storm clouds that left the impression of night, but a night seared with violent slashes of lightning. The storm provided little relief at police headquarters, where the windows were pulled shut against sheets of wind-driven rain and the hot air stagnated, cigarette smoke rising slowly to the ceiling.

Westermann drank stale coffee at his desk, looking over the report from Pulyatkin, the coroner: no matches on fingerprints or dental from Lenore; no John Does matching Vesterhue's description; no progress on the second girl's identity. This on top of the fruitless phone canvass of hospitals. Further, a note from Kraatjes: *Night walk in Godtown?*

The shift was arriving; Souza and Plouffe dragging in, looking put out, their pants soaked where the wind had blown the rain past their umbrellas.

Westermann decided that there was no point in delaying the inevitable and took the stairs to the fifth floor and Kraatjes's modest corner office. Rain rocketed against Kraatjes's windows like buckshot. Kraatjes's eyes were as dark as the weather.

"The Chief got a call this morning."

Westermann exhaled loudly. "The mayor?"

"You want to explain why you had Morphy and Grip, of all people, doing a night walk through Godtown?"

Westermann was expecting the question and he'd thought about the answer, deciding to keep it theoretical, try to avoid the specifics.

"Let me ask you a question first," he said. "This case, two dead prostitutes, just a first name on one and nothing on the second; but two things: One is that they've both got some kind of disease the doctors can't seem to get a handle on. The other—and this is the one that's interesting—is that at least one of them's connected to two parts of town that as far as our stats go, there isn't any crime. Ever. So, I figure there's two things here: Why aren't there any crimes reported in these two neighborhoods, and why is this crime connected to both of these places?"

Kraatjes nodded, pulling off his glasses and wiping them with the front of his shirt. He didn't say anything, but Westermann knew the implied question.

"Why isn't there any crime in Godtown? Prosper Maddox says he doesn't want the police canvassing his neighborhood because his people aren't worldly enough to answer our questions."

Kraatjes coughed. "That might not be the correct interpretation."

Westermann frowned. "Even if it isn't, a place like that: no B and E, no street robbery? Come on. And then, last night, no one's even in their houses. The whole goddamn neighborhood is empty except for Maddox's man. It's begging to be looted."

"Maddox's man. You mean Ole Koss?"

"Right. You see the point?"

Kraatjes nodded, looking thoughtful. "But, in the end, what did you accomplish?"

"I'm still working on it."

"Working on it," Kraatjes sighed. "Piet, we talked yesterday. I gave you a pass on the newspaper piece because I hadn't told you to lay off Maddox, yet. But you were in the *Gazette*, and I know you were in the right and just doing your job, but the photo and the article—they weren't helpful. If it wasn't you, Piet, the Chief wouldn't be so . . . charitable. But, after we talk, sending goddamn Grip and Morphy that same night? That's reckless, Piet. Reckless."

"Tell me you think there's nothing strange there; no reason to look into Godtown."

"I don't dispute it. But, you know the connection is weak and the situation that you're putting the Chief in with the mayor."

"But the Chief said he would interfere—"

"Okay, Piet. Okay. But for God's sake, do us—do yourself—a favor and at least make it look like you don't have some kind of bee in your bonnet about Maddox. Show the mayor you're working other angles."

Bee in your bonnet? "Okay."

Kraatjes apparently didn't sense enough conviction in Westermann's answer. "Listen, we are cutting you a remarkable amount of slack. For your sake and the sake of the people who are putting their necks out for you, don't ball this up. And for God's sake, don't send Grip and Morphy to handle anything requiring tact."

Westermann nodded.

The rain outside had stopped.

56.

Grip leaned into Morphy as they approached the entrance to the Community shantytown. "There's something different. You feel it?"

"Feel what?" Steam was rising off the broken asphalt of the roads around the shanties, the traces of the morning's rain evaporating, the air becoming suffocating.

The answer was *Something different*, but Grip knew this sounded stupid and instead mumbled something about the noise. Now that he'd thought of it, there did seem to be more noise coming from the shanties. Nothing in particular, just more of the ambient shanty din; behind it, the whine of insects in the field, the giant whoosh of feathers as enormous turkey vultures dipped and then ascended again, waiting for something unseen in the weeds to die.

He'd put out word that morning that he needed to speak with Ed Wayne and was disconcerted to find that no one knew, exactly, where he was. Headquarters had instituted the usual protocol for cops missing-without-leave. Grip thought about the skull graffiti and the man with the funny walk. He'd feel better once he heard that Wayne had been tracked down.

As seemed always the case, Community kids were playing in the weeded lot outside the shanty entrance, their skin gleaming with perspiration as they ran in the heat. Grip pulled from his pocket a piece of paper with a rough copy of the skull-and-top-hat design. He pulled out a handful of dimes.

Morphy, as they'd planned, slipped inside the shantytown and stood by the entrance, notebook in hand, to delay anyone coming out. Grip shook the coins in his hand and smiled kindly as the kids forgot their game and gathered around him, wondering how they could get at the money. Grip didn't even have to ask; just showing his drawing got the kids going.

"Samedi. Baron Samedi."

Grip threw some dimes out. The kids muscled each other to catch them.

"Who's Baron Samedi?" Grip asked, jingling the dimes.

The kids looked at him as if they could hardly believe his ignorance.

One of the older ones, maybe ten years old, flashed a hopeful grin. "Samedi's a *lwa*. A spirit."

"Okay, a *lwa*. Sure. Why would someone paint him on a door?"

The kid shrugged. Grip tossed him several dimes.

The kid shifted them around in his open palm, counting. "Maybe Samedi is someone's *lwa*. Maybe somebody wants Samedi to visit the person behind the door."

"What do you mean?" Grip asked, tossing a few more dimes over, aware that he only had a few left.

"When Samedi visits you? I don't know. Is Samedi your *lwa*? If Samedi isn't your *lwa*, you don't want him to visit."

Grip tossed him the remaining dimes. "You know a man, kind of thin; not like me," Grip said, forcing a carefree chuckle of sorts. "Walks funny? Like a puppet?"

The kids looked among themselves, not really confused, just consulting. Finally the same kid said, "Could be anyone, any of the *lwas*."

"What do you mean, *lwa*?" Grip asked, but the kid was turning away from him, laughing. The kid threw some of his dimes up in the air, and his friends scrambled madly to pick them up where they lay, glistening in the sun, like tiny pools of water.

57.

Panos sat behind his big editor's desk, reading a memo, while he distractedly popped grapes into his mouth. Frings stood in the doorway and gave a stage cough to get Panos's attention. Panos didn't look up from the memo or stop eating grapes, but inclined his head toward the chair nearest the door. Frings was surprised to see Deyna in the next chair, smirking. Frings ignored him, grabbing a copy of the morning's *Gazette* off Panos's desk. He scanned the headlines, nothing out of the ordinary: City official on the take; citizens need to curb excess water use to ensure water supplies remain stable; school-bus accident, driver was drunk; etc. He felt Deyna's eyes on him.

Panos finally finished his memo and looked up at Frings. "Frank, Deyna here has done some reporting. You remember that, no? He's working sources, knocking on doors, all that. Tell him, Deyna, what you've found."

Deyna shifted his chair a little so he was almost turned to Frings. "They found a second body on the river; this one upriver from the first; right by the Uhuru Community."

Frings felt the two men watching him, waiting for a reaction. "Okay," he said slowly.

"The police are playing this close to the vest. Big pressure to keep it quiet."

"Why do you think that is?"

"You're the genius, Frings, why do you think?"

"You really want to know?"

Deyna stared at him, challenging.

Frings looked at Panos. "Should I tell him what I think?"

With a flourish of his hand, Panos told him to go on.

Frings turned to Deyna. "I think you're getting this bullshit from Ed Wayne."

Deyna's jaw dropped, but he recovered quickly. "Fuck you."

"Have some respect," Panos growled.

Deyna held his hand up in apology to Panos. "Sorry." To Frings, Deyna said, "I've—"

Frings cut him off. "You want to know something about your 'source'?" Frings turned to Panos. "Remember that story I pitched you about the assaults over by the Uhuru Community?"

Panos sighed. "How do I forget? This was two, three days ago."

"I've got some sources myself. Sources who aren't full of shit. One of these sources just called me, said he was on a two-ambulance call last night down by the Uhuru Community. Said there were four guys—white guys—beat up and laid out side by side, waiting to be picked up."

Deyna glared, but Frings saw that this was new to him.

"So I asked him, could these be the ginks who've been assaulting Negroes down by the Uhuru Community? Are they thugs?

"My guy said they've got those lumpy knuckles and that there were a couple of baseball bats and tire irons laid out next to them and a car at the scene with what he described as 'blunt instruments' in the backseat. Also, anticommunist leaflets and so on."

Panos said, "So these hooligans, they get their comeuppance? Is that the story? What's the punch line, Frank?"

Deyna continued the hard stare, but with maybe a little doubt creeping in; seeing where this was heading.

Frings smiled. "So my guy, he said it took a while, but he talked to some people, looked at some charts, and he's got the four names." Frings leaned back in his chair, laced his fingers behind his head.

"Get to the point," Deyna muttered.

Panos smiled, amused.

"Okay," Frings said, leaning forward again. "Three of the names, I don't recognize. But one . . . one is a gink by the name of Ed Wayne."

Panos's eyebrows went up.

Frings said to Panos, "Another thing Deyna might not know is that Wayne's got the Uhuru Community beat. There've been a couple of calls over the past two weeks—assault calls. Wayne sat on them."

Deyna said, "I've got a second source."

Frings shook his head. "You've got one source, maybe. Wayne's already shown his hostility to the Uhuru Community. You can't source anything to him."

Deyna looked at Panos.

Panos smiled and shrugged. "You've got the story. Finding another source, how hard can that be?"

Deyna stood. "Okay. Right." He paused to stare down at Frings. Frings saw the hate. Deyna closed the door quietly behind him.

Panos shook his head. "This kid, he's going to find another source, Frank. He's damn good. And when he finds that source, we'll run the story."

"Panos."

"We have to run the story. That way no one can say we are commie lovers when we go after Truffant. We sit on this story, nobody takes us seriously."

"You're going to sell out the Uhuru Community so we can write some nasty editorials about Truffant?"

Panos slammed his fist on the desk. "Damn it, Frank. Girls are being killed."

58.

Westermann drank coffee from a yellow-stained mug in Kostas' Diner in Praeger's Hill, the glass front plastered with anticommunist posters—head shots of Stalin and Mao over the single word VIGILANCE—and blue-and-red TRUFFANT FOR MAYOR signs. Across the booth from him was Nicky Patridis, a small-time crook carrying a rap sheet that included busts for burglary, fencing, pimping, assault, and the rest of the usual, depressing list. Patridis dripping sweat into the gray eggs and dry toast he was eating on Westermann's dime.

Westermann wiped his neck with a napkin. "Keeping your nose clean, Nicky?"

"Don't give me that shit," Nicky said, his mouth full of eggs. "What do you want? You buy me eggs, doesn't mean I've got to put up with this shit."

Westermann gave him a stare. Nicky was a true sociopath; no point in being reasonable with him because he didn't respond to reason. Only one calculation mattered to Nicky—how anything affected *him*. Even when he was cooperating, it was with an eye to his own gain. He was small and hairy and ugly, and Westermann supposed that during his life people had rarely been predisposed to liking him. Westermann hadn't been predisposed to liking Nicky the first time they had met, and nothing since then had changed his mind.

"Okay," Westermann said, pushing his coffee cup out of easy reach because the acid was eating into his stomach. "I'm trying to get a read on Godtown."

Nicky shrugged, took a bite of toast.

"You ever work anything around Godtown?"

Nicky held up a finger until he finished chewing. "Nobody works Godtown."

"Nobody works Godtown, Nicky? All those religious fanatics and nobody's interested? From what I hear, they spend most nights in church; nobody home. Can it get any easier for skeeves like you?"

Nicky waved his fork no, speaking with his mouth full. "You'd think so, but it doesn't work that way." He swallowed. "Word is that the place is buttoned up. Rudi Odeline and a couple of his boys took a crack at it, like maybe a year back, maybe two. Maddox has got some kind of security or something because it didn't work out so well for them. Anyway, word got around after that and nobody cases Godtown. It ain't worth the risk, if you see what I mean."

Westermann did see what he meant, thinking about Ole Koss. But he pushed Nicky anyway.

"I don't know, Nicky. Rudi Odeline getting scared off? It doesn't wash."

Nicky's eyes went wide with indignation. "Doesn't wash? Shit. You don't believe me, ask fucking Odeline. He'll tell you."

"You know where he is?"

"Of course. He's in that kraut fucking garage that he runs."

Westermann had been there before. Rudi Odeline was a successful entrepreneur in the City's underground economy, running an illegal book out of the garage office; probably stolen goods as well, though they'd never got the timing right on a bust.

Nicky's eyes strayed over Westermann's shoulder. Westermann turned and saw the waitress hovering a few feet back; dirty-blond hair, probably attractive if she got a decent night's sleep. Her bangs hung greasy in her face; her waitress uniform didn't fit.

Nicky leaned forward and whispered, "That broad can't keep her peepers off you."

Westermann shook his head, not wanting to get into it with Nicky about this.

"Jesus," Nicky said, "I had your looks, I'd be getting cooz all the time. You get a lot of cooz?"

Westermann tensed, uncomfortable, the conversation getting away from him. He didn't know how to talk with lowlifes like Nicky. Nicky was the dregs.

"No?" Nicky was wide-eyed. Westermann noticed with distaste a speck of congealed egg on the corner of Nicky's mouth.

"I'm not going to talk to you about this, Nicky."

"What, you a queer or something?"

"Don't push it." Westermann shook his head, took his cup of coffee, and poured what remained of it on Nicky's eggs.

"All right, all right. I'm making conversation here. Don't get all bent."

Westermann threw some bills on the table, pausing for a last glare at Nicky.

Nicky said, "Hey, what with you and me pals and all, you think your dad'd take me on pro bono if I get nicked?"

Westermann considered responding, then thought better of it. What would be the point?

At the door, Westermann turned around, saw Nicky back at his eggs, picking them out of the puddle of coffee and eating them as if all were right with the world. It was tough thing dealing with Nicky; he was too indifferent to stay intimidated. He snitched to Westermann out of a calculation that he'd get more out of the relationship than he would lose. Westermann kept reminding Nicky of exactly what he had to lose, but was under no illusions that he scared Nicky. Nicky just added the threats to his calculations and either snitched or, occasionally, didn't.

59.

City Hospital was a chaos of the suffering, the ill, and their anxious families. An unsettling din of pain and disease and succor oppressively droned. The heat amplified the misery; the place smelled of sweat and urine.

Frings pushed through crowds arrayed around the entrance, flashed his press pass at a security guard who was willing to admit anyone with the nerve to bluff him; passed through the double swinging doors into the sudden quiet of an actual ward. The hallway smelled of bleach and sweat and the yellow-tiled walls were damp with the humidity. Frings stopped an exhausted nurse with dark rings under her eyes and got directions to F ward, where Wayne was roomed.

He trotted down a hall, sliding by nurses and broad-shouldered orderlies; took a left turn into another hall, empty but for a couple of younger guys in suits, looking at a collection of pills one held in his hand. They watched Frings warily as he passed. He took another turn and found the elevator bank.

Fourth floor. A pair of nurses chatted behind a desk blocking the way from the elevator to F ward. They glanced briefly at Frings and went back to whatever it was that they were doing. He asked for Wayne's room and the younger of the two jerked a thumb down the hall and said to look for the room with the cops outside. Frings had hoped to beat the cops to Wayne, when he might have had a chance to get Wayne to talk. With other cops around, there was no way. Defeat.

Frings found an alley in the working-class neighborhood, away from where kids in sleeveless undershirts threw a ragged baseball and women talked, the short sleeves of their dresses rolled up to their shoulders, hair pinned up, necks exposed to whatever wind blew through the streets. He found a reefer in his jacket pocket and lit it with a match scraped across the sole of his shoe. The smoke tasted green and alive, and Frings waited for his frustrations to melt away.

Minutes passed. His body relaxed. Frings looked down with mild surprise to see that he still held the lit reefer. He stubbed the cherry on the brick wall and dropped what remained into the inside pocket of his jacket. He left the alley, a destination in mind but in no real hurry. A couple of calls to the *Gazette* had given him Wayne's home address, and he'd written the man a short note, letting Wayne know that he'd been pegged for the Uhuru Community assaults.

Frings walked with his hands in his pockets, taking in the scene on the street, the voices coming from open windows. Two hoods sat on a stoop, talking at high volume and petting a thick-necked dog with a chain collar. A half dozen girls—somewhere in their teens—stood in an entranceway, gossiping and laughing. An old man sat in a wheelchair at the top of a stoop, watching the street, expressionless.

Wayne's building was on a nice enough block, modest apartment buildings on either side of the street. The door to Wayne's building was locked and Frings didn't see anyone inside. Several dozen blackbirds perched on an electrical wire overhead and screamed at the sky.

Frings lit a cigarette and walked west until he found a florist. He bought a five-dollar bouquet and walked back to Wayne's building. He had to wait for fifteen minutes before an elderly woman pushing a small cart filled with groceries approached the door.

Frings pulled a slip of paper with Wayne's address on it out of his pocket and put on his best smile. "Excuse me, ma'am. Does Sergeant Ed Wayne live in this building?"

The old woman was frail, her back stooped. She narrowed her eyes. "Sergeant Wayne?"

"That's right." Frings made a show of studying the slip of paper. "This is the address they gave me. Policemen's Beneficent League, sending flowers, what with Sergeant Wayne in the hospital."

"In the hospital?" The woman seemed unimpressed.

"Assaulted in the line of duty, I hear."

She nodded. "That's too bad, I suppose. Not the best of the tenants, Sergeant Wayne. But that's a bad business." She took a set of keys from her purse. Frings held the door for her as she pushed her cart past the threshold.

"Much obliged," Frings said.

The woman retreated down the hall, shaking her head and making a tutting sound.

The lobby was clean and well lit, if modest. Wayne's apartment was on the fourth of six floors, and Frings took the stairs. He heard dogs growling behind the door on the third-floor landing, took the remaining stairs two at a time.

Two doors were set into each side of the short hall on the fourth floor. Frings found Wayne's door and paused, staring at some kind of marking on the door—a skull under a top hat. He thought of the paintings in the shanties and registered the dissonance of this symbol on Wayne's door. Or maybe it had been put there by somebody else, raising different, unsettling questions.

He reached out to touch the graffiti, stopped himself for no real reason, and then, as he had originally come here to do, stooped to slide the note through the crack under the door. He was surprised to hear the sound of a radio inside, and footsteps. Frings stood. He hadn't even considered that Wayne might be married, that someone else might be home. He pocketed his note and knocked.

The door was answered by a woman, cute face in a round sort of way, her hair tied back in a scarf, shabby summer dress that fit a little too tight, as if she'd bought it ten pounds ago. She looked tired and Frings thought that maybe she hadn't slept that night, waiting for her husband to return.

"Can I help you?"

He smiled. "My name is Frank Frings. With the *Gazette*." He handed her the flowers.

"I've heard of you," she said, brightening a little and taking the flowers.

"Your husband's fine," Frings assured her. "Has he been in touch with you?"

"He's at the hospital. But you probably know that."

"That's right. I'm very sorry that it happened. I'm glad that he'll be okay." He held her eyes. "Listen, it would be great for me to get a chance to speak with him. I just need to get his perspective on a couple of things; make sure he gets *his* story out."

"What story?" She wasn't suspicious, just curious.

"I'd rather wait to talk to him," Frings said, flashing an apologetic smile. "I'd be obliged if you'd give him this note."

She took the note and looked at it, turning it over, but not opening it. "Okay."

"I appreciate that." He turned to leave.

She laughed a little self-consciously. "Do all you *Gazette* people bring flowers?"

Frings stopped. "What's that?"

"Do all you people bring flowers?" She reached into a pocket in her dress. "This guy brought flowers, too." She handed him a card.

Art Deyna.

60.

Morphy parked the prowl car in a shaded lot on the edge of the Hollows. Some kids played a makeshift game of baseball on the far side of the lot, their voices pitched high and boisterous. Broken glass in the lot caught the sun and looked like a thousand multicolored fireflies.

Morphy and Grip pulled the grease paper from sandwiches they'd picked up at a deli that catered to cops and pried the caps from two cone-tops of beer. They ate in silence, half-watching the kids. Crows on the periphery of the game shrieked at the players. The police radio in the prowl car squawked in the background. They'd both developed that cop sense to process noise from the radio subconsciously, becoming alert when some word or phrase tipped them that it was relevant. This time they didn't need the sense. The radio dispatcher used Grip's name.

"Shit," Grip said, looking at the half of his sandwich that remained. He downed the rest of his beer and leaned through the open window for the mike.

"This is Grip." He released the talk button and belched, giving Morphy a half grin.

The dispatcher's voice came with a hail of static. "That shithole bar you drink at?"

"Yeah?"

"Owner asked for you. Wants you to swing by, you get a chance."

"You know what about?"

"That's all I got."

"Okay." Grip tossed the mike onto the car seat. To Morphy he said, "We've got to swing by Crippen's."

Morphy finished his beer and tossed the can over his shoulder. "What about?"

Grip shrugged. An altercation started across the field at the baseball

205

game, two kids grappling while the others formed a circle around them, cheering them on.

Grip felt better now with a couple of beers in him and Wayne located, albeit in the hospital. He needed more information on that, but at least Wayne wasn't still missing.

Crippen's didn't have official hours and there were times, such as this, when it was open but not really functioning. A couple of older guys, serious boozers, were lighting into tall glasses of whiskey and ice. The bartender washed glasses behind the bar, listening to the usual static and bile coming from the radio. Morphy waited by the door.

The bartender saw Grip coming and dried his hands on a cloth. "I figured you'd keep me waiting."

Grip gave him a sour look. "What's the rumble? I'm on duty."

"Don't smell like it." The bartender went to the register and opened the drawer, still talking. "You know how I came in yesterday and found those specs with the shot glass and feathers and all that?"

"Yeah?"

The bartender returned with something in his hand. "There was something waiting for me today, too."

Grip opened his arms impatiently. "You going to show me, or what?"

The bartender laid a police badge on the bar. Grip tapped it around with his finger so that it was facing him.

"Jesus."

Morphy was beside him now. "That your buddy Wayne's?"

"Yeah."

Morphy asked the bartender, "Did he leave it here last night or something?"

"Yeah, well, I don't think so. Check the other side."

Morphy picked it up and flipped it over. "Yeah?"

"You gotta get the light to hit it right."

Morphy moved it around a little until he got the proper angle and then it was visible. Someone had etched a crude skull and top hat into the back.

61.

Westermann drove farther into Praeger's Hill, making his way through the slow late-afternoon traffic to Rudi Odeline's garage on a largely deserted block it shared with a series of run-down storage units. Rudi's was more of a storage facility than a garage, a white cinder-block box with only the word AUTO painted over the side door to indicate its presumed function. It was an open secret that the garage made its money as a front for a fencing operation, but Rudi was smart or lucky enough that they'd never been able to make it stick.

The garage was closed up tight. Westermann put his ear against the door, heard muffled voices from within, and pounded hard. Nobody came. He pounded again and put his ear to the door. Silence. A group of kids, a couple of them smoking, watched from the end of the block. The garage wall was pasted with the mayor's campaign signs. The sun was hot on his neck.

He pounded the door a last time and followed it with a yell. "Rudi, it's Detective Westermann. I'm not here on a bust; just some questions. Don't make me go to the trouble of getting a warrant."

He put his ear back to the door and pictured Rudi thinking it over. Eventually he heard approaching footsteps. He stepped away before the door opened to the massive presence of Rudi Odeline; at least six and a half feet tall and, even at that height, stocky. His blond hair was cut nearly to the scalp, his face chiseled and severe. Westermann noticed that the top third of Rudi's right ear was missing. Had it been missing the last time they'd met?

"What do you want, Piet?" His voice always surprised Westermann with its high pitch.

"A few questions. You want to do it out here or inside?"

Rudi blew out a big sigh. "Okay, okay. We do it outside, yes?"

Rudi found a comfortable position leaning back against the cinder-block wall, a pose of unconcern—even boredom. His white T-shirt was saturated with sweat; his green mechanic's pants clung to his massive legs. Westermann glanced down the block. Rudi's appearance had scared off the kids, but a pack of five dogs stood alert at the end of the street. Rudi was watching them, too.

"Rudi," Westermann started, getting back the big man's attention, "I'm going to ask you about something from the past. I give you my word that I'm not interested in bringing you in on this crime. Do you understand? I'm not interested in your part in it."

Rudi nodded, not happy, but weighing the possibility of getting a chit in his favor with Westermann. His face was sunburned. Westermann could make out white scar tissue over his eyes.

"A few months ago you cased a B and E up in Godtown."

Rudi looked as if he was about to protest, decided against it, and nodded.

"So I'm guessing that you, what, you heard about Godtown, it sounded interesting, and you went up there to watch the place, get a sense of how things go there. Maybe you picked a roof on one of those abandoned buildings and watched. And you saw that these people, they cut out for church every night for hours and the whole block was just empty. How's that so far?"

Rudi grunted. "Close enough."

"So this is where I kind of lose the plot, Rudi. It looked like an easy score, right? You wait until everyone heads off to church and go house to house—no hurry, no hassles. But it didn't work that way and that's what I don't get."

Rudi talked quietly, but his eyes blazed. "Who did you talk to?"

"Don't worry about that. He knew that I wouldn't come down on you. Just trying to get chits; you know how that goes. So what *happened*, Rudi? Why wasn't this the perfect score?"

Rudi shook his head. "Not so good, going down to Godtown. Not a good place. See, I went down there with another guy—"

"Who?"

"Christ, is it important?"

"I won't know unless you tell me."

Rudi sighed.

"I'm not going to roust him, Rudi," Westermann said quietly. "It probably means nothing."

"It was Klaus Hess."

The name wasn't familiar. "Do I know him?"

Rudi shrugged. "He's not so big. Some people call him Der Flederklaus. Ugly bastard." Rudi half-smiled, not feeling it.

"Okay."

"Klaus, he does locks. So him and me, we're in Godtown, thinking just like you said, we're going to go down the block, take what looks good. Like shopping, okay? But we start on the first house, we're up on the stoop and my friend is working the lock, and I hear this tapping from across the street, so I turn and look to see what it is, and it's this guy, big boy, tapping his piece against this steel rail." Rudi grimaced. "Look, what's this got to do with?"

"Keep going, Rudi. You're doing great. Nothing's going to happen to you."

"Yeah," he said ruefully. "So I tell Klaus, I tell him *look over there*, and we both look over at this guy, and he's looking back at us, holding his gun at his side, okay?" Rudi seemed genuinely astonished by the incident; even now. "We're not carrying, you know. No reason to tack on time if we're caught, and I take care of myself, you know? Gun or no gun."

Westermann nodded. Rudi was sweating hard, beads rolling down his temples, dropping off his jaw.

"Then this guy, this big boy, he takes his gun and points it at us. He's, like, maybe thirty yards away, something like that. He points it at us and just kind of slowly jerks it up, points it again and jerks it up; like he's just shot us both. Then he just stands there, holding the gun."

"What'd you do?"

"What the fuck would you do? We got out of there. Not running or anything like that. But we got down off that stoop and we walked away."

"And that was that?"

"Look, Detective, don't take this wrong, but you're not a street guy. Everyone knows that. You're tough and smart and all that, but you didn't grow up with it, okay? That guy up in Godtown, you don't want to take a piss with him. Some people, you're better off steering clear. Like this guy."

"So he just backed you off?"

"You been listening to a thing I said?" Rudi sighed in frustration. He probably didn't have many stories where he was the victim.

"This guy, he a big guy? Big as you? Blond hair? Cat tattoo?"

"I wasn't close enough to see no tattoo, but, yeah, that could be him. Very big."

Westermann thought about Koss and his aggressive posture; how he had all the cops' nerves jangling.

"And you haven't gone back?"

"Would you?"

Westermann ignored that one. "Then you put the word out."

"That's right. Stay the fuck away from Godtown."

62.

Frings found a spot in the shade under a maple tree in a leafy residential neighborhood; the kind of place where old women fed squirrels that were half-domesticated. One of these squirrels was perched on a limb several feet above Frings, making a chittering sound while Frings sipped from a paper coffee cup. Two elderly men had put a table on a stoop and were playing chess, while a small group of bright-eyed children played catch and occasionally stopped to look at whatever move had been made.

At five o'clock, the first wave of domestic help left the brownstones for the journey back to their more modest homes. Frings watched them file by. He'd perfected the art of looking as if he belonged wherever he was, even if he was not actually doing anything. Nobody looked at him funny; no one seemed to even notice him.

He half-expected to see Deyna somewhere, shadowing him. But Deyna would be looking for a second source; the source to get his story on the front page. Frings thought about who might be a second source, wondering if he could maybe head Deyna off.

He was nearly done with his coffee when he saw Ellen Aust across the street, walking wearily in her formless maid's dress. He hadn't seen her in five years or so, but she was easy to pick out; shoulders forward and chin tucked into her chest as if someone had her by the scruff of the neck. Frings poured the rest of his coffee into the dirt at the foot of the tree, put the crumpled cup into his pocket, and crossed the street to intercept her.

Ellen turned, eyes wild with fear at the sound of her name. It took her a moment to place Frings, her body relaxing, her eyes going dull.

"Mr. . . . I mean, Frank?" Her face was flattened out, pale, her eyes set a little too far apart.

"Ellen, how are you?"

She paused, wary, knowing that there must be more here than a chance encounter. "I'm doing fine," she said cautiously. "Why are you here?"

Frings flashed her a smile and let it die. "I was hoping maybe you'd have coffee with me. Or, better yet, dinner."

Frings could see her exhaustion, something deep and more than just physical. Her eyes were weary. "Coffee would be okay. I have church soon."

"You sure? You don't want dinner, get something good?"

"Just coffee is fine."

Frings walked her down to a glass-fronted diner that looked onto a dingy postcard stamp of a park. They sat at a table by the window and the waitress brought two coffees. Frings could taste the cigarette smoke in his.

"You sure you don't want something to eat?"

She declined again, looking worried. She sat with her back straight, her hands flat on the table before her.

"How have you been?" Frings asked, and realized he had asked the same question minutes before.

"Been fine, I guess. Like I said." He could tell that she knew this small talk wasn't the point, that he wouldn't have been waiting for her so that they could talk about the weather. But Frings made small talk anyway, getting the cadence established, getting her used to talking to him, as she had five years before when Frings was working the Maddox article. But it was hard; harder than he remembered. She responded to his questions with one- or two-word answers, rarely looking him in the eye. She hadn't exactly been playful five years ago, but the change was stark.

She'd had enough of the back-and-forth by the time she'd finished her coffee. Maybe she'd given him that much time, the empty cup the signal to get to the point.

"What do you want, Frank? I'm tired. I need to be getting home."

"Okay, I'll get right to it. Do you know a Mavis Talley or someone named Lenore?"

She frowned, shaking her head. "Can't say that I do."

"You're sure?"

She nodded.

"It was a long shot. Anyway, how's the church these days?"

She turned suspicious. "What do you mean?"

"I don't know. I hear the flock has grown, people joining from the City."

She nodded again.

"Is that a problem, you know, with the Fort Deposit people, all these new people coming in?"

She shook her head. "Are you trying to sow the seeds of dissension, Frank?"

Frank signaled for a coffee refill. "Ellen, let me be straight with you. Those two women I mentioned? They're dead. Both of them. And they both had pamphlets from your church, Maddox's church. Did someone from the church murder them? I don't know. But for some reason, Dr. Maddox has not been helpful in the investigation, and I'm just trying to get a sense of what's happening there."

Ellen nodded, looking small and drawn. "Are you asking me if anything's changed?"

"Sure, we can do it that way. Has anything?"

She sighed. "Things are harder. Our flock is in a time of tribulation." It came out sounding like a question.

"Tribulation?"

"The Last Days are advancing upon us."

He had nothing to say to that.

"History is coming to an end."

Frings moved his head, trying to catch her eyes. "What do you mean by that?"

Ellen looked confused, her eyes suspicious. Frings backed off, letting her think about it a little.

"Okay, these women, the two that were killed, they were prostitutes. Have you noticed women like that at the church?"

Ellen was spent, absently spinning the coffee cup between her hands, staring at the whorls she made.

He said, "Listen, maybe tomorrow? I'll take you for coffee again. We can chat some more."

She looked dubious. "I don't know what I'm going to be able to tell you, Frank."

He flashed her the Frings smile. "We'll figure something out."

63.

Westermann walked along the periphery of a silent Godtown, taking his
time. He'd arranged for two uniforms to do a night walk. Their orders:
Keep Koss occupied, if only briefly. Westermann had left them less than
five minutes ago and was giving them time to attract Koss's attention before
he moved in. Not exactly what Kraatjes had in mind, Westermann thought,
but a hell of a lot better than sending Morphy and Grip again.

Koss was taking on new dimensions in Westermann's mind. His intimidation of Rudi Odeline was startling. Rudi was notoriously tough; maybe
psychotically so. And Koss backed him down. Ran him off and Rudi
wanted no further part of him.

Westermann needed a better read on Prosper Maddox, who was emerging in his mind as the key to the investigation, like a figure materializing
from the fog; Maddox and the missing Dr. Vesterhue. Was this an accurate
assessment? Was he chasing connections where there were only coincidences?
Would he be this eager to pursue Maddox if Maddox wasn't the only way
to absolve the Community and, in doing so, absolve his own actions in moving Lenore's body?

Westermann came to the next corner and took a left, walking toward the
Church of Last Days. The lights of downtown towered over the low buildings in this part of the Hollows, an almost violent intrusion upon the dark
and quiet.

He stopped at the church, rubbing the sweat from the back of his neck,
listening to the singing coming from inside. A hymn he didn't recognize;
the words hard to decipher in the wave of voices. He walked to the opposite
side of the street and sat on the high curb, leaning back on his elbows, legs
in the street, crossed at the ankles. He listened to this hymn and then another, dimly recognizing the tune. He sensed eyes on him—probably
Koss—but he was beyond caring, so exhausted that he could have leaned
back and fallen asleep. But he heard footsteps and watched as Ole Koss

appeared around the corner across the street and to his right. Koss ambled over, arms slightly away from his body as if his musculature wouldn't allow them to fall any closer.

"Lieutenant," Koss said.

"Evening."

Koss approached, his eyes alive, scanning the street, turning once to check behind his back. He sat down next to Westermann, leaning forward, his corded forearms resting on his knees. The man radiated physical strength.

"Any more of you out tonight, more than you and the two officers?"

Westermann shook his head.

"Why're you people suddenly in our place all the time?"

"I think you know." The singing had stopped. The street was silent but for their conversation.

"Those girls? Those girls didn't come here, sir. They'd have stuck out. This is a small community, Lieutenant."

"How'd they get the flyers from the church?"

"Dr. Vesterhue? Maybe spreading the Good Word? Lots of ways it could have happened." Koss was tense, head turning from side to side, looking for something.

"Well, it's my job to figure exactly how it did happen."

"Lieutenant, I don't know if you realize the amount of consternation and stress you're causing in Dr. Maddox's flock. These are God-fearing, honest, simple people. They're not used to the ways of the world."

Westermann looked at Koss, trying to read if he was aping Maddox.

"Mr. Maddox gives us that congregation list we're asking for, maybe we can end this intrusion and things here can get back to normal."

Koss turned his head away from Westermann and spat. "Well, I don't speak for *Dr.* Maddox, but my strong impression was that he's not going to provide that list."

"Okay."

"And I don't think pushing the issue is going to do you any good."

They sat for a moment until the silence was shattered by noise from inside the church, like a group yell. Or scream. Or howl. It continued for maybe thirty intense seconds. Westermann felt the charge in his neck and scalp. He looked over at Koss, who stared hard at his hands. The howling ceased and the street returned to silence.

Westermann said, "What the hell was that?"

Koss looked over at him, lids heavy, and Westermann caught the vibe of imminent violence that must have spooked Rudi Odeline.

The howling started again and Koss's head shot to the church. Westermann watched him. Clearly, this communal outpouring of noise bothered him.

The sound ceased again and this time Koss rose to stand over Westermann. Behind Koss, Westermann thought he saw movement in the shadows, but Koss commanded his attention and the impression was lost.

"I think it might be time for you to be on your way, Lieutenant."

Westermann stood, too. "Tell Mr. Maddox that I'll be in touch."

Koss nodded. The howling began again.

64.

A solitary Negro sat on a stool playing guitar on the Palace stage, teasing a slide over the frets and coaxing a fierce wail from the amplifier on the floor next to him. He wasn't singing, just hunched over his guitar, eyes shut, sweating as if he were in the ring. Frings twisted his beer glass in slow rotations on the table, listening to the music; waiting for it to stop so he could talk. Renate sat next to him, tracing circles on his neck with her fingertips. It was this way when she was around, as if there were no one else. This is what troubled Frings, not her infidelity, but that she behaved as though it hadn't happened, or that it was normal. While he didn't hold her infidelity against her, he was puzzled that she so lacked any sense of culpability; it was almost pathological.

Across from them sat Carla and Mel Washington. Carla, like Renate, was drinking a martini. Washington didn't drink alcohol and kept his fingers occupied with cigarettes. Washington was enjoying the music, a side of him that Frings had never seen, Washington experiencing happiness.

Floyd Christian came by, asking Frings if he wanted to use the back room for a meeting. Frings thanked him, no. He wanted to coast for a few minutes, let his mind rest. He closed his eyes, the notes impacting his stoned mind like little bullets, bursting into colors on impact. Renate talking over the music in Portuguese at Washington, a language he apparently understood. Father Womé hung in the periphery of Frings's mind. Not his face. Not even his physical being. The *idea* of Father Womé; the presence. He was the sea in which the guitar sounds swam; the air that they breathed. Womé churning, insinuating himself into Frings's thoughts. Frings opened his eyes, breaking this trance. Carla was looking at him, maybe concerned. He smiled, but wasn't confident that he was making the right expression.

The music stopped, replaced by the din of dozens of conversations as the houselights came on. Washington leaned across the table. The other three leaned in, too, forming a conspiratorial circle.

"Where are we with the investigation, Frank?"

"That second girl's really a problem. Piet has—had—a different angle, keeping things away from the Community." Frings explained about Mavis Talley and about the second girl also having the sores. He told Washington about the links between Lenore and Mavis and the Church of Last Days. "Piet is going after Prosper Maddox, but it's harder now with the second girl. It's much harder to keep the investigation away from the Community."

Washington looked peeved. "You're not thinking—"

"Come on, Mel. I'm giving the Community the benefit of the doubt, but seriously, on its face, the case that it's someone in the Uhuru Community seems reasonable. Piet's doing the best he can, but he can't push too hard away from the Community, for reasons that I think you know." Frings didn't mention Deyna's progress; Washington's nerves were already jagged.

Washington pulled off his glasses and rubbed the bridge of his nose. "I know, Frank. I understand. Things are coming fast right now. Truffant running for mayor. The girls. The assaults."

"It sounds like you guys got a bit of revenge there."

"Us guys? Nothing to do with me. The Samedi people, I think. Some of those guys—"

"Not Community?" Frings asked, surprised.

"No, they're Community. Just a group in the Community. Haitians, some of them. But there's a bunch."

Frings felt Renate's hand grip his arm and turned to her, following her gaze to where Christian was hurrying toward them. Christian never hurried. Frings stood to meet him.

Christian leaned into Frings so that his mouth was by Frings's ear. "We've got to get Mel out of here now."

"Okay," Frings said, knowing that Christian would have his reasons.

Christian took Washington by the arm, leading him on a quick traverse of the room, back toward Christian's office, where, presumably, Washington could hole up. Maybe some kind of hiding place.

"We'd better split," Frings said to Renate and Carla, who were already gathering their purses. They were standing when the cops came hard through the front door and the place descended into bedlam.

Frings watched as the police fanned out around the room and caught the instinctive postures of self-defense taken by the Negroes at the sight of truncheons. A group of three cops headed toward his table; two uniforms led by a guy built like a fire hydrant in a suit showing sweat stains under the arms. Frings stepped forward to meet them, trying to head them off before they got to Renate and, especially, Carla.

The cop in the suit was aggressive from the start, getting into Frings's space, making him work to hold his ground.

"Where is he?"

Frings was a couple of inches taller, but the cop probably had him by forty hard pounds. "Who's that?"

"Don't fuck with me."

Frings stared back hard at the cop. No way this gink was going to get physical with a top newspaper guy out in public like this.

The cop leaned in closer and spoke slowly, seething. "Where's Mel Washington? You were meeting with him. Where'd he go?"

Frings kept the stare but didn't like the look that got in the cop's eyes, as if something was switching off—or on.

The cop grabbed Frings's open collar and pulled him closer and down, so that their foreheads were nearly touching. From the periphery, Frings caught a glimpse of Renate making a move toward him, a cop blocking her way. Carla was shouting something.

The cop said, "Don't make this difficult. We *will* find him. No reason for you to go down, too." Sweat was pouring off the cop's crimson face.

Frings held his ground. "Don't make things difficult on *yourself.* Do you know who I am? I'll have your name all over the front page of the *Gazette.* Harassment."

The cop gave an ugly smile. "Your paper's making a habit of that."

"What's your name?" Carla yelled at the cop.

He ignored her. "Last time. Where's. Mel. Washington?"

"I don't know, and if you don't get away from me, I will make trouble for you. You got that? What's your name?"

"You're not going to be able to hide behind your paper, you commie fuck. Look over there. You don't think I know Carla Bierhoff? Red Carla? You're here meeting with two of the biggest Reds in the goddamn City. Sharing drinks. We've had our eye on you for a while, Frings. A long fucking while, and it looks like maybe your true color is showing: Red."

Frings wondered about the "we" who'd had their eyes on him. The police?

Carla was still yelling for the detective's name.

The cop snorted. "My name? Why the fuck not? It's Grip. Torsten Grip." He looked to Frings with an ugly smile. "I'll check the paper tomorrow."

Renate trembled against Frings in the backseat of a cab. Frings's thoughts came fast—what did this manhunt for Washington mean? Washington claimed that he hadn't been involved with the attacks by the Uhuru Community ginks, and this seemed right to Frings. Other people could take care of the Community's hard stuff.

The City lights, so often a source of inspiration to Frings, tonight seemed merely ghoulish. As they passed through neighborhood after fatigued neighborhood, Renate stroked his arm.

He'd balled it up; missed his opportunity. He should have seen it coming, written the story while he had a chance instead of chasing Ed Wayne. The police had taken control of the Community-assaults story, and it wasn't going to play out as *rogue cop assaults law-abiding citizens and buries the investigation.* Instead, the story would be *violent Uhuru Community thugs assault off-duty policeman.*

He wondered where Art Deyna was.

65.

It was cooler up in the hills on the winding, rutted road headed to Fort Deposit, Prosper Maddox's hometown. Coming from the City, Westermann was surprised by how full the country seemed, even in the absence of people and anything man-made. He'd stopped earlier at a bend in the road high above a winding, river-carved valley, listening to the wind as it swayed the tops of huge evergreens; a vast sound. A sound on a different scale from anything he had heard in the City.

Now the road followed a river dotted with a scattering of crude shacks—shelter and not much else. Some lacked windows. None, Westermann presumed, had plumbing. He wondered idly how these people made their living. This wasn't farmland and the mines were still miles off.

The country was liberating, even if he was only away from the City for a couple of days. Leaving had been hectic and, in the end, unnerving. Grip had shown up with his eyes red and swollen from exhaustion. Ed Wayne had apparently taken a beating down by the Uhuru Community, and Grip had stayed on into the night to search for Mel Washington, who, for some reason, was thought to be involved. Westermann had played this news cool; not asking questions. But Grip had gone on, relating his confrontation with Frings, joking that he hadn't seen his name in the paper that morning.

Westermann had hovered on the edge of panic. Grip had made the connection between Washington and Frings.

Washington and Frings.

The true location of Lenore's corpse.

Grip.

Deyna.

If there had been any doubt about his decision to leave for Fort Deposit, this news had cemented his plan. He needed to get away, get some breathing room; let Frings take the heat for a while.

Westermann thought about this as he descended the switchbacks into the steep valley that hid Fort Deposit.

Fort Deposit was a mining town. The main street ran parallel to a fast-flowing river, and ramshackle houses on perpendicular roads crawled up the side of the encompassing hills in uneven columns. These dwellings were better, perhaps, than the shanties in the Uhuru Community, but the poverty here was clear. Westermann drove down the main street, looking for the police station. The buildings looked old, battered; paint peeling, letters missing from signs, doors hanging crooked. He counted three bars, three churches, a butcher, a grocer's, a general store of sorts, town hall, a diner, and a handful of other businesses identified only by the owner's name, the merchandise obscure. Dusty and rusted cars were parked along the street. Two women in drab clothes carried sacks of groceries toward a truck.

Westermann parked in front of the police department, which shared a wall with a barbershop on the far edge of town. Inside, he found a broad-shouldered cop in uniform sitting behind a desk, reading a newspaper. He looked up and seemed quite surprised to see someone that he didn't recognize.

"Can I help you?"

Westermann showed his badge, explained who he was. "I'm doing some background work on a case, just wanted to check in, let you know I was in town."

The cop looked as if he couldn't believe what he'd heard. "You're doing background work on a City crime out here? In Fort Deposit?"

Westermann nodded. "Is the chief around?"

The chief was not around, but the cop behind the desk was able to find him after a couple of phone calls.

"He's coming," the cop said.

Westermann decided to wait outside, resting his hat beside him on the wooden bench in front of the barbershop. Afternoon shadows were beginning to reach across the road toward him, but the bench was still in the sun. A breeze blew from the west, and for the first time in weeks Westermann felt comfortable outdoors, maybe even a little cool.

A couple of old-timers—gaunt men with sunken cheeks and hard eyes—shuffled by, nodding in silent greeting to Westermann. They walked with a forward bend, as if they were shipping heavy packs. Their arms, though, were still roped, and one had crude blue tattoos on both forearms. They passed silently into the barber's, the opening of the door triggering a bell that announced their presence.

A young man in police uniform strode down the street toward him. Westermann stood, ready for this kid to take him to the chief, and was surprised when the kid introduced himself.

"Chief McIlvaine," he said, extending a hand. "I have to admit that I didn't catch your name when Loughlin in there called."

"Westermann." Westermann took the hand. "Lieutenant Westermann. Call me Piet."

"Then you'd best call me Mac. Christian name's Douglas, but with a last name like McIlvaine . . ."

"That's fine," Westermann said, not sure what else to say to that. "I'm up here doing some background on an investigation I have going in the City."

"Prosper Maddox?"

"Why do you say that?"

"Come on, let's go and talk down by the river."

Westermann followed McIlvaine down the block and then to the right as they followed an abbreviated dirt road to a kind of boat launch leading to the river. Ducks swam slowly, dunking their heads and then shaking off the water. Waterbugs danced on the surface. McIlvaine led Westermann to a bench just off the river.

"It's better down here," McIlvaine said. "The view's one of the few benefits of living in Fort Deposit. No reason to deprive you of it."

It *was* beautiful. The water was crystalline, the rocks clearly visible under the surface, and on the far side the reflections of the trees on the opposite bank were brilliant.

"So," Westermann said, "Prosper Maddox."

"Yeah, I figured. Not that there's anything wrong with him, as far as I know. He was up and gone before I took this job. But everyone here knows Maddox and everyone has an opinion on him."

"Why's that?"

McIlvaine scratched at his temple. "This is a dying town, Piet. There's a coal mine a bit up the road that used to provide for the people here. But too many people moved in and the vein wasn't what they'd hoped it was. I mean, just look around. You saw it coming in.

"Well, Maddox saw this early on. Saw that there wasn't a future here for people. So he led his flock away. Took them to the City. Some people, they thought it was the best thing that could have happened. Fewer people without work. And Maddox's people were kind of at the bottom of the heap here, if you know what I mean. Other people, though, they weren't so happy about it, having family or friends just taken away. Homes abandoned, and all of a sudden at that; left to just fall down. And then there were the people who'd split with his church."

"How's that?" Westermann asked.

"I don't know the details. Before my time. But maybe ten years ago, something like that, Maddox's church split into two groups. His group stuck around for a while but they ended up in the City. The other group, they're still here. You want to find out more about Maddox, you'd probably want to talk to them."

"Okay. But what can *you* tell me? How was he while he was here? You must have heard stories at least."

"I really don't know too much about him. See, Lieutenant, there are two kinds of people in this town—people who go to church at night and people who go to bars. I think you know who gets most of my time. You want to find out about Maddox, you should talk to the people at the Holiness Church."

"The Holiness Church?"

"Yeah, that's Maddox's original church. He's not the most popular guy there, but there are some people who could give you a little more insight. Some might even be objective."

"So where do I find the Holiness Church?"

"Oh, I'll show you when we get back up to Main Street. They'll be starting worship up around seven, I'd guess."

Westermann looked at him. "On a Thursday?"

McIlvaine laughed. "The Holiness Church doesn't take too many days off. But then again, neither does the Lord." He shot Westermann a wink.

66.

Frings waited at a window table in the diner where he'd had a coffee with Ellen Aust the previous day. He wasn't sure what to expect from her. He'd come here instead of meeting her on the street, giving her some room; letting her make the move if she wanted to continue to talk. Either she'd want to or she wouldn't. It didn't make a difference how aggressively he pursued it.

A couple of older men sat at the counter talking about the horses while Frings sipped his coffee and watched the ladies walk by on the sidewalk. A man in shirt and tie, his hair slicked back with sweat, paused by the window and plastered a sign against the pane, the glue spreading out under the pressure. Frings could see through it from the back. TRUFFANT FOR MAYOR.

He was giving Ellen until a quarter past the hour and then he'd split. He didn't have to wait nearly that long.

Ellen looked different today; wearing makeup, he thought. Her dress was nicer, too, though still maid-wear. She must have seen him through the window because she made straight for his table. Frings held up a finger for another coffee and stood up to greet her.

When they were sitting, Ellen said, "I'd like to apologize for yesterday. You caught me by surprise."

Frings shook his head. "Please, I should apologize to you for showing up like that; no warning."

She smiled, keeping her lips tight to hide her teeth. "Dr. Maddox, he tells us to be wary and vigilant in the world; that the Trickster comes in many guises and holds sway over many people. But I know you, Frank. I know you from before and I believe I can trust you."

Frings smiled.

"And I think maybe there are things you'd want to know. Is this going to be in the newspaper?" This last bit seemed to worry her.

Frings shook his head. "Not if you don't want it to be. Ellen, depending on what I hear, I might want to find out more from other people. I'll have to see. You don't need to worry about your name or your words being printed, though."

She thought about this, staring down into her coffee. "It's not just being in the paper, Frank."

Frings sensed her quandary, was surprised that she was willing to talk to him. She had her congregation and little else besides. No good could come out of talking to Frings about it; potentially some bad. There must be a reason she wanted to talk. There must be something she needed to tell him. He decided to wait her out, let her take it at her speed. He sipped his coffee.

She lifted her eyes to Frings, looking decisive. "I think Dr. Maddox is troubled."

"How's that?"

"Understand that he is a man of God, Frank; that he concerns himself with holy things. But he's under so much pressure, he's been distracted, even withdrawn. It's not just me that sees it, neither. He's drawing into himself, nurturing his relationship with the Lord while he ignores this life. But that's not it, or at least not all of it. He fasts and prays in seclusion all day, then comes out and preaches for four, five hours at a time."

"What about?"

Her eyes were fatigued, terrified. "Enemies. Enemies of the church. The police come into our neighborhood now, almost every night. That never used to happen. Dr. Maddox says that they are watching us, seeing if we are making preparations for the Last Days. He says that our enemies watch us from the abandoned buildings around our neighborhood; that they stalk the perimeter at night. We pray, sometimes nearly all night, for them to be driven away. But every night Dr. Maddox says that they are still out there."

"You don't believe that, do you?"

"I'm scared. The police are in our neighborhood all the time now. They never used to be. People don't leave the neighborhood after dark; don't even walk in the neighborhood alone after dark."

Frings nodded.

Ellen shrugged and Frings could see the debate that played out in her mind between her respect for Prosper Maddox's authority and insight and her own common sense.

Frings pushed. "What is it? What do you want to tell me?"

Ellen's face flushed. "We are living in the Last Days, Frank. It's happening right now." Her voice was urgent. "Dr. Maddox says all the signs are there, and the Antichrist, he is among us."

"Among *us?*"

"Here. The City. Dr. Maddox had studied prophecy and prayed and it was revealed to him that Father Womé is the Antichrist."

Frings blinked twice, shook his head. "Father Womé?"

"Yes! Christ is returning, Frank, and you are not saved."

67.

Evening began to fall as Grip walked, mind wandering, toward Ed Wayne's apartment. Heat lightning lit the sky in uneven bursts. In his left hand he carried a bottle of whiskey, still in its liquor-store bag. In his right he had his desk flask of whiskey and he sipped on it frequently as he tried to make sense of that afternoon.

He'd been in a shit mood all day because he'd spent the previous night in the search for goddamn Mel Washington and had only caught a couple of hours of sleep. They hadn't found him either, though Grip had been sure they'd come close. Most likely at the Palace, but they hadn't been able to find the hiding place. Grip had made a note to find a reason to toss the place sometime in the future; pay back Floyd Christian for playing coy with them all night. That goddamn Frings wasn't any better, though Grip knew that getting in a pissing match with a reporter wouldn't do his career much good, or the lieut's for that matter. The Chief liked the force to keep a good image in the press, and the lieut had already balled that up once.

So he'd been in a shit mood and the lieut had headed out of town, and Morphy had been a son of a bitch all day, hassling Grip about everything. *Jesus.*

By the time he arrived at Ed Wayne's building, he was half in the bag; drunk enough that he almost missed the skull-and-top-hat graffiti, not quite washed off Wayne's door. *Almost.* He stared at it for a moment, feeling the hollowness in his gut. Wayne's wife answered the door. She was pretty well fancied up, for her. She'd probably been receiving visitors all day. Grip smiled at her drunkenly, noticing why Wayne must like her; the generous body, a cute, girl's face. One thing, drunk or not, he was glad to be out of that hall.

She smiled back at him, took the bottle of whiskey that Grip had forgotten he was holding, and showed him back to the living room where Wayne was half-sitting on the couch, awash in bandages.

"Torsten," he said, and Grip could tell Wayne was drunk, too.

"Jesus, Ed. You look like hell." Grip couldn't quite evoke the cheeriness necessary to make it sound like anything other than an honest appraisal.

Wayne coughed. "Yeah, well . . ." Both of his eyes were swollen and discolored. His lips were ragged and stitched.

"I saw that skull on your door. Same one as they did on your badge. When'd they do it?"

"My badge?"

"Yeah. You didn't know? Someone scratched that skull and hat into the back of your badge and left it in Crippen's."

"Shit," Wayne said, thinking.

"Yeah, shit. When did your door get marked?"

"Three days ago, maybe? Right after they did the one at Crippen's."

The same day as Grip's own door. "You know who did it?"

"Community thugs. Same as jumped me."

Grip knew Wayne was guessing; that he had no idea. "The fuck were you doing down there, Ed? You the guys jumping those kids every night?"

"Of course."

Grip shook his head.

"Don't give me that holier-than-thou bullshit. If you spent more time busting Reds and less time taking orders from them . . ."

Grip tensed. "What's that?"

"What? You hard of hearing now?"

"Who am I taking orders from?"

"Westermann."

"He's Red now? That's your latest beef with him?"

"I'm telling you."

"Listen. I know you're all beat to hell, but that doesn't mean I'm going to listen to this bullshit."

"Bullshit? How hard's your buddy Westermann pushing the investigation into the Uhuru Community's involvement with these girls who were found on the river? Huh?"

Grip didn't have much to say to that.

"What I hear, he's got a hard-on for Prosper Maddox. Now, where I stand, that's covering up for a bunch of goddamn Reds by going after a good Christian man; an anticommunist, at that."

"Shut up, Ed."

Wayne managed a gruesome approximation of a smile with his damaged mouth. "That's right. Shut up, Ed. You've got nothing else to say. Tell you what. Next time you get a chance, why don't you tail your boss when he gets off work? See where he goes, who he sees."

"You know something I ought to know?"

"Nah. I'm just suggesting you do it. Maybe it turns out interesting."

The wind had picked up when Grip emerged from Wayne's building. Grip, still on edge, wiped the sweat from his face with the sleeve of his coat. He saw that someone had plastered Truffant signs over the mayor's signs on the wall of Wayne's apartment building. He also saw someone walking across the street toward him, his hand on his hat and his head down against the wind, something about him familiar.

"Detective Grip."

Grip got a look at the guy now and recognized him from the night they'd braced Joey Stanic; that reporter now wearing a grin as if he knew something.

"Fuck off," Grip said, walking down the block.

Undeterred, the reporter walked along with him. "I'm Art Deyna, with the *Gazette*. I don't think I've introduced myself before. I won't take much of your time, I just have a question or two."

Grip kept walking.

"I've got it on good authority that the bodies of two women have been found on the riverbank near the Uhuru Community. I'm trying to find out if they were found in the same spot—"

"You've got the wrong guy, asshole. I don't know anything about any bodies."

Deyna smiled. "That's perfect. Exactly what I would have expected you to say. Come on, Detective, you're assigned to the case. You're part of the investigation."

"I am, am I? That's news to me."

Deyna kept it pleasant. "Is this all I'm going to get from you, Detective Grip?"

Grip ignored this.

Deyna continued, "I've asked around about you, talked to some people, and it seems like you've got no love for the Reds. That's good—neither do I. Something you might not know, though, is that your boss, Lieutenant Westermann, doesn't exactly share your viewpoint."

Grip stopped; adrenaline raging. "Get the fuck away from me before this gets ugly."

"Yeah, I'll go away. I want you to see something first; something for you to think about. Then I'm gone." Deyna reached into his jacket pocket, pulling out a photo that he handed to Grip.

Grip stared at the photo, his breathing shallow from the booze and now this.

Deyna said, "You know Lieutenant Westermann, of course, and the two Negroes. One's Mel Washington and the other's Warren Eddings. I don't need to tell you who they are."

Grip pushed the photo back into Deyna's chest. "I've looked. Now screw."

Deyna pocketed the photo. "Nice to meet you, Detective. We'll talk again."

68.

Westermann followed McIlvaine's directions and found the church just outside town on a semipaved road that meandered up the side of the eastern hill. The church looked as if it might once have been some kind of storage facility: low, windowless, built for function not aesthetics. There was none of the architectural striving that even the humblest houses of worship in the City aspired to. Westermann parked his car between two pickups that showed the wear of hard years. The parking lot was little more than a patch of worn and yellowed grass. Westermann counted eight parked vehicles, none looking as if they had much life left.

He hesitated in front of the door, hearing muffled voices from within. Looking back toward his car, he saw the orange-tinged moon through a latticework of branches. He noticed for the first time the scream of thousands of crickets, like ringing in his ears. They were shockingly loud, and Westermann, maybe because he was at a church, thought vaguely of locust plagues. Headlights approached slowly; an ancient Ford pulled into the lot. The appearance of the car chased Westermann from his reluctance and he opened the door and entered the church.

His arrival attracted the attention of the congregation inside. Maybe fifteen or twenty people sat on folding chairs arranged in rows bisected by an aisle leading to a podium. A young woman in a formless summer dress sat between two children with wild red hair. Older women, several appallingly overweight, another two rail-thin and sinewy, sat in concentrated silence. There were older men, too, with feverish eyes, bodies hewn by a lifetime of manual labor. A plump, middle-aged man wearing a tan suit over a white shirt stood behind the podium. His wide baby's face dwarfed the round, wireless glasses perched delicately on his nose. This man walked out from behind the podium and started down the aisle toward Westermann wearing a placid, benign smile.

"I don't believe I know you, brother," the man said, extending his hand.

Westermann took it, feeling tense with all these eyes on him.

"Pete West," he said, not sure why he was lying.

"Brother West, welcome." The man held Westermann's hand in both of his. "I am Brother Allison. Welcome to our humble church."

Westermann watched tiny streams of perspiration running down Allison's temple, making a dark stain on his collar. Allison kept hold of Westermann's hand until Westermann felt compelled to step back, the continuous physical contact making him uncomfortable. The air inside was stale and hot, smelled of sweat and something else—candles?—that seemed to seep into his pores, forcing drops of sweat to bud on his skin.

Westermann heard the door open behind him. Brother Allison looked over his shoulder, his face lighting up.

"The children have arrived," he said, smiling.

Westermann turned to see two teenagers, probably brother and sister, both beautiful in a slightly unreal blond-haired, blue-eyed perfection. The boy had a crew cut and wore a plaid, short-sleeve shirt and jeans. His presumed sister's blond hair cascaded down onto her shoulders and the straps of a white summer dress. Westermann noticed she was barefoot. The excitement among the rest of the crowd was palpable. The boy carried a guitar case.

"Brother West, please excuse me," Allison said, and escorted the two teenagers to the podium. Westermann sat down in a folding chair in the same row as one of the obese women, who eyed him warily and nodded slightly, Westermann taking it as a reluctant welcome.

While the brother tuned his guitar, Westermann watched the other people in the audience, some staring blankly forward, others looking down at their clasped hands, mouthing what Westermann assumed were whispered prayers. The young mother spoke quietly to her two children, whose eyelids, Westermann now noticed, were drooping with fatigue. More people arrived, exchanged low greetings, taking seats behind Westermann.

He was far from the City.

Brother Allison grabbed the podium with both hands. "Now, I haven't had to lead worship too often in the past, so you might have to bear with me a little. I stopped by Brother Symmes's abode this evening and he told me that he was unable to make it tonight. He had another obligation and said that it was rare that he missed worship but that tonight he could not be here. So I am sorry that Brother Symmes is not here, but I believe that we will be in the Lord's presence tonight anyway. Praise the Lord!"

The crowd responded by murmuring "Praise the Lord," and Brother Allison stood with his head down, perhaps gathering himself.

"Well, what I think I'll do is turn this over to Roger and Annie and let them play the Lord's music for a while and see if we can call on the Holy Spirit to make his presence known. Praise God!"

The boy's guitar sounded both hollow and vast coming out of the small amplifier. Westermann felt the rhythmic, pulsing chords in his chest. The people watched motionless, riveted, entranced. Westermann could feel the metronomic repetition of the music beginning to work on his mind, and he found himself staring at the boy. The golden siblings began singing in a harmony that was just off, but more beautiful for the imperfection. They finished one song, and without pausing, the boy altered the chords and the rhythm of his playing. Westermann registered the change with his chest and his ears, equally heartbroken by the passing of the first song and excited by the promise of the new. He watched the two of them sing, exquisite in their placidity, nearly motionless—their eyes sometimes shut and sometimes staring over everybody's heads and into the distance. Westermann wondered what he would do once the music stopped, thinking it would be unbearably sad.

He looked around, saw that the music was catalyzing the room; individuals seemed to fall into private reverie. Two of the older woman sat with their hands flapping spastically, moving their mouths with manic energy, uttering inaudible words. Another old woman was up and swaying with the music, clutching a cross that hung from her neck on a leather string. Her eyes were clenched shut, tears flowed down her cheeks. Younger people—adults in their thirties or forties—were here now; the crowd grown to three dozen or more. When had they all arrived?

He pulled himself out of his chair and stood at the periphery, his breathing shallow. His shirt was wet with sweat. A middle-aged woman was on the floor behind the rows of chairs, shaking as another woman held her head in her lap and gently stroked her hair.

The song ended and the brother and sister took seats in the front row, watching Brother Allison at the podium, talking, soothing. With the music stopped, the sounds of the other worshippers became audible: intense whispers of prayers and shouts of "Praise the Lord" and "He is here" mixed with women speaking strange words at a crazed pace. The sound was disorienting. His ears began to hum as the sensory environment became overwhelming. And the heat. He found an empty chair and closed his eyes against the intensity of his surroundings, but the noises seemed only stranger, more intense; frightening and thrilling him. He lost himself, his mind emptying, and was almost surprised when he opened his eyes to find the church.

Many people were up now, wandering around, speaking to each other or to themselves. Westermann saw three women lying on the floor, repeating some semicoherent chant.

"I can feel the Lord's presence, I surely can. Praise Jesus! I can feel him working in me." Brother Allison made an awkward, jerking movement, like a record that had skipped, and then recovered himself. "Yes. Yes." He raised his eyes in ecstasy. "I can feel the Holy Ghost filling this room. Praise God!"

The boy had his guitar again and was strumming chords. *Trance music.*

Brother Allison smiled at someone in the crowd. "You think it's time, brother? Okay. Okay. Praise Jesus! Maybe, yeah." He was looking for someone among the assembled. "Harvey, could you come forward and help me with the crates? Brother Wallace, are you here?"

The two men walked to the unlit back of the room. Westermann unbuttoned the front of his shirt, wiped his hand across his damp chest, pulled it away cold. He felt a new tension in the room as people redoubled the earnestness of their prayers; others hugged; and the boy continued to strum.

Brother Allison appeared with his hands above his head, and from each hand dangled two rattlesnakes. The snakes' movements were somehow incongruous with the people in reverie, the angry rattling at once electric and menacing. A thin man with patchy brown hair limped behind Allison with a rattlesnake in each hand and another snake—no rattle—draped across his shoulders. Two younger women next to Westermann were speaking in tongues and shaking their heads manically; a huge man wearing mechanic's coveralls was weeping into his hands. The guitar pulsed and the sister swayed, creating wordless sound designs with her angelic voice. Allison had his head cocked and was looking quizzically at one of the rattlers who probed the air with its tongue and rattled a menacing trill.

Westermann stood, transfixed by the serpents as they undulated and twisted on the two men's arms. Harvey Wallace tossed a rattler through the air to a gaunt man with a port-wine stain that crept up his neck from under his flannel shirt like an encroaching tide. The man batted the snake three times on its head, sending the rattle into spasms. Two other men had each taken a snake from Allison, who stood with his arms out wide and his face to the ceiling while the two remaining snakes entwined his arms and wound past his neck. Westermann found himself walking forward toward Allison, the aural chaos seeming to crescendo—tongues, prayer, the girl's wordless singing, the rattles—all tethered by the hypnotic rhythm of the boy's guitar. Westermann faced Allison, watching the snakes probe with their tongues around the man's cherubic, sweating face. Allison opened his eyes abruptly and trapped Westermann's with their intensity. Westermann held out both hands for a snake. Allison's eyes widened.

Allison had to shout to be heard above the din. "You want the serpent?"

Westermann nodded. His knees shook. Sweat poured down his face. He was so close that he caught the sweet, damp smell of the snakes.

"Are you good with the Lord?" Allison shouted.

Westermann stood mute, knowing the answer, wishing it were not true, his heart hammering.

"Are you good with the Lord, Brother West?" Allison repeated, his dank breath lingering in the air. The longer of the two rattlers—maybe five feet long, brown and gold, with a broad head the size of a child's fist—was in striking distance of Westermann. Westermann stared at the snake as it pierced the air with its tongue in flickering jabs. He felt himself sway.

Allison said something; probably asking again if Westermann was right with the Lord. He took a backward step and another and then fled into the cool night.

69.

The terrain of Praeger's Hill at night seemed, to Grip, oddly hostile. He was aware that he and Morphy reeked of cop and would be met with nothing but fear and anger in these blocks of prostitutes, johns, and other parts of the City's dark clockwork. Tonight, though, there seemed an extra element of threat. Grip tried to get a purchase on this sense; tried to determine whether to pawn it off on his own inebriation or on the accumulation of so many sleepless nights for so many people being manifested as some kind of directionless rage. But, whatever the reason, Grip was puzzled and unnerved as they worked their way through groups of defeated-looking prostitutes, asking if they'd ever been seen by Dr. Vesterhue or had a connection with the Church of Last Days.

Grip watched Morphy work the prostitutes. The guy could talk to women; you had to give him that. The younger pros perked up when they saw him coming, the older ones had long since stopped giving a shit about who their customers were, as long as they had the cash.

Something about Morphy's interactions with these women bothered Grip. He was so natural. Grip was troubled by Morphy's ability to so convincingly act like someone he wasn't. It was just as convincing as when Morphy was being himself. Grip wasn't sure what to make of it.

He had initially planned to talk with Morphy about the recent doubts he'd been having about Westermann: the photo of Westermann and Mel Washington, his resistance to investigating the Uhuru Community, and his vigor in going after Prosper Maddox—his alleged communist leanings. He'd always trusted the lieut. Did his maybe being a Red change this?

He'd wanted to talk to Morphy about these things, but seeing him in action, he wasn't sure he could trust his partner, either. How could he when Morphy could so easily fool these hardened women of the street who must have seen it all?

Another source of disquiet: Were they—or rather, was he—being followed? Plenty of Negroes in this part of town, and while Grip, whatever his flaws, didn't harbor anything beyond the usual racial unease, he was fighting the sense that the jangly-limbed man was here and the proliferation of black faces was making him hard to locate. Grip felt he might have seen the man, his eyes yellow beneath a narrow-brimmed cap, among groups of men drinking or throwing dice. This sense was strong, as if he'd seen the man up close, noticed details in his face, but Grip was never that close to the man—never, indeed, was sure that he'd actually seen the right man.

A red neon light flickered on another block—a strobe effect—and this was almost more than Grip's electric nerves could handle. He took another drag off his whiskey flask and offered it to Morphy, who declined with a wave of his hand, but took a cigarette. They stopped to light up and Grip did another crowd scan, thought he saw the man, and then, when he focused on the spot, saw nothing. He shook his head.

"What?" Morphy asked.

"Nothing."

Morphy grunted but didn't pursue the matter and they continued on.

Another block and they found a group of three prostitutes, no different from countless other groups, except maybe a little younger, a little less weary. They could flash the dead-eye as quick as the others though when they saw the two cops approach, at least until they got a better look at Morphy and warmed a bit. They'd staked out a bar called Drake's, but it was too early for people to be leaving in any numbers.

"Evening, ladies," Morphy said, grinning, charming. "We won't take any of your time, but we're trying to track down any girls who saw a doctor name of Vesterhue."

One of the girls, small, dark, a pixie face, and shabby cocktail dress, met Morphy's gaze. "Sure. What's it to you?"

70.

Outside the Holiness Church, the cars were mostly gone but the din of the crickets was, if anything, louder. Westermann had no idea of the time, but it must have been on into the early morning, the moon bright enough to lend a shimmer to the silhouettes of the trees and hills. He leaned against his car, heart rate back to normal, head throbbing. He should have been in bed in the dingy room he had let above a dim bar on Main Street. But he wouldn't be able to sleep in this state of exhilaration. He needed to talk to somebody to settle himself down.

Allison was next to him, leaning against the car as well, his tie undone and his shirt collar open to the cool night. His hair was lank with dried sweat, his body sagged, his eyes shone.

"The Lord got ahold of you," Allison said, marveling.

"Did he?"

"I suppose you'd be the proper judge of that. But from where I stood, I'd say something had you."

Westermann nodded. *Something.* Outside, in surroundings less alien, less confined, he wasn't so sure what it had been. *The Holy Ghost?* The heat, the music, the intensity of belief in the people around him—all these things, he thought, had drawn him along, pulling him outside himself. Circumstances, not the Divine. Or was it the Divine that created the circumstance? He couldn't analyze it. He had no frame of reference.

"I take it you're not normally a churchgoing man. Or at least not a church like this."

Westermann shook his head.

"Well, there's never a bad time to come to the Lord, Brother West. I truly believe that your presence tonight was a gift from the Lord to you. He has a plan for you. He brought you here, praise God."

"I came here because of Prosper Maddox."

This took Allison by surprise. "Prosper Maddox? You're seven years too late, brother."

"No. I know he's not here now. I just . . . there's been a problem and I think he can help us, but he doesn't seem to want to."

Allison pondered this. "You police?"

Westermann nodded.

Allison frowned. "Brother West, I don't bear you any ill will, but you have attended our church under false pretenses, and I think that you will have to excuse me if I take my leave now."

Westermann held up his hand in apology, exhaustion threatening to overwhelm him. "I'm sorry. I hadn't meant it to go this way. I was just going to come in, have a word. But, as you said, I got caught up in it."

Allison frowned and nodded, conceding this point.

"Could you just tell me who I might talk to about Prosper Maddox, about why he left town? Then I'll be out of your hair."

Westermann waited while Allison, also drained, thought this over. Westermann wondered how often his congregation met. McIlvaine had made it sound as if it was nearly every night. Westermann couldn't imagine maintaining this state of heightened emotion night after night.

"You might could talk to Boyce Symmes. He wasn't here tonight, but he's another old-timer might could tell you about Prosper."

"I appreciate that, sir," Westermann said, and held out his hand to Allison. Allison looked at it, then took it.

71.

Grip spent two uneasy hours sleeping on a cot in Westermann's small office just off the squad room. Morphy had gone home to his wife, but they'd both agreed that someone should be on premises in case something came up. Grip wasn't unhappy that he would be away from his apartment, with the skull still painted on the door and the memory of the presence in his room the other night.

The prostitute they'd found that evening—the one who knew Vesterhue—had agreed to go back to the station with them after they promised her a decent meal and a payoff to her pimp. She claimed her name was Angel, and she was sleeping on a cot in a locked interview room. Grip needed a clearer head before they talked.

She'd given up the names of four girls she thought had also seen Vesterhue; even the addresses for two of them. Exhausted and coming down off his whiskey binge, Grip had given the information to two uniforms and sent them out into the night.

While the men were gone, Grip fell into a deep, troubled sleep, sweating as if he had a fever. He was awakened twice in the two hours, pale cop faces looking down at him, telling him they'd brought in another girl, set her up in a cot in a spare interview room. Two girls and Angel. It had the feel of something big. A break in the case. But Grip's mind was carried by strange, unfocused currents, and he fell asleep again to be greeted with still more disturbing dreams.

72.

Grip woke after two hours of troubled sleep to a young cop named O'Lear leaning over him, shaking his shoulder. Grip wandered to the bathroom and rinsed his face, the water smelling of sulfur. Leopold leaned against the wall outside Interview Room Three, holding two paper cups of coffee for Grip. They'd decided to start with one of the women who Angel had pointed them toward. The uniforms that had picked her up were concerned about her health, had told Grip that she was in bad shape.

"She's been up fifteen minutes, used the restroom. Should be ready to go."

Grip thanked him and used his back to open the door, which swung back shut once he was inside. They'd rousted the woman from her apartment, where she'd been sleeping and feverish. Her name was Joan Draper and she sat with her elbows on the table, her hands in her snarled, brownish hair. She wore a heavy shirt and slacks, even in this heat, and Grip could see that beneath the cloth there was little to her. Her wrists, where they protruded from her sleeves, were barely more than skin over bone. Her face was slack and the capillaries in her right eye had burst, framing her blue iris in red.

Grip sat down opposite her and set one of the coffee cups on her side of the table.

"Miss Draper?"

She stared at him; not defiant, just exhausted. "You got any aspirin?"

Grip returned with two aspirin and a cup of water and started again.

"You know why you're here?"

"Something about Dr. Vesterhue?"

"That's right."

"He in trouble?"

"I don't know. Have you seen him recently?"

She thought about this. "A couple of weeks? I'm not too good on dates."

"That's okay. Why did you see Dr. Vesterhue? Were you sick?"

She nodded. "I'm sick. But that's not why I saw him, or not the only reason. Dr. Vesterhue came around to some of the girls every so often, took a look at us, gave us medicine if we needed it."

"What? The clap? Something like that?"

She stared at Grip for a couple of beats, letting him know she didn't like that. "It's not just social diseases with us."

Grip regretted the remark and held up his hands. "I apologize. No insult intended. I'm just trying to understand what he was doing."

"He was a doctor."

"Okay. I get it. So, he makes house calls."

She nodded. "He didn't want us in his clinic. At least when we were really sick."

"Because?"

"He ran a Christian practice, or something. I don't remember exactly what he called it. He had a lot of religious people come to his clinic."

"What religious people? Do you know?"

"Sure. He gave me stuff—gave us all stuff—from his church, all the time. The Church of Last Days. It's a joke with some of the girls."

"It is?"

"Yeah, that this church is paying him to look after us."

"Wait. The church is . . ."

"Dr. Vesterhue would give us little books to read and say they're paying him to see us, like maybe that'd get us to read them."

"But you didn't?"

She laughed and it turned into a coughing fit. "I don't read."

"Why do you think the Church of Last Days is paying a doctor to look after you?"

She shrugged.

"Christian charity," he muttered under his breath.

"What's that?"

"Nothing," he said, thinking about getting Prosper Maddox into this room; asking him some questions.

Grip rubbed his eyes. Joan's head sagged between her lean shoulders.

"You said you're sick right now, Miss Draper?"

She nodded; her eyes focused on the table between them.

"If it's okay to ask, do you know what you have?"

She shook her head.

"Did Dr. Vesterhue know you were sick?"

"Yes. He said it was like a cold. Nothing to be done about it."

"Do you know how you got it?"

"No. A couple of the other girls have it—had it."

"Lenore?"

She looked up. "Who?"

"Mavis Talley?"

"Yeah, she's one. Who's Lenore?"

Grip ignored the question. "Miss Draper, I'm going to want to get the names of the other girls you know who you think might be sick. But let me ask you first, did all these girls see Dr. Vesterhue?"

She thought about it. "I guess so."

"Are there other girls who saw Dr. Vesterhue but aren't sick?"

She didn't need to think about this one. "Sure."

Grip played it cool, but his mind raced. "Miss Draper, I really think we need to get you to a hospital."

This suggestion alarmed her.

"What is it?"

"The boss. He won't like it."

"You let me take care of that. I need to get you to a hospital. I'm going to send an officer in here to take the names of the other sick girls. Then I'm going to get someone to drive you to a hospital and make sure you get looked at. We'll keep someone at your door, just in case."

He thought he saw fear and bewilderment in her expression; but mostly he thought he saw relief.

Kraatjes was waiting outside the interview room, frowning. Startled, Grip checked the wall clock over Kraatjes's shoulder. Four a.m.

"Sir?" Grip wondered what the hell would get the deputy chief in here at this early hour.

"Westermann hasn't returned, has he?"

Grip shook his head.

"Still in Fort Deposit?"

"As far as I know."

"I need you to get in touch with him. Tell him to get back here as soon as he can. No delays."

"Sure. What's up?"

"Detective, if I wanted you to know, I would have told you already."

73.

A light rain fell in the City the next morning, almost like steam in the humid air. Frings carried an umbrella, but his clothes were still somehow getting wet. It was early, not yet nine, and the streets were quiet, even for this part of town. Frings took his time despite the rain, his head still a little foggy from sleep, the heat slowing him down.

He'd left Renate sleeping, her hair spread across the pillow, reminding him of Lenore in the river, her hair floating around her pale face. He'd been about to kiss Renate on the forehead, an almost rote gesture, but he hadn't. Because of the association with Lenore? Or something else? He tried to make sense of this as he walked through the misting rain.

The weather seemed to have scared off the crowd from Father Womé's stoop, but two huge bodyguards nevertheless loomed underneath the awning on either side of the front door, scowling and making quiet conversation, eyeing Frings's approach.

As Frings turned to ascend the steps, the guards bounded down, guns drawn, Frings's head in their sights. Frings dropped his umbrella and put his hands up.

"What's your business here?"

Frings looked from one man to the other, getting nothing back. "I want to speak with Father Womé."

The man who seemed to be in charge frowned and shook his head. "Not going to happen."

"Come on, fellas. I'm with the *Gazette*, my name's Frank Frings. I've spoken with him before."

The guard shrugged as if it couldn't have made less difference. Without his umbrella, Frings was becoming soaked through; Womé's men, too.

"Look, can you put the guns away? I'm not armed."

The guard in charge nodded to the other, who holstered his gun and gave Frings a quick, professional pat-down. Finished, he nodded to the guard in charge, and he, in turn, holstered his piece. Frings put his hands down, feeling the tension ease a notch.

"How about this? Can one of you go in and ask Father Womé if I can have a few minutes of his time? I'm with the biggest newspaper in the City. We've talked before. If he doesn't want to talk, I'll leave." He looked from one to the other.

The guard in charge said, "This about last night?"

"Last night?"

The guard in charge shrugged. "Nothing."

"Yeah, well, last time I was here, he told me about the assaults down by the shanties; asked me to look into them. I did. I want to tell him what I found out. Can you give him that message? Let *him* make the decision?"

The guard in charge nodded and the other man climbed the stairs and disappeared into the house.

Frings wasn't led upstairs this time. Instead, he followed a guard down a narrow hall draped with what appeared, in the dim light, to be cloth hangings, probably African. Frings was presented to Father Womé in a small room off an enormous kitchen. Womé sat at a modest white table, eating a breakfast of fruit and cheese. A cup of steaming coffee was placed by an empty chair. Womé looked up at Frings and nodded to the chair, his face showing none of the warmth of their previous meeting. His lids threatened to close altogether, his lips were pressed into a tight, concise line.

"Mr. Frings."

"Father Womé."

"How can I help you?" Womé's voice seemed to come from far away. Something about him was off.

"Last time I came here you asked me to look into the assaults by the shanties."

Womé didn't answer, focusing on peeling an orange with a small knife.

"Well, I did; and you were right. The police sat on the investigation. And there's a reason why they did."

Womé pulled his eyes from the orange to fix Frings with a tired stare.

Frings said, "The officer in charge of the investigation; he was one of the men committing the assaults."

Womé nodded.

Frings said, "You probably already know that, what with your people beating the hell out of him and his friends the other night."

"My people?" Womé slid a slice of orange into his mouth and began to chew.

"Uhuru Community people."

"Yes. That's true."

"I'm not sure I understand why you don't consider them your people."

Frings waited for Womé to finish with his bite of orange.

Womé wiped his mouth with a napkin. "The Community people are indeed my people. But you—all of you—mistakenly see the Community people as unified, everyone the same. These people who took revenge on the group of violent fanatics, they are not the same as the women who work with your friend Carla Bierhoff, who are not the same people as the leaders in the Square. These are all my people, but . . . Am I clear?"

Frings nodded. "So, who took care of those 'fanatics'?"

"Young men. Followers of Samedi."

"Samedi?"

Womé waved away the question. "You have never been to the Square. In two days' time you must come to the shanties with your friend Carla Bierhoff. You must witness the Square. You can't understand the Uhuru Community without seeing the Square."

"What's the Square?"

Womé shook his head. "Two days' time."

This was as far as Frings was going to get on this topic.

"Things will most likely get worse, you realize. We're sitting on the story about the second body they found, but not for much longer. It's going to come out. And that cop? He's going to be a martyr."

Womé was ripping apart a roll now, releasing the smell of fresh bread into the room. Frings remembered his coffee and took a sip—dark, bitter.

Womé said, "Again, the perils of living in white man's society. This is why the Community is so important. When we are strong, our strength is twisted against us. Do I know that things will get worse? Of course. A group of men endeavored to set fire to the shanties last night. But they met resistance."

"From Samedi's people?"

Womé shrugged. "Them. Others. We aren't victims, Mr. Frings. We are merely disadvantaged in our struggle."

"How about Mel Washington?"

"Mel Washington is one of my people and I love him as I love the rest."

Frings wondered what Mel would think about being characterized as one of Womé's people. "You understand that his presence in the Commmunity just encourages the anticommunists and rightists to come after you."

Womé laughed a short, sour laugh. "Anticommunists and rightists? These are but a small number of the people who hate the Uhuru Community and what it stands for. Do you think that if Mel Washington and Betty Askins and Warren Eddings were sent away from the Community, that these people you mentioned would suddenly support us; want to help us; even tolerate us? Mel Washington is a very important member of the Uhuru Community even though, like me, he does not live in the shanties. Would I turn my back on him to curry favor with my enemies?" Womé ripped another roll in two. "Don't make the mistake of thinking we will allow ourselves to be victims. We aspire to peace through isolation. But if our community is put in jeopardy, we will do what is necessary. I think people will be surprised by our capacity in this regard."

Frings nodded, thinking about the symbol painted on Ed Wayne's door. "What about the girls?"

"Girls?"

"The dead girls . . . on the riverbank."

"Two girls?"

"The two girls they found on the riverbank by the Community. The first girl, downriver, nobody paid much attention. This second, once the story gets out, will be trouble."

Womé put down his roll. "Two girls. Two girls when we are weighing the fate of an entire community. Are Negro lives really so lacking in value?"

74.

Westermann drove a rutted dirt road in the cool of morning, looking for what Allison had called "the colored trees." Westermann had looked to him for an explanation and Allison had said, "Trust me." Westermann still wasn't sure what to make of it, but continued on, driving slowly, worried about the car's axles.

He was still unsettled from the previous night at the Holiness Church, the feelings that he had experienced there. He couldn't find a purchase on it. It challenged his concept of himself. He'd felt something similar to this once before, in the aftermath of his killing Sam "Blood Whiskers" McAdam after McAdam had killed Officer Klasnic. Then he had been forced to face both his cowardice and his capacity to end someone's life. It had been unpleasant. This, though, was something different, more like a reassessment of what had been his certainties about the world. Not damning like after McAdam, but maybe even more distressing.

In this frame of mind, he rounded a curve in the road to see the sparkling of hundreds of points of shimmering color, as if a rainbow had dropped from the sky and shattered. He slowed further and came to a spot where an even more primitive dirt track branched off to the left. He could now see that the lights were actually hundreds of shards of broken glass in myriad colors, strung from tree branches.

Westermann pulled off onto this new track and saw a shack in the distance. He parked as far to the side of the road as he could without risking getting stuck and covered the rest of the distance on foot.

Glass shards dripped from trees all the way to the shack. The effect of their manic twinkling was nearly hypnotic; the sound of his footsteps on the dirt and rock of the road was unnaturally clear. Westermann felt exposed as he stood before the shack, a tattered structure that seemed constructed—or at least repaired—with whatever had happened to be around: logs, plywood, sheet tin, scrap lumber. The sturdiest part seemed to be a narrow porch that ran the length of the front, chairs scattered about it. Behind the shack, Westermann could see edges of a garden and hear the sounds of chickens coming from an outbuilding that seemed to be barely standing.

"Hello," Westermann called out to the shack. "Mr. Symmes? I'm looking for Mr. Symmes."

Westermann heard voices inside the house and the groan of the floor under footsteps. The front door opened and a thin man in overalls stepped out, holding a shotgun by the barrel; just to let Westermann know he had it.

"Mr. Boyce Symmes?"

The man had mottled cheeks and a narrow jaw. He looked to be in his sixties, the horseshoe of hair around his skull shaved nearly to the skin. He stared back at Westermann with suspicious eyes.

"Mr. Symmes, I'm Lieutenant Westermann. Brother Allison sent me here to talk to you."

The man nodded, but didn't move.

"I'm hoping to talk to you about Prosper Maddox."

This time the man spoke. "Maddox?"

"Yes, sir."

"You ain't from around here."

"No, I'm not. I came up from the City."

The man nodded. "Well, I guess you might as well come have a seat." He turned to the open door and yelled inside. "James, put some water on and bring us two mugs of coffee." Westermann climbed three buckling steps to the porch, and Symmes nodded to a chair that he might have fashioned himself.

"Maddox having his troubles in the City?"

"Well, I don't know that I'd put it quite that way."

"There were those—myself among them—that counseled him not to go. Even though he weren't really Holiness Church anymore; at least not the way most of us were."

Westermann shifted in his chair, trying to get comfortable. "Can you explain what you mean by that, sir?" Wind agitated the tops of the trees and they creaked quietly with the strain.

Symmes considered this for a minute. "I understand you attended the prayer meeting last night."

"That's right."

"You see how things are. There's leaders, but it's not like the Baptist Church or what have you, where you've got a preacher. Maddox, he was a leader in our meetings. One of them. We also get traveling preachers from time to time, doing the circuit of Holiness churches. Well, a number of years ago, one comes by the name of Purcell. He comes and he preaches his message, and that is that we are in the End of Days, awaiting Jesus' return. This is far from our usual fare, Lieutenant. In other words, End Times preaching just ain't something we concern ourselves with. But Prosper, he was real keen on this."

A younger man emerged from the house, carrying two steaming mugs on a tray with his left hand.

"Thank you, James," Symmes said, not introducing Westermann.

James was tall and broad-shouldered, but the right side of his face drooped and he limped badly. He was wearing a short-sleeve shirt and Westermann could see that his right arm was atrophied and he held it awkwardly to his chest. A large, solid-blue rectangle was tattooed on his right arm. Westermann took his mug and nodded his thanks. James nodded in return and limped back inside.

"My son. The war," Symmes said, and left it at that. "Maddox, like I said, was keen on Purcell's preaching, and he took to studying Revelation and such. He's a smart boy, Prosper. And he starts preaching Revelation at prayer meetings, and to be truthful, some people kind of wearied of it. Like I said, it's not normally our concern. Eventually, Maddox started holding his own meetings, mostly for younger folks, but some older, too. My son was one. One day, this was during the war, Prosper says he's moving the flock to the City. He's got some places there or some such. So a couple dozen of them just up and left. Never looked back."

"Not your son?"

"He was still with the army. Came back, his church was split in two."

"Was there any other reason why Maddox might have felt like he needed to leave?"

The sound of a car approaching on the dirt road was suddenly audible. From the periphery of his vision, Westermann could see that James was standing in the doorway. He saw Symmes check the location of the shotgun. Nobody spoke. Westermann watched the approach to the house, the dirt track running between the trees, alive with colored glass.

The sound came closer and the front of a police car became visible crawling slowly toward them. Symmes stayed tense, but didn't move for the shotgun. The police car pulled to a stop fifty feet from the house. McIlvaine emerged.

"Boyce. James. Lieutenant Westermann."

Symmes nodded. Westermann registered the tension.

"Lieutenant," McIlvaine said, "we got a call for you from a"—he consulted a piece of paper in his hand—"Detective Grip. Said he needs to speak with you. Urgently."

75.

Grip and Morphy met a road-weary Westermann at the squad room. They filled him in on the information they'd received from the three prostitutes. They were gone now; Joan Draper to the hospital and the other two back to the streets. Westermann listened. They made it quick, walking with him, because the Chief was waiting.

Grip told Westermann about the girl he'd sent to the hospital. "I asked them to get that doctor who'd looked at Mavis Talley to have a look at her, see if maybe she has the same thing."

"What do you think it means if she does?"

"What?"

They stopped in the hall. "What do you think it means? What does it mean if this girl Draper and Mavis Talley and Lenore, they all have the same disease, and they all got treated by Vesterhue, and Vesterhue says he's paid to do it by Prosper Maddox's church?"

"I think it means that we have to get Maddox in here for a talk."

That wasn't the kind of answer that Westermann had been looking for, but just asking the question helped him think some things through.

The Chief's secretary saw them coming and got out of his chair. "Piet, the Chief's waiting for you."

The Chief looked up from his reading when Westermann entered. Kraatjes stood by an open window, smoking and flipping through the contents of a folder he'd propped against his chest. He tossed the folder on a chair, giving Westermann his full attention.

Kraatjes said, "They found a third body last night."

Westermann looked from Kraatjes to the Chief and back again. There was no mistaking their concern. "The same place on the riverbank?"

"Same place. Same MO as the second girl; strangled not drowned."

"Was she sick like the other girls? Did she have those sores?"

Kraatjes nodded.

The Chief said, "The cat's out of the bag, Piet."

Westermann's heart hammered. "What do you mean?"

The Chief coughed into his hand.

Kraatjes said, "The cops who were first at the scene were indiscreet. They're part of Ed Wayne's squad. We gave them hell, but they weren't going to let this slide."

The Chief said, "We're trying to figure out who they talked to, but word made its way to Truffant. He's making an announcement to the press this afternoon and it'll be ugly. It's not going to be any better when he says that we've been spending resources harassing—that's how he'll put it—Prosper Maddox."

Westermann stared at the Chief.

Kraatjes cleared his throat. "Piet, why don't you tell us what the hell is going on. Why are you so intent on going after Maddox?"

Westermann gave Kraatjes and the Chief the full picture. He told them about the connection between the girls and Dr. Vesterhue, and about how some of the girls had contracted an illness that had defied the admittedly lackluster efforts made at diagnosis. He explained the connection between Vesterhue and Prosper Maddox, specifically, how it was Maddox's church that was paying Vesterhue to minister to the women. When he'd finished, he sat back and watched Kraatjes and the Chief exchange glances.

Kraatjes got up from his chair and propped himself on a corner of the Chief's desk so that they were both facing Westermann.

Kraatjes said, "Do you have a theory about how all this information fits together; how it helps us find out who killed these girls?

"I don't have a theory. Not yet. But we're making progress. The connection between Maddox and the girls through Vesterhue; the illness that several of those girls seem to share. This is a real connection."

The Chief asked, "Has anyone else—anyone who hasn't seen this Dr. Vesterhue—been identified as having this illness?"

Westermann shook his head. "Not that we've found."

"And you haven't found Vesterhue?"

"No."

"Do you have thoughts about that?"

"I'm not sure. He's missing."

Kraatjes sighed. "So, the key person, the person who connects the murdered girl and these other, apparently sick, girls to Prosper Maddox and his church, this person is missing?"

"Yes."

Kraatjes again. "That's a problem."

"But that's why it seems so suspicious, right? That the person who Maddox would most fear is missing?"

"What are you implying?"

Westermann shrugged. It was obvious what he was implying. "Things seem—"

"Suspicious," the Chief said.

"Yes, sir."

"Remind me why we are putting so much time and effort into this case. There must be dozens of similar cases that go unsolved because we don't put forth ten percent of this effort. Why this one?"

"Where she was found. Maddox's stonewalling."

The Chief nodded.

Kraatjes asked, "What about the Uhuru Community? That's where two of the bodies were found and the third was just downriver."

"We've been looking into that angle, too. But we haven't turned up anything. The strong impression is that if it was somebody from the Community, that it would be a hard secret to keep."

Kraatjes and the Chief exchanged a look, unconvinced.

Kraatjes said, "The first girl was drowned and the other two strangled. How does that play in your thoughts?"

"I don't know. It's puzzling."

The Chief shifted, straightening in his chair. "Look, Piet, you realize the pressure we are under. If we go after Maddox and we can't make anything stick—someone's going to be held accountable, because when people look at this case, it's going to seem to them that the Uhuru Community is the most likely place to find a culprit. And, Piet, they'll wonder why the Community wasn't the main focus of the investigation."

Westermann looked from Kraatjes to the Chief, wondering where this was going.

The Chief said, "What do you want to do?"

"Bring in Maddox and ask him some questions."

The Chief nodded; looked at Kraatjes. "Okay. We'll bring in Maddox.

I'll call his lawyer. We're not going to have Grip and Morphy rousting him at his church. And when he gets here, it will be you and Kraatjes in the room with Maddox and his lawyer."

Westermann nodded, feeling a surge, as if there was a chance to really get a purchase on this case. "Thank you, sir. One more thing."

The Chief raised his eyebrows.

"I'd like to pick up Maddox's muscle, Ole Koss. I want him out of the way so we can send a few detectives around the neighborhood; maybe get a chance to ask some questions without Maddox or Koss interfering."

"In for a dime, in for a dollar, I guess. Is this going to come back and bite us, Piet?"

"I think this is the right thing, sir. I really do."

The Chief looked at Kraatjes again, then back at Westermann. "We trust your judgment, Piet. We trust your judgment."

76.

Carla approached the front steps of City Hall, past beat reporters and photographers setting up below a podium placed at a landing halfway up to the front entrance. A crowd had begun to gather at the lower stairs, though it wasn't clear whether they had been drawn by the newsmen's presence or because they knew what was about to happen or they just wanted to stay in the shade of City Hall. A mustard-colored haze leaked out of the storm drains, bringing with it a sulfurous odor.

Three youngish men stood smoking on the lower steps. One of the men, Carla realized, was watching her as she neared the steps. She identified him not by his face, which she had never seen up close, but by the attention he paid her and by his posture; the posture she had seen outside her apartment window earlier that day.

Early that morning, looking down the street from Carla's apartment, Washington had spotted Art Deyna, standing just inside an alley across the street, watching the building. Gerhard, her husband, had been incensed, storming down to the street and confronting Deyna, demanding to know where he came off staking out their building. Carla had taken advantage of the commotion and snuck Washington out a service entrance that would have been in the Deyna's line of vision had he not been receiving a tongue-lashing from one of the City's most prominent scientists. Afterward, Gerhard had said that Deyna's calm had been unnerving—just taking Gerhard's rant with a funny smile, then saying, "So Mel Washington is up there, correct?"

Deyna winked at Carla as she passed. Startled, she brushed through the front door, greeted the guard briefly by name, and headed for the stairs at the back of the lobby.

A small group had congregated outside Truffant's office: two cops and three men Carla recognized as Truffant's assistants. One in particular eyed

SCORCH CITY | 259

her worriedly, knowing that Carla meeting with Truffant could have no good outcome. That she was even able to get here was a result of her good relations with the City Hall guards, who were on orders that afternoon not to let the press or public down Truffant's hall.

Carla considered asking the two cops to tell her whom Truffant was meeting with, but decided against it, not wanting to seem anxious in front of his aides. Instead, she paced slowly up and down the hall, eyeing the painted mural of fabled politicians from the City's founding up to the turn of the century—men with impressive brows and luxuriant beards.

Truffant's door opened and conversation spilled out into the corridor. Truffant was agitated, his voice pitched high. A man was with him, Truffant's height but slim and pleasant-looking, wearing small, round glasses. Carla knew she recognized him and realized that it was Prosper Maddox. She watched Maddox shake hands with Truffant, patting the councilor's arm with his left hand and leaning in to say some last thing. He pulled away and Truffant caught a glimpse of Carla. Maddox turned as well and smiled at her, showing no sign of recognition.

Truffant excused himself, walked over to Carla, and kissed her lightly on the cheek.

"Carla, how are you?"

"I'm good, Vic. I was wondering if you had a minute."

Truffant looked at his watch. "I don't . . ."

"A minute," Carla said with more force this time.

Truffant reflexively looked to his aides, saw frowns and shaking heads.

"For you," he said, smiling, but reluctant, "a minute."

They walked past Maddox, who gave her the smile again, and Truffant closed the door behind them. He stood with his hands cupped together before him.

"What is it, Carla?"

"The Uhuru Community—"

Truffant laughed, holding up his hands as if in self-defense. "Carla, I was worried that this was what you were here about. I'm making an announcement as soon as we're done. Was the podium set up when you came in?"

"Vic, you don't understand. Those girls, there's really nothing—"

"Whoa, whoa, whoa. There's nothing? Carla, I know you have spent time there trying to help, and I respect you for it. I really do. But the Uhuru Community has become a center of violence. First the attack on the police officer and now the deaths, it turns out, of three young women. Deaths, I might add, that have been kept under wraps by the mayor and the police force."

"The police officer, he instigated the violence that night."

"I don't think you have the story here."

Carla sighed in frustration. "I don't?"

Truffant shook his head. "Carla, an off-duty police officer was beaten near to death while trying to help three citizens being assaulted by a mob. A mob from the Uhuru Community. Now I realize that you work with these people, but that doesn't change the facts. And these three young women—murdered, Carla. Murdered within a shout of the Uhuru Community."

Carla's felt the heat in her face. She tried to keep her voice steady. "You know there's no proof, Vic."

She saw that Truffant was losing his cool as well. "You're going to tell me what I know?"

"Those four men, including the police officer, were involved in several assaults on Uhuru Community residents over the past week. The assaults on those four men were the Community trying to defend itself."

"Come on, Carla."

"No. You know this is the truth. You know that there is no evidence—evidence, Vic—that ties those murders to the Community."

"What I know is that tomorrow's papers are going to run with the story that those Uhuru Community Negroes assaulted white citizens and a cop. They are going to report that three young women—young white women—were murdered essentially in the Community. The good people of this City are going to finally see these idol-worshipping, communist, un-American fiends for what they really are, Carla. *That* is the truth."

"This is going to end badly, Vic. You are going to be turning people loose."

"No, Carla, *you're* wrong. Things are going to work out precisely because I *am* turning people loose. I know your sympathies, Carla. You're a nice woman, but what you believe is dangerous, and I'll be damned if I let you or anyone else talk me out of doing what needs to be done to save this City and our country."

Truffant pulled the door open with abrupt force. Faces turned toward them from the hall. Carla could feel herself trembling, her jaw clenched.

77.

Panos was up and looking out his window, leaning against the sill; a situation both unusual and alarming. Panos's physical state was diminished enough that he was rarely out of his chair unless it was absolutely required. The exception was when he needed to burn nervous energy, which meant that something was up. Frings was pretty sure he knew what it was.

"Chief?" Frings asked.

Panos, rolling his body against the sill, turned to him. "Frank, have a seat."

Frings sat and watched Panos lean from the window until he could put a hand on his desk and then edge slowly to his chair and sit.

"Frank, I know you to have been following the girls who've been killed on the riverbank. There is news."

Frings leaned forward in his chair. "I know."

"You know? I'm sorry, Frank, how do you come to know this?"

"I've got a source."

Panos watched Frings. Frings stared at his hands.

"Ask me the question, Frank."

"What question?"

"The big question—how do *I* know?"

Frings didn't think it mattered much. Everyone would know soon enough and the trouble would really begin.

Panos said, "Truffant is holding a press conference." He glanced at his heavy watch. "Right now."

Frings stared, feeling slightly unreal.

"Deyna is there. You know, Frank, you killed his story. He had the scoop and you talked me into killing it. Now everyone will have it."

"You want an apology?"

"No. I want you to understand, Deyna is young; this was his first big one. You stopped it."

"It had to be stopped."

"Well, there's no chance of that now."

"I know."

"We're running the story."

Frings nodded.

"Deyna will be on the front page."

"Let me get you something, too."

"Of course, Frank. Of course."

Frings walked out into the sun and pulled his hat down to shield his eyes. He turned up the block but heard someone calling his name from across the street; a woman's voice. He stopped and, to his alarm, saw Ellen Aust sitting on a bench, discreetly waving to him, barely moving her hand.

Ellen stood to greet him as he approached. She wore her maid gear: form-less dress, flat shoes, hair up. Frings saw the tension in her shoulders and in the way she was fighting to keep her expression neutral.

"Ellen, this isn't a great idea, meeting here."

"I need to get out." Her voice was barely audible.

"Okay, but let's go somewhere and talk." He put his hand on her shoulder and ushered her along the sidewalk to a diner a couple of blocks down. They took a table at the back, Ellen facing away from the door. The place smelled of stale coffee and bacon grease. The patrons were mostly gray men, sitting quietly, sweating over their newspapers.

"What's going on?" Frings asked carefully.

"I . . . I don't know what I believe anymore. Dr. Maddox is so *sure* that the end is near. He says the signs are all there, but I don't know. He's like a different person. Maybe it's the fear or his work, but I don't know that he's not gone crazy."

"Ellen." Frings spoke softly, trying to calm her by keeping his own voice steady. "What is scaring you? What has changed?"

"Dr. Maddox, he changes from moment to moment; he'll be screaming from the altar and then he'll just stop and say nothing, like he's in a trance. Sometimes he weeps and he can't stop. Is he going crazy? I don't know what he'll do. But what if he's not crazy? What if he's right?"

"He's not right."

Ellen talked fast. "I don't know if I would have even thought about it if I hadn't seen you. We never really talk to people from *outside*. When I talked to you, that seemed normal—like what I remember of normal. Now it's different. Now it's dark and there's fear and there are enemies coming for us, at least that's what Dr. Maddox says. And it all seems right when you are in the middle of it. But when you are out, even for just a little bit, the whole . . . situation starts to seem strange. And then there are the howls."

"I'm not sure what you mean."

"I told you that Dr. Maddox says we are surrounded by enemies that lurk in the abandoned buildings, watching us, waiting for us to let our guard down."

Frings nodded.

"We howl at night, to scare them away. We gather in the sanctuary and have candles all around so that it's kind of light inside, but it looks dark from the outside. And then we howl; he has us scream as loud as we can. We sometimes do it for nearly an hour. To scare off our enemies, he says."

There was a question in her expression: *Is this crazy?* Frings wasn't sure what to say. If her account was accurate, Maddox was insane. But could he tell her that? Is that what she needed to hear?

Frings shrugged.

"I need to leave." Ellen's face was pale; her eyelids drooped. She seemed to be barely holding herself together. "I haven't slept . . ." Her voice trailed off.

Frings thought about the depth of fear that would lead her to abandon everything she knew in the City to seek refuge with a relative stranger. He moved his head to the side a little to make sure she was looking at him. She was chewing hard on her lip and Frings thought it might bleed at any moment. "Listen, Ellen. We can go from here right to my apartment. My girlfriend will look after you. You'll be safe there. We'll figure something out."

She looked at him, dazed, and nodded.

78.

A professor friend of Gerhard Bierhoff's—a Red back in the thirties—owned a town house near the Tech. The friend was intrigued by the communal experiment at the Uhuru Community, and Carla had arranged for Mel Washington to stay with him for the time being. The professor was off teaching an evening class. Carla, Washington, and Frings sat in the living room, all green floral fabrics and high windows. The heavy curtains had been drawn. Usually fastidious, Washington looked terrible—unshaven, eyes red-rimmed with exhaustion and stress—even a few days underground had taken their toll. Carla and Frings joined the usually teetotaling Washington for a glass of the professor's brandy, trying to get him to relax.

"Any word? The cops still looking for me?"

"We'll know more when Piet gets here," Frings said.

Carla put her hand on Washington's arm. "You're safe here."

Washington looked at her with hard eyes. "I'm a prisoner here. I need to get out. This is a critical time."

There wasn't much to say about that, so Carla and Frings were quiet, sipping their brandies.

Westermann arrived. Nobody shook hands and Westermann waved off the brandy.

"Anyone on the street?" Washington asked.

"Watching this house?" Westermann said. "No. I don't think so. They've lowered the priority on finding you, Mel. They took in a couple of kids from the Community. But it's part of a bigger picture: Uhuru Community violence. You know about the third girl?"

Washington nodded.

"It's getting tight. Really tight. But we are making some progress going after Maddox."

This brought the other three to attention.

Westermann continued, "We're bringing him in tomorrow."

Washington looked dubious.

Carla asked, "What's his connection?"

Westermann looked to Frings, who gave him nothing. "That's just what it is—a connection. Or, I guess, connections. He keeps popping up."

"Nothing concrete, though," Washington said.

"We're getting there. Look, it's our only chance. If it isn't Maddox, then it's going to fall on the Community. That's just a fact. But that's not why I'm here, right?"

Frings walked to the window and pulled the corner of the curtain back to peer out the window to the street. An older woman walked a small dog along the tree-lined street, waited while the dog relieved itself on a tree. A couple walked hand in hand behind two blond kids, who raced ahead of them and then ran back. Cars were parked the length of the block, but he couldn't see any that were occupied. He felt the eyes of the other three on him.

"Piet, Ellen Aust came to visit me today."

"Oh, yeah?"

"She's leaving Maddox's church; said they are getting out of control." Frings sat back down.

"Out of control?"

"Maddox seems to have gone off the deep end. He thinks the police coming through Godtown now, that they're agents of the devil or something like that. He's gone paranoid, thinks there are people hiding in the buildings around Godtown. Ellen says Maddox has the congregation howl at night to scare them off."

Westermann said, "I've heard that."

"From who?"

"No, I heard them howling. Down in Godtown."

Frings looked at him. "The other thing is that Maddox thinks the world is going to end soon and that"—he looked at Washington—"Father Womé is the Antichrist. Maddox thinks it's all about to play out."

Washington looked stricken.

Carla said, "What does that mean?"

Frings shrugged. "I have no idea, but it can't be good, can it? Maddox thinks he's in a battle of good against evil. Who knows what he thinks he needs to do. At the very least, it's another connection between Maddox and the Uhuru Community. It might even have something to do with those girls."

Carla said, "I think we need to assume that the shanties are under real threat. We need to distribute food, vaccines, figure out an alternative place for people to go if the shanties get bulldozed or—"

Westermann stood up, tried to stretch away some of the tension. "We're going to rattle Maddox's cage a little more tomorrow. We'll see what happens."

Frings massaged the back of his neck, wondering if this would be a good move or disastrous.

79.

At the end of the block, Grip leaned against an elm tree, smoking a cigarette and waiting for someone to come out of the town house Westermann had entered earlier. Something about shadowing his boss made Grip feel sordid. But Ed Wayne had planted suspicion in Grip's mind and he needed to see this through, if only to prove Westermann's guiltlessness to himself. Grip found his flask and considered a nip before deciding that he didn't feel like whiskey on top of the heat and his fatigue.

A hell of a lot of pedestrians were out at this time of the evening. They'd probably been waiting for the temperature to drop only to be rewarded with this stifling night in which to walk their dogs, venture to the grocer's, or whatever it was they were doing. Grip drew a few glances from people not used to a tough-looking stranger loitering on this block. Grip smiled absently, keeping his attention on the town house.

A month ago, he would have considered letting Morphy in on this. But Grip was increasingly reluctant to confide in Morphy. It wasn't necessarily that Grip distrusted him, more that he was growing to increasingly believe that he didn't understand his partner. It was possible, he thought, that Morphy was genuinely unfathomable, that he didn't have a stable enough personality to get a fix on. Whom could Grip trust? He would have said the lieut, but here he was staking the man out. *Shit.*

He was dismayed to find that he was down to three cigarettes. He lit one, figuring he'd deal with getting more when the time came. Hopefully the night would pick up and he wouldn't be smoking out of boredom. He wondered who was inside with Westermann; classy neighborhood like this, near the Tech. Maybe he had a girl here, Grip thought. The lieut must have a girl—or girls—somewhere. With his looks . . .

The door to the town house opened and two men and a woman emerged. They paused briefly on the sidewalk, exchanging a few words. The lieut was there, of course, and two others who looked familiar. Westermann left the other two, walking away from Grip. The other two headed toward him. He pushed away from the tree and strode for the corner, realizing now who the two were: Frank Frings and Carla Bierhoff. Not only was Bierhoff a known communist, but just a couple of nights before he'd seen those two exact people at Floyd Christian's place, where he felt sure he'd just missed Mel Washington. Now they were meeting with the lieut.

Washington.

Frings.

Red Carla.

The lieut.

Grip cursed Ed Wayne.

He hurried down a parallel block and took a right, moving quickly so that he could get within sighting distance of Westermann. Sweat flowed down his face with the effort. Halfway down the second block he saw Westermann step out from the corner in front of him. Grip slowed down abruptly and moved to the side, getting closer to the row of houses. Westermann didn't seem to glance in his direction, instead crossing the road and continuing down the block to Grip's left. Grip stopped for a second, giving his heart a chance to recover and Westermann time to put some distance between them.

Grip followed Westermann for close to a half hour through exhausted neighborhoods. Westermann's size made him an ideal tail, easily followed from a block behind. Keeping up was still a bitch, though, because Westermann's stride was so much longer than Grip's. He had to work hard to keep up the pace. The effort and the temperature wore him down.

Five blocks from Morphy's row house, Grip sussed out Westermann's destination. He felt strange, as if he were being left out of something. Why would the lieut be visiting Morphy at home? He'd never visited Grip at home. Was this a frequent occurrence, and if so, why didn't either of them ever mention it to Grip—especially Morphy?

Grip continued to tail Westermann for another block, preoccupied with these thoughts, until he remembered that Morphy wasn't home, which meant that he had followed Westermann all this way for essentially nothing—other than the disquieting knowledge that Westermann and Morphy were meeting behind his back.

They arrived at Morphy's block and Westermann paused on the side-walk, smoothing his hair with both hands. Grip stood in the shadow of a stoop and watched Westermann knock on Morphy's door. They both waited. The door opened, and from that distance, Grip caught a glimpse of Mrs. Morphy. He waited for her to tell the lieut that Morphy wasn't home, but the body language didn't jibe with that particular conversation. Wes-termann stepped in, and Grip was fairly sure that he saw the lieut touch Morphy's wife's hip with his open hand before the door closed. He was watching this over a distance, but he felt sure that was what he had seen.

He sat down on the steps, his mind racing. Only one thing could really be happening in that house. It seemed in some ways a betrayal, and in other ways it just seemed crazy. It was one thing to sleep with another man's wife—immoral, courting trouble. But Morphy's wife? It was like Russian roulette—the best possible luck got you nothing; anything less got you killed. And why would Westermann, who Grip assumed would have no trouble pulling birds, take this kind of risk? Morphy's wife was paralyzingly sexual—at least to Grip—but still . . .

Grip sat on the steps for a half hour, until there was no possibility that he had misread the situation. Satisfied that he understood, Grip walked to a nearby liquor store, picking up a bottle and a pack of cigarettes for the walk home.

80.

Winston's voice was shot from singing five nights a week, so this night he was just playing guitar. Floyd Christian's clientele didn't seem to mind, which was all that really mattered to Winston. Christian seemed like a good guy to play for; he paid Winston up front in cash—much more than Cephus ever had—and came across as a decent cat. The kind of cat you'd show up and play for even if your voice was nothing but a wheeze.

It was at least one thirty under the spots. Winston switched to a slide and plucked at the strings with fingers too slick with sweat to grip a pick.

As he sometimes did, Winston closed his eyes and let his thoughts roam. He thought about the previous night—he'd only been scheduled for the first set and had spent the rest of the night outside the shanties with about a dozen other Samedi cats who'd taken on the task of guarding the Community against the crazy ofays who wouldn't leave well enough alone.

It was spooky, standing in the flat no-man's-land outside the shanties, watching the men melt away into the shadows under a purple sky spattered with high, red clouds; watching the man they sometimes called Glélé and sometimes called Samedi walking around like a goddamn puppet, the strings being pulled by the *lwa* himself. Winston could call up the essence of what he had felt in Glélé's presence, a feeling of supernatural confidence—of invulnerability. It puzzled him, this feeling. He was not superstitious, not even particularly religious given his upbringing. But he sensed something with these Uhuru Community gods, something different from what they had preached in his church down South. More like ghosts. Not that he really believed in ghosts, but he'd seen how the Community people felt about the *lwa*, and they were in a better position to judge than he was. He saw no reason to dismiss their beliefs, especially since he saw the evidence for himself in the Square and in Samedi; more evidence than he'd ever seen of his mother's God.

He could feel as much as hear the screaming that he was coaxing from his guitar, and the feeling conjured the sensation of Samedi's presence—the presence of the *lwa*.

Last night, a car rumbled through—a DeSoto he thought, though he was not good with those things—packed with white kids. He'd experienced the action with a kind of hyperclarity, like a slow-motion dream or looking through aquarium glass. The car stopped and the kids got out, holding bottles with something sticking out of the tops. Lighters flared. Winston watched what the boys couldn't see—shapes of men emerging out of the shadows, advancing silently on the car. When the white kids had their bottles lit, a wild ululation came from somewhere—Winston guessed Glélé—and the Samedi men, Winston among them, ran at the ofays.

Winston now worked the slide violently, his fingers frantic on the strings, howling coming from the amp.

The boys panicked, throwing their Molotov cocktails wildly. The Samedi cats closed the distance quickly, but the first boys had already made the car. One took the wheel. A bottle exploded with a pop. Another. The car began moving, four boys inside, two more running alongside, hands on the open windows. More pops; more bottles exploding. Winston ran at an angle to intercept the car and thought he might have a chance to jump on the hood or get his arm in a window. The fifth boy was pulled inside the car by his shirt and the sixth was halfway in, his legs dangling out the window as his buddies tried to pull him in. The car accelerated. Winston cocked his stick back as he ran and then swung it as hard as he could as the car swept past. He made contact with something that made a sound like a tree branch being snapped over someone's knee, then heard a scream.

Winston's right hand now dropped away from the strings and he massaged a few last whimpers out of the fret with the slide, then let that hand drop, too. He opened his eyes to the smoke and the half-seen faces in the crowd. There was a silent moment, then the cheers came hard.

81.

Arriving to work, Panos found Frings sitting in one of the leather chairs in his office with his feet up on the desk and the newspaper in his hands. The place smelled of stale coffee. Panos hung his jacket on a hook on the back of the door and lowered himself slowly into his chair. He stared at where Frings's coffee cup sat on his desk. Frings set the cup on the floor under his chair.

"Don't keep me in suspense, Frank. Tell me your troubles."

Frings read from the paper. "This is, what? . . . One, two, three, fourth paragraph: 'Councilor Truffant alleged that the police and the mayor conspired to cover up the murders of three young Caucasian women whose bodies were found in the vicinity of a Negro shantytown known as the Uhuru Community.' *Caucasian*, Panos?"

Panos nodded. "It's accurate, Frank."

Back to the paper. "'Truffant alleged that the Uhuru Community is a communist enterprise, pointing to self-proclaimed communists Melvin Washington and Warren Eddings as leaders in the Uhuru Community.'" Frings skipped ahead. "Truffant, quote, 'Based on the cover-up of the three murdered girls and the savage beating of an off-duty police officer, one has to wonder where the mayor's sympathies lie, with the people of the City or these violent Negro communists.'"

Panos gave a pained smile.

"'Truffant asserted that his first action as mayor would be to bulldoze the shanties.' Quote, 'This would be the top priority for me. But I understand that, if I win the election, I will not take office until three months from now. I would not blame any citizen for thinking that this was too long of a wait to address this problem.' End quote.

"Panos, this is an incitement to riot and we ran it in the paper. That's reckless. We'll have a lot to answer for if something happens in the shanties."

"Frank, it's news. The *Sun* has this. The *Post* has this."

"We're better than that, Panos. This could get people killed. Look"—Frings held the paper up to Panos—"the front page has a picture of god-damn Piet Westermann talking to Mel Washington down at the shanties. Jesus, Panos, think of the implication. The guy's not supposed to interview Mel Washington because he's supposedly a commie?"

Panos banged his fist on his desk. "Enough. Enough, Frank. I under-stand you don't like it, okay? But, Frank, why does your pal Westermann bring Prosper Maddox into police headquarters to talk, but he meets with Mel Washington on the outside, when he thinks no one is looking? Ah? What does it mean? Maybe nothing. But, Frank, you can't pretend that it doesn't happen."

"Listen, Truffant is an asshole. You see this; I see this. We print this story, the people who know better, they, too, will see this. People who don't . . . There are problems in this City, Frank. I don't know if most people think like you and I."

"We ran your column, Frank. I think that makes our standpoint clear."

Frings shook his head. "We didn't run it on the front page, Panos. Not on the front page."

THE *GAZETTE*
Editorial, August 12, 1950

FLIMFLAMMERY

History is written by the victors and news is written by the powerful. Only a naïf can read the newspaper with the expectation that he is receiving "The Truth," a concept that in and of itself seems to be negotiable in these unsteady times. Would that this paper were immune to this practice, but the briefest perusal of today's front page shows its—our—complicity.

I refer specifically to allegations aired by Councilor Vic Truffant regard-ing the tragic murders of three young women and the somewhat less troubling beatings of four men, all in the general vicinity of the Uhuru Community, of which we have previously written. It is a testament to Vic Truffant's strategic acumen, if not to his honesty, that he was able to pre-empt any journalistic investigation of the story by holding a press conference where he presented his conspiratorial version of these events; this version—a fetid brew of half-truths and innuendo—because of a combination of apathy and laziness, graced the front pages of all the major papers, this one not excepted.

But while Vic Truffant correctly anticipated the retarded work ethic of most City reporters, his version does not deserve to go unchallenged, as it is as lacking in actual evidence as it is awash in bad faith. To be brief, Councilor Truffant claims that the perpetrators of these felonious actions were one or more Negro men from the Uhuru Community. The evidence: the proximity of the victims to the Uhuru Community and the alleged communist ties of certain Community residents. Yet questions exist that stymie the logic of this conclusion. I will focus the rest of this column on the assault on the four Caucasian men and make explicit the flaws in Truffant's specious claims.

Why, one asks, would these Caucasian men be in those environs in the dead of night? The reason for this may be illuminated by a different series of assaults, events deemed not sufficiently important to merit a mention in any of the City's major papers—again, this paper included. Over three nights, three separate assaults were carried out against Uhuru Community residents—unprovoked attacks against unarmed citizens. It will be no surprise to frequent readers of this column that the police were decidedly indifferent in their response.

So let me posit another scenario, one that I believe is more consistent with the facts and with the context of the events of the past week. Four Caucasian men return to the scene of their previous attacks, anticipating another night of preying upon unsuspecting and defenseless Negroes. They have not foreseen that the Uhuru Community will resist this attempt at intimidation and are therefore caught unawares when members of the Uhuru Community take steps to preempt the next violent incident.

In the absence of any witnesses beyond the participants in this incident, the reader must discern which scenario most likely played out. If you accept the scenario that Vic Truffant has described, you are placing your faith in the author of the story rather than in a plausible reading of the facts.

There is a larger motive here, I believe, to Vic Truffant's advocacy of these four men's soft martyrdom. That motive is Councilor Truffant's oft-stated and well-known wish for the destruction of the Uhuru Community shanties. Perversely, he seeks to use the very people who terrorized Community residents as the victims who will garner public support for this aim. Do not fall victim to this flimflammery.

F. Frings

82.

An air of expectancy greeted Westermann the next morning as he arrived at Headquarters, maybe ten minutes after Maddox and Koss and their lawyers. Cops hung around the squad room, ignoring the reports they had to type or the beats they had to walk. They chatted in groups of four or five, drinking coffee, sucking on cigarettes. Westermann felt their eyes on him and understood the complicated expectations. For the most part, these people didn't like him, and his failure with a high-profile figure such as Maddox would quietly be cheered. But cops reflexively rooted for the big bust—bagging big game. In some ways, this was a no-lose situation, and they stuck around, knowing that any outcome would be worth the wait.

Souza and Kraatjes met Westermann at the interview rooms. Souza looked harried, a cigar smoldering in the corner of his mouth. Kraatjes stood calmly, eyes in a slight squint, head cocked back a little. He was ready to go, but something was bothering him, too.

Kraatjes said, "Chief's office."

Westermann didn't believe it.

"Part of the negotiation. Maddox doesn't want to be treated like a suspect."

"We're—"

"Piet."

"What?"

"Maddox's lawyer, in the Chief's office—it's your father."

Westermann stared at Kraatjes, bit his lip, felt the adrenaline. How could this have happened? Did his father not know that he was handling the case? He must have, it had been in the papers. What the hell was he thinking? *Another test. Another goddamn test.*

"You okay?" Kraatjes asked.

"Sure."

"You want someone to take your place?"

277

"No."

Krattjes kept Westermann's eyes until he seemed to make a judgment. "Okay. Let's go."

"Just a question—how can this be allowed?"

"We're just questioning, Piet. This isn't a trial. Maddox hasn't been arrested. They're just trying to mess with you—with us."

Westermann shook his head, confused by this betrayal, wishing he were surprised.

"Where's the Chief?"

"He's at City Hall, keeping Truffant and His Honor away. Let's not ball this up, okay?"

Westermann shook his head. Pissed.

Maddox and Big Rolf were sitting in leather chairs that had been brought in specially for the questioning. Big Rolf stood, shook hands with Kraatjes.

Big Rolf looked at Westermann. "Our first professional encounter. I suppose I should feel a father's pride."

"Hello, Rolf."

They shook hands. It was strange.

Maddox watched this from his chair, hands placidly laced in his lap. He looked unhealthy, his skin oily and pale.

Kraatjes said, "Thank you for coming today." As if he were going to launch into some kind of stand-up routine.

Maddox unlaced his fingers and turned his hands palms up in a practiced motion, a gesture of clerical grace.

Everyone sat.

"Have you been told why you're here?" Kraatjes asked.

Big Rolf said, "Our understanding is that Dr. Maddox might be able to assist you in a murder investigation."

Kraatjes nodded. "The murder of three young women." His voice was quiet, deferential; almost apologetic. "One's name was Lenore. We still don't have her last name. The other two remain unidentified."

"A tragedy," Big Rolf said.

Westermann clenched his teeth, not rising to the bait. He watched Maddox, whose mind seemed elsewhere. Maddox looked vaguely in his direction, but didn't seem to be particularly focused on anything.

Kraatjes turned to engage Maddox directly. "Do you know a Dr. Raymond Vesterhue?"

Maddox turned his head toward Kraatjes, but kept the unfocused stare. "Of course."

"Can you elaborate on that, Dr. Maddox?"

"We retain him, as an excellent doctor and a Christian, to tend to the medical needs of our congregation."

"Do you engage him in other ways?"

"We pay him to perform charitable acts on behalf of the church—to minister to the poor."

"By poor, Dr. Maddox, are you referring to prostitutes?"

Maddox made the palms-up gesture again, and this time Westermann took it as an acknowledgment.

Kraatjes continued the questioning. "Were you aware that Dr. Vesterhue provided medical services to the murdered woman named Lenore?"

Big Rolf seemed about to say something, but Maddox put up a hand. Westermann wasn't sure he'd ever seen anyone do that to his father before and was surprised that his father seemed to accept it.

"I'm afraid that I must confess a failing in this regard," Maddox said. "While we provide money to Dr. Vesterhue to cover his time and expenses during his work with these unfortunate women, I do not, in fact, have any contact with them, nor do I follow their medical travails. Dr. Vesterhue, as a condition of our agreement with him, gives the women materials from our church. Sadly, to date, none has taken advantage of our offer of salvation."

"Did these materials include anticommunist pamphlets in addition to religious ones?"

Maddox smiled. "I don't believe I need to tell you or the lieutenant that communists prey on those who are already morally degraded. To not alert them to this danger would be derelict on my part."

"Do you know a Mavis Talley?" This question—Westermann breaking Maddox's rhythm with Kraatjes—seemed to startle Maddox a little.

"I assume that she is one of Dr. Vesterhue's patients as well, and as I said before, I was less than vigilant regarding Raymond and his patients."

"We've learned that several of Dr. Vesterhue's patients have contracted an illness that the hospital can't seem to identify."

Kraatjes cut in; picking up the pace. "Has anyone in your congregation been ill? Seriously ill? We believe that this disease is potentially fatal."

"I'm afraid not." Maddox smiled apologetically.

Westermann said, "Tell me about the Uhuru Community."

Big Rolf stood up. "Dr. Maddox did not come here, of his own volition, to be harassed by you. We *will* cease to cooperate if this continues."

Kraatjes gave him a startled stare, and Big Rolf looked to Maddox, back to Kraatjes, then sat down. He'd done his job, giving Maddox a chance to breathe.

"The Uhuru Community?" Maddox asked.

Kraatjes nodded. "Why do you want the Uhuru Community shut down?"

"*Do* I want the Uhuru Community shut down?"

"You were meeting with Councilor Truffant before the press conference yesterday; before he more or less called for the Community to be razed."

Maddox considered this behind half-closed lids. "As I said before—"

Westermann pressed, "Communism. We got that. You say you think that the Uhuru Community is a serious communist threat? I don't believe you really do."

Big Rolf started to speak but Maddox held up his hand again.

"Lieutenant, I'm not a fool. Nor do I go looking for threats under beds and such. But Scripture is very clear about the attributes of the Antichrist and his dominion. We have the privilege of living during the End of Times, Lieutenant. This fact may have escaped you, but it is as plain as the leaves on the trees. The Jews have returned to Israel. Russia is risen. The conditions are just as foretold, and we—or I—am in a unique position to thwart the Antichrist's ascent."

"Father Womé?" Westermann said, incredulous.

Maddox stared at Westermann. Westermann looked to Kraatjes, who kept a neutral expression.

Big Rolf broke the silence. "I'm sorry. What does this have to do with the murdered girls?"

"Nothing," Kraatjes said, his voice distant.

83.

Godtown was again empty under hazy, yellow skies. Westermann's detectives split into three pairs, fanning out over the two square blocks. Grip tracked the progress of the other two pairs of detectives, thinking that it was like watching people moving around an empty movie set, knocking on the doors of prop houses. *No one* was out. The whole neighborhood was functionally deserted. The knocks on doors sounded like rifle shots. Grip was tense, the heat suffocating.

Grip and Morphy started with Mary Little's row house. Grip fought to stay focused on the canvassing at hand, but his mind kept drifting to the scene from the previous night: Westermann touching Jane Morphy's hip—a comfortable, familiar gesture; Westermann's disappearance into Morphy's house. Grip was exhausted. He'd been unable to sleep last night. What he'd seen troubled him, as did the question of what, if anything, he should do about it. He felt pulled in opposite directions by his loyalties to Morphy and to the lieut, neither of whom he was eager to betray, either through acts of commission or omission. Did Westermann's actions forfeit his claim to Grip's loyalty? Where did his, Grip's, best interests lie? In the end, those two considerations had led him to decide that he had to tell Morphy, because Westermann didn't deserve Grip's silence, and because if Morphy found out about his wife and found out that Grip knew and hadn't told him . . . Grip didn't want to spend much time ruminating about what that would lead to. Now he had to find the right moment to let Morphy know.

With this distraction, Grip banged on Mary Little's door; hard, but not intimidating. No answer. Grip put his ear to the door, heard nothing. He banged again, identified himself as police. Still nothing. Morphy played with the window to the right of the door and found it locked. Grip turned, shook his head, and they descended the steps.

They walked up the next set of steps, Grip wondering if maybe the best time to tell Morphy was now, when they were busy; when maybe Morphy's reaction would be tempered by being in public and in the midst of his duties. Grip banged on this new door. Again no answer. Again he put his ear to the door and was met with silence. Again, he yelled that he was police and to please come to the door and open up. But nobody was home. Grip watched a stray German shepherd weaving down the street, a dead rat hanging limp in his jaws. Grip noticed Morphy watching, too, the dog dripping red foam from his mouth. Grip pulled his gun from its holster, but Morphy put a hand on his arm and Grip put it back.

They looked up the block to see that the other two pairs of detectives had encountered similar results. No one was on the streets in Godtown; no one was home.

Morphy waited for the big dog to turn a corner, put two fingers in his mouth, and let out a piercing whistle. The other detectives looked their way, and Morphy pointed to the street, calling a meeting. Grip pulled a pack of cigarettes, shook two free, gave one to Morphy.

"Morph," he said, "we need to talk for a minute when we get done here."

"Okay," Morphy said, seeming unconcerned.

They met the other detectives in the street and talked things over, though there wasn't really much to say. The houses were empty. The people had to be at the church. Grip thought that with Koss and Maddox down at headquarters, they might be able to bully their way in past whoever was minding the door.

They walked back to their prowl cars and drove them around to the front of the church. It was quiet on the street, though when the last engine was cut, Grip thought he could hear a low murmur, as if people were murmuring hushed prayers inside.

Morphy and Grip went to the huge double doors while the other detectives took places behind their squad cars, guns drawn but not visible from the church. Grip pounded on the door. People were definitely inside. He put his ear to the door, but didn't hear approaching footsteps. He banged again and yelled, "Police," but still no footsteps. Instead, the murmuring ended, replaced by a moment of silence and then by a burst of noise, like dozens, if not hundreds, of people screaming. Grip felt the chill on his back. He looked at Morphy, who was chewing on his lip, eyes narrow, as if he was pondering some moderately difficult riddle. The detectives behind the cars shifted around, nervous and antsy.

"The fuck?" Grip said.

Morphy grabbed the door handle and shook it. Locked. The volume seemed to crest. They didn't have a warrant; the only windows were stained glass.

Grip and Morphy returned to the cars.

"What the hell is going on in there?" Dzeko asked.

"The fuck does it sound like?" Grip responded, edgy. "There's a boatload of people in their screaming their asses off."

"Why?"

Grip rolled his eyes and made a disgusted noise.

"I'm just asking."

"There's nothing here for us," Morphy said. The other detectives nodded, eager to get out of there. They got back into their cars to make the trip back to Headquarters, having failed in their modest goal to talk to somebody—anybody.

Grip drove several blocks in silence, waiting for Morphy to ask him what they needed to talk about. But Morphy didn't say anything. He seemed lost in his thoughts, whatever those were. Grip realized that he could just let the whole thing drop, that Morphy might very well never ask him about it. But he'd made his decision and had enough conviction that he wouldn't drop it just because it was going to be hard as hell.

"Larry," Grip said.

"Yeah?"

"About what I had to tell you?"

"Okay."

"I shadowed the lieut last night."

Morphy looked at him, surprised. "You did what?"

"Shadowed the lieut."

"Why's that?"

"Long story. Ed Wayne's got some bug up his ass that the lieut's a commie."

"Is he?"

"Don't know. Maybe. He met with Carla Bierhoff . . ."

"She's a Red, right?"

"Yeah. He met with her and that reporter Frings. Maybe others. I don't know."

"That's strange."

"I *know*, but that's not the thing. I followed him after that meeting, you know, to see where he went next. So I did, and he ended up at your place."

Morphy looked over at Grip. "I wasn't there last night."

"Yeah. I know."

"So what? What happened?"

"He knocked on the door, Jane answered." Grip paused, dreading the next part.

"And?"

"He went in. Didn't come out in the half hour that I stuck around."

Morphy's gaze kept steady. "Am I hearing you right?"

Grip nodded.

"That's interesting," Morphy said, sounding as if he'd just heard that someone had eaten his sandwich.

"What are you going to do about it?" Grip asked. But Morphy was back to staring out the windshield, lost in thoughts that Grip was happy not to know.

84.

Carla had come to expect a certain pace to the activity in the shanties—a certain pitch to the noise, a certain number of people in the narrow alleys. This day, though, the shanties were different—busier, louder, but also something less tangible—an urgency she hadn't sensed in the past.

The air was beginning to develop the grasping heat of late morning. Humidity rose off the weeds and concrete, and Carla felt her skin flush, sweat dampen her forehead. A group of young men stood at the intersection of two alleys, passing a reefer between them. Carla recognized Billy Lambert, his face less swollen, among the group. It was funny, she thought, she hadn't realized he was part of the Samedi group.

She waved to the men and they mostly waved back, recognizing her from past visits. She walked on into the maze, surprised to see the number of people and the purpose with which they moved. She walked sideways, hugging the walls for long stretches to avoid colliding with others carrying small farm animals, children, baskets of goods. Chatter came in quick patois bursts, the pitch somehow alarming. Even the menace that she so often felt walking through the shanties—or any other desperately poor place— alone, even this was different. The young men who so often seemed dangerous were preoccupied, not even noticing Carla. The place smelled of smoke from pungent wood. It felt like a prelude to an evacuation—or a siege.

Eunice Prendergrast met Carla outside her shack, her round face drawn with stress. Betty Askins's mouth was a tight line. None of the other usual women seemed to be around.

"Eunice, what's happening here?" Carla asked.

Betty Askins answered, her voice quavering as she tried to suppress her rage. "There's a rumor going around that Father Womé dreamed that the Community burned to the ground. People are preparing to leave."

Eunice wouldn't meet Carla's eyes. "There's a ceremony in the Square tomorrow. We'll be asking the *lwa* for protection."

Betty gave an exasperated sigh and looked to Carla. "We need to do what we can today and tomorrow. Food, medicine, clothing; whatever we had planned, we need to do it before tomorrow night."

Eunice nodded. "After the Square, I don't know what will happen."

A group of children slowed as they passed Eunice's house, walking with backs straight and chins high. Once past, they ran again, laughing.

"You've got them trained well," Betty said.

Eunice didn't so much as smile. Carla made a mental list of contacts she'd have to make, people she would have to coax into action, to speed up their charitable efforts.

"I'll send someone back later," Carla said, "with an idea about when different things can be scheduled. Then you two can get your people to spread the word. We'll do everything we can before tomorrow night."

Eunice smiled grimly. "I'm worried about the Community. I'm worried this could end very quickly."

Carla nodded. "I know."

85.

The crowd outside the interview rooms was even larger now, and boisterous. Cigarette haze was heavy; some of the night-shift cops were liquored up. Bodies were close; the room was claustrophobic and smelled of sweat.

Westermann had walked out of the Chief's office angry and frustrated. Maddox had maintained his cool, made no mistakes. The presence of Big Rolf had confused Westermann—initially because of the betrayal he'd felt, but even more perplexing was the way Maddox had treated Big Rolf: like a servant, without the deference he usually commanded. Westermann's head throbbed with stress.

Kraatjes, though, had been more sanguine. "He's hiding something, Piet. I know you wanted to get the big admission or a slip or something, but he's too smart and your father would have stopped him even if he'd started to slip. You could tell from the moment we walked in—he feels protected; doesn't think there are consequences to stonewalling us. So he went with that not-of-this-world shit and what can you do? But he's hiding something, and I wasn't sure about *that* until today."

"You have a theory?"

"No. Not yet. Maybe we'll get something out of Koss. He strikes me as someone we might be able to persuade to say more than he intends to."

Koss was sitting straight in his chair, shoulders squared to the door, when Kraatjes and Westermann came in. Koss's face was flushed with the heat. His lawyer, a normally fastidious man, had his jacket on the back of his chair and his shirt was already soaked through. Westermann and Kraatjes sat down opposite Koss and his lawyer. Koss nodded to Westermann; cocky, familiar. Kraatjes registered this, then introduced himself to Koss and then both himself and Westermann to the lawyer. In the cramped confines of the IR, Koss seemed even bigger, his shoulders barely contained by the collared shirt he wore.

Kraatjes said, "I assume you've been briefed about why you're here."

Koss nodded. "Sure. The girls they found on the bank."

"Three of them. One ID'd as Lenore, last name unknown," Kraatjes said.

"Right."

"Did you know her?"

"Sure. Of course."

Westermann leaned forward in his chair. "Say that again."

Koss shrugged. "I knew her. I knew Lenore. Not well, but I knew her."

Kraatjes said, "Explain how you knew her."

"Dr. Vesterhue, I don't know if you know, but he did work with a lot of the whores for the church. We paid him to do it. I was the liaison. I paid him, helped out when necessary. I met a lot of the girls."

"Do you know where Vesterhue is?"

Koss frowned. "Why? Is he missing?" Maddox had professed surprise, too. Westermann ignored the question. "These girls that you met, do you remember a Mavis Talley?"

Koss's eyes darted to Westermann. "Mavis? Sure, I know her, too. Again, not well. I just know who they are."

Kraatjes picked up again. "What's Lenore's last name?"

Koss shrugged. "I wouldn't have known Mavis's if you hadn't just told me."

"Were you aware that Lenore was very ill?"

"I don't think so."

"How about Mavis Talley?"

Koss shook his head. "Dr. Vesterhue made his visits. I don't remember him visiting anybody specifically because they were sick. Maybe . . . no, I don't think so. I don't know."

Westermann was aware of something at the back of his mind, a question that he needed to ask. He couldn't pull it forward; too much else happening.

Kraatjes asked, "Did you visit Mavis Talley at City Hospital and subsequently have her discharged?"

"Mavis was in the hospital?" Koss made a good show of really thinking this one over. "I don't believe I knew she was there. I can tell you for certain that I didn't visit her."

"Did—," Kraatjes began.

Koss's lawyer spoke up. "I'm afraid I have to interject. My understanding regarding this interview was that Mr. Koss was going to provide you with some help vis-à-vis the investigation into the young woman's—"

"*Women's*," Westermann said.

"Thank you. *Women's* deaths. This seems as though he is being treated as a suspect."

Kraatjes nodded. "I'm sorry if we have given that impression. We are trying to determine the nature of the church's—and your client's—relationship with these young women."

"Whores," Koss said, and everyone looked at him.

The lawyer's eyes bulged. "I think that maybe this interview should end now."

Westermann wiped the sweat from his brow, concentrating on the table. Koss began to stand.

"One last question?" Then, before the lawyer could object, Westermann asked, "Do you know a guy named James Symmes?"

Koss smiled. "Sure. Jimmy Symmes. Of course. We were in the army together."

86.

Warren Eddings sat slumped in a chair in the corner of a coffee shop in Little Lisbon that was, depending on one's viewpoint, either famous or infamous as a gathering place for unionists and communists. The place was in decline, but it was still considered friendly ground, and Warren Eddings was as safe here as anywhere else in the City.

Frings removed his hat and placed it on the next seat. The inside band was saturated with sweat; Frings's hair dripped onto his collar. The owner, an ancient man with a tangled beard that hung to his sternum, brought over two tiny cups of espresso. A radio played tinny Gypsy music.

Eddings looked drawn, as if he hadn't slept in a week. He hadn't shaved in days, his cheeks and upper lip showing stubble above his beard, which he'd bound with string.

Frings cocked his head, trying to get Eddings's eye. "Warren. What's going on here?"

Eddings looked up, lids almost too heavy to keep open. "It's falling apart very quickly."

"The Community?"

Eddings snorted, nodding.

Frings said, "I really think that we can get through this."

"No. It's not Truffant. It's the Community. The people, they're going to end it."

"I don't follow."

"You know how I've been trying to tell you that the Community, it's not ours? We don't run it; we just try to do what we can to keep it going?"

"Yeah, I get that, Warren. You made it pretty clear."

"Mmmh," Eddings said, looking into his cup. Frings took a sip of his and felt the heat in his face.

Eddings said, "The Community, whatever else it is, it's a religious

community—superstitious and religious. People in the shanties are preparing to leave because of some dream that Womé had. A goddamn dream."

"I don't—"

Eddings banged his fist on the table. "Open your eyes, Frank. Look
around. You think those people need any more convincing their world is
going to come down around them? Truffant. Fucking crackers throwing
Molotov cocktails at the shanties at night? This dream, it just confirms
what they already know."

Frings nodded.

Eddings took a deep breath, settling down. "They're going to do one of
their ceremonies at the Square tomorrow night. More superstitious bullshit,
but maybe it will give them some courage; get them to try to make this
work."

"You going to be there?"

This drew a rueful laugh. "Yeah, I suppose I will. Those are our people,
for better or worse, right?"

"I'm going, too."

Eddings looked up. "Really?"

"Womé more or less invited me to come."

"Okay."

They drank in silence for a few moments. Frings thought about what
Eddings had said.

"Warren?"

"Yeah?"

"Where's Mel? I don't think I know where he went after our meeting last
night."

"He's safe."

"You can trust me, Warren. I kept him safe for days."

Eddings considered this. "He's at the old rail yard, staying in the Black
Comet Line."

87.

Winston walked with his eyes cast to the sidewalk before him. He was troubled. He had his guitar slung over his shoulder in its jerry-rigged case. The intensity in his eyes had people on the sidewalk moving out of his way, though he was unaware of this, caught up as he was in his thoughts.

The second body found in the rocks had put him on edge, unsure what he was supposed to make of it. But in the Community—a place that did not, as far as he could tell, operate under the normal laws of cause-and-effect or even reason—this had seemed just another event Winston couldn't make sense of. He was certain that his understanding of the world was at best shaky, and at worst plainly wrong, so he'd resigned himself to *not* understanding. The discovery of a second body was just another increment in his growing sense of disquiet.

The third body was too much. Where he had been willing to grant the strange gods of the Uhuru Community a cloak of inscrutability, he was now filled with a dread certainty that they were malevolent. At least toward him. Was there another explanation? Winston had spent the previous night alternating between an unsuccessful attempt to understand the appearance of the two girls on the riverbank and a deep sleep that had strangely left him exhausted.

The Palace was just a block away. A beggar afflicted with St. Vitus' dance shimmied manically up and down the sidewalk.

Winston needed to leave the City. He'd gone as far as he could go, from the Checkerboard up to the Palace. The Palace was the pinnacle in the City and look at him—still sleeping on the dirt floor in a shantytown shack on the nights when he wasn't with a woman. Things weren't going to get better here. It was time to get out before they got worse. But he had to leave the City on good terms with the Uhuru Community gods, and that meant staying for the next day's Square. That was his chance to gain their goodwill, though he had no idea how to go about it.

88.

Westermann paced around Headquarters, working off nervous energy. He'd called out to Fort Deposit and asked McIlvaine to track down James Symmes, Boyce Symmes's crippled son. Westermann would come out that night to talk to him. "Too late," McIlvaine had said, "he's already coming your way. Hopped on a bus less than an hour ago." Kraatjes had authorized a tail team for Koss and a couple of uniforms were dispatched to meet Symmes at the bus station and bring him in. Things were moving fast, picking up an end-of-the-road momentum.

Westermann found Grip smoking a cigarette at Westermann's desk.

"I heard your father was in the room with Maddox."

"Yeah."

Grip shook his head. "Jesus."

"Where's Morphy?" Westermann asked, changing the subject.

"He went to get us lunch. Look, I need to talk to you about something."

"Okay."

"You see"—Grip struggled for the right words, worrying, for once, about nuance—"you know my political views, that I'm concerned about—"

"The communist menace," Westermann said, semi-ironically.

"That's right. I know you don't share my . . . enthusiasm for the politics of it." Grip paused, not sure how to proceed.

"Where's this going?"

"You know Ed Wayne. From what he says, sounds like you two got into it a little."

Westermann's mouth went dry. He found himself licking his lips, trying to work up some moisture like a punk on his first bust.

Grip squinted a little and Westermann got the feeling he was getting a read. "He's an asshole, Wayne, but he's also with the cause, and we run into each other because of that. Anyway, he's got it in his mind that maybe you're Red, and he starts getting on me about it. 'Your lieut's a commie bastard,' stupid shit like that. And I know it's because he doesn't like you and that's just the kind of asshole he is. But last night he gets one of the guys down at the bar," Grip said, technically not lying, "to shadow you; see what you got up to."

Westermann, his pulse pounding in his ears, stared at Grip.

"I don't know how to say this, but he says you went to a meeting with Frank Frings, the reporter, and Carla Bierhoff. And I was going to say I don't believe that shit, but just a couple nights ago I ran into those two exact same people—together—when I was looking for Mel Washington. That makes me think maybe it isn't bullshit. It makes me wonder if Mel Washington was there, too, and that gets me thinking about this investigation—and don't take this wrong—but how you've been playing down the Uhuru Community angle the whole way. You know? I don't know what to think."

Westermann's voice sounded strange coming out. "We're getting close on this—the Maddox angle."

Grip grimaced, not enjoying this conversation. "Are we? Is this a better angle than the bodies being found right by the shanties?"

Westermann felt the sweat on his face. "Twenty-four hours. If we don't have this nailed down in twenty-four hours, we'll go after the Uhuru Community as hard as you want."

Grip nodded, thinking. "You still didn't answer me about Mel Washington."

Westermann had found his footing again. "You really want to push this, Torsten?"

Grip frowned and shook his head. "I know enough. This isn't a conversation I wanted to have."

Westermann could see that. "Okay."

"But there's another thing. That guy, the one Ed Wayne got to follow you, he didn't just leave after your meeting. He kept following you."

Westermann knew what was coming next.

"He says he followed you to a certain address and that you entered that address and didn't come out again by the time he'd left, he said, maybe about an hour later."

"Okay."

"You know the address I'm talking about?"

"Sure."

"I know that Morphy was working a security gig last night."

The energy drained from Westermann's body, the excitement he'd felt just a few minutes before displaced by a type of dread. It was hard for him to register what was happening, the stress was too much. He asked the big question, feeling like an observer, watching this happening to someone else.

"Does Morphy know?"

Grip nodded.

"What do you think he'll do? You think he'll try to kill me?"

Grip sighed. "Lieut, you ever have a clue what Morphy will do? I talked to him. I'll talk to him some more. But I'd watch it, if I were you. He might not do anything. He's just . . . it's Morphy. I thought you should know."

Grip left. Westermann sat back in his chair staring blankly ahead. Nothing seemed real, yet the weight of all these things seemed almost too much to bear.

Morphy.

Wayne and Deyna.

Big Rolf.

Maddox.

Lenore slowly swirling downstream.

Westermann closed his eyes and his head swam; the Holiness Church nipped at the edge of his thoughts—the complete release he'd felt there, release from his worries. He stood and walked to his window, watching the street traffic below, clearing his head. Because it was the easiest thing to think about, he wondered why James Symmes was coming to the City.

89.

Moses Winston showed up for his last performance at the Palace a couple of hours early, wanting to be sure that everything was okay between himself and Floyd Christian, who had been nothing but straight-up with him over the past few days. He'd agreed to do shows for two weeks, but things were getting hot, and when things got hot, it was time to move on.

The Palace wasn't really a dinner joint, but people did show up before the music started to have a light meal, and the house was maybe a quarter full. Houselights up, smoke-free air; it was demystifying, Winston thought, a different place from when the show was on.

He asked a waiter where he could find Christian and was pointed to the back office. The door was closed—this was unusual—and Winston knocked tentatively. From inside, he heard Christian ask who was knocking.

"Moses Winston, Mr. Christian."

He waited for a moment and the door was opened by an ofay that Winston thought he'd maybe seen before.

Christian beckoned him in and he sat down next to the white cat, across the desk from Christian. Christian's office was smoky; smelled of reefer. Christian introduced the white guy—name of Frings—and they shook hands, the white guy telling him how much he liked his guitar playing. Winston wasn't quite sure how to respond, so he smiled and didn't meet the man's eyes.

Christian cleared his throat. "Moses, you live down in the Uhuru Community, right?"

"Sometimes, Mr. Christian. I've got a friend who's been letting me stay there. Sometimes I have other places to stay . . ." Winston let that go, not wanting to get into his many lady friends with Frings there.

"You there the last few nights?"

Winston nodded.

"I'm trying to figure out what's going on down there, Moses. I'm hearing things—from Frank, here, and from others—that the Community may be closing down. People are preparing to leave. Is that accurate?"

Winston scowled in thought. "I think so, Mr. Christian. There's a lot of rumors going around the shanties. Folks talking about moving on while they can."

"And you?"

"Me? It's time for me to move on anyway, but I don't like what's happening down there. Crackers driving by, chucking bottle grenades at the shanties. White thugs. I've seen it before. Nothing good comes of it. I'm staying around tomorrow night because those crazy islanders are having a ritual in the Square and I said I'd be around for it, maybe beat on a drum. I've been helping out a little with some of those boys, trying to keep the Community safe; paying them back for their kindness."

Frings asked, "Samedi's people?"

This startled Winston, and he looked from Frings to Christian, who nodded that it was okay.

"Yeah, Samedi. I'm not one of them, but I help them out. They're crazy but they're all right."

Frings said, "Where are you moving on to?"

Winston shrugged. "Heading north. See where the road takes me."

"I'll miss seeing you play. I really mean that. I've seen a lot of people play. You're as good as any of them."

Winston thanked Frings, looking him in the eye, then looking away again. Something about Frings bothered him; made him think maybe Frings was a threat.

90.

Two uniforms brought James Symmes in that evening. Symmes walked with the help of a cane crafted from a knobby branch. He might as well have had COUNTRY tattooed on his forehead. They brought him to an interview room, gave him a cup of coffee, and went to find Westermann.

Westermann was at his desk; the two uniforms paused at the threshold of his office, unsure whether to disturb him. Westermann was staring at an open file on his desk, but clearly not reading. The men could also tell he was unaware of their presence. One of the uniforms finally tapped on the doorframe, and Westermann, startled, looked up. They told him that Symmes was waiting in the interview room. Westermann waved them in.

"Any trouble?"

The senior of the two cops, a short guy with a barrel chest named Konchesky, did the talking. "No, sir. He was surprised to see us, but didn't seem too bothered."

"Good."

"He had a gun, though, sir. Army-issue Colt."

Westermann frowned. "He say anything about it?"

"Said there was no way he was coming into the City without being able to protect himself."

"Country mouse," the other chimed in.

"Okay," Westermann said, thinking about Symmes's shack; how the entire population of Fort Deposit wouldn't fill some of the apartment buildings here. "He say anything else?"

"No, sir. We saved him for you, just like we were told."

"Thank you." Westermann let them go. He closed his eyes, willing his mind to empty of competing thoughts; to focus on the task at hand. He called Kraatjes.

* * *

Kraatjes placed a pack of Luckies on the IR table and invited James Symmes to take one. He shook his head.

"Am I under arrest?"

Westermann was surprised by Symmes's eyes. They betrayed no fear; no intimidation at being brought in, without explanation, to police headquarters in a strange city. He wasn't scared, didn't even seem curious. The question came off as an attempt to clarify a minor detail.

"We just have a few questions for you. I was going to come back out to Fort Deposit, but the chief out there told me you were headed this way, so it saved me the trip."

Symmes grimaced with the good side of his face. This close, it looked as if the right side of Symmes's face was slowly sloughing off, his eye drooping, his mouth frozen in a permanent half frown, his cheek slack. He held his atrophied right arm close to his chest, as if he were clutching books.

With his left hand, Symmes scratched next to his left eye. "What questions?"

"Why don't I start with why you came to the City today?"

"To see Dr. Maddox."

"About what?"

"Am I in trouble here?"

"No."

"I wanted to talk to him."

"About what?"

"Ole Koss."

"What about Ole Koss?"

Symmes snorted a laugh. "How much time you got?"

Westermann shrugged. "All the time you need, James."

"Jimmy."

"Okay, Jimmy."

"You want to know about Ole Koss?"

"Sure."

"Well, we was in the service together, after the war. They sent a dozen of us over to Africa, watch over this open-pit mine they had. We didn't actually do much; they had other troops on guard. We just dried out in the sun, rested, drank. We'd had a rough go in Germany."

Westermann stole a look at Kraatjes, who was leaning forward in his chair, forearms on the table and fingers laced. Symmes took a sip of coffee and used his left hand to wipe away some that had dribbled from the right side of his mouth.

Kraatjes said, "Excuse me, Mr. Symmes. I don't mean to be insensitive, but it doesn't seem to me that you would pass an entrance physical. Is this something that happened to you in Africa?"

Symmes closed his eyes and nodded. "I'm getting to that.

"We didn't have much to do, like I said. So, sometimes we went looking for something. One time, this carpenter we knew, called Van Oot, he asks us if we want to go out in the bush, see a friend of his that's got a ranch somewhere. Van Oot traded some pills to a hophead at dispatch for a few days' use of a jeep, and we loaded it up with gas cans and beer. The bush, there are tracks but there aren't really roads. Van Oot drove and I don't know how he found it, but it took us a half day to get out to the ranch and we drank the whole way. Van Oot's friend Danny lived on this ranch that was over a river, and he had a team of Africans that worked for him. We sat out on his porch that overlooked the river and drank beer and watched the crocs and hippos in the water.

"So, the next day we woke up with hangovers and had breakfast and this tea that's half-whiskey. Danny, he was big, maybe like six foot five, he asked if we wanted to go deeper into the bush, see this African he said would take us on a lion hunt. So, yeah, sure. We headed out in two jeeps this time; me and Joe Turner following the other three in Danny's Rover. We drove for hours, passed some villages; stopped for lunch at this watering hole where there were some elephants." Symmes shook his head at the memory of it.

"We kept on and in the late afternoon we came to this village. The other villages, we'd gone around them, you know. Waved to the people we saw, but basically stayed away. Here, Danny led us right to the village edge and we parked the jeeps. It was quiet there, except for some dogs that came out to us and some livestock noises, like all those villages.

"I've seen a lot," Symmes said, shifting his gaze to the table, "what with the war and all. But this was something different. I don't know. Maybe when you look back at things you think that you remember this or that and maybe it was that way and maybe it wasn't. But we knew before we got there that something was wrong. We didn't see anyone outside the village. And when we went in—this village was really just a bunch of huts around a clearing—

there were a couple of bodies lying out in the open. I don't know if they had just died there or whether the hyenas dragged them out, but animals had started on them, but then just left them alone. We could hear the sound of the flies coming from everywhere. We found the villagers dead in their huts. It looked like they had been vomiting blood, or maybe bleeding from their mouths.

"Danny got frantic, looking for someone, running in and out of huts; saying that people were missing; that maybe they'd left. But he finally found her, a woman. He was grabbing her and holding her and getting blood all over himself. Koss and Van Oot and I pulled him off, but he fought like hell, busted us up pretty good. He was big, you know. And he'd lost it.

"When we'd gotten over the shock of it, we put bandannas over our mouths. Joe Turner had been checking the perimeter, and when he joined us, you could see that he hadn't found anybody alive. You could also see what we must have looked like, with all this blood on us. Some of it was the woman's, but some of it was ours, too. Like I said, Danny was big and we had a hard time pulling him off. We finally forced some whiskey into him and he calmed down enough that we got him in the jeep. Koss made us wait for a minute and he went back into the village. We saw smoke, blue smoke rising into that low sky, and Koss walking out with this wall of flames behind him."

91.

Frings read the *Gazette* on his couch and drank a beer. Behind the closed bedroom door, Ellen Aust slept in his bed. According to Renate, Ellen had slept most of the day. Frings had gone in to have a look at her, her face plumper in the laxness of sleep; making her look like a little girl. She seemed to bring out some maternal instinct in Renate, though the women were essentially the same age. Renate had drawn Ellen a bath and made her soup and coffee during the few hours that she was awake. Renate had also lent a sympathetic ear. When Frings arrived home, she related their conversation in hushed tones as if it were some kind of conspiracy.

"Ellen, she is very frightened; *very* frightened. She says that leaving her church *enrages* her preacher. She says that anyone who leaves can never come back, and that the preacher, Madd . . ." Renate paused, uncertain.

"Maddox."

"Ah, right. Mad-dox. This Maddox, he says that people who leave are going to burn in hell and everyone prays together *very, very* hard to keep their church together. She cries very hard when she thinks of this; she doesn't like these memories. She cries that she has nowhere to go, that she knows no one."

Frings nodded, thinking about how terrifying it must be for her to be suddenly alone in the City.

Frings heard movement back in the bedroom and finished his beer and put the kettle on to boil. He wondered what he should make her. Breakfast? He found a carton of eggs in the refrigerator and some cheese and an onion. He put a frying pan on the stove to heat and diced up a portion of the onion and pulled the cheese over a grater. He needed to figure out what to do with Ellen in the long term. Maybe he could locate a cheap apartment near the house where she worked. He wondered if it was safe for her to return to that job. Would Maddox's people go looking for her? What would they do if they found her? Surely, the first place they would check would be at her job. Maybe he could find her another place to work.

Ellen emerged from the bedroom wearing one of Renate's robes. She had taken the time to straighten her hair, and her face was splotched red from cold water. Frings smiled at her and she gave a wavering smile back. She wasn't comfortable alone with men.

Frings cooked the omelet and Ellen paused before eating it, Frings thinking that maybe she was saying a silent grace or something. She ate quickly but neatly and seemed refreshed when it was over. Frings poured two cups of coffee and sat down opposite her at the small kitchen table.

Frings said, "I talked to Renate."

"She's very nice."

"She is. She's concerned about you."

Ellen nodded.

"Ellen, what do you think is going to happen with the church?"

Frings saw her shoulders tense, her eyes drifting down to the table between them.

"I mean, why did you leave now? You've been there for years. You told me about the howling, about how Maddox is becoming more fearful. But what do you think Maddox is going to do? He can't keep this up forever."

"He's waiting. We . . . *they* are all waiting."

"For what?" Frings leaned across the table despite himself.

"The End of Days. The Final Battle. Maddox says it can happen at any time; that all the signs are there. We need to be ready."

"And the people in the church—you and the others—were . . ."

She looked up at him, her eyes bright with some unidentifiable emotion. "Scared. We are all scared."

They sat for another half hour. Frings tried to make small talk, but Ellen had retreated into herself. Frings finally gave up and they sat in silence, drinking coffee, until Ellen decided to return to bed. Frings put a pillow on the couch, turned off the lights, and must have fallen asleep because he surfaced—briefly, but clear-minded—long enough to realize the question that he needed to ask her. Then he fell back asleep again, wondering in the last, confused moments of consciousness whether Renate would be home that night.

92.

A uniform knocked on the door and brought in fresh coffee. None of the men needed it; the energy in the room was high.

"We drove all the way back to the ranch after that, a lot of the drive in the dark, which was very tough. Koss was in the lead car with Van Oot, who was driving, and Danny. They drank hard the whole way back. I was in the other jeep and Joe Turner was driving. We didn't drink and we didn't talk much. I just wanted to get back to the mine, forget the whole thing. But it didn't turn out that way.

"When we got back to the ranch, Van Oot and Danny were falling-down drunk and they found their way to beds somehow. Turner and me, we sat on the porch with Koss and he told us what he'd learned on the ride back—that the woman was Danny's girlfriend, or something like that. We'd already figured that. He also said they thought this disease must have moved through pretty fast and that maybe half the village had fled. Nobody talked about it being contagious, but that was what everyone was thinking about. Nobody wanted to end up like the people we saw there.

"We spent the night at the ranch. Everyone was exhausted and slept through until the afternoon. When we finally woke up, Danny was vomiting and having cold sweats. It might have been a hangover, but everyone was real nervous. Then it hit me and we knew that we were in trouble. It started with the vomiting and then the chills. Turner wanted us to get in the jeep and head back to the mine; go to the infirmary there. I couldn't go. I've been in combat. I know what my limits are and I just couldn't go. Then it hit Van Oot and there was definitely no way we could do it with only two men healthy; so we were stuck."

Somebody was banging on the door. Westermann exhaled hard in frustration and got up. He cracked the door to find one of the deputy chiefs, a career cop named Flamini, looking pissed.

"Get out here," Flamini hissed.

Westermann gave Kraatjes a look, then left the room to meet with Flamini.

Flamini, within grasping distance of his pension, had one of those bodies with a thick torso and thin, bowed legs. His eyes were narrow with anger.

"What the fuck is going on in there? I've got a lawyer, one of Truffant's guys, down here who wants to know why you've pulled this kid in. Says he wants to be in the room."

"He's not a suspect, sir. He's a possible source in an investigation."

"Yeah? If that's so, why the fuck is Truffant sending one of his lawyers down here—paying a fucking mint in the process—to get this kid out?"

"I don't have an answer for that."

"Well, you can consider your interview over or you can charge him with a crime and let the lawyer in."

The uniforms who were hanging around checked out the confrontation. Westermann looked around, saw Deyna leaning against the wall in the back. Their eyes met. Deyna winked.

Flamini said, "What's it going to be, Lieutenant?"

Without turning, Westermann knocked twice on the door and waited until Kraatjes emerged.

Flamini reddened. "Jesus fucking Christ, what are you doing in there, Jack?"

Kraatjes stared at him. "We're conducting an interview. What are you doing here?"

Westermann said, "There's press here."

"What?" Flamini snapped.

Westermann nodded toward Deyna, and Westermann's two superiors looked over. Deyna played it cool.

Kraatjes spoke more quietly. "What are you doing here?"

Flamini told him about the lawyer.

Kraatjes kept his eyes on Flamini. "You can take this up with the Chief, but this interview is going to continue."

"This is coming from higher up than the Chief."

Kraatjes shook his head. "In this building, nobody's higher up than the Chief." Kraatjes turned back and opened the door. Westermann followed him in, leaving Flamini steaming but powerless.

"I'm sorry about that, Jimmy," Kraatjes said quietly, taking his seat. "You were telling us that you and Danny were both sick."

306 | TOBY BALL

"Van Oot got sick, too. Not long after me—the vomiting, chills. I'm not sure how the days went, the three of us were really out of it, and Turner and Koss were trying to take care of us because the Africans who worked on the ranch got spooked when they saw us, the condition we were in, and just kind of disappeared. I remember—or I think I remember—being outside as it was becoming dark. I don't know why I would have been. But the ranch had this huge porch, I think he called it a veranda, and it had these big wicker chairs and tables, and I remember looking at it in that yellow light and it being empty and thinking that we were totally alone out there; and we were dying.

"I don't know, maybe four, five days after we got back, Danny was really sick—there was blood on the floor from where he'd been vomiting. We couldn't wake him up. There was this wind that was howling and kicking up sand and dust, a real storm. These Africans showed up in two army jeeps. They pull up and there were maybe three with machine guns who stayed on the porch, and this other guy, real dark-skinned and wearing sunglasses, he came in and talked to Turner and Koss. They took him to see Danny and then Van Oot and me. We were all in bed. This guy was real thin and he wore his shirt unbuttoned and he had this wooden cross on a leather thong. Danny, this guy said, the life had already left him, like his body was just going through the motions of dying. Me and Van Oot, he gave us some kind of drink that he made, I didn't see what was in it, but it was foul-tasting and I've drank strychnine in church, so I know. I threw a lot of it up, but some of it stayed down. I came out to see the rest of them on the porch. Van Oot and Danny were too sick to get out of bed, but Turner and Koss and the Africans were drinking beer.

"The guy with the sunglasses said his name was Senah Glélé—I remember the name, Koss wouldn't shut up about him. Anyway, Glélé said that he'd been sent by Legba to save the children of Jesus. I had a pretty good fever; he seemed strange but no stranger than anything else."

"Who's Legba?" Westermann asked. "A tribal chief?"

"What? A chief?" Jimmy laughed cynically. "No, Legba's an African god. They had a lot of gods over there."

Westermann nodded. "Sorry, Jimmy, please go on."

"Yeah, well, Glélé, he said Koss had the disease, too, but he wasn't affected by it, maybe because he was so close to God. I remember that he stared for a long time at Koss, like studying or something, and that wasn't something Koss normally would have been good with. But he let Glélé do it.

"They left, but by then Danny was gone and Van Oot died the next morning. I started recovering quickly after the visit, but you can see how it left me." Symmes pointed to his sagging face, his withered arm.

"Koss knew that I was a Christian, but what most interested him was what Glélé had said about him not being affected by the disease because he was so close to God. He really took that to heart, started thinking he was special, or chosen, or something. The thing was, when we made it back to the mine and they were able to take blood samples and all that, it turned out later that he *did* have the virus, but he didn't show any symptoms. So Glélé had been right."

Kraatjes had his hands together, fingers and palms flat against each other. He looked somewhere over Symmes's shoulder, trusting that Westermann would catch Symmes's reactions.

"Do you think, James, that your Christian faith saved you?"

Symmes's shoulders drooped. "I've thought about that a lot. I know what Koss thinks, that he's some kind of special child of God or some such. Me, I don't know. Van Oot and his friend were so far gone by the time Glélé arrived, it might have just been too late for that medicine to help them. I'll tell you this though; before then, Koss wasn't one for religion, so I don't know why the Lord would have spared him. But I don't know."

Westermann asked, "Do you know that Ole Koss is in Prosper Maddox's congregation?"

"I do."

"What do you think of that?"

"Koss, well, he found religion real fast once he thought he had a special part in it. He knew about Dr. Maddox from me, from killing time out at the mine. So, I guess it doesn't surprise me too much."

Westermann was about to follow up when there was a perfunctory knock and the door was flung open. A uniform stepped in, followed by Flamini.

"This interview is over," Flamini said, smirking.

Kraatjes was out of his chair. Westermann stayed seated, deferring to his authority.

"You get in touch with the Chief?"

"The mayor did."

"Yeah?"

"The Chief knows the pecking order."

Kraatjes nodded and turned to Symmes. "You want to leave?"

Symmes seemed confused by the situation and stared mutely at Kraatjes.

Flamini said, "Let's get him out of the room, there's someone here to take him."

Outside, Ole Koss stood with his arms crossed, and next to him, Big Rolf. Westermann stared at his father, feeling the anger rising in him.

"Hey, Jimmy," Koss said, as if they were just two good friends meeting after a long separation.

Symmes was silent, his eyes darting desperately back and forth between Kraatjes and Koss.

"Jimmy?" Koss pressed.

"Ole." Symmes's voice sounded hollow, lost.

Westermann put his hand on Symmes's shoulder, leaned in so that he could talk in his ear. "You want to leave with Ole Koss? We can set you up with a bunk here, if you want, or a hotel where we put up witnesses. You don't have to leave with him."

Symmes nodded, seeming to understand.

Big Rolf looked to Kraatjes. "My client would like a word with Mr. Symmes. I assume you have no objection."

"Go ahead."

Koss and Symmes walked to a corner of the squad room. A group of uniforms eyed Koss, gave him room.

Westermann seethed. "Rolf." He nodded to his office. His father followed him in. Westermann left the door open; saw some uniforms looking in from across the squad room.

"What the hell are you doing?"

Big Rolf played it neutral. "I'm Prosper Maddox's lawyer, Piet. I'm representing his interests."

"But why this? Why now? You haven't represented him in the past, have you?"

"My client hasn't been the target of police harassment in the past. He hasn't needed representation."

Westermann shook his head. "Do you have any idea what is going on here?"

Big Rolf reddened. "How dare you?"

Westermann saw then that his father had no idea; no idea at all.

"Rolf," he said slowly, "if Jimmy Symmes walks out of here with Koss, whatever happens after that is on your conscience."

Big Rolf opened his mouth to speak, but Westermann brushed past him.

Koss and Symmes stood with Kraatjes.

Westermann said, "Are you staying with us, Jimmy?"

Symmes shook his head.

Kraatjes said, "He's decided to leave with Mr. Koss."

Westermann saw that Koss had Symmes's bag. "You sure?"

Koss stepped forward. "He's made his decision."

Big Rolf joined them. Koss took Symmes by the arm and led him toward the exit, Symmes hobbling along with the help of his cane. Big Rolf took a step to follow, stopped, and looked at Westermann. Westermann met his father's eyes and saw things he'd never before seen there: confusion, uncertainty, fear.

93.

Frings woke to a noise, confused for a moment by the topography of the living room. He pushed himself up on an elbow and saw Renate's silhouette in the kitchen doorway. He found her drinking a glass of water, her face pale without makeup in the harsh light of the kitchen.

"Our friend is sleeping in the bed?" Renate's shoulders sagged with exhaustion.

Frings nodded. "She needed the sleep and I would have been stuck in the bedroom if she was out here."

Renate nodded, showing Frings her palm, not happy but without the energy to fight about it.

"You can sleep in the bed with her," Frings suggested.

Renate was about to reply—doubtless something petulant—when the bedroom door opened and Ellen emerged, again in Renate's robe. Renate's mood changed instantly, as it often did, and she rushed over to Ellen, putting her hands on the woman's shoulders, asking her how she was. Ellen smiled shyly and the two women sat at the table. Ellen offered to sleep on the couch, but Renate wouldn't hear of it. Frings wondered if Renate was going to share the bed with Ellen or whether he was going to end up on the floor with Renate sleeping on the couch. Either way, he pulled another beer from the refrigerator.

The women were deep in conversation, so Frings went out to the living room and found half a reefer in the ashtray. He smoked, listening to the traffic noise, trying to empty his mind, but thinking about the shanties and wondering what might be happening there this night.

Eventually Ellen and Renate left the kitchen, turning off the light as they did. Renate told him that the two women would sleep in the bed; he could have the couch.

"Before you go," Frings said.

"Yes?"

"Ellen, did you have a doctor? Was his name Vesterhue?"

"It was Dr. Vesterhue sometimes."

"But sometimes it was a different doctor?"

"Sometimes I saw Dr. Berdych. Why?"

"Just wondering," Frings said, but his body tingled with adrenaline. "I'll grab the alarm clock from the bedroom. I need to be up early."

94.

Grip had never seen Crippen's filled the way it was tonight. More young people drinking than he'd seen here before, rowdy and loud. The radio hate was jacked up from the back room, the static adding to the din. Violence was in the air. Grip didn't like it.

Ed Wayne sat at a corner table, eyes glazed where you could see them through the swelling. Empty shot glasses were arrayed before him. Grip maneuvered his way over, keeping the cop look to deter the drunks in the crowd. At Wayne's table he hovered until an older guy got the picture and left after shaking Wayne's hand. Grip sat down as a guy came back with a tray of beer bottles and whiskey shots.

"The fuck you doing here, Ed?"

"I was crawling the fucking walls; thought I was going to kill my old lady."

Grip wasn't surprised by what Wayne said, but still felt the disgust. "What's with all the kids?" Nodding back toward the room.

"There was a meeting a couple hours ago, talking about the Uhuru Community and communism and some religious shit. The guys stuck around afterward. Fucking crazy, some of them. Glad they're on our side."

"Who was running the meeting?"

"Fitzy," Wayne said, pointing over to the geezer Grip had displaced. "But then your buddy Prosper Maddox talked a little bit."

"*Maddox?*"

"Yeah, he didn't stick around. Didn't really fit in with the rest of the clientele, if you follow; talked some crazy shit about the end of the world or something. I was drinking pretty hard during that shit, not really paying attention."

"So what's going on? They had this meeting; now what?"

Wayne's eyes were too swollen to squint, but Grip saw the suspicion. "I don't know, Torsten. You've got me worried a little, sticking up for your Red lieut, and all."

Grip leaned across the table. "Do not fucking question my commitment, Ed. Just because I'm not a goddamn jackass doesn't mean I'm soft. What the fuck is going on?"

Wayne scowled. "We're going to burn those fucking shanties to the ground."

95.

Westermann walked through deserted streets in the night heat, people holed up inside from pure fatigue. He was exhausted, feeling it in his legs and in the way he had to concentrate to keep his mind from wandering. He was closing in, just missing details.

Big Rolf.

Deyna.

Jimmy Symmes leaving with Koss.

The twins singing at the Holiness Church.

Focus.

He was certain that the disease that afflicted Mavis Talley and Lenore and the two other girls was the same disease that Symmes and Van Oot had picked up in Africa and that Koss apparently carried. This cemented the connection between Prosper Maddox's church, Dr. Vesterhue, and the sick prostitutes. They must have contracted the disease from Koss. Was he sleeping with these prostitutes with Vesterhue trying to treat them once it became apparent Koss was infecting them? That didn't really explain Lenore's drowning death—or the other two, for that matter—or why it had happened down at the river. And where was Vesterhue?

Photos with Washington.

Lenore rotating slowly as she drifts downriver.

Are you good with the Lord?

He was pulled from his thoughts by a sense that he was being followed or watched. He turned around, but the street was empty save for a couple of winos sitting against a storefront, too tired even to talk. He kept moving, distracted now and trying to figure out if he was really being followed or just spooked by what Grip had told him about the night he *was* tailed.

He began to worry that it might be Morphy, wondered what Morphy intended to do. Kill him? Would Morphy do that?

A block from his building he felt the grip of panic, his proximity to safety cutting his breath short. He turned again. Still no one. He broke into a half trot, feeling stupid for running like this, but at the same time desperate to reach the safety of his building. Half a block away, he saw that someone was sitting on the steps, mostly in the shadows. He slowed down to a fast walk and pulled his gun.

The figure stood up, putting his hands in the air, one holding a lit cigarette. "Don't shoot, sir," the man said, gently mocking.

Jesus Christ.

96.

"It's me, Frings." Frings watched Westermann decelerate, still holding the gun but pointing it down now.

Pale and out of breath, Westermann asked, "What're you doing here?"

"I told you that Ellen Aust is at my place."

"I remember." Westermann took a look over his shoulder at the empty street.

"Well, I was talking to her tonight because I knew that some of the Godtown people were treated by Vesterhue, and I wondered if maybe there was another doctor who they saw, too. Especially with Vesterhue MIA. So she says sure, she sees a guy named Berdych."

Westermann had dark patches under his glazed eyes, his shoulders sagged. He looked at Frings and Frings understood that Westermann didn't know who Berdych was.

Frings said, "Carla and Betty Askins and some businessmen have arranged for food and clothing and all that to be distributed down in the shanties?"

Westermann nodded.

"Well, they're vaccinating kids at the same time, and the doctor who's volunteered—"

"Is Berdych." Frings saw Westermann's eyes narrow as he understood the implications. "Let's go upstairs."

Frings had lain awake that night, thinking about Berdych, working through the implications. He remembered him from the meeting at Carla's: a tall guy, skinny, short blond hair, little round glasses. Carried himself as if he were high caste. Frings wasn't sure what to make of his connections to both the Church of Last Days and the Uhuru Community. The benign explanation was that he was a charitable doctor who, in his good deeds, happened to work with two groups, two groups with very different philosophical foundations, that seemed to figure in Lenore's death. A coincidence, though that wasn't quite the right word. An improbability.

The other possibility, the one that had kept Frings from sleeping, was that Berdych's loyalties lay with Prosper Maddox, and volunteering his services to the Community was some sort of subterfuge. Frings knew from Carla that Berdych would be vaccinating shanty kids in just a few hours. *Hours.* Grabbing a couple of reefers, he'd headed out into the night.

He'd grabbed a jitney to Westermann's building, riding in the back with his eyes closed, mind racing, wind from the open windows making crazed vortices around his head.

Westermann wasn't home, and uncertain of his next move, he'd sat on Westermann's stoop and smoked another reefer until he'd heard the sound of approaching footsteps and seen the figure moving at him with a gun in his hand.

Frings wasn't sure what he'd been expecting at this tony address but the largely barren apartment had not been it. The place was beautiful, no doubt, but looked as if someone were moving in or moving out, as if no one actually *lived* there.

They drank beer while Westermann recounted for Frings the interview with Jimmy Symmes. Frings listened, eyes closed, picturing in his mind the scene Westermann described. He thought about Symmes unburdening himself of this knowledge, but certain things weren't making sense to him—not so much the story, but Symmes's intentions.

"What is Symmes doing here? Why did he come?"

Westermann frowned, scratched at his temple. "That's the question, isn't it? We didn't get the chance to ask him."

"Do you have a guess? Was he coming to see you, tell you his story?"

"That wasn't my impression."

"Did you say he brought a gun?"

"Yeah. Said he wanted it for protection. You know, a kid from the sticks in the City and all that."

"He needs protection? That ring true to you? This gink was in the war, saw combat, and he's scared to come to the goddamn City? You buy that?"

Westermann frowned. "He has some physical problems. I don't know."

Frings stood, suddenly restless, thinking that things might start moving fast. "So let me see if I can tell what you're thinking. You think that some-how they—Koss, Vesterhue, maybe Maddox—figured how to infect people with this virus that Symmes and the others caught in Africa. Probably something to do with Koss, maybe giving them shots of his infected blood, something like that. Probably Vesterhue was experimenting with it on those girls and seeing what happened. Right?"

Westermann nodded. "But where are Vesterhue and the other girls?"

"That's not part of what I'm working out right now. Anyway, I think that Maddox's problems with commies in general and the Uhuru Commu-nity in particular are pretty well established. So I think you're worried that Berdych is going to infect those kids when he's supposed to be vaccinating them at the Community tomorrow."

"You don't think so?"

"No, I do. I really do. But it's important that you think so because I can't stop him. You can. Go arrest him, question him, whatever; but don't let him get to those kids."

97.

A red haze seeped into the eastern sky as Westermann arrived at Head-quarters. The duty officer gave him a heavy-lidded gaze, fatigue robbing him of the energy to muster actual hostility. Upstairs, the squad room was empty and Westermann helped himself to three aspirin from Souza's desk drawer. No sleep, a hangover coming on as his drunkenness faded. He opened his office window in time to hear a delivery truck rattle by. He rubbed his eyes with the heels of both hands, willing himself to clarity in this stagnant heat. He needed to get his mind around the logistics.

Koss.

Maddox.

Where was Vesterhue?

Where was Mavis Talley?

He needed to convince Kraatjes first. If he convinced Kraatjes, the two of them could go to the Chief. But if it went wrong, this was a career-killer.

Kraatjes always arrived early, when the sun still hid behind the skyline. He rapped on the doorframe, pulling Westermann from his thoughts.

"I saw your note." Kraatjes looked apprehensive. "You look like hell."

Westermann knew how he appeared: unshaven, yesterday's clothes wrinkled and withered, hair lank from twenty-four hours of sweat.

Kraatjes took a seat, looking cautiously over at him. "Okay, Piet. What's up?"

Westermann laid it out for him.

The Chief's lights were off and the sun came through the open windows, casting an orange light across the room. Westermann unloaded the case just as he had to Kraatjes—what he knew, what he intended to do—while Kraatjes paced, smoking, nodding along.

When Westermann was done, the Chief leaned back in his chair, stared at the ceiling. Kraatjes settled over by the window, blowing cigarette smoke into the stagnant City air. Westermann, his story told, slumped in his chair, his hand supporting his forehead.

The Chief asked Kraatjes, "You think Asplundh will grant us the warrants?"

Kraatjes nodded, having thought this through. "You guarantee that one of us falls on his sword if it goes south, then, yeah, I think he'll do it. He doesn't want a bunch of dead kids on his conscience."

The Chief sighed. Westermann could feel the Chief's appraising eyes and knew that his shabby appearance didn't inspire confidence. The Chief leaned his elbows on his desk and steepled his fingers.

Kraatjes finished his cigarette and stubbed the filter into a glass ashtray on the Chief's desk. "I'll take the fall if this goes wrong."

The Chief looked at Kraatjes, then Westermann, then back to Kraatjes. The Chief shook his head. "I appreciate what you're trying to do, but this is on Piet. We'll do this, but Piet gets the credit or he takes the fall. That's how it's got to work."

Westermann nodded, his thoughts drifting, fatigue blurring his focus.

Morphy.

Morphy.

Morphy.

The Chief stood. "Let's get this moving."

98.

Morphy, Grip, and a dozen uniforms rolled through Godtown, no lights, no sirens. The sidewalks were empty; they were always empty. Grip had his window down, listening to the sound of the tires on asphalt, a sound usually drowned out by the noise of the City. His nerves were electric—this was not going to be a normal arrest; he didn't know why, but it just wasn't.

They pulled up in front of the church, and Grip and Morphy waited while a half dozen of the uniforms took up positions by the two alternative exits. Down the street, Grip saw a mound of fur and thought it might be the body of the German shepherd they had seen. Why was it just lying there? Wouldn't somebody move it?

Singing was coming from inside. Grip racked his brain for the hymn but couldn't find it. He pounded the front door. Nobody came. The sun scalded his neck. He pounded again, yelling, "Police. We have a warrant. Open the door." More singing, but no one came. He tried the door, but it was locked.

Grip descended the steps, moving stiffly, and sent two uniforms up with a battering ram. The four others drew their weapons.

"Do it," Grip said.

One blow with the ram and the doors burst open. The cops dropped the battering ram and moved to the side, giving the others a clear shot into the empty foyer of the church. The singing now came to them much louder. Grip led them in, pointing pairs of cops in various directions, telling them to look for Ole Koss.

Grip, Morphy, and two uniforms paused before the doors leading to the sanctuary, pulling their guns. Grip eased the door open and they stepped through to find the pews filled with people in plain dress, standing and singing. Above the pulpit, lit by the morning sun, a stained-glass Jesus cast his hands over his disciples in piercing primary colors.

A few people in the back noticed the cops and stopped singing. Grip, Morphy, and the two uniforms stood where they were. More people noticed the police and also stopped singing. Grip watched as the awareness of their presence filtered up toward the front pews. The organist stopped and then the last few singers, and then the place was silent, a couple hundred people staring wordlessly at the four police.

Grip walked down the aisle between the pews, his footsteps loud in the crowded silence. None of the congregants moved or spoke. He saw their faces—old, young, plain, beautiful, disfigured, innocent—watch him as he walked. Grip wiped sweat from his forehead with his sleeve. His hands shook. He led Morphy and the two uniforms behind the pulpit and found a short hallway leading back. Grip beckoned the uniforms, whispered to them to keep watch on the sanctuary. They nodded, not looking happy.

Grip and Morphy walked down the hallway to where it ended at a door. They stood to either side, backs to the wall, as Morphy gently pushed the door open. Nothing. Grip peered around the corner; saw Maddox sitting behind a small writing desk, stage-lit by the sun cascading through a high window. Seeing Grip, Maddox leaned back in his chair, eyes glazed.

Grip kept his gun down, touching his thigh. "Prosper Maddox, we have a warrant for your arrest."

Maddox looked toward them with unfocused eyes. "I can't sleep, can't let down my guard."

He did look terrible—pasty skin, heavy lids, unhealthy slump to his shoulders.

"Where's Koss?" Grip asked.

Maddox didn't seem to have heard.

"Where's Ole Koss?" Grip asked again.

Maddox shifted his half-lidded gaze from Grip to Morphy and back to Grip.

Morphy seemed, in his own way, concerned. The uniforms arrived. Grip shot them a furious look.

"The sanctuary's covered."

"Did they find Koss?"

The uniform shook his head.

"Go to your car, radio for some support. I don't know what's going to happen when we get Maddox out of here."

Grip followed them to the sanctuary, leaving Morphy watching Maddox. The scene hadn't changed much. Four uniforms stood by the entrance, guns out but pointed down, nervously scanning the crowd. Grip waved two of them over and situated them by the pulpit.

"We're waiting for reinforcements," Grip whispered, "and then we're walking Maddox out of here."

The cop wouldn't take his eyes off the crowd to look at Grip. "You want us to clear the sanctuary?"

Grip had thought about this. "I think we're better off having them all in one place. We can let them go after we get Maddox out."

"Okay."

Grip walked back to Maddox's office. Maddox was sitting with his hands in his lap, head down, eyes closed. Morphy leaned against the wall, watching.

"He asleep?"

Morphy shook his head. "Praying, I think."

They waited fifteen minutes for support, Maddox almost in a trance, Grip and Morphy nervously biding time. Grip found Morphy's anxiety disconcerting, it wasn't like him. But the silence of the place, considering the number of people in the sanctuary, was eerie.

A uniform came back, pale and jittery. "We've got a dozen cops out there now."

Grip nodded. The uniform left.

Morphy walked behind Maddox and lifted him gently under the arm, guiding him around the desk. Morphy turned Maddox's shoulders so that they faced each other.

"We're going to walk through the sanctuary and to the door. You won't say anything to anyone. You open your mouth, I will kill someone; maybe you, maybe somebody else, maybe a kid. But I *will* kill somebody."

Maddox gazed dazedly at Morphy. Grip hoped that Maddox would keep his mouth shut.

They walked around the pulpit and into the center aisle, Grip in front, Maddox, Morphy behind. The congregants were seated and silent, but seeing Maddox they rose. Grip tightened his hold on his gun, kept walking, watching the uniforms as they fidgeted.

It started with one man; for just a moment his voice was alone, but they all joined him, howling. The uniforms had their guns pointed into the pews, but no one took a shot. Trembling, Grip grabbed Maddox's sleeve and rushed him up the aisle, everyone's eyes on them, the noise deafening. Grip pulled Maddox through the door to the vestibule then outside. In the open, the howling was much quieter, no longer overwhelming. Grip and Morphy each took an arm and walked Maddox toward their prowl car.

Maddox spoke quietly, as if to himself. "They will be greatly shamed, for they will not succeed. Their eternal honor will never be forgotten."

Morphy glared. "Shut up."

"But the Lord is with me as a dread warrior; therefore my persecutors will stumble; they shall not overcome me."

Shut up.

99.

Carla arrived at the shanties shortly after seven that morning, a formidable day coordinating the distribution of food, clothing, medicine, and information ahead of her, even with the help of Eunice Prendergrast's network. Time was also going to be an issue; when the Square got going sometime in the late afternoon, everything else would stop.

Carla grew increasingly troubled as the morning wore on. The truck arrived with clothes, and Eunice's women were ready with distribution lists, but the scene inside the shanties was making deliveries nearly impossible. The narrow lanes hummed with the movement, not of children, but of adults carrying loads or calling out to this person or that, making plans. Many people weren't in their shacks, and the women just left the clothes in the hopes that the occupant would return to get them.

"Are all these people going to leave?" Carla asked Eunice as they stood outside Eunice's shack drinking her thick coffee.

Betty Askins, who had been assembling the children and adults in need of medicine or vaccines in the Square, arrived, looking stricken.

"The kids, they're in the Square?" Carla asked.

Betty nodded. Eunice ducked into her shack to get Betty a cup of coffee.

Betty whispered so that Eunice could not hear her. "I can't believe that people are abandoning the Community because of a dream; a superstition." Betty was trembling with frustration.

Carla nodded, having no words.

Eunice returned with the coffee, and the three women drank in silence amid the chaos around them. Finally Eunice said, "Betty, are you coming to the Square? It may be the last time."

Betty looked at her.

"Come to the Square, dear," Eunice said. "You'll see why you're not really one of us."

* * *

Frings arrived. Carla watched him approach, the sweat darkening his jacket, running down his face; the exhaustion in his pouchy eyes. Something else, too—a grimness to him.

Frings greeted Betty and Eunice with tight nods, met Carla's eyes.

Carla said, "Excuse us for a minute. Dr. Berdych should be getting to the Square soon. I'll meet you there."

Frings escorted Carla gently by the forearm down the alley. She let herself be guided, concerned by what she sensed in Frings. They found a gap between two shanties and slipped in. It was tight and the sun reflecting off the tin walls made it almost unbearably hot.

"What is it, Frank?"

Frings put his hands on her shoulders and told her.

100.

Winston stayed on the shaded side of the street as he made his way to the shanties. He'd spent the night with a waitress from the Palace in her one-room apartment above a liquor store, and had not slept. Her place had been bare, mattress on the floor and all that, but it had smelled nice and so had she. All night.

He pushed a shopping cart he'd boosted from a bum sleeping one off down an alley, leaving the cat's stuff in a neat pile. Now it was loaded with his guitar and amp. His other possessions—such as they were—were back in the shanties at Billy Lambert's. He was getting the hell out of the City tonight. All those women, some with boyfriends, husbands, and even worse, mad-as-shit brothers. Then there were the troubles in the shanties— the attacks by the white folk and everyone getting ready to leave. And something else, something that might not catch up to him, but who knew?

He planned to stick around for the Square before he left. He dug the Square. When Eunice Prendergrast learned he was a musician, she got him a drum and told him to flow along with the rest of them. It had been good; really good. Almost like those times onstage when it really came together, but in a different way. Better. Hard to explain. Hard to even dredge up the feeling when it wasn't actually happening. He was looking forward to one last time. Maybe smoke some mesca with Billy, get in the mood.

He came to the field that led to the shanties. The cart rattled as he steered off the cement sidewalk and onto the jumble of broken asphalt, dirt from God knew where, and weeds that passed for a field around here. The Samedi cats were out, rolling oil drums and lugging scrap wood to dump in them. A couple of them were painting that weird skull and top hat on the barrels. Watching all this, in a chair against the shanties' edge, was Senah Glélé, wearing a black bowler and smoking a cigar, his eyes hidden by dark glasses.

Winston found a guy he kind of knew named Étienne. "What's going on?"

Étienne was pouring sweat. His eyes were yellowed and rimmed red. "Getting ready, boss. Getting ready."

"For what?"

"Things happening today, boy. Getting ready."

Winston chewed on his lip, not sure he was willing to put much stock into Father Womé's prophecies. These Samedi guys certainly did, though, and they knew Womé better than he did.

Étienne said, "Heard you're checking out."

"That's right."

More of the guys had stopped now, using Winston as an excuse to take a break.

"Where you headed?"

Winston shrugged. "Don't know."

"Don't put down roots, right? Just ease along."

There was a lot of head nodding and people slapping him on the back, shaking his hand.

"You sticking around for the Square at least?" Étienne asked.

"Yeah. I'm sticking around for that and then making my way."

Inside the shanties, Winston weaved his cart through the confusion of people. He found Billy Lambert's shack and pushed the cart through the door. Billy was sitting in the corner on a seat he'd made from a stack of newspapers. Daylight leaked in through some narrow slits that Billy had cut through his tin wall. From the smell, Winston knew that Billy'd already started with the mesca.

101.

Westermann didn't expect the move on Dr. Berdych to be complicated. A plainclothes guy, a Negro, was hanging around the shanties, and another was a block down where he could relay hand signals from the first. When the signal was given, the prowl cars would move in from a couple of blocks away. No problems.

Westermann sat in a prowl car with Souza, doors open, and listened to the police radio as Grip reported back on Maddox's arrest. Grip and Morphy would deposit Maddox at Headquarters, where the Chief would keep Truffant at bay, for a few hours, at least.

The waiting was eating at Westermann. "You a religious guy, Lou?"

Souza laughed. "The old lady drags me to church every Sunday, if that's what you're getting at."

"Yeah, but do you go just because your wife drags you? What are you, Catholic? Are you a believer?"

Souza made a face. "Jeez, Lieut, I don't know. I guess I never thought about it that way. It's just something I do."

Westermann let it go. He had other things on his mind.

Maddox.

Vesterhue.

Morphy.

It concerned him that Grip and Morphy hadn't turned up Koss, or for that matter, Symmes. He didn't like the idea of Koss finding out that Maddox was in custody again, or that they'd arrested Berdych. They needed to find Koss quickly. APB, maybe. Approach with caution. Or he could put Grip and Morphy on it. That had the added attraction of keeping Morphy the hell away from him. Then again, he couldn't duck Morphy forever.

"Hey, Lieut, I hear the heat's supposed to break tomorrow," Souza said, blowing smoke out of the side of his mouth.

"That right?"

"That's what they say."

Westermann climbed out of the car and walked down the block. He was worried that they still hadn't figured everything out, how it all fit together; yet they were still moving forward with arrests. His head swam from fatigue, his chest tightened.

He would have to face Morphy.

Souza's call—his voice echoing in the empty street—came as a relief. Westermann jogged back to the patrol cars. He slid into the shotgun seat and Souza leaned on the horn, signaling the cars to move out.

Four prowl cars moved in, sirens off. The panel truck wasn't running. Two clean-cut guys in collared shirts were talking to a round Negro woman wearing a bright orange scarf wrapped around her hair. Behind them, in the distance, young Negro men were rolling oil drums, carrying wood planks.

Westermann, glad to be doing something, took the lead. Souza and the uniforms trailed, hands on their holstered guns.

Westermann approached the clean-cut men. "Dr. Berdych?"

The one on the right, short blond hair and a mustache hiding a harelip, said, "No. The doctor's in the truck," nodding toward the back of the panel truck where stairs led to an open door.

The uniforms took charge of the two men. Souza followed Westermann to the truck.

Westermann put a foot on the bottom step. "Dr. Berdych?"

He waited, heard nothing. He walked to the top of the steps and leaned through the door. "Dr. Berd—" Westermann felt a pinch in his arm, a flood of warmth, and he pulled away, falling backward off the truck, grabbing at the syringe that was stuck through his jacket and into his arm. The needle broke in his arm as he hit the ground hard. Berdych stepped into the doorway, tall and stooped, his eyes wide. Westermann heard three pops in succession and watched as Berdych took two bullets to the chest and one above the eye, falling back into the truck.

Westermann lay on his back, looking up at the panel truck, thinking, *This is balled up.*

Things happened fast, kids from the shanties watching from the perimeter. Crime-scene cops showed up, took photos, samples, and, finally, Berdych's corpse, zipped up in a body bag. Internal Affairs cops in expensive suits separated the uniforms and questioned them individually about what they'd seen.

Westermann sat in the shade, sweat pouring off him, something from that syringe in his body. A crime scene guy had bagged up the syringe barrel and rushed it to Pulyatkin to compare what was left with Lenore's disease. Westermann felt empty, not just because of his fear about the substance in the needle, but because without Berdych, how could they connect Maddox with the dead girls?

Grip and Morphy arrived, standing in the street before Westermann.

Grip said, "Souza really kill that doctor?"

Westermann nodded. "He had to. No choice, but it's not easy. He's spooked."

The three of them took in Souza sitting on the bumper of a prowl car, Plouffe talking to him with a hand on his shoulder. Two uniforms, older guys that Souza must have known, stood with him, too. Souza's tie was undone. He was waiting to sign something for IA, then Plouffe would drive him home.

Grip said, "And Berdych got you with a needle?"

Westermann nodded. Morphy gazed into the distance, mind elsewhere. "You know what was in it?"

"No. Too many bottles in the truck. Pulyatkin's looking at it."

"Jesus." Grip changed the subject. "Lieut, you know what's going on with those oil drums?"

"One of the uniforms checked it out. Sounds like they think there's going to be trouble."

"Yeah, but I mean that thing they painted on each of them. The skull. It was painted on my door and scratched into Ed Wayne's badge. What the hell is it?"

Westermann shrugged. "I don't know. You've been in the shanties. They've got all kinds of paintings like that. Symbols."

Grip nodded; thinking. "You know, about the trouble they're worried about?"

"Yeah?"

"They might be right."

Crows perched on the roof of the panel truck shrieked at the uniforms.

Bigger birds, vultures, circled over the field between the shanties and the warehouses downriver.

Westermann saw someone new on the scene, skinny guy with his fedora pulled low, walking around the taped-off panel truck. Grip turned to where Westermann was looking.

"Damn it."

Art Deyna.

102.

Frings and Carla stood with Eunice in the shade of a tin shack on the edge of the Square. They ate fried plantains a friend of Eunice's had prepared. Only the clothes had arrived for distribution. Nothing else had made it.

The Community seemed to be leaking away before their eyes. The commotion was still intense, the shanty alleys still crowded, but not *as* crowded.

The square was clear, except for a half dozen men setting up stools next to brightly decorated drums of various heights and shapes. Another man, lean and tall, wearing a white suit and white, flat-brimmed hat, paced around the drummers, keeping up a conversation. Occasionally one of the men would idly slap his drum three or four times, making a hollow sound.

People peered through the thresholds where shanty alleys emptied onto the Square, some stepping in to watch for a moment or two; most disappeared back into the warren.

People walked past them talking in their Caribbean patois, Frings struggling to pick out a piece here and there with little success. He felt somehow rooted to this spot, transfixed by the preparations for the ceremony.

Two strikingly beautiful young women arrived, wearing long, colorful dresses that wrapped tightly down the women's slender bodies. Their hair was wrapped as well, coning back.

"Those are the priest's assistants," Eunice said. The women were talking to the man in white, while a couple of drummers played a beat and others chatted. The man in white walked to the center of the Square with a piece of chalk and carefully drew an X in the dirt.

Frings looked to Eunice.

"The crossroads. Where the spirit world meets our world. That man is the assistant priest. He's making preparations for the ceremony."

The man continued to draw, now tracing a circle with the center of the X as its midpoint.

"Who's the priest?" Frings asked.

Eunice looked at him in surprise. "Well, Father Womé, of course."

103.

The IA cops were gone, along with the crime-scene cops, the panel truck, and a disconsolate Souza. A dozen uniforms hung around outside the shanties, watching the Community men light fires in the oil drums, black smoke rising in thick plumes.

Grip said, "They have those things in this heat?"

Morphy chuckled and two uniforms they were chatting with smiled. There was a lull, the lieut in the shade with a doctor, getting the broken syringe removed and his arm bandaged. Grip, Morphy, and the other cops waited, eyeing the white men gathering in the field, knowing there would be more work to do.

Something in the distance, across the field toward the warehouses, caught Grip's eye and he excused himself. Drums—sporadic, not coordinated—came from the shanties as he crossed the field. The only other sounds were the crows, the light crush of his feet in the weeds and gravel, the distant flow of the river. The ground seemed to radiate heat, and the sun on Grip's neck had sweat pouring off him. Ahead, the two girls, dressed in canary-yellow dresses, stood several feet from their cow, which lay on its side, strangely deflated.

He heard the sound of the flies. The girls didn't come to meet him, but watched. They weren't twins, but roughly the same ages with their hair in neat braids. They were calm. Grip wondered how long they'd been there.

The cow, he saw, seemed to have burst open, blood pooled under its body and in it, viscera. The side up seemed untouched.

Grip approached the girls, kneeling to be at their eye level. "What happened?"

One of the girls said, "He popped." The other nodded earnestly.

"Popped?"

The girl who had spoken nodded. The other said, "He was the Mack Doll."

Grip looked to the shantytown, its form distorted by the waves of heat rising from the field. He wiped his forehead with his sleeve.

"Where are your mothers?"

One of the girls nodded toward the shanties.

"Maybe you ought to go find them."

The girls nodded and, without so much as glancing back at the dead cow, walked toward the shanties. Grip watched them for a couple of minutes, knowing that as soon as he left, the crows would converge.

Westermann gathered his men—Grip, Morphy, and Dzeko—in the shade of a factory building that had caved in on itself, the crumbled brick walls on top looking vaguely like a castle's crenellations. They heard rats scuttling in the ruins, smelled something decaying. Westermann laid down their only priority: Find Ole Koss. Things were falling apart around Koss and his reaction was unpredictable and likely dangerous. Grip and Morphy headed to Crippen's to shake the tree, see what fell out.

Morphy surprised Grip by taking the wheel, and Grip decided not to say anything about it. Morphy gave it the full siren-and-lights treatment, trusting that other cars would get the hell out of the way.

"Jesus, Morph. Let's get there in one piece."

Morphy looked sideways at Grip and shook his head. Grip hoped no one gave Morphy shit at Crippen's.

A block away, they could see the crowd at Crippen's spilling out onto the sidewalk.

"The fuck is that?" Grip said.

"It ever get like this?"

"Never. Not close."

Morphy killed the sound and lights and pulled the prowl car to the curb down the block. Grip led Morphy into the crowd—all men—nodding to guys he recognized, several cops among them. People were drunk, their body language belligerent.

Grip pushed his way inside, knocking a guy's arm out of the way, spilling beer on the guy's shirt. The guy started to make a move at Grip—not a small guy, either—but Morphy got ahold of his shirt and got in the guy's mug and he backed down fast. Morphy grabbed a glass off a table and threw the beer in the guy's face; the guy looked unsure; the man who'd just lost his glass got a good look at Morphy and decided to get another beer from the bar.

Grip grabbed Morphy by the arm and pulled him hard. "Come on. We've got business."

Ed Wayne was at his usual table. Grip nodded for Wayne to get up. Wayne stared at him, glassy-eyed. Morphy shoved by a couple younger guys and picked up Wayne by the back of his shirt. The crowd checked out the commotion.

Grip got in Wayne's face. "You know where Ole Koss is, Ed?"

Wayne drew back, as if the question surprised him. "How the hell would I know that?"

Grip bit his lip in frustration. "The fuck is going on here?"

"Free liquor. No one's supposed to know, but Gerald told me Truffant's footing the bill."

"Why?"

"Where the fuck have you been?" Wayne sneered.

Grip caught the subtle movement of Morphy's arm as he gave Wayne a shot to the kidney, Wayne wincing and his eyes rolling drunkenly. "All right. Jesus. There's a group—these guys, others—going to take apart the Uhuru Community tonight. Tonight. Burn it to the ground."

Grip shook his head. "That's not a great idea, I don't think."

"Fuck you."

Morphy shoved Wayne forward onto the table, his weight tipping the table over and sending him and the beer glasses sprawling into the laps of his friends.

Grip and Morphy pushed their way back out to the street again. No one had seen Koss.

"This is getting out of control," Grip said as they walked back to their car. "There's a lot of kids in those shanties; women; old people."

Morphy shrugged. "I don't drink there."

Grip winced at him.

Morphy drove back to the shanties, siren and lights going again, but almost serene at the wheel as he careened through the crowded streets. Grip recognized the attitude and kept quiet, knowing that Morphy was mulling something over.

* * *

Westermann was by the shanties, drinking coffee from a paper cup and talking to Dzeko, who looked as if he was about to drop from heatstroke. Grip heard drums coming from the shanties, the rhythm not quite organized. The ground seemed to bake in the sun.

Morphy strode toward Westermann and Souza, forcing Grip to skip a little to stay close. He had no idea what Morphy had in mind.

"Lieut," Morphy said, still moving, "I've been thinking about Koss."

Westermann turned to them. Everyone was sweating, but Dzeko's face was the color of a slice of watermelon.

Morphy said, "He's coming here. He's got to know those assholes at Grip's bar are going to tear the shanties apart tonight."

"What?"

"Oh, shit." Grip looked around, registering the dozen or so cops, shaking his head. "We need a lot more support down here. There's a group getting ugly uptown, going to come here and raise some hell."

Westermann looked to Dzeko. "Phone it in."

Dzeko shuffled off toward the squad car.

"You going to make it?" Grip called after him.

"Go to hell," Dzeko shouted over his shoulder; but Grip hadn't been kidding, the guy looked about to keel over.

Westermann turned back to Morphy. "You were saying about Koss?"

"Yeah, no way he lets this go. If we're right and they were really trying to infect all these people, then Koss is going to do whatever it is he wants to do before the shanties get torn down and all the people disperse."

"Isn't that the point?" Grip asked.

"No. *The point* is they fucking think Womé is the Antichrist. *The point* is that Koss is going to come here to do some killing."

Westermann nodded thoughtfully. "Okay. So we post people around? Keep an eye out?"

Morphy shrugged. "You're the lieut."

104.

Father Womé arrived as three men in loose, button-down shirts were planting an eight-foot pole where the assistant priest had chalked the *X*. Frings registered that people noticed Womé, but went back to what they were doing. There was respect but not awe, and for some reason that surprised him. Maybe they were used to seeing Womé, or maybe Frings had fundamentally misunderstood what Womé meant to the people in the Community.

The crowd hugging the edges of the Square was growing, their bodies making it even hotter. Womé wore a light tan suit along with a homburg and round sunglasses. He leaned on a brass-tipped cane as he conferred with the assistant priest and the two women. More drummers set up on wooden crates or sat cross-legged in the dirt. The crowd hummed with expectancy.

Carla pulled on Frings's sleeve and nodded toward Eunice, whose eyelids drooped as she listened to another woman, as if she were falling asleep; but her broad shoulders were tense. The woman left and Eunice was motionless until Carla gently touched her arm.

"She said there's a group of white men gathering in the field, more coming all the time. Said the police killed some doctor, a white man."

Berdych? Frings nodded. "Okay. I'll find out what's going on."

He pushed out of the Square and headed toward the shantytown exit, trying to keep a constant direction. A goat was loose and a couple of boys chased after it with a rope.

He didn't like the idea of white men gathering outside the shanties. On top of what he now figured was the shooting of Berdych, the situation seemed to be getting out of hand.

After a couple of false turns, he found his way to the outside. A warm breeze blew off the river, carrying something that approached fresh air. Uniforms gathered around a dozen police cars, smoking and talking shit. Two cops were posted at each corner of the shantytown. Frings stepped out

339

to get a better view of the field and saw a group of two or three dozen white men, maybe fifty yards away, drinking bottles of beer, their boisterous talk drifting on the wind. Between the shanties and the men, a line of cops and, behind them, young Negroes pacing back and forth between the fires burning in oil drums.

Shit.

Frings found Westermann talking with three other cops, including the one who'd braced Frings the other night in the Palace. He kept his distance, edging over so that he was in Westermann's line of sight. Westermann eventually saw him and nodded. The other three men turned to look. The cop from the Palace looked from Frings back to Westermann and then back to Frings. Westermann excused himself and walked over.

"I can't be talking to you here."

"What's going on with those ginks in the field?"

Westermann looked at him.

"Off-the-fucking-record," Frings said.

"Detective Grip over there"—Westermann nodded to where the three men were watching them—"says that there's a sizable group of men planning to take down the shanties."

Frings shook his head. "And the cops are here to what, guard the shanties?"

Westermann nodded. "If it comes to that."

The drums were going again.

Westermann asked, "You know what's going on in there?"

"Yeah. Come have a look at who you're protecting."

People stood three deep around the perimeter of the Square when Frings and Westermann arrived. Kids sat on the roofs of the surrounding shanties. The drummers were all going now, the rhythm fast and hypnotic. Frings led the way through the crowd to Carla and Eunice. Carla and Westermann exchanged looks but didn't speak.

In the Square, Father Womé was shaking a rattle and moving in choreographed steps with the assistant priest, who carried a sword and was flanked by the two women, now carrying white standards attached to poles. The three would advance together and Womé would retreat, stop, and then advance on the three, who would retreat in turn. Women on the edges of the crowd were dancing subtle dances, not coordinated with each other, but moving with the same beat. People were singing, or maybe chanting in what Frings thought must be some African language. He felt out of place and conspicuous; looked over at Carla and saw that she felt it, too.

Westermann grabbed Frings's arm. "Who's that?"

Frings followed Westermann's gaze to Moses Winston, slapping a drum with his bare hands, his head cocked slightly to the side, eyes closed.

"Moses Winston. He's a musician."

"He lives here, in the shanties?"

Frings was surprised by the question and turned to Westermann, not liking what he saw in the lieutenant's unfocused eyes.

"He's staying here, from what I've heard," Frings said slowly. "He's a traveling musician, just living here while he's in the City. Why?"

Westermann frowned and seemed to sink further into himself.

In the Square, the assistant priest and the two women discarded their props and began dancing around the pole, the man, especially, moving libidinously; the women only slightly more chaste. The tempo picked up and two men from the crowd—thin, shirtless, gleaming with sweat—entered the Square whirling, their arms out, eyes rolling around in their heads.

This was what was going to save the Community? Would this ceremony stoke their courage? Inspire resistance?

Beyond Carla, Frings saw Eunice with her eyes closed, her head swaying slightly to the rhythm, mouthing the words of whatever song was being sung.

105.

Westermann stood motionless, frightened by the intensity with which he was experiencing the ceremony, this frenzy of sound, motion, release. He felt Frings's eyes on him but couldn't pull his gaze away from the scene in the Square.

Father Womé, his jacket off, his white shirt soaked with sweat, circled the pole, head down, doing a funny shuffle that emanated from his hips. The assistant priest twirled one of the women around and her dancing grew increasingly frantic.

Lenore rotating as she floats downstream.

Something foreign in his blood.

Ed Wayne and Art Deyna.

Marijuana smoke rose from all sides of the Square. Westermann wiped sweat from his brow with his sleeve. Another man entered the square, a loose shirt hanging from his skeletal frame. He wore dark glasses and a shapeless hat and had the strangest walk that Westermann had ever seen, limbs seemingly controlled from without, not quite moving naturally or in concert. He carried a cane that he mostly waved as he whirled around and made little jumps while leaning way back from the waist. His appearance was greeted with a cheer from across the Square.

Photos with Mel Washington.

Sam "Blood Whiskers" McAdam standing over Klasnic, whose chest is blown open.

Big Rolf looking confused, scared.

Close to twenty people danced now. Womé was making the rounds, talking animatedly to this person or that, dancing all the while. Some danced subtly, moving their hips and heads; others whirled and shook and occasionally fell, writhing, only to be picked up by people from the crowd. The man with the funny walk weaved through all this, rubbing up against the women, clasping hands with the men, and spinning in circles with them.

Are you good with the Lord?

Are you good with Legba?

Westermann swallowed great gulps of air, feeling somehow outside himself. He had to leave.

The drums lost nothing of their power out in the shanty alleys, but he was away from the intensity of the people and the feeling that had threatened to overwhelm him. He careened through the maze of alleys; his thoughts seemed beyond his control, the drums disorienting. A few people still walked through the shanty passageways and he felt their wary eyes on him. He'd lost track of how long he'd been walking when he happened upon a gap in the shanty walls. He slipped through in a daze, greeted on the outside by two uniforms, guns drawn.

Recognizing him, they lowered their guns, but remained on guard, nervous. Behind them, in the near distance, Westermann heard the powerful rush of the river. He'd emerged on the opposite side he intended.

"Lieutenant, I think you'd better find Detectives Morphy and Grip." One of the cops motioned around the corner of the shantytown wall.

Spurred by the cops' urgency, Westermann hurried around the corner, but was brought up short by the scene before him. Flames licked over the edge of the oil drums, dense black smoke rising to the sky like skeletal fingers, while a group of about twenty young men from the shanties paced manically back and forth, some carrying sticks or clubs. Past them was a group of cops, spread out along the length of the shanties. Some watched the men by the oil drums and the others watched the crowd of white men—now close to a hundred strong, Westermann guessed—two dozen yards or so off.

The drums were loud even out here, and the men from the shanties and the group of white men had to shout for their epithets and threats to be heard. The cops between the two groups of men moved tensely, unsure where to focus their attention. Westermann jogged between the oil drums and the shanty walls to the front of the shanties. There weren't enough cops here.

Ten yards from the corner, he saw Morphy and Grip coming in a hurry.

"Jesus," Grip said. "Where've you been?"

Westermann nodded toward the shanties.

Grip stared at him. Westermann saw the concern in his eyes.

"What's going on here?" Westermann asked. "Is support coming?"

"Yeah, that's what they say. Lieutenant Ving is calling the shots with the uniforms."

"Okay. Good." Ving was competent.

Grip shook his head. "No. Not good. A couple of the uniforms say they saw Koss, got a couple of shots off at him, but missed."

"Yeah?"

Morphy jabbed a thumb toward the shanties. "He's in there."

Jane Morphy, stretched naked on her bed.

Do you love me?

106.

Betty guided Frings through the shanties, Frings holding her gently by the arm as they walked. She was smaller than she seemed. They walked in silence until they reached the threshold of the front entrance. Through the door they could see the array of police cars and edgy cops.

Frings looked around, searching for a face he might know. Anders Ving walked over to him, grim.

"Frank."

"Andy."

Ving ushered the two of them away from the shanties, to where they had a better perspective on the field and what lay beyond. Frings watched Betty's reaction as she saw the horde of drunken white men massing mere yards from the shanties, only a couple dozen cops and the Samedi men as resistance. She seemed remarkably calm, calmer than Frings felt.

Frings leaned toward Ving. "We need to get Mel Washington out here."

Ving was astonished. "Mel Washington? This situation isn't charged enough for you?"

"Listen. The only way this doesn't end up really badly is if we get the Community people out of the shanties before those assholes move, because there's no way you're going to hold them back forever. Mel has been working with these people for months. We need him if we're going to get this place cleared out."

Ving shook his head. "Jesus, Frank. You really think that's a good move for me? A good career move, if nothing else?"

Shit. "Andy, I'll frame it in the paper. You know: 'The resourceful Lieutenant Ving trying anything in his power to avoid a riot; the kind of innovative thinking we need in the police force.' And so on."

"Right, right, right, you'll shovel on the horseshit."

"People eat it up. The brass aren't going to screw a big hero. Come on."

Ving sighed. "Frank, you really owe me on this one. Maybe you can fix me up with one of your girlfriend's friends or something?"

"Your Nordic good looks, Andy, and you need fixing up?" Frings winked. "You know I take care of people."

"Yeah, okay, if you say so. Where do I find your buddy Mel?"

Frings nodded to Betty. "She'll take you to him."

107.

Grip moved quickly through the shanties and was soon disoriented; the drums, the smells, the strange *sameness* of these little alleys. He hated this fucking place and it didn't help that Ole Koss was in here somewhere along with three edgy cops with guns—Westermann, Morphy, and a single beat cop.

Grip held his gun pointed forward and kept his left shoulder to the shanty walls as he hurried along. *The goddamn drums!* He felt eyes on him from the darkness behind open doors.

He heard footsteps and grunts down a perpendicular alley and tightened his finger on the trigger. He spun around the corner, ready to fire, but found a kid with a rope dragging a resisting goat. Grip managed a nod at the kid, but his nerves were through the roof.

Up ahead, in a blur, he saw someone, a Caucasian, cross on a perpendicular alley. Grip closed his eyes, counted to three, and took off after him.

Westermann had branched off to the left, away from the river, while Grip had gone right and Morphy and the uniform had headed straight in and then split.

Westermann tried to concentrate, address the real danger of the situation, but exhaustion, fear, the impact of the ceremony in the Square . . . they overwhelmed him. He moved in a daze, his eyes doing slow sweeps of the alley before him, his gun out but pressed against his thigh. The drums played with his perceptions, made his legs weak. He heard voices from the shacks, but they were either women's or had that Caribbean patois.

Jimmy Symmes walking away with Ole Koss.

Klasnic lying dead in a pool of blood.

Old women speaking in tongues, hands shaking.

He crept through the alleys, trying to get a hold on the situation, but the drums seemed to fracture his thoughts. His breathing went shallow. He edged up to another intersection, turned to peek around the corner, and felt the barrel of a gun against his forehead.

"I could hear you coming a mile away, Lieut." Morphy was almost apologetic as he forced Westermann back into the alley he had just left.

"Larry, this isn't the time—"

Morphy's temper exploded from nowhere. "Shut the fuck up and drop your gun."

Westermann knelt, placed his gun gently on the ground. His hands shook.

Morphy put his lips to Westermann's ear, whispering. "The past few days, I wake up, I ask myself if today's the day that I kill the lieut. Every day the answer is no. But one day, the answer won't be no, and I won't have to ask the question anymore."

Westermann nodded, trying to pull away from where the barrel pressed into his forehead.

"You dropped off the edge," Morphy said.

"I know."

Morphy pulled the gun back and walked away, heading left down an alley. Westermann stood with his eyes closed, shaking, until he remembered why he was there in the first place, picked up his gun with his still-shaking hands, and walked unsteadily forward.

108.

If Winston's arms ached after this hour of drumming, he was beyond noticing. He was where he wanted to be spiritually, mentally. The rhythm of the drums propelled his efforts, and the collective sound seemed to seep into him, separating his mind from his body.

Earlier, he'd been distracted, worried that he wouldn't know how to approach this ceremony, knowing that there was something that he wanted to achieve: getting on the good side of the Community gods. But this concern had melted away as the drums worked on him. He understood that he just needed to be carried along with the ceremony; that things would work out that way.

He watched the dancers in various degrees of frenzy: some shook violently as they danced, others seemed as if asleep except for their gentle swaying. Father Womé sat in a chair, receiving people as they came to him in their trances, offering some words before the people danced away to be replaced by others. Winston experienced the scene before him as a shimmer, like looking through the crystal-clear waters of a fast-moving creek, everything bright and clear but not distinct.

Glélé—though now, Winston was sure, he had become Samedi—wove his way between the dancers, making little circles with his cane and lewd movements toward the younger women.

Winston heard a different kind of noise from the crowd to his left; a sound of surprise and protest. He turned to the source and saw a white man—no, he knew who it was, not just a white man, but Ole Koss—stumble out of the crowd and into the Square, a figure isolated by the color of his skin and by the quality of his movements, somehow dissonant with those of the dancers, who continued, oblivious, around him. Koss had a gun in his hand.

Winston felt the cold on his skin, knowing what would happen before Koss stalked toward Father Womé. The crowd noise changed, no longer rapturous. Koss had his gun aimed at Womé when he stopped, his attention suddenly diverted, recognition in his eyes. Winston followed Koss's sight line and saw Samedi, motionless, staring at Koss, a wide smile on his lips.

As Moses knew would happen, Koss turned on Samedi, gun outstretched, and advanced on him, shooting three times into the man's chest. The noise came to Winston as three cracks followed by three more as Koss stood above Samedi, shooting into his supine body.

Another cat burst into the square, also white, also carrying a gun. Winston heard screams from the crowd. Most of the people in the ceremony were still dancing, and Winston realized that he was still drumming but didn't stop. He watched the second white cat run at Koss from behind and bring the butt of his gun down hard on Koss's head. Koss went down on his hands and knees, blood rushing from the wound down his neck. The white cat hit him again and Koss was facedown in the dirt, the cat with his knee in Koss's back, the gun trained at the back of Koss's head.

109.

Grip had his knee hard in Koss's back, his gun in the nape of Koss's neck. His hand was steady and he was in control. He noticed that the drumming had mostly stopped, replaced by the sounds of fear—screams, sobbing, confused murmurs. From his knees, he looked around at the maybe two hundred Community Negroes, wondering what they made of all this. They could tear him apart if they wanted to. He looked at the dead man next to him, saw that it was the jangly-legged man, and wondered if he was surprised by this or not. He cuffed Koss's unresisting wrists.

A white guy emerged from the crowd, his shirt discolored with sweat. Grip recognized Frank Frings and found himself relieved to see him. Nobody seemed to be leaving. All eyes were on him. The Square seemed to shrink.

Frings squatted next to him, patting Koss on the shoulder. "You need to get him out of here."

Grip nodded. "You think they'll try to stop us?"

Frings shook his head.

Morphy and Westermann arrived near simultaneously, both assessing the situation warily. The uniform showed up seconds later.

Grip stood. "Let's get the hell out of here."

110.

Purposeless. Frings stood with Carla and Eunice Prendergrast before Father Womé, who, still in his chair, stared back at them with vacant eyes. Eunice crouched down to Womé's level and urged him to speak, to show some consciousness of the situation around him. Womé didn't respond. Frings tried to figure out the problem: Shock? Drugs? A trance? Spiritual exhaustion? All of these?

It should have been pathetic, Womé in this state during a moment of acute crisis. But somehow it wasn't. He was still a presence.

The drums were all silent, their noise replaced by the din of people outside the shanties. Frings heard violence in the pitch, but it might have been because he knew who was out there; what their intent was.

Frings conferred with Carla and Eunice. The crowd was beginning to ebb away, probably unaware of the mob outside the shanties, so consuming had been the ceremony. Eunice didn't seem to know if most of these people still planned to abandon the shanties that night or if the ritual in the Square had fortified them enough to stay. Frings couldn't believe they'd stick around after the murder they'd witnessed on top of everything else.

Carla leaned against Frings, sagging with fatigue. Eunice called over those in her group of women who remained in the Square.

Frings rubbed the back of his neck, feeling the urgency of the situation and also his inconsequence. He watched Eunice talk with her women until he heard a murmur from the remaining crowd behind him and turned to see Mel Washington, bearded and drawn, walking toward Eunice with Betty Askins and Warren Eddings in his wake.

111.

Morphy and Grip each held one of Koss's heavy arms. Koss was conscious and staggered along as they pulled him through the shantytown alleys. Westermann walked in front and the uniform took up the rear. The crowd noise from outside had everyone on edge.

Where is Vesterhue?

Something is in my blood.

Big Rolf looking back, scared.

Koss's senses returned. He began muttering to Morphy and, especially, Grip. "Let me go. You're really going to arrest me for killing that Negro demon? That demon that followed me here from Africa? I was doing the Lord's work. He walked Godtown every night, a soldier of the devil. A soldier of Womé."

Westermann registered that Grip was letting Koss talk, which wasn't Grip's way. Grip's patience for perps sounding off was minimal; but he let Koss run his mouth. Westermann didn't like it.

"Shut him up," Westermann said over his shoulder.

"You'd like that," Koss spit back.

Westermann waited to hear Koss grunt from a Grip kidney-punch, but it didn't come.

Lenore's body slowly rotating as it floats downstream.

Jane Does on coroner's tables, covered in sores.

"Yeah, you've got some things to answer for," Koss taunted.

Still no move by Morphy or Grip to silence him. Westermann kept moving, at a loss about what to do. Koss was going to talk at some point. Maybe it was better to get it out now, get a handle on what Koss had on him before everything was on the record. But he was showing weakness in front of Morphy and Grip. Worse, they were abetting his humiliation.

"I'm going to take the juice," Koss continued. "I have no problem with that. I'm good with the Lord. But I'm not going to leave any secrets, Lieutenant. I'm going to tell what I know."

"You'll have your chance" was all Westermann could think to say.

"I'll have my chance," Koss said, mocking Westermann. "You want to know what I'm going to say? You want to know what I have on you, Lieutenant? Red Lieutenant? I bet you Grip, here, would like to hear; wouldn't you, Torsten?"

We can just push her back into the river.

Front-page photo of Mel Washington talking to him.

The twins singing, Brother Allison sweating piously.

"You're just digging yourself a hole," Westermann said.

"A hole? How about this hole: I killed Vesterhue; I killed Jimmy Symmes; I killed three of those whores. That's enough to see me burn. But you know who I didn't kill? I didn't kill Lenore Ivanova. And you know what, Lieutenant? I know where she was killed and it wasn't where you found her; but you know that, don't you? I did what I could to point you in the right direction. How many bodies do you need to find before you start looking in the Uhuru Community?

"It got me wondering, why is Lieutenant Westermann poking around Godtown when all the bodies are by the Uhuru Community? It didn't make sense."

Westermann turned on Koss, fists balled. Grip put a hand in Westermann's chest, holding him away from Koss. Westermann's heart hammered.

Grip's voice was subdued. "Let's do this here. Before we go out, Lieut. It'll be easier that way."

Morphy turned to the uniform. "Get out of here, and you didn't hear anything."

The uniform nodded and hurried off.

The enemy among us.

Big Rolf walking with his arm around Vic Truffant.

Grip and Morphy weren't holding Koss now, and even with his hands cuffed behind his back, he exuded physical strength. He tilted his chin up and showed Westermann a cocky smirk.

"Like I said, I was wondering why you were in Godtown. But then I found out you were spending time flapping your gums with Frank Frings and maybe his little girlfriend Red Carla. That's kind of interesting. And those two, well, it's no secret that Red Carla is close with Mel Washington and spends time down in the shanties. You connect the dots."

Westermann tried a confident laugh, but it came out false. He tried changing the subject. "You're confessing to, what, five murders? Six? Seven? Where are the bodies?"

"You found two on the river. The others are hidden. Look, I'll bring you to them, don't worry. I've got nothing to hide. It's all done in the Lord's name. All of it. But you, Lieutenant, I don't know why you do what you do, but you are about to reap what you've sown. The Lord does not reward subterfuge and abetting the godless. You knew that somebody moved Lenore Ivanova's body. You might have done it yourself. But whether it was you or someone else, it was done to get that body away from the shanties because you and your Red friends didn't want this murder tied to the Community."

Westermann fought panic, his words coming out without thought. "You're lying. You're trying to pin that murder on someone else."

"I've just confessed to five. You said so yourself. I'm going to lie about this one?"

Westermann glanced from Morphy to Grip. They stared back. He'd lost them.

"Then who killed her?"

Koss shrugged his massive shoulders. "That's on you, Lieutenant."

They stood in silence for a moment, Westermann feeling the heat in his face, the wobble in his knees. It was coming apart.

Grip said, "Lieut, you haven't denied it. Did you move the body?"

Westermann stared back at him, debating the lie.

Are you good with the Lord?

"You've got to say something," Grip pleaded.

Westermann looked to Morphy and saw the hate. Grip was looking at Koss, who smiled, pleased with himself.

Are you good with the Lord?

Are you good with Legba?

Westermann pulled the badge from his pocket, threw it at Grip's feet, and walked away.

112.

Frings stood on the roof of a building across the street from the Uhuru Community, resting his forearms on the low wall that ran along the edge. The sun had set and the sky was a fading scarlet dotted with wispy orange clouds. Frings smoked a reefer in the breeze and watched the last few members of the Uhuru Community walk out of the shanties through an opening made by tearing down two shacks. They retreated out the side away from the field, slinking off where they couldn't be seen by the mob that had grown to at least a couple hundred. Even up here, Frings could sense the latent violence waiting to be unleashed. He spotted Deyna, notebook out, talking with Ed Wayne. Deyna was crossing a line Frings had crossed long ago, but he was crossing it to the other side.

Washington had arranged this evacuation, the only way he could see to prevent a tragedy. Womé had been barely better than catatonic as he was led away by two bodyguards, Frings still not sure if he was spent from the rituals or if he'd been overwhelmed by the situation, by the raw physical presence of it.

Mel Washington was down there now, talking to Lieutenant Ving and Kraatjes. Washington had earned the right to be free of police persecution. He'd assessed the situation and formulated the course of action. Frings had volunteered to accompany him, introduce him to Ving. Washington had shaken his head. "This is our affair."

Frings understood and moved aside.

He watched Washington's approach to Ving, then the body language of the two men as their inaudible conversation progressed, thinking Washington was lucky to be dealing with Ving, who was smart and not afraid to take bold steps. Frings watched as Ving nodded along with whatever Mel was proposing. They shook hands and Ving strode across the field, alone.

Ving had returned with three white guys, Ed Wayne among them. Washington met them by an oil drum, smoke still billowing, the Samedi ginks long gone. They worked out the compromise. The mob would give the people in the shanties time to leave—a couple of hours—then they would level the shanties or burn them or whatever it was they wanted to do. There was no way to save the Community, Washington realized, but this way he could at least save the people.

Frings tossed the last bit of his reefer over the edge of the roof and stretched, feeling the strain of the day ebbing from his body. Below, one of the prowl cars gave a quick siren blast, which must have been the signal because the mob began to move on the shanties. Their noise drifted up to Frings like a primal roar, and he thought that this was what happened in the City: Grace was devoured by brutishness, utopias by the ignorant.

He watched as the mob took to the shantytown like ants to a carcass.

EPILOGUE

113.

Weeks later.

Standing at Panos's window, Frings saw Grip loitering across the street from the *Gazette*'s main entrance, smoking a cigarette and eyeing the passing women.

Panos noticed the sudden tension in Frings's posture. "What is it, Frank?"

Frings made a noncommittal noise and turned to Panos. "I've got to go, Chief."

"Someone waiting for you?"

"Yeah. Maybe."

Frings didn't mind making Grip wait and thought that maybe a reefer would relax him, make it easier to talk. So he sought out Bronstein, who never passed up a visit to the fire escape. They sat on the grated stairs, passing a reefer and watching the street. It was finally cool, a breeze making it almost cold. Two blocks down, they could see the aftermath of a car accident, an improbable volume of steam rising from one of the engines.

Frings took a drag off the reefer, then pointed it down toward Grip. "You know him?"

Bronstein squinted. "Yeah, I think so. Detective Morphy or . . . no, not Morphy."

"Grip," Frings grunted, keeping the smoke in.

"Yeah, that's right, Grip. Son of a bitch, Grip. Not as bad as his partner, though. That's who I was thinking of, Morphy."

Frings nodded. The stoned pigeons had sensed what was happening on the landing and perched on the railing expectantly. Frings blew smoke their way.

Bronstein took a hit, thought for a minute, then blew smoke at the birds. "He waiting for you?"

"I think so."

"Jesus," Bronstein said, handing the reefer back. "You'd better have some more of this."

Grip and Frings sat in the same diner, at the same table, that Frings had weeks before with Ellen Aust. They waited in uncomfortable silence for their coffee.

When it arrived, Grip asked, "You heard from Lieutenant Westermann?"

Frings shook his head.

"You tell me if you had?"

Frings shrugged. "I don't know. But I guess I *would* tell you if I *hadn't*, because I *haven't* and I *am* telling you."

Grip nodded at this. "I'm sure you know he's missing."

"That's what I hear."

"No body's turned up; he hasn't been back to his apartment; hasn't contacted friends."

"You think maybe he's in a hospital somewhere? Berdych's needle . . ."

Grip shook his head. "Nah, Pulyatkin took a look at what was in the syringe. The lieut doesn't have to worry about getting the mumps."

"Look, what are you after, Detective?"

"We off-the-record?"

"Why not?" Frings said, wondering where this was going.

"The lieut took off after we cuffed Koss, right? He and Koss had some words as we were getting out of those fucking shanties, and then the lieut just vamoosed. Well, we took Koss downtown of course and grilled him about what had happened. We had a lot of questions you know—not about the lieut, really, because we didn't know that he wouldn't turn up again and we figured we had time."

Frings nodded.

"So we started in on Koss and the first thing was why did he kill that guy in the Square—guy's name turned out to be Glélé, don't ask me to spell it. Koss says he was after Womé but when he got into the Square he sees this Glélé character and he recognizes him; says he met him in Africa and then damned if the guy doesn't show up here, in the City. Koss said this guy was bird-dogging him down in Godtown. Drove him nuts; thought he might be going crazy—seeing things. But this guy—Glélé—left the skull-and-hat symbol on the church walls sometimes, so he knew there must be someone. You know this guy—Glélé?"

Frings shook his head.

"Look, I know you and the lieut worked this thing together somehow. I don't know why. Maybe it's a Red thing; maybe something else."

"Yeah, we were working together."

Grip waited for Frings to expand and, when he didn't, said, "Koss rolled over on everything: Symmes, Vesterhue, Berdych, the dead girls. Says he and Vesterhue were infecting the girls, seeing how the disease worked: how long it took to go through someone, how it could be transmitted, all that.

"We pushed him, you understand. You can't tell me that this whole thing, that Prosper Maddox didn't know about it; wasn't a part of it. But Koss stuck to his story: it was him and Vesterhue. Morphy even got a little rough with him, but the guy was in the Leopard Corps; we weren't going to break him with a little rough stuff. So Maddox is going to skate. Vesterhue and Berdych are dead, and Koss is going to fry."

Frings said, "I know all of this."

Grip leaned forward on the table. "Koss said he needed to kill those girls because he was worried that if they started showing up at the hospital, a bunch of them, that he'd have a problem. Mavis Talley did, and that got him spooked. So he was going to kill Lenore, but someone beat him to it."

"How's that?"

"Koss said he went looking for Lenore at the Checkerboard—that's the joint she worked out of—but he got there and the other whores said she'd left with this musician she liked. Koss said he found out where they sometimes went, the rocks on the riverbank by the shanties, so he went there looking for her. When he got there, she was dead. He said it was perfect because not only was Lenore already dead, but the investigation would have to focus on the Uhuru Community, a place he didn't much like to begin with. But that's not what happened—the body ended up downstream. So Koss, he was already going to kill those other girls—the ones who were sick—Koss goes ahead and dumps their bodies at that same spot. He figured that with all these bodies showing up, we'd be all over the Community. But we both know how the investigation went. Lieutenant Westermann ignored the Uhuru Community as much as he could get away with."

Grip paused, but Frings didn't volunteer anything.

"I thought at first maybe he was trying to cover for the Community, keep them out of the investigation. But I don't know that I think so anymore. He ran the right investigation, found the guy that'd been doing all the killing, except Lenore. So I thought about it some more, and there was only one way it made sense to me, that maybe it was the lieut who moved the body. But why would he do that? Which made me think of you."

Frings took a sip of his coffee.

"I'm not here to take you down, Frings. All this shit, Koss has taken the weight, and while it pisses me off that Maddox is walking free, you got to roll with the punches, right? I just want to know if I got it right."

"Does it make a difference?"

Grip scratched at the back of his head. "Does to me."

114.

Frings stood on the edge of the field that had overwhelmed the old railway yard. He was with Mel Washington and Betty Askins, all looking over at the four gleaming black railcars with BLACK COMET LINE inscribed in gold above the windows. A front was moving toward the City, the sky divided between a bright summer blue and the encroaching purple. Beneath the clouds, the gray haze of rain seemed to hang in the air. Wind eddies blew litter around the field. Occasionally a piece lifted high above the rest, as if making a break for the sky, before being sucked back down again.

A small group of Negroes, maybe two dozen, had gathered by the cars and were making conversation through open windows with people inside. Blackbirds hovered overhead, making a racket and drawing looks. A large mechanical noise was nearing, signaling the approach of something that was shielded by the buildings to Frings's left.

"This is how it ends, huh?" Frings asked.

Mel Washington was wearing a suit, as though this was some kind of occasion; and it probably was for him. "In some ways."

A train engine appeared around the edge of some buildings, moving in reverse. A little cheer came up from the group by the railroad cars.

"I can't believe that it'll actually work." Frings lit a reefer. "Any idea where he's going?"

Washington shook his head.

Betty said, "Does it matter?"

They left it like that and watched the engine approach the Black Comet Line cars. It slowed as it got closer to the cars, eventually inching until the couplings met. The engineer and two other men congregated around the coupling, making an inspection. The air pressure dropped and the wind changed direction, turning cool.

Satisfied that the coupling was adequate, the engineer returned to his post. The crowd around the cars pulled away. A window in the back came down and Frings saw Father Womé, looking out at the field. The engine rocked back, compressing the couplings between each car; then moved slowly forward, a blast of steam coming from the smokestack. Father Womé brought his hand up and held it as a kind of wave to the group he was leaving behind. As the train picked up speed, Frings kept his attention on Womé and, just for a moment, thought that their eyes met. Just as quickly, the moment passed and Frings was left watching the engine pull its short string of brilliant black pearls away from the small crowd.

"I guess that's it," Washington said as the train disappeared behind the buildings.

"I guess so." Frings turned to walk back to his car.

115.

Westermann sat at a table toward the back of a dark roadhouse out in the sticks. He was thinner now and his beard had come in red. He wore workman's clothes, dirty and damp from the misty air outside. He'd never actually met Moses Winston before and saw the irony that when it finally happened—now—it was out of the City, way out. Their paths hadn't crossed so much as Westermann had tracked Winston down, wanting to clear up some unresolved business.

The place was small but full of impoverished laborers and farmhands, drinking clear liquid from mismatched glasses. The place stank of sweat and foul alcohol. Westermann drank a beer; he was the only one drinking beer so far as he could tell. Winston was sitting on a stool, an electric guitar in his lap, picking with his right hand and working a slide with his left; occasionally singing some blues number.

Westermann had spent a couple of long weeks waiting to see if the disease would show itself, monitoring every ache, every unusual sensation, like a hypochondriac. But nothing had happened. Either the syringe hadn't contained the disease or he was somehow immune, as Koss had been.

He was hungry and exhausted, but no longer plagued by interloping thoughts. He wouldn't be able to keep this up forever—his money was already running low—but he felt he had somehow found room to think, to experience without the crushing pressure and stress that he felt in the City.

Winston announced that he'd be breaking after one more song, so Westermann ordered two beers and waited. Winston finished to enthusiastic applause and left the stage, walking out a screen door at the back. Westermann followed, holding the necks of both beer bottles between the fingers of one hand. The door creaked as he stepped out to the narrow stairs that descended to the ground. Winston sat on the third step, hunched over, steam rising off him in the cool, damp air. Winston didn't turn until Westermann sat on the step beside him, offering a beer. Winston took it, a little suspicious.

"Hello, Moses. Do you know who I am?"

Winston shook his head, waited.

"My name's Piet Westermann. I was a City cop up until recently." He paused. Winston pulled on his beer, looking off into the distance. Westermann watched him, trying to read his reaction, getting nothing.

"I worked a case—a series of cases—of girls we found murdered on the riverbank down by the Uhuru Community. You know about those murders, right?"

"I do."

"You were staying in the Uhuru Community when these murders occurred, right?"

Winston nodded without much interest.

"And you left the City when? After they tore the shanties down? I was there that night, Moses. You were, too."

Winston looked at Westermann now. "So you say."

"Let me tell you something. I'm not a cop anymore. I'm not going to be again. But there's something that I've been thinking about and I thought maybe you could help me."

"That right?"

"Ole Koss—the guy we arrested that night in the shanties—he confessed to several murders. A good number. But he says that he didn't kill the first girl we found on the riverbank, a girl named Lenore."

Winston flinched, caught himself, frowned.

Westermann nodded. His face was wet from the cold mist, his clothes beginning to cling to him. "You see, that made some sense because the girls he murdered, he strangled somewhere else and dumped them at the riverbank. Lenore, she was drowned. So, we didn't solve Lenore's murder. But even though I left the police, Moses, I can't get past the fact that we didn't get her justice, you know? And I thought about her being killed on the riverbank by the Community, but it not being someone from the Community, because then word would've gotten around."

Winston nodded.

"But you weren't really part of the Community, so it makes sense that you could've done it and nobody's the wiser."

"What you want, man?"

Westermann paused, looking at the dark silhouettes of the trees against the starless night. After all that had happened, all the sacrifices, the answer was right here—an itinerant musician and a prostitute. Suddenly exhausted, he returned his gaze to Winston, locking eyes. "Did you kill her, Moses?"

Winston thought about it for a minute. "You ain't a cop?"

"Look at me." Westermann pulled on his frayed shirt, held up his bearded chin, his neck thin, his shoulders gaunt. "I'm not here to hassle you. I just want to know what happened to that girl."

Winston tipped his beer into the side of his mouth and then started to talk.

"I got a weakness for the ladies, and they seem to have a weakness for me. Some ladies, they take me home, sometimes not. I pay if I have to; no shame in that. When I got to the City, I was playing street corners, you know? I didn't have a place to start, but I knew when people heard me play, I'd get a paying gig somewhere. I always do. So, this cat Cephus, he gets me playing at his club, Checkerboard. He runs whores out of there, too. I figure y'all know about that because a couple blues come in every week for their piece. Anyway, I got friendly with Lenore—she was one of Cephus's whores. Real nice girl. I paid for it with her a couple times, but then I didn't pay no more. We enjoyed each other's company, I guess you'd say. But she was sick, real sick—lost weight, had these sores. Cephus, he's not such a bad cat, he tried to do what he could for her, and she was seeing this doctor some church sent to her. Anyway, it was hard for her."

The screen door opened. An older man—white, skinny, missing teeth—said, "Moses, you're due back onstage."

Winston didn't turn around but raised his beer in acknowledgment. "Couple of minutes, Mr. Harvey. I need to finish up with this."

The old man clucked but returned inside.

"One night, okay, after my show, she comes find me, says she's too sick to work; says she wants to talk. So we pick up a bottle at a liquor store and walk down to the riverbank, down by the shanties, and we just sat back in the rocks and smoked some mesca, drank some whiskey, listened to the river, you know. And we got real lit up—real lit up—and just talked like crazy drunks, and then she went down to the river and washed her face, and when she got back, all her makeup's gone and she's got these sores on her face. I said, 'Child, it's just getting worse,' and she rolls up her sleeves and she's got the sores there, too. She's just not getting better. She has a couple friends real sick like this, too, and another one that died."

Winston paused, taking a pull on his beer. Westermann looked at his hands. Such a small thing. Such a small thing, and it had led to everything.

"She says to me that she knows she's dying and that this doctor that checks in on her, sees how she's doing, she says she thinks it's this guy that's got her sick, and she says she don't want to do it anymore. She looks at me and she asks me, can I drown her? All up in my face, crying. And I'm drunk and been smoking mesca and I don't know what to think, and she's crying and saying, 'Please, please, do it.'"

Winston shook his head, tears at the corners of his eyes.

Westermann felt as if he were fading away. "You did it?"

Winston nodded. "Drowned her. She took a big drink off that whiskey and her eyes all rolled up, you know. So I kind of set her down in the water, held her there. It didn't seem real, but it was. I drowned her and I walked away."

Westermann nodded and they were silent for a moment.

Westermann said, "That's a lot to carry around with you."

Winston nodded.

The old man poked his head out the door again, barked, "Winston."

"Time to go," Winston muttered, took another drink of beer, and walked into the roadhouse, leaving Westermann alone. He stood on the stoop, his back to the light and noise of the bar, and stared into the darkness. He took another drink of beer and closed his eyes, trying to call up the release he had felt in the Holiness Church and finding that he couldn't. Not even close.